KISS OF ENCHANTMENT

DEBORAH COOKE

DEBORAH A. COOKE

Kiss of Enchantment
By Deborah Cooke

Copyright © 2023 by Deborah A. Cooke

Cover by Kim Killion

All rights reserved

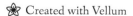 Created with Vellum

MORE PARANORMAL ROMANCE BY DEBORAH COOKE

The Dragonfire Novels

KISS OF FIRE

KISS OF FURY

KISS OF FATE

WINTER KISS

Harmonia's Kiss

WHISPER KISS

DARKFIRE KISS

FLASHFIRE

EMBER'S KISS

Kiss of Danger

Kiss of Darkness

Kiss of Destiny

SERPENT'S KISS

FIRESTORM FOREVER

HERE BE DRAGONS: A Dragonfire Companion

The DragonFate Novels

Maeve's Book of Beasts

DRAGON'S KISS

DRAGON'S HEART

DRAGON'S MATE

Paranormal Young Adult:

———

KISS OF ENCHANTMENT

CHAPTER ONE

O rion had come to hate the darkfire crystal. Each time that the *Pyr* of the Dragon Legion were bathed in its blue-green light, he braced himself for disaster. The best possible scenario was that he would be tossed through time and space with his fellow warriors, buffeted by wind and cold until all suddenly stilled. The worst, the part he dreaded, was that he would be left behind, abandoned in some unknown place and time.

He stood by his earlier suggestion that the stone should be cast aside, but Drake, the commander of their company, was resolute. The darkfire would take them where they needed to be. They must be steadfast and go where it commanded.

Five men had been lost early from their company of seventeen. He had known three of them—Lidio, Cletus and Milo—as comrades and companions and he mourned their loss. Were they where they needed to be or simply lost?

Orion resented that he did not know.

Then Alexander had recognized his old home and insisted upon seeking his wife there. Drake had granted permission to his second-in-command, but the crystal had heated as soon as Alexander stepped away from the company. Instead of returning to them, Alexander had run, intent upon discovering the fate of his mate. The crystal had swept them away before Orion could see the truth. Had Katina even been there? Had she welcomed him? Or had Alexander been left alone, as well?

It was unsettling to confront a challenge when its result could not be discerned. The darkfire glinted and shone, following its own enigmatic impetus, and there was nothing any of them could do about it.

What better reason to despise the stone and the force that illuminated it at intervals?

This time, when the darkfire faded, the Dragon Legion warriors were in a sunny plaza. It was early in the morning, dew fresh on the flowers in the heavy planters that were scattered across the space. One man was watering the flowers and jumped in alarm at their sudden appearance. A large fountain was in the middle of the square, water splashing from it and sparkling in the sunshine. There were buildings around the square, their windows shuttered or dark. It looked modern, closer to the time of the *Pyr* who had released Drake's men from Cadmus' spell. Orion straightened with interest. Was the darkfire crystal finished with them?

The Dragon Legion had manifested in the shadows near what was clearly a restaurant. It was closed now, but the tables and chairs were still set up under awnings on its patio. At Drake's direction, the company of dragon shifter warriors pulled together a pair of tables and sat down together, flicking anxious glances around themselves. Orion wondered whether the others noticed Drake's strain.

There were only eight of them remaining: Drake and Damien, Thad and Ty, Peter and Ashe, Orion and Ignatio. Orion missed Aeson, who had been a good friend. He sat beside Damien, who he had known the longest of anyone in the company.

"Aeson," Ty noted.

"One more lost," Peter agreed. "Besides Alexander, that is." He glared at Drake. "You shouldn't have let him go."

"I have no wish to deny a man his greatest desire," Drake said. He held up the dark crystal, then closed his hand over it. "I wish it hadn't lit so soon. I wish we could have waited for him."

"He *chose* to look for Katina," Ashe said to Peter, his tone defensive. "It's our responsibility to defend our mates after we've had a firestorm. Alexander did what was right."

"He ran to her," Ty added. "Making sure the crystal left him behind."

"Well, I hope she was there," Ashe said, practical as ever. Drake cleared his throat but the younger man glanced up. "Well, I do! It would be terrible if he'd taken that chance only to find her gone."

That had been precisely Orion's concern. Alexander was a warrior who could be relied upon in any battle. He didn't want to know that Alexander had been disappointed. He wanted to imagine him happily reunited with Katina.

The trouble was that he was beginning to wonder whether any of them would have happy endings. It wasn't supposed to be this way. The firestorm was supposed to lead each one of them to a destined mate, a chance to conceive a son, and a future worth paying any price.

No doubt Alexander had believed that.

"Alexander might have ended up alone," Damien said and Orion realized he'd missed some of the conversation and speculation.

"That would suit you," Iggy said to Damien, obviously trying to lighten the mood of his fellows. "Love them and leave them, that's our Damien. Mr. Heartbreaker."

Damien smiled, untroubled by the accusation, probably because it was true.

"Do you even have a heart?" Ty joked. "I remember that one in Paris." He whistled through his teeth and Iggy grinned. "She could have had my heart and soul just for the asking, but not Damien."

"He takes what they offer and leaves them behind," Iggy concluded.

"And we'll refrain from commentary on how that serves the good of mankind," Peter muttered.

"They're happy for a little bit," Damien said. "It's not like I trick them. They know what they're getting."

Orion watched as a pair of older women came into the square at the opposite end, unlocking a door and moving inside. Their clothing looked similar to the time when Drake's men had been awakened by the *Pyr*. Maybe they were getting closer to that era. Orion had found it challenging, because of the tremendous change from the world they had known, but there had been other *Pyr* there, gathered together to fight *Slayers*. A bigger company of dragon shifters on a quest to improve the world had been comforting.

"It's a bakery," Ashe whispered, watching the women. "Get ready for temptation when they get that oven going."

There was an almost-silent groan from the men. "If we're still here, we'll go see if we can buy something," Drake said.

"Or make a deal." Iggy nudged Damien. "If our money's no good, maybe Mr. Charm can get us some breakfast." Iggy and Ty began to tease Damien.

"By Zeus, maybe that's the point," Thad said suddenly, interrupting the conversation. The others turned to look at him. "What if the darkfire crystal isn't as unpredictable as we think? What if it's got a plan to fulfill?"

"Such as?" Peter demanded. "What possible reason could be behind this insanity? Every time it flashes, we get picked up and flung down somewhere else. We don't know where we are..."

"We don't know *when* we are," Ashe interjected.

"I'd say Italy, roughly 1972," Damien murmured.

Drake peered at a church tower and shrugged. "Rome."

Peter flicked a look at the pair of them that spoke volumes, then shoved a hand through his silvered hair. "We can't eat, we can't sleep, we don't dare wander away from Drake and the stupid crystal in case it lights when we're too far away and we get left behind. What kind of plan could there possibly be?"

Thad looked untroubled by the older man's scathing tone. "Maybe it's not an accident. Maybe the crystal is returning each of us to the place we belong. Scattering us like salt through the ages."

"But how would it know?" Peter demanded.

"The firestorm," Drake murmured, and the other warriors looked at him.

Orion frowned. "You mean that the darkfire crystal took us to Alexander's village, precisely so he could be reunited with Katina?"

Thad nodded with enthusiasm. "It makes sense! Darkfire doesn't have to be irrational. It's disruptive and it's unpredictable, if you don't understand what it's doing or why, but mostly, I think it makes unlikely things happen." He nodded at the others. "And it's linked to us. It's a force associated with the *Pyr*. Why wouldn't it enable the firestorm?"

"So, it sent Alexander back in time more than two thousand years to be with his wife and son," Ashe said thoughtfully.

"So, he could keep his duty to defend them," Iggy agreed. "Makes sense to me."

"If they're there," Peter said. "If she still wants him."

"That's all well and good," Orion said, getting up to pace. He wanted to do something, anything other than sit and wait. "But what can we do? How can we guide it? How can we guess where we are and why, or control where we go next?"

"Who else has had a firestorm?" Ty asked. "If Thad is right, the crystal will take us back to the mate."

"I left a wife and son," Drake admitted, his words soft. "Theo was a little older than Alexander's son and Cassandra..." His voice faded and he stared into the distance.

"I don't think you should tease yourselves," Damien said flatly.

"Why not?" Iggy demanded.

"It's better than doing nothing," Orion said.

"Because now one of you is thinking that your destined mate must be here," Damien said, his tone harder than usual. "And each of you who hasn't had a firestorm is going to want to break rank, no matter where we end up. You don't know what the darkfire crystal is planning, if it's planning anything. You could end up doing something stupid."

Peter gave him a hard look. "Did you have a firestorm?"

"Yes," Damien admitted. "And no power is ever going to take us to where she is."

Orion averted his gaze, remembering the spark of Damien's firestorm and how potent it had been even to be in its proximity. He couldn't even begin to imagine how overwhelming its force would be, if connected to him.

As if he had summoned it with his thoughts, Orion felt a spark. Warmth spilled through his body, like light running through his veins, making him feel alive and vital—and aroused. He caught his breath, inhaling deeply of the golden heat of what had to be his firestorm. He lifted his hand and felt his eyes widen as fire began to glow around his fingertips. The flames grew, becoming a dancing halo of flame.

She was here!

"Great Wyvern," he whispered in awe. "So, this is what it feels like."

Then he looked. Sure enough, a woman had come into the square and was knocking on the door that the older women had unlocked. Her hair was dark and long, and he guessed she was in her mid-twenties. Her shoes were flat and her skirt short. Even at a distance, she was beautiful, and he would have noticed her without the firestorm's heat.

A spark exploded from Orion's fingertip and arched through the air toward her. An answering spark rose from the woman, and the two sparks collided in a brilliant burst of yellow light over top of the fountain.

She turned to look in astonishment and he saw that she was carrying a backpack. She had it cradled against her chest, as if there was something precious inside it.

His mate.

"She's the one," Orion said and began to march across the square. He watched her stare at him, her eyes wide and her lips parted. Her eyes were hazel with thick dark lashes. She retreated a step, holding that backpack close, as the golden glow of the firestorm caught her in a halo of light.

Then she pivoted and ran.

"Stop!" Orion called, then wondered whether she even understood the Greek of his homeland. He wished he had learned more of the language of the modern *Pyr*, though there was no guarantee she would have understood it either.

He felt rather than saw the flash of the darkfire crystal behind him, and turned as a wind stirred the dust in the plaza. He saw his fellows illuminated by blue-green light, but like Alexander, he raced away from them.

She was his mate.

This was his firestorm.

And no matter where and when this was, it was exactly where Orion was meant to be. He only hoped he could outrun the darkfire's reach.

———

Earlier that morning in Rome, April 1972...

SIX THOUSAND YEARS of civilization and some things never changed.

Well, one thing in particular seemed to be set in stone.

Men were pigs.

It was a beautiful sunny morning in Rome, but Francesca's mood didn't match the weather. It was one thing to be given this menial job, and quite another that Dr. Thomas had insisted she wear a skirt. The patron was traditional, he said, implying that there was something outrageous about a woman wearing jeans. Jeans were practical! Especially when Francesca spent most days digging in the ruins or preparing archeological artefacts for display.

Besides, whether or not she improved the patron's view had nothing to do with anything. She was a person, a scholar, and not just a piece of eye candy for old men.

She'd fumed as she dressed, not prepared to defy Dr. Thomas when he held so much sway over her future. Then when she had come down to the breakfast room in their *pensione*, both Dr. Thomas and Larry had stared at her as if their eyes were going to fall out of their heads. They practically drooled on the floor at a glimpse of her legs—and Larry had kept touching her at the table. His hand brushed hers when he offered the cream for the coffee. His thigh collided with hers a little too often. Dr. Thomas just stared. Ugh.

Now, the men of Rome were gawking and whistling, making her feel like she was navigating a meat market. If she got pinched again in a crowd, she'd kick the offender where it would hurt.

How had she even gotten stuck with this errand in the first place? Easy—she was the only woman on the team.

Francesca almost growled at the truth in that. The world had come a long way according to her mom, but it hadn't come nearly far enough for Francesca. She was the most senior grad student. She was the one on the verge of completing her dissertation. Yet she was also the only female, so she'd been sent to collect an artifact for the exhibition in Cumae, when Larry should have been given the job as the most junior member of the team. He hadn't even finished his undergrad degree.

While she was being ogled in the streets, Larry and Dr. Thomas enjoyed their breakfasts and newspapers.

She hoped they choked on their pastries.

If the patron, Mr. Montmorency, with his *traditional* values, expected more than her simple collection of the vase he was lending to the exhibit, he'd get a surprise. Francesca didn't even care if that meant he withdrew his support.

Men were all the same. It seemed a universal truth that they expected to be served by whatever woman was in the vicinity, whether it was technically her job or not. At the museum, she'd soon learned that she was expected to make coffee, run errands, and wash the dishes in the shared kitchen, as well as continue with her own research. She made coffee for herself, which felt mean, but she wasn't a servant. She had flatly declined to clean the dishes, which had clearly been a surprise to Larry and Dr. Thomas. She also refused to pick up lunch each day.

That was probably why she'd ended up with this errand. They'd closed ranks against her, insisting that Mr. Montmorency preferred to deal with women.

She marched through the streets, hoping that didn't mean what she suspected it meant.

Maybe there were two exceptions to this universal truth. Francesca's older brothers weren't perfect and they sure weren't angels, but they helped. Rafe switched off with his wife, Maddy, in taking care of their infant son so they both could keep their jobs. He was as good with a diaper and a bottle as anyone Francesca had even seen. Gabe ferried the kids to school and picked them up since his wife, Kathy, had a longer commute to work, and he made a mean spaghetti sauce for dinner. Her brothers played for the team, as Rafe said, just as Dad had done.

Francesca was starting to wonder whether the men in the Marino family were a species so rare as to be nearly extinct.

Mr. Montmorency's apartment was in the Trastevere, not that

far of a walk from the area around the Vatican where they were staying. Francesca liked this old Roman neighborhood with its ochre and yellow walls, its cobbled streets and its tiled roofs. The past was close in this corner of the Eternal City and her mood improved with every step. It seemed like a neighborhood where she could live happily, especially once the streets became quiet. She allowed herself a fantasy of completing her doctorate and continuing her research in the Vatican collections, buying a little apartment in the Trastevere with a private patio and a sun-baked kitchen.

By the time she reached Mr. Montmorency's apartment, Francesca was feeling her usual cheerful self. Collecting the artefact would give her the chance to peek at it alone first, after all. Dr. Thomas was sure it was fake, but what if he was wrong? She tingled with anticipation as she rang the bell.

"*Bon giorno*," a handsome older gentleman said when he opened the door. His gaze swept over her with undisguised appreciation, but she didn't let her smile waver. She'd only be here for a moment.

He was well dressed for a servant, but if Mr. Montmorency collected Roman artefacts, he had to be wealthy. This man looked as if he'd just taken off the jacket of an elegantly tailored dark suit: his tie was perfectly knotted and his shoes polished to a gleam. If he hadn't been in his fifties, he could have been a model: he was fit but not thin, his hair was dark and trimmed short, and his confidence was supreme. "You must be the American, Miss Francesca Marino," he said smoothly, without a trace of accent in his English. He then stepped back and gestured to the apartment. Even from the doorway, Francesca thought the interior resembled Aladdin's cave, thick with treasures.

"Is Signor Montmorency at home?" she asked politely as she stepped inside. He closed the door behind her and at the sound of the lock shooting home, she felt a little flicker of panic, as if she'd made a mistake.

His smile seemed a little more hungry than it had a moment before and his eyes glittered.

No. She was letting her imagination get the better of her. He wasn't any worse than the others.

"I *am* Magnus Montmorency," he said, as if confiding a secret.

"I'm sorry, sir. I expected you to have a manservant or butler."

He waved his hand, dismissive of the very notion, and led her into the apartment. "Servants talk," he said. "I prefer my privacy."

There was something to be said for that.

Francesca followed him, her curiosity overwhelming her uncertainty with every step. There were framed paintings on the walls of the corridor, each with a little spotlight, and she blinked in amazement. Instead of the usual Madonnas and crucifixions, they all showed dragons, mostly being tamed by a woman. This first one could have been a Giotto from the fourteenth century. The next reminded her of the work of the Lorenzetti brothers. Francesca was no expert in medieval painters but she'd seen a lot of wonderful examples in the course of her studies. Was this last one a Tintoretto? She had to stop and stare for a moment.

"You admire my collection," Mr. Montmorency said with pride and she smiled at him.

"St. Margaret of Antioch and the dragon," she said. "I haven't seen all of these depictions before."

"Some of them have never been photographed," he said with pride, running a fingertip down the frame of the one she thought was a Tintoretto. His eyes glittered when he flicked a glance at her. "They're mine, all mine."

Francesca noted his possessiveness of his treasures and made a mental note not to rouse it further. "They're beautiful," she said because they were.

He smiled and beckoned. "But not why you are here."

Francesca followed him into what had to be the main room of the apartment and once again found herself staring. She might have entered a cathedral given the ceiling soaring overhead, its surface covered with sparkling mosaics. But this was no shrine to Christianity: the image on the ceiling depicted a battle between a dragon and a soldier, and looked like Byzantine work. The dragon raged out of a stormy sea, breathing fire and fury, while the hero in question brandished his sword and held up a round shield. He defended a maiden in flowing white robes, who had been chained to a rock. The entire scene was lit with the golden glow of the fire breathed by the dragon. It even surrounded the maiden with a halo of sorts, reminding Francesca of the corona painted around the heads of religious figures in Christian art.

"Perseus," Francesca guessed, unable to tear her gaze away.

"How clever of you," Signor Montmorency murmured and she found him very close to her.

She took a step to one side, putting more distance between them. "I sense a theme," she dared to say and watched him.

"A fascination, if you will." He continued to stare at the ceiling, but the corner of his mouth lifted in a little smile that Francesca did not trust.

Wasn't there anyone else in the apartment?

"It's remarkable," she said.

"It is," he agreed easily. "That was why I had to have it." He turned to face her and his eyes shone with conviction. "Anyone can collect items that are valuable."

"Anyone with enough money to spare," she felt obliged to note.

That smile widened, which wasn't reassuring at all. "Indeed," he agreed and Francesca retreated another step. There was something about Mr. Montgomery that seemed...dangerous. He quickly looked at the ceiling again, almost as if he felt she'd glimpsed a secret. "I choose to collect items that are magnificent, whether others perceive their value or not."

Francesca looked around the room. It was sparsely furnished, the better to highlight his treasures. One wall was lined with large windows that opened to a private terrace, tiled in terra cotta, walled and mostly bare. On the opposite wall was a magnificent fireplace carved of dark marble—in any other home, she'd have assumed it was a modern replica of a Renaissance masterpiece, but in Mr. Montmorency's home, Francesca guessed that it was the real thing. Carved dragons twined over it, serpentine and sinuous, both ornamental and fierce, their details accented with painted gold. That was probably real 18 karat gold, too. A fire burned low in the grate, little more than coals, even though it was a warm day. The floor was made of marble squares in alternating black and white, making Francesca feel as if she'd stepped into a chess game.

The wall behind her and the one in front of her mirrored each other. There was a closed door opposite the opening where they stood: that one probably led to private rooms. There was an alcove on either side of the doorway opposite her, each containing a single stone pedestal topped by a glass-walled display case. All four stone pedestals matched the fireplace in a way, each being carved out of the same dark stone and having a dragon wrapped around it. The dragons were twisted around the pillar, tail at the bottom, head on one side of the pillar with jaws open as if each one would devour the displayed treasure on the pillar's top. There was a similar pair of pillars on either side of the doorway Francesca had entered with her host.

He gestured and they walked together to the display case to the right of the door opposite, the one closest to the windows. In the case was a tall vase, twelve to fourteen inches tall and about six inches wide. The top of it would have been open but there was a stopper in it, one that had been sealed with wax and stamped with marks. Francesca admired the iridescent glimmer which was characteristic of Roman glass and tried to discern the markings on the seal. She couldn't quite make them out. Maybe a signature or a warning.

"Roman glass always looks as if they captured a rainbow," she said and her companion chuckled.

"Or as if they harnessed the moon and stars," he said, a surprisingly poetic turn of phrase and one that prompted Francesca to look at him. His eyes were gleaming and she was startled to find him watching her.

Predatory was about the size of it. His gaze swept over her again, his nostrils flaring slightly, and she knew it was time to go.

Francesca removed her backpack, setting it on the floor before opening it. "I brought some padding to wrap it up," she said, taking it out. "Dr. Thomas wanted me to tell you how honored he is that you are entrusting us with this piece for the exhibit."

"It is time that more had the chance to appreciate it," Mr. Montgomery said, a sentiment that Francesca found admirable and somewhat inconsistent with his other comments. He put his hands in his trouser pockets, the move drawing her attention to his very expensive gold watch.

Was she supposed to stand here and admire it with him all day? They still had to drive back to Baiae, and the others were waiting for her.

Mr. Montgomery didn't move, though.

Francesca cleared her throat. "Could you unlock the display case, please? I don't want to take too much of your time."

"No," he said softly. He unlocked the case and stepped back. "Modern women are always in a hurry."

Francesca couldn't hold back her words. "As opposed to all the medieval women you've known? Or the ones from antiquity?"

"Precisely," he said, as if he meant it and she glanced up. His thoughts were hidden now, his expression impassive. "You know the story, of course?"

Francesca opened her mouth and closed it again. She did know the story because Dr. Thomas had laughed about it. The exhibition would make a mockery of Mr. Montmorency's theories about his prized artefact and she still felt uneasy about that now that she'd met him. He didn't seem like the kind of man who would appreciate that revelation. "Why don't you tell me?" she invited, reasoning it was a small thing to give him. "The version I heard might be different."

He beamed at her and she knew she'd made the right answer. While he spoke, she opened the unlocked case and began to wrap the vase, well aware of how intently he watched her.

"Once upon a time, Apollo desired the Cumaean Sibyl but she refused to be seduced," he said, his voice low. "This was unacceptable to the handsome god, to be denied by any female, never mind a mortal woman."

"Albeit one with the power of foresight," Francesca felt compelled to say.

He inclined his head slightly. "So, Apollo persisted in his suit and told her to name her price. She seized a handful of sand and told him that she wished to live as many years as the number of grains of sand in her grasp. He agreed, but she still refused to surrender to him, wanting proof that he had kept his promise before she submitted. In time, no matter how often he checked, it became clear that she had no intention of surrendering to him at all. And so, Apollo let her age, saying that she had not been so clever as to ask to remain youthful for those centuries. The Sibyl faded and grew ever smaller, the price of her betrayal of the god's will, until she was almost as dust herself. She was trapped then in this jar and ultimately only her voice remained, the last remaining voice of prophecy, sealed in this vessel forever."

It was a creepy story, to Francesca's thinking, and one that showed the lack of choice that men expected women to have. Even a woman with as much power as the Sibyl had been limited in their agency, or their ability to change their own circumstances. She felt the older man's gaze upon her but tried to hold her tongue. She doubted she'd manage that for long.

"The story displeases you," Mr. Montmorency mused after a moment.

Francesca shrugged. "She turned down a guy and ended up sealed in a jar. That seems pretty harsh to me."

"Not just any guy," he countered, accenting the last word. "The god Apollo himself."

"Does it matter? He would have just taken her virginity and abandoned her, just like a mortal man. Shouldn't she have had a choice?"

There was a moment of silence between them and Francesca felt him watching her as she put the swaddled vase into her backpack.

"Your heart has been broken."

"No," Francesca said, daring to meet his gaze. His eyes were darker now, which made him look more threatening. She stood taller, refusing to be afraid of a man at least thirty years older than her. She was fast and strong. "I just know how that story goes." She put on the backpack but backwards, so that the weight of it was against her chest. She could wrap her arms around it this way and be sure it wasn't jostled in a crowd—even though the streets weren't very busy at this hour.

"One might have expected more," he said quietly and Francesca felt herself flush as she took offense.

The only reason she'd been sent on foot, rather than a team of curators from the museum with a carton and a truck, was that no one believed the vase was more than a nice piece of old glass.

No one except Mr. Montmorency.

"It's very busy right now at the museums," she said. "I'm honored to have been trusted to pick up your vase for the exhibit."

He eyed her, then nodded once, turning away to indicate the display case in the niche on the other side of the door. "Will you have a look at one more treasure?" he invited and there was no way Francesca could decline temptation. This guy had a serious hoard of a collection but she was never coming back.

Mr. Montmorency had moved to stand before the display case on the other side of the door, the one closer to the fireplace, and was seemingly lost in thought.

It was a funerary urn, one inscribed with a name. Francesca squinted at the Roman letters. AURELIA. Was it an actual Roman funerary urn or had he repurposed it for his wife's ashes? Francesca fought against her urge to shudder.

To her surprise, he unlocked the display case and removed the lid from the vessel, setting it down beside the vessel. Was he going to show off the ashes? Francesca once again retreated a step. But when Mr. Montmorency tipped the urn, a round stone rolled into his palm.

His eyes glittered again as he smiled at her. "Surprised?"

"Yes. But you knew I would be."

"I can be disappointed that you were predictable, Miss Marino," he murmured, then replaced the urn in the case, lifting the stone and turning it in the light. It was about the size of an egg but perfectly spherical. It was a greyish-green color, and mottled with tiny specs of red. "A bloodstone," he said before she could ask. "Known to the ancients as heliotrope."

"Sunstone," Francesca said.

"A healing stone believed to be imbued with the power of the gods. A protective stone, used on battlefields to staunch blood." He extended his arm so she could see it better. "This one is inscribed."

"With the symbols for the four elements," Francesca said, recognizing them. "What was it for?"

His dark brow lifted, making him look diabolical. "Aurelia insisted it could raise the dead, a fitting association for a stone subsequently believed to have been formed from falling drops of the blood of Christ as he died on the cross."

Francesca smiled. "So, it's a *magic* stone. Lucky you." She couldn't entirely keep the laughter from her tone but Mr. Montmorency didn't share her amusement.

His own smile faded and his eyes narrowed to menacing slits. "Aurelia was many things but she was not a liar. This stone, in fact, is a copy, precisely because skeptics like you don't deserve to even see the real one."

"I see." She had to get out of the apartment before she really offended him. Dr. Thomas should have sent someone who was more of a diplomat.

Her host's tone turned dismissive. "No, you don't, but I have neither the time nor the inclination to show you more." He gestured toward the front door, flicking his hand as if she was a child being sent to play outside. He said something beneath his breath and she thought she discerned the words "impossibly stupid species," by which she assumed he meant either grad students or Americans.

Either way, Francesca was only too glad to take the hint to leave. She headed for the door with purpose, relieved that he didn't accompany her. Mr. Montmorency remained behind—in his audience room, shrine or baby museum—and she turned at the doorway to find him watching her. There was a trick of the light just then, a blue light that seemed to flicker around the silhouette of his figure, even as he exuded displeasure.

"Thank you very much, *signor*," she said cheerfully as she unbolted the door.

"Damage my prize at your peril," he said quietly but the words—and the threat—carried clearly to Francesca's ears. It seemed to echo in her thoughts, so menacing that she felt cold.

Francesca stepped out of the apartment and hurried down the stairs, not even looking back until she was in the sunlight again. She shivered and held the bag close as she hurried away from the apartment and its owner.

Good thing Mr. Montmorency had no idea that Dr. Thomas intended to trash his story about the Cumaean Sibyl's voice once and for all.

But then, the man seemed to have a taste for imaginative (and even irrational) stories. No doubt he'd collect a few more.

Thank goodness he hadn't made a move on her. She might have

dismissed her trepidation as just her imagination, but she remembered the glitter of his eyes and shivered again.

The sun was brighter and the street a little busier than it had been just moments before. People were heading to work and more shutters were open. Francesca could hear the chatter of conversation and saw one woman hanging out her laundry. Another was singing softly as she watered the plants on her terrace—from this angle, it looked like a lush oasis. She was headed back toward the *pensione*, then halted.

She deserved a reward.

She wanted a coffee. A good one. And a pastry.

There was a little bakery in the next square. She'd noticed it as she passed through. Larry and Dr. Thomas could wait ten minutes for her to get a good breakfast.

Maybe twenty while she enjoyed it.

She'd earned that, for sure.

CHAPTER TWO

I t didn't take Francesca long to reach her destination. The square with the bakery was still pretty empty. There was an older man cleaning the fountain in the center, absorbed in his task, and many of the windows were still shuttered. A group of men sat on the chairs of a closed restaurant on the other side of the square. Most of them looked to be in their twenties and thirties, except for one who could have been their leader or boss. They were dressed casually but even at a distance, Francesca could see that they were really fit.

A soccer team, maybe?

If they were tourists, they had to be European. Maybe Greek, given their dark coloring, olive skin and quiet intensity. They didn't seem to be talking to each other—just watching her. It could have been because she was the only person moving in the square, but Francesca guessed that it was because of her gender. She shot a glare across the piazza, which made exactly no difference to anything, hugged the backpack with one arm and tried the door of the bakery. It was locked, so she knocked.

Then she froze at a tinkle inside the backpack. Had she broken the vase? Terror shot through her as she remembered Mr. Montmorency's warning, then the hair prickled on the back of her neck.

As if a storm was coming.

But it was early in the day and the sky was perfectly blue.

Francesca glanced over her shoulder and saw a bright orange spark. She stared in astonishment as it sailed through the air, bright against the vivid blue sky, a plume of yellow-orange heat on a mission —and headed right for her.

One of the men was on his feet, his hand raised as if he had flung it toward her. She opened her mouth to tell him off just as a second spark erupted from the backpack. It launched into the air like a rocket and the two lights collided over the fountain, sending a shower of sparks down into the plaza. Some of them sizzled as they landed in the water of the fountain. The older man watering the flowers flinched, but seemed unhurt. Francesca took a stumbling step backward, unable to explain her sense that she was surrounded by a halo of golden light.

Cradled by its warmth.

Turned on.

Oh.

The guy who'd been on his feet was crossing the piazza when she looked again, his determination evident in every step. He wore khaki pants and a dark T-shirt, one that didn't hide the fact that he was completely ripped. His gaze was fixed upon her, his resolve so evident that she shivered.

Strangely enough, there was a blue-green shimmer of light sliding across the ground and his companions had completely vanished.

Francesca stared at him for a moment, unable to make sense of what was happening—then she realized he had to be a thief.

Dr. Thomas had warned her to be careful, but she hadn't believed anyone would want Mr. Montmorency's vase until this moment. She knew that even without the story of the Sibyl, old Roman glass had value to collectors.

She also knew that if this man caught her, he would overpower her easily. He had to be over six feet tall and all muscle. He marched toward her with the vigor of a trained athlete, so intent upon catching her that she felt the universe might be on his side. He looked both purposeful and relentless, so much so that she doubted that anyone successfully denied him anything. He had dark hair and a killer tan, shoulders that stretched his dark T-shirt taut, but his eyes were an unexpected silvery-blue.

Like the ocean in sunlight.

Now she was going crazy.

Or being mesmerized, maybe just as he planned.

Francesca pivoted and ran, hugging the backpack to her chest. The jar seemed to have heated from the impact of the spark, which made no sense at all. It got hotter with every step, and she interpreted that as a sign that he was gaining on her. It could have been glowing like a coal fire, but she wasn't in a position to unwrap it and have a look.

She could hear his footfalls gaining fast and ran faster. She flung herself down an alley, not daring to look back and see whether he followed, then through a crowded morning market. At least she knew this part of the city like the back of her own hand, after her time studying here. She was sure she'd evade him, then she heard his voice.

Low and soft, as intense as he was, as deep as the ocean.

"Stop, I beg of you. Stop. I can explain." His voice was melodic, almost musical, and seductive as hell.

Because he was calling to her in Ancient Greek.

Francesca frowned as her steps slowed. No one spoke Ancient Greek any more, especially not in Rome. Well, except for her, Larry, and Dr. Thomas, and Larry's Greek was dubious.

None of them spoke it like this, so beautifully. It was like poetry to listen to him chastise himself, even when he cursed.

"How can I tell her? How can I convince her to trust in the power of the firestorm?" he demanded with quiet heat. "I am a fool! I do not deserve such fortune." Francesca glanced back, then realized a bit late that she'd turned into a dead end.

How could she have been so stupid?

She'd been entranced by his voice.

She spun to face him, the backpack against her chest as if it would protect her. The walls rose four stories high on either side of the alley and there was a high brick wall behind her. Shutters and blinds were closed on every window and there was no one else in the alley.

Except him.

He halted, silhouetted against the open end of the alley, then pushed a hand through his hair. There was a golden glow between them, one that Francesca couldn't explain at all, and it brightened as he took a step closer. It also burned a little hotter, making the backpack so warm that the inside of her arms had to be burning.

If that wasn't strange enough, a languorous heat spread through her body from the backpack. She felt aroused, which made no sense, and she was sure her nipples had tightened. Her heart skipped, but not from the effort of running, her breath came quickly and she felt herself flush. It was a flush that came from deep inside her, one that made her toes curl and her mouth go dry.

One that made her realize how long it had been since she'd had company at night.

One that kept her rooted to the spot, watching him.

He walked closer, moving slowly as if he was afraid of startling her.

And he kept talking, even as he stretched out a hand in entreaty.

It was the Greek that melted Francesca's resistance, though, not his good looks or even his gesture.

"O, curse of my days and nights," he said. "How did I come to be in this time, where I cannot speak to my destined mate, let alone court her favor? How could the darkfire so betray me, by delivering me to a firestorm that can never be satisfied? What have I done to merit such cruelty?"

Absolutely, undoubtedly, Ancient Greek. She hadn't been wrong. There was no iotonisation in his vowels: he was speaking as they had in the second century BC. And so fluidly! The words flowed from his tongue with an elegance that Francesca envied. She'd never heard anyone speak the language like this.

She was transfixed.

He stopped two paces away from her, his gaze searching her face. His expression was one of wonder and despite his size and power, Francesca was convinced he meant her no harm. In fact, he looked to be shaken by her presence.

His hand shook as he stretched that hand toward her, then he stopped, as if he was daunted by her.

Those eyes with their ethereal blue seemed to see to her very heart. Francesca couldn't even take a breath.

"So beautiful," he murmured, his gaze roving over her, his admiration clear. Oddly enough, Francesca felt flattered, not ogled. "So precious and such a gift unexpected. And yet, and *yet*, Zeus might have made this jest upon me by ensuring that I cannot tell her of our entwined fates. How am I to convince her of the merit of the firestorm?" He lifted his hand and a radiance glowed from his palm, a flurry of sparks leaping toward her, the light so bright that Francesca narrowed her eyes.

They inhaled sharply in unison and their gazes met.

"Maybe you should tell me about the firestorm," Francesca said in Ancient Greek.

His eyes lit with understanding and he smiled, a smile so dazzling that Francesca could only stare. He had to be the most handsome man she'd ever seen. He closed the distance between them with a purposeful step and caught her face in his hands. His grip was gentle, his hands warm, his expression so intense that Francesca couldn't look away from him. He was studying her as if she was the greatest marvel in the world and it was hard—no impossible—to steel herself from responding. Francesca couldn't even summon her usual skepticism, not when he looked at her like that, not when his thumbs slid across her cheeks in a slow caress.

"You understand," he said with satisfaction, then chuckled a little. It was a dark sexy sound, so intimate that it could have melted her knees. "Of course. The firestorm leaves nothing to chance."

And then, before she could ask any of the obvious questions, he bent and captured her mouth beneath his own.

He kissed her.

His was a perfect kiss, compelling, gentle, persuasive and demanding, thrilling. A complete stranger kissed her in the street— and he did it so well that Francesca could only kiss him back.

OF COURSE, Orion's destined mate understood him. Even in this time and place so distant from his own origins, the firestorm had removed any barrier between them.

The modern *Pyr*, the ones he had met in America, were right. The firestorm was so much more than the mating of *Pyr* and mate, so much more than the chance to conceive a son. It was an opportunity for a profound partnership, the chance to forge a connection that would sustain them both for all their days and nights.

It was a gift beyond all expectation.

And this woman, so feminine and yet so bold, with her flashing eyes and her welcoming kiss, was more of a marvel than Orion had ever hoped to encounter. Her kiss muddled his thoughts, filled him with desire, aroused every protective instinct within him. She was a treasure to be cherished, and like his modern kin, he wanted to savor their courtship.

That would make the satisfaction of the firestorm all the sweeter. There was a heat in his veins, like molten gold, and a fire in his heart like nothing he had ever felt before. She was both soft and strong in his embrace, even with the bulk of the backpack between them. It had grown hot, undoubtedly due to the firestorm, and in another time, he might have wondered whether it would leave a burn on his chest.

In this moment, there was only his mate. He broke their kiss to stare down at her, mesmerized. Her eyes were shining and she was smiling just a little. Her eyes were hazel, flicked with green and gold, and thickly lashed, while her lips were full, painted a soft pink. Her lipstick was smeared a little, the result of his kiss, and Orion felt a surge of satisfaction that she bore some small mark of his claim.

"Oh," she said, then cleared her throat. Her fingertips strayed over his shoulders and she watched their progress. The orange glow of the firestorm heated an increment, becoming more yellow and radiant. It burned through him, a surge of fire and need, one so potent and right that he halfway wished it would last forever.

Then he wondered how he would endure it.

"Does this always happen when you kiss someone?" she asked in a husky whisper. Her Greek was good, a little stiff, but easily understood. He felt blessed again.

"No," Orion confessed with a shake of his head, then smiled at her. "Only with you."

She shook her head a little, her brows drawing together. "Why would that be?"

"Because you are my destined mate. It is the gift of the firestorm to illuminate our bond, to provide a guiding light to our shared future."

She frowned and took a step back, pulling out of his embrace. "That's a new one," she said, which made no sense to Orion. His reaction must have shown because her lips tightened. "No one has ever tried to seduce me with that line before." Her smile turned impish and her gaze dropped to his mouth. "You were doing better before you said anything."

Orion claimed her hand and rubbed his thumb across the back of it, admiring how the glow of the firestorm bathed her skin in golden light. "The firestorm is not only about seduction or even pleasure," he insisted, hoping she would understand that he was sincere. "It is about partnership and union beyond the mere physical."

"What about the sparks?"

"They are its sign, one that cannot be missed." He dared to move closer, raising his fingertips to her cheek. He felt an immediate rush of need with closer proximity, one that made him catch his breath in awe. He watched as her eyes widened in surprise. Her cheek was soft beyond belief, and she needed no paint to accentuate her beauty. Her lips parted as she stared up at him and Orion bent closer, wanting only another kiss.

"They are a mark of our shared destiny," he whispered before touching his lips to hers.

She made a minute sound that might have been born of skepticism, then Orion smelled *Slayer*.

He spun away from her and tucked her behind him, determined to defend her at any price, then surveyed the alley. A man stood silhouetted at the end of the alley, and Orion assessed him as being older but still powerful.

"Mr. Montmorency," his mate whispered.

Orion did not glance back at her. He could see the glitter of the *Slayer's* eyes and knew better than to let his attention slip. "You know this man?" he asked quietly.

"I met him this morning. He's a patron, lending an artefact to the exhibit I'm helping to curate."

Orion glanced back, not understanding, and she patted the pack she was carrying.

Whatever this *Slayer* had entrusted to her was in that bag. Was he retrieving the item or interfering in Orion's firestorm? He bristled as he watched the *Slayer* saunter into the alley, confident and purposeful.

Immediately, he calculated and assessed his position. The sky was clear overhead, except for a wire that crossed between the buildings at the entrance to the alley. Perhaps a telephone or electrical line. He knew only that it should be avoided. Orion was aware of all the windows facing this cul-de-sac, all the possible human observers if he chose to shift shape. He could take flight, but there was little margin for error if he could fly, and less to maneuver on the ground.

"Why is there a blue shimmer around you?" his mate asked in a whisper, but this was not the time to explain the details of his nature.

Orion knew the scent of this *Slayer*. He couldn't make sense of it. He didn't recognize him in his human form, and knew they could not have met in the past. *Slayers* had not existed in Orion's own time.

"Who are you?" Orion demanded, realizing belatedly that his opponent might not speak Greek.

The *Slayer* smiled and walked closer. He was shimmering blue as well, no doubt assessing Orion. "Signora Marino," he said lightly, then continued in Greek, ignoring Orion's question. "I trust my prize is safe in your possession." The shimmer of blue around his form revealed that he wasn't truly ignoring either Orion or the threat he posed. *"Who are you?"* he demanded in old-speak, the words echoing in Orion's thoughts, even as he smiled at Orion's mate.

Orion chose not to reply. How could he know this *Slayer's* scent?

"Of course!" his mate said, stepping out from behind Orion— exactly as he had feared she might. She began to walk toward the *Slayer*, showing a confidence in his intentions that Orion did not share. "You can see that I have it safely right here."

The *Slayer* eyed her bag. "I had understood that you were a serious academic, not a woman who formed liaisons in the street, Signora Marino."

"And you understood correctly," she said, ice in her tone. "I simply paused for a moment."

Slayer and mate turned as one to survey Orion.

In that instant, Orion realized that he recognized his challenger from the *future*. The darkfire crystal had flung Drake and his followers into the past, scattering them through the centuries, but his memory of this *Slayer* hadn't yet occurred. It had occurred in America, when he and Drake's followers had joined forces with their modern brethren.

That explained why his opponent didn't recognize Orion.

It also meant that Orion was uncertain of the consequences of his actions in this time and place. If he attacked the *Slayer*, if he injured or killed him, how would that change the future? Would it influence the outcome of the war between *Pyr* and *Slayer*? Orion couldn't imagine that it would be irrelevant.

"I am Magnus Montmorency," the *Slayer* said, walking steadily closer to Orion with one hand outstretched. There was an intensity in his manner that Orion perceived as a threat. He also recognized the name.

"I know," he said, not providing his own name. The two glared at each other, sizing up each other's powers. Magnus, undoubtedly deliberately, dimmed his blue shimmer so that it vanished to nothing. Orion didn't doubt that he could still shift quickly, but his choice left Orion's mate turning her attention to Orion. Her suspicion of that light was clear.

He stepped back from the cusp of change by force of will and the light flickered, then died.

Magnus chuckled, then switched to old-speak. *"I knew there was something special about Miss Marino. She will be a delightful sacrifice."* He smiled then, a hungry flash of his teeth, and the sight made Orion's fists clench.

He would not let his mate be injured and this *Slayer* should know as much.

Magnus held his gaze, as if daring him to shift first.

"Why is there thunder on a clear day?" Orion's mate asked, looking up at the visible patch of sky. Of course, she heard the rumble of the old-speak.

"Perhaps you have a destination to reach," Orion suggested and the *Slayer* chuckled.

"Yes, I would not wish my prize to be damaged by the rain," he said, leaving it unclear whether he referred to whatever Orion's mate carried or the mate herself.

His stance was confrontational and Orion's mate looked between the two of them with uncertainty. "You're not going to have a fight with a patron of our exhibition," she said in an undertone.

"I will respond in kind, if he begins one," Orion growled. *"If he is fool enough to touch my mate,"* he added in old-speak.

"I do love a challenge," the *Slayer* replied and took a step closer.

"This thunder is crazy," Orion's mate protested just as the *Slayer* began to shimmer blue again.

Orion seized his mate's hand and flung her toward the opening of the alley. The firestorm flared to brilliant white light, temporarily blinding all three of them. "Run!" he ordered and to his satisfaction and relief, she walked quickly, followed his instruction.

He heard her steps fading as he blocked the end of the alley, ensuring that the *Slayer* couldn't follow.

"Have we met?" the *Slayer* asked, his voice silky. *"Because your adversity seems disproportionate for a first encounter."*

"Even though you threatened my mate?"

"Even so."

"I recognized your name."

"Indeed?"

"Rafferty Powell is a friend of mine."

"Ah! And any enemy of Rafferty Powell is thus an opponent of yours." Magnus smiled, his eyes gleaming. *"Let's make it official, shall we?"* He removed something from his pocket that gleamed,

then flicked it at Orion. It flashed in the light, a small disk of metal that spun end over end. Orion knew it had to be the *Slayer's* challenge coin, even before he snatched it out of the air with satisfaction.

A duel to the death.

The traditional terms suited him admirably.

"I like having matters clearly defined," he said and pocketed the coin. He might have shifted shape and pursued the challenge immediately, but there was a bang overhead as shutters were opened in a hurry and collided with the wall. Someone cried out, reminding him that there could be human witnesses.

Magnus dropped his old-speak to a hiss that echoed in Orion's thoughts. *"Until we meet again,"* he vowed, then spun on his heel and strode out of the alley. By the time, Orion stepped after the *Slayer*, he had vanished among the pedestrians.

Orion ran a hand over his brow, striving to recall all he had known about the *Slayer*, Magnus Montmorency. Magnus could take the salamander form. He had created the Dragon's Blood Elixir and consumed it, giving him a kind of immortality—or at least a powerful ability to heal from his injuries. He was the sworn enemy of Rafferty Powell, the *Pyr* who had freed all of the Dragon's Tooth Warriors from Cadmus' curse.

How much of that was true in this time and how much of it hadn't occurred yet?

Orion pulled the challenge coin from his pocket. He didn't recognize the currency but it didn't matter. He, too, was the sworn enemy of Magnus Montmorency, and one day, they would battle to the death. He had no doubt he would see the *Slayer* again—not only did he know his scent, but there was some connection between the *Slayer* and Orion's mate.

And whatever was in the backpack she carried.

Signora Marino.

At least the *Slayer* had done him the favor of surrendering his mate's name. A name wasn't a lot of information, but along with the spark of the firestorm, it might be sufficient for Orion to find her.

———

WAS it three impossible things one should believe before breakfast or six? Francesca couldn't remember, but she was sure that she had fulfilled the list either way on this particular morning.

Never mind the affluent patron with no staff, the one who believed in magic. That wasn't so impossible to believe. But there was that inexplicable spark that had been flung at her, and the one that had erupted from her backpack, as if the first had summoned the second.

That was one impossible thing. Sparks couldn't be tossed around like baseballs, and they didn't answer each other's summons.

Next, there was the golden glow that appeared between herself and the guy who had followed her, the one she had assumed to be a thief, except for his amazing ability to speak Ancient Greek.

Definitely two.

There had been that kiss, an unexpected caress that had threatened to melt her bones. She should have pushed him away. Francesca never let any stranger touch her, let alone kiss her, but that kiss had been worth the price of admission. She could count either the incredible kiss or her own capitulation to it as the third impossible thing.

There had been his ridiculous line about the firestorm and destined mates—okay, an outrageous line wasn't an impossible thing to believe—then the way the glow had brightened between them. Had he been controlling it? If so, how? The jury was out on how impossible that was.

But the way he had shimmered blue was another thing entirely. It couldn't have been a trick of the light, not when Mr. Montmorency did the same thing. Why had that patron followed her in the first place? Why hadn't *she* been surrounded by a shimmering blue light? What was that about?

Either way, she had a solid four impossible things. At least.

The sound of thunder on a clear morning made for five inexplicable details in one morning.

Francesca supposed that it wasn't impossible to believe that the two men had fought, because there certainly had been a crackle of adversity in the air. Did they know each other? It seemed as if they did, but then Mr. Montmorency had introduced himself. Men, and her older brothers, often made no sense, but the charge between the two of them hadn't exactly been impossible. Unlikely, maybe. Uncomfortable, definitely.

Despite how independent she was, Francesca did like that the guy had come to her defense. Maybe he'd only meant to ensure she got out of the alley safely, but she didn't really trust Mr. Montmorency either. Why had he followed her at all?

But what exactly had been the danger? The threat had been palpable, but Francesca couldn't explain it. Mr. Montgomery hadn't been antagonistic when she'd left him just minutes before. It had to be something between the two men, some history she didn't know. What could it be to make them so hostile to each other? And why had she been in peril? She had nothing to do with any male feud. What had been that brilliant white flare of light when the guy had taken her hand? It had sent a shock through her that left her simmering.

With a desire beyond anything she'd felt before.

That gave her a solid six things.

She really needed some breakfast.

Francesca was halfway back to the *pensione* before she realized that the strange golden light had vanished. She felt cold, even though it was a warm day and she was walking briskly. The backpack had chilled, too, and felt as she would have expected a bag containing a glass vase to feel.

Maybe she was losing her mind, which wasn't the most optimistic thought ever.

The rental car was idling in front of the *pensione*, Larry leaning against the fender finishing a cigarette while Dr. Thomas packed his leather satchel into the back. They both looked a little rumpled, though Larry was closer to unkempt. Dr. Thomas was a good-looking man who had no interest in clothing or the details of daily life. Larry was just a slob. The rental car was a compact with a hatchback, bright green in color, with a very uncomfortable back seat. Their luggage was jammed in the back and half of the back seat.

Francesca had never been so glad to see a vehicle in her life.

"Got it?" Larry asked, throwing away his cigarette butt.

"Yes," Francesca replied, leaving it at that.

"Then let's head out," Dr. Thomas said, his gaze dropping to the bag she was hugging. "We can look at the vase in the museum," he concluded, without a lot of interest.

Francesca, though, kept the bag between her knees in the back seat, not wanting to let it go.

She should have been reassured by the normalcy of everything, but she was still rattled. She couldn't have imagined it all. She was still simmering from that kiss and still really turned on. She still had six things she couldn't explain and she didn't like that one bit.

It was a strange start to her day and, for once, she was glad to be packed into the cramped back seat of the small car.

She was even more glad to be leaving Rome.

She turned and looked out the back windshield as they left the *pensione*, not entirely sure she was glad to be leaving Mr. Ancient Greek behind.

That kiss was going to keep her warm at night for a week.

———

ORION FOLLOWED the glow of the firestorm and the scent of his mate, only to emerge on a narrow street in a busier and more affluent neighborhood. There were people, but none of them were his mate. None of them were speaking Ancient Greek either. The flow of conversation around him was incomprehensible. He could smell salty food and the exhaust of automobiles, both familiar from his time with his future brethren, and the cobbled streets had some similarities to the ones he had known in the past.

There were bicycles and carts, but no sign of Miss Marino. She couldn't have vanished!

But her scent was gone. He had followed it to this point, where it simply disappeared. Orion stood and looked around himself.

She could have vanished if the *Slayer* had caught her. But Orion had followed her quickly and not seen the *Slayer* on the way. He would have sworn his opponent had gone in the opposite direction— even though there was still a faint scent of *Slayer* in his vicinity.

No, she must have gone inside a building or maybe gotten into a vehicle.

A vehicle departing would explain the sudden absence of her scent.

Orion didn't know how to guide one of these vehicles and he didn't know where to hire a ride. He probably didn't have the right currency anyway. Not speaking the language might be the least of his troubles.

He looked right and left, even considered the merit of shifting shape and flying in search of his mate. He could just follow the spark of the firestorm, but in this moment, he couldn't even feel it. She had moved away quickly, which means she had to be in a motorized vehicle.

How would he find her again?

He didn't have the skill to beguile humans, and it was easy to imagine that Drake or Erik would heartily disapprove of him shifting shape in such a public place, even for the sake of his firestorm.

She must have come to this location for a reason. Maybe to meet someone. Maybe to return to wherever she was staying. There was an establishment directly beside him that reminded him of an inn. Baggage was piled in the main room and entryway. A clerk spoke to people from behind a desk, as bored as innkeepers had always been in his own time.

He practiced his mate's name silently as he entered the inn.

"*Si?*" The clerk was a woman with long painted nails. She eyed him with impatience, then drummed those nails on the desktop. "*Si?*" she said again and he decided it was a query.

"Signora Marino?" Orion repeated carefully. He was aware of a younger man coming to stand behind him. He had sandy hair and a backpack, as well as a friendly smile. He reminded Orion of the people he had encountered with his future brethren.

Always smiling.

Soft but friendly.

But with a definite scent of *Slayer*. Orion resisted the urge to turn and look more closely. Did *Slayers* work together in this time? This one might know his mate's location. He might know the other *Slayer* or be allied with him. Had Orion already erred in mentioning his mate's name aloud?

"Ah!" Clearly the woman recognized the name, which was encouraging, but Orion had no chance of understanding her rapid and long reply. She pointed to the street, explaining again with a little more impatience, but he couldn't understand her.

His mate had left. He already knew that much. But where had she gone?

His confusion must have been clear because the *Slayer* behind him gave him a nudge. "She's gone," he said, raising his voice as if Orion was deaf. He was speaking the tongue of the future brethren, the ones in that land of Chicago and Minneapolis. Orion understood it better than he could speak it.

He nodded.

"Cumae," the younger man said, then said it again, louder, enunciating so that his teeth were displayed clearly.

"Cumae," Orion repeated. Could he mean Kymai? He knew of the colony, of course, founded on a distant coast by his kin from Evvia, but he had no notion where it was exactly, much less how to get there from his current location. He also was uncertain whether it might still exist. "Kymai," he asked in Greek, hopeful, but the other man just nodded.

"That's it!" He leaned closer. "Do you need to go there, to Cumae? Do you want a ride?"

Once again, Orion was uncertain of his meaning. "Signora Marino," he said with resolve. "Kymai." He pointed to himself then to the city outside the doors with one finger. "Kymai."

"You want to go to Cumae and find her," the *Slayer* concluded with satisfaction. He was young and plump. Orion had no fear of him despite his nature. "Got it. I'll give you a ride. I'm headed to Naples myself."

"Neapolis?" Orion suggested, knowing that was another nearby colony.

"That's the one," the younger man said with glee.

"Napoli," the woman said but the young man only smiled at her.

"It's okay. I'll give him a ride." The *Slayer* turned back to Orion. "A ride." He lifted his hands to grip an invisible circle and moved them as if he was rotating it. Orion had no idea what he meant, but he knew the *Slayer* was trying to convince him of something. "A drive to Cumae. Me." He pointed to himself. "And you." He pointed to Orion, then at a small blue car parked outside the hotel. He made the motion with his hands again. "Cumae. Signora Marino. Si?"

"Kymai," Orion agreed, recognizing that he was being offered transportation to his mate. If this *Slayer* thought to take advantage of him on the way, he would be surprised by the vigor of Orion's response. Let him believe that Orion had no notion of his nature.

"*Si,*" he said with resolve. The woman clapped her hands with pleasure and the *Slayer* grinned.

This would work.

Maybe Drake had been right about the darkfire taking each of them where they needed to be.

The woman gave the *Slayer* a piece of paper, which he signed, then she gave him a different one which he shoved into his pocket. He grabbed his bag and headed for the blue car, pulling a set of keys from his pocket. He unlocked the back of it and smiled at Orion. "It's small but it was the cheapest one they had. I'm all about the budget. Of course, if I'd known I would have company, I would have gone for a bigger model." He had an accent, one that made him sound a bit like Erik Sorensson, leader of the *Pyr* in that future era.

Was Erik alive in this time and place? It was a definite possibility. The leader of the *Pyr* had been centuries old, as Orion recalled. Could he find Erik?

Could he find more *Pyr*? One *Slayer* had already found him, drawn by his firestorm, and this one had either stumbled across him or sought him out. If there were *Slayers*, there had to be *Pyr* as well.

Perhaps more of his own kind would be drawn to his firestorm. It was an encouraging possibility.

Orion patted the car, trying to show his appreciation and relief. "Good," he said, remembering that word from the future. He then said it again in Ancient Greek, hoping he might be understood.

"Good," his companion repeated in Greek and laughed. He shut the hatchback and offered his hand, switching languages to Orion's relief. "I'm Sigmund Guthrie."

Orion understood that this was an introduction and took the *Slayer's* hand. "Orion."

"Just Orion?"

"Orion," he said, not feeling inclined to provide more information to a *Slayer*.

"I guess I shouldn't be surprised that a guy with a Greek name would want to go to a colony founded by the Ancient Greeks," Sigmund said cheerfully. He opened one door of the car and Orion opened the other, getting in beside him. When Sigmund started the engine and put his hands on the wheel that directed the vehicle, Orion understood his earlier gesture. "That must be what you and Signora Marino have in common."

Orion was puzzled and didn't hide it.

"She's a grad student, working with Dr. Thomas on an upcoming exhibition about Cumae. It'll be in Baiae."

Orion smiled. He didn't understand everything his companion had said, but was reassured that he'd be able to find her in Baiae. "Baiae?" he asked.

"A Roman retreat from the city and resort dedicated to the pursuit of pleasure. *Palatium Baianum.* My kind of place, but a bit later than the Ancient Greeks. Third century AD." Sigmund guided the car into traffic as Orion nodded. "So, you're visiting former Greek colonies." He smiled. "And maybe Signora Marino, too."

Orion had an odd feeling then, as if the *Slayer* knew more about his own mate than he did. The possibility made him uneasy, and anxious to reach his destination.

He wished he knew how long it would take to reach Kymai.

He turned to the window when he felt the glow of the firestorm again, a sign that they were drawing closer to his mate. He would find her and he would win her and their partnership would be glorious.

He had to believe.

CHAPTER THREE

Francesca was sitting behind Larry, who was driving, and even the floor behind the professor was filled by his larger briefcase. The car seemed to be low on the road, probably because of all their luggage. The backpack was between her knees on the floor, the only place to put it, but she would have kept it close either way.

Dr. Zachary Thomas pushed back the brim of his hat and glanced back at her with a smile. He was the best-looking professor in the Classics department but that wasn't why she was lucky to have him as her graduate advisor. Many people under-estimated his intelligence either because of his good looks or his crumpled clothes, but he was a brilliant scholar, too. It was perfect that he was cross-appointed to the Medieval Studies department and seemed to know everyone whose help was of use to her in the research for her thesis.

She smiled back.

"Everything went well?"

"Perfectly," she lied. "Mr. Montmorency was very gracious."

The professor nodded and raised his brows. "Did he show you his exhibit room?"

"The one with the mosaic ceiling?" She watched him nod. "It's quite something."

"He's a very enthusiastic amateur collector. Self-taught." Dr. Thomas said this in a tone that wasn't flattering. "I'm not looking forward to the day that he discovers he's wrong about his own arte-fact, but there's no point in evading the truth."

"I'm not sure he'll be easily persuaded," Francesca said and saw Larry glance at her in the rear view mirror. "He's very sure about its history."

"The voice of the Cumaean Sibyl, trapped in glass for almost two thousand years," Larry said, his voice mocking.

Dr. Thomas' smile was indulgent.

"It's a beautiful example of Roman glass," Francesca said. "And the stopper is intact."

"Of course, it looks as if it is," Dr. Thomas said soothingly. "It might have been added just a few years ago."

She leaned forward. "Do you think Mr. Montmorency is a coun-terfeiter?"

Her professor shook his head. "No, but there are plenty of them at work. He could have been deceived. I hope he didn't pay too much for the piece."

Francesca sat back and thought about the bloodstone, the one with the symbols that Mr. Montmorency thought could raise the dead. Maybe he was gullible.

How gullible was *she*? It wasn't possible for both him and the Greek guy to have shimmered blue right before her eyes.

As if to test her grip upon her own sanity, Francesca felt a glow of heat emanate from the backpack. She looked down as it began to radiate, the light seeping out the seams, like there was a fireball trapped inside it.

And not just any light, but the one that made her tingle. She found her thoughts filled with the memory of that guy's kiss and the feel of his fingertips brushing her cheek. She wished she'd asked his name or really anything about him, but that kiss...

"What are you doing?" Larry demanded and Francesca straightened.

"Me?"

"Do you have a flashlight back there or a mirror?" he asked, twisting in his seat. "There's a flashing light and it's really distracting."

"Not from me. Maybe, um, the sun glinted off the buckles on the backpack straps." It sounded ridiculous but he didn't say anything more.

The light continued to seep from the bag, though its hue dimmed to a deep orange. It reminded her of the glowing coals of a dying fire.

What was up with this jar? Francesca was itching to open the backpack and unwrap it, but was a bit afraid of what she might find. She remembered that tinkle. What if the seal had broken? She'd be held responsible. What could be inside it that would glow when exposed to air? Some kind of phosphorus, maybe? Better to keep it hidden away and learn the worst of it later, when she was alone.

Even if the curiosity might kill her.

It would be at least two hours until they reached the museum. She could wait.

To her relief, they progressed more quickly once they reached the broader roads in the suburbs. Soon, they turned onto the highway, heading south, and Francesca turned around to look back. A small blue car merged into the traffic behind them, but it was completely unfamiliar. There was no sign of Mr. Montmorency or the guy who kissed like he'd invented it. She told herself to be relieved.

She had the jar.

Everything was going to be just fine.

Funny that she didn't quite believe it.

———

SIGMUND COULDN'T FIGURE out this Orion guy.

He was *Pyr*. Indisputably so. But Sigmund didn't recognize his companion's name. He thought he knew all of the existing *Pyr*, but not this one. He couldn't even think of any *Pyr* that might be related to this guy.

It was like he had popped out of nowhere.

Even more strange, he either didn't realize that Sigmund was a *Slayer* or he didn't care. Sigmund suspected the latter. Sigmund reasoned that even if he cheated, he'd lose any battle with Orion, and maybe Orion knew that, too.

Sigmund hadn't had a real plan for this day. He'd spent weeks trying to convince Magnus to let him see his treasures, based on his own hunch of the possibilities, but the old *Slayer* was characteristically disinterested in anyone else's view about anything. If only Sigmund could see the bloodstone himself, he could conduct his own experiments—but Magnus wasn't sharing any details. The obvious solution was to leave Rome for the moment. Maybe Magnus would be more receptive after he had time to regret a lost opportunity.

Maybe not.

Sigmund had impulsively offered Orion a ride to Cumae, recognizing that he was *Pyr*. Curiosity, as they said, often killed the cat with Sigmund. He hoped it didn't this time. Orion was all hard muscle and purpose. Where had he come from?

Was he looking for the bloodstone, too? Sigmund didn't want to have to wrestle Orion over anything.

Why was he going to Cumae? And what did the very pretty Miss Marino have to do with it? Sigmund had admired her at the hotel, even stopping to chat with her at breakfast the day before but she'd made it clear she wasn't interested.

Of course not. Her type thought they were too good for anyone.

Little had she guessed what secrets Sigmund had, and what a great ride he'd give her, offered the chance. Bitch.

Sigmund slanted a glance at his companion, who was watching the road ahead with fierce intensity. Was that a firestorm Sigmund had felt, ever so faintly? He looked again and saw a glimmer of golden light touch Orion's profile.

A firestorm would explain a great deal. There was nothing Sigmund liked better than thwarting a firestorm, and if Miss Marino suffered for his interference, well, that was what she deserved for not seeing his merit in the first place.

He pushed the gas pedal a little harder so the car accelerated, noting how Orion nodded approval. His *Pyr* companion might not approve so much of whatever happened once they reached Cumae and that made Sigmund smile.

The golden glow also brightened an increment, proof that he was right about the firestorm.

Thanks to the mysterious Orion, Sigmund had a new goal.

————

THE BACKPACK WAS DEFINITELY GETTING warmer again.

It had been cooler when she'd gotten in the car, but ever since they'd left Rome, it had been slowly heating up. Francesca had pushed it down as close to the floor as possible so the light wouldn't distract Larry, but it wasn't getting any dimmer.

The bag was warm all over, even where she wasn't touching it. When she moved her hands, she couldn't find one bit of it that was cold. It was a sunny day, but she was sitting in the shade in the car, and the bag was on the floor.

In fact, if she squinted at it, it seemed to be glowing.

It wasn't the bag. It was the vase *inside* it. Francesca thought it looked like she had a vial of sunshine swaddled up in the backpack, and the golden light was sneaking out through the cracks. That made no sense, though.

What made even less sense was the way she was feeling. She was warm in a very sensual way. A seductive heat was flowing through her, making her keenly aware of everything around her. She felt the softness of her cotton t-shirt and became aware of the way it stretched across her breasts. She felt the lace edge of her panties brushing against her skin and the worn leather of her sandals against the bottoms of her feet. The upholstery on the seat felt rough against the back of her thighs and the waft of air across her knees made her feel naked. She smelled dust and heat and the scents she associated with summer in Italy, as well as the salty tang of the sea, not so far away. The windows were open in the car and her ponytail blew, the ends of it brushing against her face at intervals, like strands of silk. She couldn't stop thinking about that kiss, the one that had singed her very soul, and how much she wanted another one.

Too bad she'd left that guy behind.

Too bad she didn't even know his name.

Dr. Thomas was oblivious to whatever spell Francesca was under. He was talking, well, lecturing really, as was his habit.

"And so we have our trinkets to tease the imagination of the public," he said with satisfaction. "The publicity people will be happy, even if it's all nonsense."

Francesca was writing her doctoral thesis on women in positions of influence in Ancient Rome, and one of the groups of women who had more control over their situations were those believed to have prophetic abilities. Dr. Thomas was her advisor since his specialty was Ancient Rome, with a particular interest in social mobility. Larry, perhaps predictably, was a student of military history. Their discussion would inevitably veer into battle tactics, weapons and who had been beaten when, which was just about the most boring possibility. Francesca only halfway listened, thinking it had been a lot more interesting the previous summer, before Larry joined their little team.

Maybe Mr. Montmorency's vase wasn't so empty after all. That would be really interesting.

She desperately wanted to open the bag and look, maybe find something that would surprise both of her companions.

"Francesca can tell us more about the sibyls," Dr. Thomas invited, as if he knew she wasn't paying attention, and she started at his utterance of her name.

She cleared her throat. "While there were many sibyls recorded in the ancient world—including the Erythraean Sibyl, the Persian Sibyl, the Libyan Sibyl and the Delphic Sibyl—"

"All of whom were immortalized by Michelangelo on the ceiling of the Sistine Chapel as well as the Cumaean Sibyl," Dr. Thomas interjected.

"The Cumaean Sibyl had the distinction of being located closest to Rome, thus we know more about her from available documentation."

Dr. Thomas wagged a finger at the windshield. "Once again, there is a domination of western records over our available sources, but it is not necessarily the case that the Cumaean Sibyl was considered dominant even by the Romans or in their time of ascendancy." His footnote made, he then waved for Francesca to continue.

"The story is that the Cumaean Sibyl came to the attention of the Romans when she appeared to Lucien Tarquinius Superbus, the last king of the Roman kingdom, offering to sell him nine books of prophecies," Francesca said. She liked this story a lot. "When he refused to buy the books, she burned three of them, then offered the remaining six to him at the same price. He refused again, and she burned three more. Tarquin then purchased the last three volumes at her original price and she vanished."

"Citation please," Dr. Thomas reminded her.

"There are three sources of the story including Dionysius of Halicarnassus, Varro in Lactantius 1:6, and Pliny's Natural History."

"Volume?"

"XIII 27."

"Good," Dr. Thomas said. "And the fate of the three books?"

"They were kept in the Temple of Jupiter on Capitoline Hill in Rome, to be consulted in emergencies, until they were destroyed in the burning of the temple in the 80's BCE."

"And we know this how?"

"Tacitus," Larry supplied before Francesca could reply. She glared at him. He was so competitive that sometimes she wanted to smack him. "Who also recorded that messengers were sent throughout the empire to gather any texts copied from the books, so they could be gathered again. This collection was kept in the Temple of Apollo on the Palatine Hill."

"Exactly. And this perhaps strengthened the association between the Cumaean Sibyl and Apollo." Dr. Thomas considered that for a moment, then nodded. "Francesca, tell us more about the sibyl's practice of prophecy."

"She accepted questions from seekers, then offered her replies written on oak leaves, arranging them outside her cave. These were often riddles, but could be made less intelligible if the wind blew and disturbed the order of the leaves. She always declined to rearrange them, leaving the seeker to divine the original order, if possible." Francesca liked that detail, too, and to her it was indicative of the Sibyl's control over her own choices because there were no stories of any retaliation against her for this refusal. Before she could say anything about that, Dr. Thomas had continued.

"One such prophecy preserved for us was her advice given to Aeneas, before his descent into the underworld in search of his father, Anchises." Dr. Thomas waved a hand again and Francesca supplied the quote, first in Latin, then in English.

"Trojan, Anchises' son, the descent of Avernus is easy.
All night long, all day, the doors of Hades stand open.
But to retrace the path, to come up to the sweet air of heaven,
That is labour indeed."

"AENEID 6.126-129," supplied Larry the keener before she could.

"Excellent, Larry." Dr. Thomas said warmly. "And thus we know that the Cumaean Sibyl was also considered a guide to the underworld, which could be accessed by the nearby crater of Avernus according to Roman superstition, and thus she offered a link between the living and the dead. This connection informed her prophecies and made her famous throughout both Rome and its empire." The finger pointed toward her. "Francesca? Bring us to the titillating exhibits, please." His tone was a little bit mocking, as if the sibyl was worthy only of dismissal and Francesca was annoyed on the prophetess' behalf.

If either man had been paying attention, he would have heard the irritation in her tone, but neither, of course, were.

"The Cumaean Sibyl was a mortal woman and a virgin. She was desired by Apollo, who offered her any gift in exchange for her maidenhead. She seized a handful of sand and asked for as many years of life as grains of sand in her grasp. He granted this wish to her, yet she still refused his advances."

"Capricious," Larry said.

"Indeed," Dr. Thomas agreed.

Francesca couldn't let it be. "But she was a mortal woman and she declined the advances of a god," she said. "That surely is a sign of her ability to shape her own circumstance. She had agency..."

"But she paid for her decision," Dr. Thomas corrected. "Which undermines any argument about her agency."

"That she even thought it a possibility to decline is significant..."

He interrupted her crisply. "What happened to her, Francesca? According to the stories?"

"She faded and grew smaller as she aged. This was at the will of Apollo and in retaliation for her refusal to submit to him. He insisted she had not asked for eternal youth. Ultimately, she was said to have been confined in a jar, a small faded remnant of her former self."

"Hardly an indication of agency, Francesca," Dr. Thomas tsked and Larry snorted.

"Eventually, all that remained of her was her voice, sealed into that jar for all eternity. That's the story from Ovid's *Metamorphosis*," she added, anticipating the question.

"A woman's voice secured in a jar," Dr. Thomas mused, then shook his head.

"Quite a story," Larry agreed.

"But a sign of her importance," Francesca argued. "No one else's voice was preserved."

"If indeed this one was," Dr. Thomas said and Francesca had no chance to offer the quote attributed to the Sibyl by Propertius. "We have four candidates for that jar in question. The Vatican has loaned one to the exhibit from their collection, as have the Archeological Museum in Athens and the British Museum." His tone turned to an academic jeer. "And then we have Francesca's unlikely contender, borrowed from Mr. Montmorency's private collection. If nothing else, it will add to the variety of the jars on display."

"You don't think the voice is in any of them, do you, sir?" Larry asked.

Dr. Thomas laughed. "Do you?"

Francesca bristled. "This jar's provenance puts it in the right locality at the right time, and the story is that it was in the possession of a Roman senator fascinated with the Cumaean Sibyl," she argued. "Whether it contains the sibyl's voice is less important, I believe, than that people *believed* her voice was secured within it." It was time for Propertius. "'To such a degree will I be changed that I will be visible to no one; but I will be recognized by my voice. My voice the Fates will leave me.'"

"Propertius," Larry provided.

"Nonsense," Dr. Thomas said. "I remind you, Francesca, that it is our task to ascertain which are facts and which are conjecture."

"There is no factual evidence that the Cumaean Sibyl ever existed," she felt obliged to point out. "Everything about her is a story. What's important is the existence of the stories and what they reveal about Roman society and contemporary perspectives, as well as the role of certain women."

"We will agree to disagree." Dr. Thomas' disinterest in Francesca's view was clear. "I'm actually more interested in why your Roman dignitary, and Mr. Montmorency for that matter, even care about the receptacle said to contain the sibyl's voice. It is akin to the ongoing search for the Holy Grail: it is less about the grail itself, or the story of it being used by Joseph of Arimathea to catch the blood of Christ, than the objectives of the seekers who desire the secret of immortality."

Larry nodded. "We'll never be able to tell for sure which of the other three is the right one," he said.

"Undoubtedly, there is no right one," Dr. Thomas said.

"Maybe we should open them and listen," Larry said, then laughed to prove that he was making a joke.

Dr. Thomas didn't laugh. "And compromise the artifacts? I think not. The seals are integral to their importance as relics of the past, even though they are clearly empty."

Larry nodded, chastened.

"At least, the vases are collected and the publicity people can photograph them to promote the exhibit." Dr. Thomas drummed his fingers on the door. "I'm anxious to return to the real work. Did I tell you that I had a message from the archeological team working at the *città sommersa*?"

Francesca looked out the window. He'd told them seven times about the new discovery at the submerged ancient city of Baiae.

"You mentioned that they had uncovered a new mosaic," Larry said with enthusiasm. "Of a marching army."

"That's what's visible so far. They're working on removing the barnacles and so forth, and I'm hoping that at least part of it can be photographed today. It may provide information about uniforms and weapons, even before the rest of the image is revealed."

"I'd love to help, sir, if that's possible."

"Francesca, can you take the vase to the museum while we continue to the harbor? I know this find is of little interest to you."

Larry smirked. "No powerful chicks. But then, maybe there aren't any of them to find in ancient Rome."

"No, the Amazons did not journey so far as that," Dr. Thomas said and the pair of them laughed together. Their skepticism about Amazons was well-established, though Francesca thought there might be truth in the tales of those warrior women.

"Of course, I'll take the vase to the museum," she agreed, glad of the opportunity to be alone with her prize. "I'll be able to clean it for the photographs."

———

THE MUSEUM in Baiae was a sanctuary for Francesca, a refuge from the bustle of the world and a place for quiet work. It was located within a fifteenth-century castle built on a rocky peak, which had a commanding view of the Bay of Pozzuoli and the Tyrrhenian Sea. It was never hard to believe that it had been a military site first. West of Naples and south of Cumae, the museum had an impressive collection of antiquities found in the area.

Ancient Baiae had been an important retreat for affluent Romans as well as near both Pompeii and Cumae, so the entire area was rich with archeological remains. Items collected from the *città sommersa*, the underwater ruins of ancient Baiae to the immediate south of the modern city, had pride of place in the museum. The Roman city had sunk due to changing elevation levels, a result of the volcanic activity in the region. The exhibit being curated by Dr. Thomas would be a seasonal display, opening for the upcoming summer, focused on the ancient Romans at leisure in Baiae. The detail about the sibyl and the practice of consulting her was a small part of it, and Francesca's contribution.

Francesca carried her backpack through the exhibit halls — which had once been the dormitories of soldiers—to the private room where they were working on the displays. Her footsteps echoed on the stone floor, the silence making her aware that she was probably alone in this part of the building. It was just after noon, so all was typically quiet as staff and visitors took their midday break. Larry and Dr. Thomas had continued to the harbor.

This was Francesca's favorite time, when she felt as if she had the place to herself. She paused to survey Emperor Claudius' nymphaeum, as she always did. A replica had taken its place under-water in the bay, but she particularly liked the statue of Ulysses with his outstretched arms. There was a yearning in his pose that made her appreciate that the desire for adventure was always countered by a wish to be home again. She felt that herself often, working in Italy but missing her family in the States.

The backpack was still glowing and warm, even in the cool interior of the museum. Once in her work area, Francesca set down the bag on the worktable. She twisted up her hair and put on her glasses, then pulled on a pair of latex gloves to protect the vase from the oil in her skin. She unwrapped it carefully, then felt her eyes narrow.

It *had* changed.

That made another impossible thing to add to her list.

It was the same vase she had wrapped that morning, but it looked different, and not just due to the hue of the light in the workroom. The glass was still iridescent but brighter and the colors were more

vivid. It was more yellow, as if it had been gilded while in her backpack—or heated, the way iron turns red in the forge.

Francesca bent closer for a better look as something moved inside
it. The vase seemed to have a firefly in it, even though the stopper
was perfectly intact. The golden pinprick of light moved incessantly
in the vase, as if seeking an escape. She double-checked the seal but it
was uncompromised, which made no sense.

That list was getting long.

The fact was that the spark of light couldn't really be an insect.
After all, there was no way that a bug could have gotten into the
sealed vessel—and if one had, it would be long dead. Francesca used
a magnifying glass for a better look. Even though it was on the move,
she managed to follow its course. It wasn't an insect. There were no
wings, as an insect might have, and no body.

Just light.

A spark in the jar.

And there hadn't been one before. She checked the seal again,
then bit her lip and frowned at the jar. Had the Greek guy somehow
put this spark in the jar in the piazza? How?

She remembered that there had been an answering spark, too.

What was going on?

"I see that you are well," said a man with a low growl of a voice
that made Francesca jump at its familiarity. The low hum that the
sound launched in her belly was definitely familiar—as was the
sound of his melodic Ancient Greek. "That is a relief."

Francesca spun to find the man who had kissed her in Rome
standing in the doorway. He stood straight, his posture making her
think of soldiers, but his arms were folded across his chest. He looked
confident, if not arrogant, and that dismissed any fleeting sense that
his appearance in this place and time was a coincidence.

He'd followed her, even though Francesca couldn't guess how.

She hadn't mistaken how attractive he was, though. There was
something imposing about him, powerful, as if he could take someone

apart with his bare hands. Francesca also knew that his strength was tempered, that he could be gentle if he so chose, though she had no idea why she was convinced of that. Maybe because of the reverent way he had touched her cheek. Something melted inside her at the memory. His shoulders were broad enough to almost fill the width of the door and he was watching her with a little smile on his lips. Not like she was funny or cute. Like he admired her. His feet were braced against the ground and his eyes gleamed with familiar interest.

She knew he liked what he saw.

Francesca liked what she saw, too. She smiled a little, glad to see him again but wishing she knew how—and why—he'd pursued her. He was dressed oddly, too, his khaki pants vaguely military but cut closer to his body than was the current style. The fabric looked lighter than cotton, too. His dark T-shirt was tight but she had no complaints about that view.

As they eyed each other, the light in the room turned golden, reminding her of the glow that had lit between them before. It was romantic, like candlelight, as was the way she felt warm yet excited too. She was humming with a desire that was familiar only because she'd already felt it on this day. She could have been on a date with a hot guy instead of at work. Francesca had little time for romantic relationships these days, but she knew she'd make an exception for Mr. Ancient Greek. She would make an exception for great sex, for sure.

Then she reminded herself of practicalities. How had he known her destination?

"It's a long way from Rome," she said. "How did you get here?"

"A Sl...stranger gave me a ride," he said, stumbling as if the words were unfamiliar.

But how had he known where to look for her?

She recalled every warning her brothers had ever given her and kept her distance, at least for the moment. He didn't seem like the stalker type, but she decided to be blunt. "Are you following me?"

He smiled, suddenly looking so handsome and trustworthy that Francesca couldn't catch her breath. "I sought you, yes," he confessed, taking a step into the room. "We were interrupted but I wished to speak with you some more." He surveyed the contents of the room, maybe giving her a chance to think about that, then his gaze locked with hers before she could ask the obvious question. "But if you do not wish such discussion, I will leave."

She wondered whether that was true.

She suspected his absence would be temporary. He didn't look like the kind of person who gave up on anything very easily.

"But how did you do it?" Francesca folded her arms across her chest, trying to sound stern even though she was again thinking about that kiss. She couldn't stop staring at his mouth, remembering the feel of it upon her own. "You followed me, several hundred miles, without any idea of my destination, and turned up just a few minutes after I got here. That makes no sense. How could you be so lucky?"

"I needed no directions," he said, his voice low and soft. Francesca shivered just a little at the seductive sound. Then he lifted one hand before himself, his manner expectant. She saw a mustering of light around his palm, then it brightened from orange to yellow. "I followed the light." When the glow was almost white, a spark launched from his fingertip.

Just like it had before. Francesca braced herself to feel it land up on her, to send that beguiling fire through her right to her toes. She was ready to melt in anticipation of another kiss.

But the spark sailed over her head and landed on the vase she'd set on the worktable, the impact prompting a slight tinkle. The vase also glowed brighter for an instant and that spark of light trapped inside it moved more quickly, as if agitated, before fading again.

As if nothing had happened.

Francesca turned back to her guest, only to find his expression one of astonishment.

He frowned. "How can this be?" he murmured, as if asking himself, then strode past her with impatience.

What had he said about the firestorm? She couldn't remember.

She watched him, mystified. He propped his hands on his hips to stare down at the vase, then bent to study it from every angle. When he straightened, he ran a hand over his face, clearly puzzled.

He seemed to have forgotten her presence completely.

"How did you do it?" she asked, moving to stand beside him. He exuded a warmth that made her want to touch him, and her lips burned a little. His kiss had been leisurely and completely seductive, his mouth firm but enticing. She flicked a glance at his face, but he was still glowering at the vase.

Obviously not thinking about that kiss.

Irritation flared within Francesca. "How?" she demanded again and he started slightly.

"I do not know," he admitted, peering at it again. He scanned the room, his gaze lighting upon her backpack. He strode to it with purpose and looked inside, then he impaled her with a look. "You were carrying this earlier."

"Yes."

His gaze slid back to the vase.

"It was inside the bag," she said, anticipating him.

"For the love of Zeus," he whispered, easing toward the vase as if it was an unpredictable force. He bent lower again to peer at it, then stretched out a finger as if he would touch it. The air glowed golden, then more yellow, then brightened to a blinding radiance as his hand moved closer to the vase. The golden lights trapped inside the vase multiplied and swirled in a frenzy, as if they wanted to break free and go to him.

He pulled his hand back abruptly and the light dimmed.

The hair prickled on the back of Francesca's neck. What was going on?

"Impossible," he whispered, seemingly unable to tear his gaze from the vessel.

Francesca bit her lip, wishing his attention was fixed on her with such intensity, then frowned at her own inappropriate thoughts. She knew nothing about him except that he could kiss, and she was supposed to be smart. His inattention gave her the chance to survey him again, which did exactly nothing to get her thoughts on track.

"What is inside the vessel?" he asked suddenly, flicking a glance at her so hot that it might have scorched her.

Francesca took a step closer, emboldened by his fascination with the vase—and apparent disinterest in her. When she was right beside him, she took a deep breath. No cologne. He smelled clean, like sunlight and wind and the sea.

She wanted another kiss with a power that surprised her. She wondered what he would do if she initiated it. "I thought you knew," she said, trying to keep her voice light. "I thought you caused it."

"Me?" Again, he turned to her, his eyes so bright that she couldn't take a breath.

Francesca managed to shrug. "That light wasn't there before I saw you in the piazza. Before the spark."

His expression changed slightly, as if that made a kind of sense to him but still he shook his head. "It cannot be."

She watched him and her mother would have said she could smell the wood burning. "You know what's going on," she guessed.

"I only suspect, but my suspicion cannot be correct." He flung out a hand. "It makes no sense!" Once again, he turned to her so abruptly that she nearly jumped. His gaze was intense. "What *is* this vessel?"

"It's a Roman glass vase, an ancient artefact on loan for an exhibit."

His eyes narrowed. "How ancient?"

"Perhaps two thousand years old."

He nodded understanding. "And this color makes it unusual?"

"No. That patina is characteristic of Roman glass. What's unusual about it is that spark trapped inside it. See? The seal on the stopper hasn't been broken."

He looked as she had instructed. "How long has it been sealed?"

Francesca shrugged. "At least a hundred years. The story is that it's been sealed much longer, maybe fifteen hundred years." He turned to look at her with surprise and she nodded. "I brought it here to find out more about it."

"You acquired it?"

"I borrowed it. From Mr. Montmorency."

His expression became guarded then. He eyed the vase again. "I wish I knew more," he murmured.

Francesca smiled. "I thought that was my anthem," she said lightly and he cast a puzzled glance at her. His eyes were very blue, and unexpectedly so. Meeting his gaze was like staring at the ocean— but better. Much better. "I'm always trying to learn more."

"You have an avid curiosity?"

"Yes! There's so much to discover. I'm not sure I'll ever know everything I want to know, or learn everything I'd like to."

His gaze warmed, turning appreciative and she almost preened. "Then perhaps we have something in common," he said softly.

She didn't retreat a step or look away. He didn't even seem to blink. His lashes were as dark as his eyes were light. That little smile lifted only one corner of his mouth. Even though he was smiling a little, he still looked fierce, like he'd be a formidable opponent.

Like he'd seen many, many things—and not all of them had been good things.

Francesca understood in that instant that this was a man who would not flinch from doing whatever he believed had to be done. There was a hardness in him that she found herself respecting, for she sensed that he had a firm moral code.

Then she scoffed at the direction of her own thoughts. All she knew about this guy was that he could kiss, which told her absolutely nothing about his character.

She didn't even know his name.

"Where are you from?" she asked, wishing it hadn't sounded so abrupt. He lifted a brow. "You don't sound like you're from around here."

He nodded once. "Greece, of course."

"Where?"

"An island called Euboea. A city called Erétria." There was pride in his voice.

Francesca smiled that he had clearly thought she might not know of it. "A very famous city in its time," she said and he nodded agreement. She reasoned that children must learn Ancient Greek in a city that was so important twenty-five hundred years ago. "It was colonists from Erétria that settled Cumae here."

"Kymai," he said, gently correcting her pronunciation. "I remember."

He had to remember from school. He couldn't *actually* remember that. Francesca had a very strange feeling suddenly, one she couldn't readily dismiss. "What brought you here?"

He started to answer, then hesitated, choosing his words. Was he going to admit the truth, whatever it was?

"Destiny," he said then with such conviction that Francesca almost laughed out loud.

"Destiny?" she echoed. "You can't be serious."

He eyed her, his expression puzzled. "Why? You would question its influence?"

"Of course! We make our own choices. There isn't any guiding force driving us in one direction or another. That's superstitious nonsense. Our lives are shaped by our choices and nothing else."

"Ah," he said and averted his gaze. Francesca sensed that he disagreed with her and wondered what he would say.

"You can't believe that everything is fated to be," she chided. "It's not rational."

He flicked a hot glance at her. "Can you not believe that some matters are fated? Would you attribute happy encounters to coincidence?" He shook his head with that same resolve. "No, I cannot believe the gods would be so cruel as to leave so much to chance."

The gods. Was he neo-pagan, or enough of an enthusiast of the ancient world that he worshipped the old gods? He had mentioned Zeus, but she'd thought that a turn of phrase.

"The gods," she echoed, unable to keep a smile from her tone. "Like Zeus and Apollo?"

He didn't smile. "Such divinities are not to be slighted. The consequences might be dire."

Francesca dropped her gaze. She didn't want to insult him, but she thought gods of any kind were a bunch of nonsense. She'd expected him to be more practical than this—she expected everyone to be. She felt the weight of his attention land upon her but didn't look up.

"You do not believe?" he whispered, as if that was unreasonable.

"I'm an atheist," she admitted, meeting his gaze steadily. "I had enough of all that when I was a kid. My family's Catholic, but I haven't gone to church in years." She smiled. "Except to look at the artefacts."

"Atheist?" His gaze searched hers and he looked suddenly stricken. "You are *godless*?"

"I don't believe in gods," she clarified, recalling that *áthe(os)* was the Greek root and meant literally 'godless'.

He shook his head and surveyed the workroom, and she knew he was troubled by this confession.

"Don't worry about it," she said. "It's only rational to believe in what I can hold in my own hands. I need to see it to believe it—if a deity turns up, *then* I'll believe."

It was meant as a joke, but he shook his head vigorously. "It is only rational to honor those who can cast adversity into your path. And you cannot truly wish to experience the presence of the divine. They are unpredictable in their actions." He was stern. "It is a comparatively small thing to show respect to beings of power. Your choice is a foolish one."

Francesca's lips parted in outrage. "Foolish? I'm not the one falling on my knees, praying for someone else to solve my troubles for me. I make my life what I want it to be..."

He laughed and surprise silenced her words. "I do not entreat the gods for favors either," he confided. "I would only ensure that they are not offended. Life has sufficient challenge without their interference." Then his eyes lit. "Though your view might explain much," he murmured.

Explain *what* exactly?

CHAPTER FOUR

F rancesca had no chance to ask what he meant before he offered his hand. "I am Orion. You are Signora Marino." His confidence appeared to have been restored, although Francesca could not understand why.

She liked that he was treating her like an equal by offering to shake hands. "You know my name?"

"It was how I found you. The S..." He corrected himself as he had once before and she wondered what he'd been meaning to say. "The *stranger* addressed you by name in the street."

Francesca flushed that she hadn't remembered that earlier. "Right. I'm Francesca, Francesca Marino," she said, putting her hand in his. Orion's strong fingers closed around her hand, gripping firmly but gently, his touch sending tingles to her toes. He frowned down at their interlocked hands, as if something was wrong, but then he shook his head and smiled into her eyes again. "You can call me Francesca," she added.

His eyes glowed with pleasure and her heart skipped a beat. "And you must call me Orion."

She stared into his eyes, snared by the warmth of his hand and the power of his presence. She thought of herself as someone with a lot of restraint, but he was the one to turn away first, and she almost sighed when he relinquished his grip on her hand.

"You did not answer my earlier query," he said, but there was no accusation in his tone. "What is in the vessel?"

"No one knows, but it's supposed to hold the voice of the Cumaean Sibyl. That's all that's left of her." She was ready for Orion to make a joke, but he didn't even smile.

"The Cumaean Sibyl," he repeated thoughtfully. "I know of four of the ancient priestesses and oracles of Apollo, but not this one."

"Which ones do you know?" It wasn't common knowledge for a layman, but then again, it might be taught to children in Greece.

"The oldest and most esteemed was the sibyl at Delphi," Orion said without hesitation. "Who was not the same oracle as the Pythia."

That was true but a mistake many scholars made, never mind the public. Francesca was impressed.

He continued. "Later there was one in Phrygia, at Gergitis."

"In Anatolia," Francesca said softly, surprised by his knowledge. Orion pronounced the locations with a slight inflection, different from the way she had learned to say them. She loved the sound of his Greek and could have listened to him all day long.

"I heard of two more: one in Erythrae, in Ionia."

"Near the island of Chios."

He smiled approval and she was dazzled. "Yes. The fourth was at Dardania in the Troad."

"The Hellespontine Sibyl," Francesca said. How intriguing that he included two who had not been immortalized by Michelangelo at the Sistine Chapel.

"I know little of them beyond that," Orion admitted. "I have never been interested in prophecies about the future, or even riddles."

"Varro said there were ten in all," she informed him.

"I do not know this Varro."

"A Roman writer." She counted them on her fingers. "The Persian, the Libyan, the Delphic, the Cimmerian, the Erythraean, the Samian, the Cumaean, the Hellespontian, the Phrygian and the Tiburtine. They were ten mortal women who could divine the future or so it was believed."

"Ten?" He ran a hand over his head and seemed bewildered. "Perhaps that happened later than...my inquiries."

"The Sibylline books were said to have been compiled by the Hellespontine Sibyl, then brought from Gergis on Mount Ida to Erythrae, then brought by the Cumaean Sibyl to what is now Italy."

"Kymai," he said, his gaze watchful.

"Yes, it is believed that the Greek colonists brought her here."

He appeared to be fascinated by the vase. "And by the tale, her voice alone survives, captive in that vase." He turned to her so quickly that she almost jumped when their gazes collided. "I am reminded of the tale of Pandora."

Francesca was intrigued. "How so?"

He lifted a fingertip toward the vase, not touching it but indicating the seal. "Have you not read the injunction here?"

"No, I haven't had a chance to look at it closely." Francesca moved to his side and was startled by the frantic movement of the light in the vessel. They both stared at it and she knew she wasn't the only one dazzled by its display. "It's getting brighter," she whispered.

He slanted her a smile that warmed her to her toes. "It likes when you are near me." Francesca glanced up in surprise and he lifted a dark brow. "As do I." He captured her hand in his and when she might have pulled away, he nodded toward the vase. The light brightened to yellow, swirling at dizzying speed inside the jar.

Francesca slipped her hand from his warm grip and put a step between them. The light became more orange again and the movement stilled slightly. "It makes no sense," she whispered.

"It does not adhere to our current notions, but that does not mean it is irrational or inexplicable." He frowned at the vase. "It means only that we lack information to understand it."

That actually made sense. She eyed him as he studied the vase. "Tell me about Pandora," she invited, wondering which version of the story he would favor.

He nodded slowly, as if choosing where to begin. "Once there were three brothers, Titans as well as sons of Iapetus and the oceanid Clymene. The eldest, Atlas, was strong. The middle son, Prometheus was clever. The youngest, Epimetheus, was a fool. Prometheus worked in clay and routinely presented his creations to Zeus for approval. One day, he made a beautiful boy who he named Phaenon. Fearing that Zeus, with his desire to possess all beauty himself, would take Phaenon away from him, Prometheus hid the boy. But Zeus saw Phaenon from above and desired him as predicted: worse, he sent an eagle to snatch the boy away. Prometheus appealed for Phaenon's return, but Zeus refused, placing him in the skies as the planet Jupiter. In defiance, Prometheus returned to his mold and cast many more replicas, creating the race of men."

Francesca knew the story, having read it in Hesiod and other sources. When Orion paused, she complimented him. "You're a good storyteller."

"I should be," he said immediately with pride. "My father was the keeper of stories of our kind. I learned at his knee."

Had his father been a poet?

He cleared his throat and continued. "The gods believed that these men should be subservient to them and worship them, making offerings of oxen for divine favor. But their demands were too great, so Prometheus came to the defense of his creations. He convinced Zeus to demand only a part of each sacrificed ox, and Zeus demanded the best piece of each one. Irked, Prometheus then tricked Zeus, slaughtering an ox then wrapping the least desirable parts in fat, while the prime pieces were wrapped in the hide. Zeus swore to accept the offering that he chose from this sacrifice for all future sacrifices, then picked the offering wrapped in fat. He realized he had been deceived, but as the god of oaths, he could not rescind his word. He was compelled to accept the lesser cuts for all eternity."

Francesca smiled, admiring the cleverness of Prometheus.

"This rankled his pride, though, and Zeus denied the gift of fire to men as a result. Prometheus once again came to the defense of his creation and stole fire from the gods, hiding it in a stalk of fennel and giving it to mortal men. In retaliation, Zeus had Prometheus chained to a rock: an eagle came each night to devour his liver and each day, his liver was restored so he would be in torment forever."

"Until Heracles killed the eagle."

Orion nodded. "Many eons later. But Zeus had not yet had his vengeance upon men. He ordered Hephaestus to create something of beauty that would plague men for all eternity. The smith-god made a woman of astonishing loveliness, but one with a wicked heart. Her name was Pandora. She wore a golden crown wrought by Hephaestus adorned with all the animals and fish of the world, so lifelike that they could almost be seen to move and be heard. And she was presented to Epimetheus as a bride and a treasure. He accepted her even though his brother Prometheus had warned him never to take any gift from the gods. In Pandora's dowry was a sealed jar with a warning on its seal that it should not be opened." He lifted a finger to indicate the glass vessel. "The same warning as this," he noted softly before returning to his story. "But Epimetheus wished to know the fullness of the wealth brought by his new bride. He broke the seal and opened the jar, releasing all the troubles of the world and unleashing them upon men."

"Except Hope," Francesca said.

Her companion smiled at her. "Which was trapped in the jar when he closed it again, after realizing his error."

Francesca eyed the jar. "I could never figure out why Hope was there in the first place. It was supposed to be a jar of evils, though some subsequent writers suggested it was blessings and evils and that the blessings were supposed to remain in the jar."

He was shaking his head. "It was destiny," he said with conviction. "Hephaestus knew that Epimetheus would open the jar. Given the temptation, his choice was inevitable and predictable. But Hephaestus also knew that Zeus' cruelty would punish men too much. He put Hope in the vessel, securing it to the bottom so that it would not be lost so soon."

"I've never heard that version before."

"It is the only one I know." He looked at her then, his expression curious. "Will you open this vessel?"

Francesca was shocked, both by the suggestion that she should tamper with an artefact and by his conviction that the tale was true. She winced. "I don't think the Cumaean Sibyl or her voice is actually in there."

He extended his hand toward the vase, holding her gaze in challenge. The light flared to brilliance again, the small lights within the vase becoming frenzied. The glass glowed with a golden iridescence that was blinding in its brilliance and Francesca stared.

Then Orion lowered his hand and it all dimmed, as if she had imagined it all.

"*Something* is in there," he said with conviction.

He was right. "But what could it be?" Francesca asked.

Orion took a deep breath and exhaled. "I thought I knew, but I must have been mistaken." He turned to her, then reached out, cautiously claiming her hand in his. Francesca knew that if she pulled away, he would have relinquished his grip. His touch sent a thrill through her, though, and she raised her gaze to his, struck again by the clear blue of his eyes. They were piercing in this light and she couldn't look away, even with the sense that he could read her thoughts. She felt spellbound and didn't even want to blink.

Orion didn't seem to be similarly affected, though. He was looking down at her hand, frowning slightly. She watched disappointment slide into his expression. "It is not you," he said, as if saddened, then sighed. "There can be no doubt." One more time, he turned to the vase but his expression was filled with yearning.

"You thought the light was my doing?"

"I thought it was your presence." His voice dropped low. "I thought it was the firestorm," he murmured, as if that confession explained everything.

In reality, his words left Francesca with a lot of questions.

But Orion abruptly inclined his head toward her, his tone becoming more formal. "I apologize for my intrusion and thank you for your patience, Francesca. I will trouble you no longer."

As Francesca watched, he turned and headed toward the door.

He couldn't just leave!

"You used that word before, Orion," she said, wanting only to encourage him to stay. "What exactly *is* the firestorm?"

———

WAS FRANCESCA NOT HIS MATE? It defied belief.

Orion had been so sure. He had found this woman so alluring. He had felt the power of the spark and he had followed its light, his heart filled with hope. It had been clear that his fate was unfolding just as it should...until he saw the spark of the firestorm illuminate the vase instead of Francesca.

His mate could not be a glass vessel.

His mate could not be trapped within that vessel—even if the tale was true and she was secured in the vase, he would not be able to satisfy the firestorm and conceive a son with a woman's voice.

No, the gods mocked him. He had left Drake and his fellows for an empty promise, only to find himself in a time and place where he had only thus far located two *Slayers*.

But Francesca's skepticism about the gods could explain all. Perhaps her refusal to honor the gods explained their desire to make a jest at the expense of the firestorm. She did not even seem to acknowledge their influence, which he could not believe they would tolerate. Cheating the firestorm might be their vengeance.

What could he do? Could he convince Francesca to modify her views? What right had he to insist that she change her view of the divine? He did not believe such a quest had a chance of success, but once again, the firestorm showed its power. He had to leave and consider his path, beyond the dizzying influence of the light in the vessel, whatever it was.

But Francesca called him back.

Orion could only hope that was a sign that she might find his argument persuasive. She would suit him well as a mate: young, attractive and clever. He liked the way her eyes lit in challenge, how she was neither shy nor brash. She had bound up her dark hair into a messy knot since they had parted ways in Rome, but the gleaming silk of it was undisguised. She was wearing glasses and her posture was unwelcoming, her tone challenging and her arms folded across her chest. Her gaze was steady, almost daring him to reply. She was confident in her own intellect and he admired that.

Orion realized that she had no notion of her feminine allure, however. Francesca could not know that her pose showed off the lean perfection of her legs, and made her breasts look ripe, inviting his caress. Sweeping up her hair left the nape of her neck exposed, a soft expanse of feminine skin that he had always found irresistible. Even her voice was husky and seductive to him, a voice made for whispered confessions in the dark. He wanted to remove the pins from her hair and push his hands through it. He wanted to see her in no more than her smile, to caress her from head to toe, to make her sigh and hear her reach the crest of pleasure.

Oh, he could have seduced her for a hundred days and nights, and ensured that she always invited him back for more. He understood that she wished to be appreciated for her keen wits, but there was so much more about Francesca to admire.

If he convinced her of the power of the gods, would that earn their favor? Might that restore the promise of his firestorm? Orion wanted to try, and not just for the sake of the firestorm.

He was tempted by Francesca, no matter what she believed.

But she could only be his mate if he regained the pleasure of the gods.

He took a step closer to Francesca and watched her catch her breath. She was as aware of him as he was of her, which offered encouragement for his plan. He took another step and she flushed a little, her lips parting as her eyes began to shine. She was remarkable. Perfect. He recalled that kiss, an embrace so perfect that it might have been destined to be, and he decided that firestorm or not, he could not walk away without another taste of Francesca.

"The firestorm is the mark of one of my kind meeting his destined mate," he said, watching her reaction.

"Your kind?" she echoed, evidently confused. "Greeks?"

Orion chuckled but did not explain. She did not believe in what she could not see, after all. She had told him as much herself.

Perhaps he would show her what he could become.

Not yet.

She studied him, perhaps aware that he hadn't told her everything. He sensed her hunger for knowledge and respected it. How much could he tell her without putting the *Pyr* in peril of being revealed? "And what happens in this firestorm?"

"A heat is kindled between two who are destined to unite as one," he said, once again taking her hand in his. There was no spark, but desire did slide through his veins, igniting a need that would soon become irresistible. Her fingers were slender, her skin lightly tanned, and she didn't pull away from him. She was both delicate and strong. "The firestorm sparks, igniting desire, a sign of their shared connection." Orion lifted her hand to his mouth and pressed a kiss into her palm. He watched Francesca's eyes widen slightly and saw that she swallowed. He guessed then that she had not fully explored the

KISS OF ENCHANTMENT 71

range of pleasure that could be shared between a man and a woman —and knew he would be glad to add to her knowledge of that. She licked her lips, as if hearing his thought, and Orion burned for another sweet kiss. He eased closer and she simply waited, an answering heat in her gaze.

Inviting him onward.

What would it take for her to seduce him instead? Orion smiled in anticipation of that possibility.

"The firestorm burns hotter with every passing moment," he murmured, placing her hand on his shoulder and drawing nearer. Her breasts were close to his chest and he could smell her perfume, a light floral scent that fueled his desire. Sweet. Feminine. Utterly seductive. "It drives all from their thoughts save the desire for each other, the need to touch and caress and claim." He bent and touched his lips to her throat beneath her ear. She sighed and trembled, which made him want to gather her into his arms and defend her from whoever was foolish enough to threaten her. Then she tipped her head back, a sensual pose that encouraged his kiss, her hand curling around his own neck to pull him closer. With her other hand, she removed her glasses and dropped them on the desk, then pushed those fingers into his hair.

The invitation had become a command.

Orion backed her into the work table, trapping her between it and his hips, and closed his arms around her with satisfaction.

She rolled her hips against him, smiling when he inhaled sharply. He liked her bold move, how she left him in no doubt of her desire. His hand tangled in her hair, setting it loose of the pins so that it fell around his fingers. His other hand was locked around her waist, holding her against his chest. He flattened his palm against her back, liking that he could almost span the back of her waist with one hand, and almost growled with satisfaction when she rose to her toes.

Her smile broadened. "Sounds hot," she whispered.

"Incendiary," he agreed, bending to kiss her ear. "Relentless," he murmured in her ear, then kissed it again, more demandingly. "Overwhelming," he breathed against her skin, feeling her shiver of delight. She arched her back so that her breasts rubbed against his chest and he felt her nails as she gripped the back of his neck.

What a glorious temptress she was.

"Irresistible?" she asked in a throaty whisper.

"Absolutely," Orion agreed, gripping a fistful of hair at her nape as he brushed his mouth over hers. She gasped but didn't move away, and that was all the invitation he needed to capture her lips beneath his own and kiss her soundly.

This time, he wouldn't break the kiss until he'd had his fill of her. That alone might make the difference.

———

SIGMUND STOPPED in the museum and closed his eyes, savoring. There was nothing like the snap, crackle and pop of a firestorm. He hadn't felt one in a while but it was an experience no dragon shifter would ever forget. The firestorm was like a beacon in the night, a warmth in the deepest cold, a summons he couldn't resist. Crossing paths with Orion had been a stroke of luck, and just feeling the tingle of the firestorm's glow in his veins made Sigmund feel much younger than his years.

This was the good stuff.

He was comparatively young for a *Pyr*, just having passed his first century mark, but there were days when he felt ancient. This wasn't one of them. The insistent heat of the firestorm filled him with optimism for the triumph of his dark schemes, and the inevitability of his vengeance upon his father. It wasn't fair that only *Pyr* had firestorms, that *Slayers* were cheated of this gift by some trick of fate. It wasn't right that he, as a superior specimen of dragon shifter, would be unable to reproduce. If anything, the world needed more dragons just like him. How else would the secrets of the past be discovered, documented and unfurled for future use? What *Pyr* had written a book compiling countless shreds of knowledge about their own kind? Not one of them! He had been the one to undertake that task. In fact, it had been under his father's leadership that the stories and details had been scattered, many of them lost and forgotten. Even the prospect of a long life, longer than most humans, left Sigmund with the conviction that he'd never have enough time to find and learn all the dragon lore.

But even he had to take a break from his work to meddle with a firestorm. What a bonus that it was with Francesca! And Orion, the aloof *Pyr* who had used him for a ride, not even deigning to make conversation. Sigmund had to interfere with a firestorm, any firestorm, or he wouldn't have been a worthy *Slayer,* but this one would be particularly satisfactory to foil.

All the same, it was a shame that anything that felt so very, very good had to be stopped, even on principle. He closed his eyes and savored, reminded of the sun coming out from behind the clouds or the sensation of stepping from a dark cellar into the midday heat of a summer day. He felt warmed through, as he hadn't since turning *Slayer.*

One more breath. One more moment. Then he'd do what had to be done.

He smiled that Francesca had thought she disliked him before.

Sigmund's eyes flew open, then he moved quietly toward the firestorm's golden glow.

ORION'S KISS was even better the second time. Francesca closed her eyes and surrendered to his caress, loving the grip of his strong hand in her hair and the tender power of his kiss. She was trapped between him and the desk and there was nowhere else she wanted to be. He was so hard and hot, but he moved slowly, as if he believed he had to convince her to accept him.

Francesca was more than ready to take him home for the night.

His kiss changed constantly, exploring and teasing, first assertive then gentle, and she felt as if she was being sampled thoroughly, as if he couldn't get enough of her, as if they could kiss like this for half of forever. Time stopped and the workroom was filled with the faint golden glow from the vase and the heat of Orion's beguiling touch.

Eventually, the hand against her back slid around to cup her breast, Orion's thumb easing back and forth across her nipple so that it was teased to a peak. His sensory assault went on and on, making her squirm against him with need. Francesca felt pampered and cherished, appreciated and seduced as she never had before.

Finally, he broke his kiss and dipped his head, popping the top button of her blouse. Francesca saw him inhale sharply as the white lace of her bra was revealed to his gaze, and smiled, glad of this hint that she wasn't the only one affected by their embrace. Then he cupped her breast in his broad palm and took the taut nipple in his mouth, teasing it with his lips, teeth and tongue, even through the cloth. The sensation was heavenly. Francesca could only close her eyes and enjoy. By the time he turned his attention to the other breast, she was so hot and wet that she thought she'd lose her mind. She held on to his shoulders, her nails digging into him as he tormented her with pleasure.

Where had he been all of her life?

When Orion's hand slid under the hem of her skirt, sweeping up her thigh with a possessive ease that made her heart flutter, Francesca actually heard herself moan—then his fingertips were moving against her panties. Wanting more, she took a step to one side, but Orion swept her up in his arms and placed her on the desk. He chuckled at her purr of satisfaction as his fingers eased beneath the edge of her panties and the warmth of his fingertips touched her softness. Their gazes locked and she felt her throat work, her heart racing.

"I would love you all the night long," he growled with heat and his fingers slid against her gently. Francesca gasped at his sure touch. "I would give you every pleasure possible."

She could hardly argue with that. His eyes flashed silver and he kissed her again, his caress turning rougher and more possessive. Francesca locked her arms around his neck, not wanting this moment to end and he deepened his kiss, devouring the sound of her pleasure.

This was the good stuff.

"Sorry to interrupt," a man said, his tone unapologetic and his accent American. Francesca jumped so suddenly that she might have fallen off the table. As it was, Orion locked an arm around her waist and held tight. Whoever it was couldn't have any doubt what they'd been doing as she was practically wrapped around Orion. Francesca reached for her glasses and put them on, hoping they made her look a little more dignified.

She was pretty sure it didn't work.

Orion spun to confront the intruder after breaking his kiss, sheltering her from view with a protectiveness that she could have appreciated more if she'd been the kind of woman who thought she couldn't take care of herself. She pulled her knees together and eased away from him an increment to straighten her clothes.

Then she saw that the blue shimmer of light was back again, radiating around him—or was it coming *from* him? Who glowed blue? No one she knew, but there was no mistaking the light in the dim light of the workroom. It couldn't be a trick of the sun here either. Francesca removed her glasses, polished them and put them on again, but the blue light didn't change. Was the light in front of Orion, creating a halo around his shadow? Was he radioactive or...luminescent?

It was the same as in the alley where Mr. Montmorency had found them. It was easy to recall the crackle of animosity between

Orion and Mr. Montmorency, even though she hadn't understood its reason.

Did Orion just dislike anyone getting near her? Protectiveness was one thing but possessiveness was another—especially since they hardly knew each other. She put more distance between them and his hand landed on her knee as if to urge her to stay close.

Francesca did.

"Why did you follow me?" Orion demanded of the new arrival. He was tense and alert, ready to fight. Even his voice was a low rumble of power, filled with threat.

Follow him? For the first time, Francesca looked over her shoulder at the intruder and gasped in recognition. It was the creepy guy from the hotel in Rome. What was *he* doing here? He considered Orion and was smart enough to retreat a step.

"You know him?" she whispered to Orion who nodded once, tersely.

"He is the stranger who gave me a ride from Rome."

Some points were getting together to make a line, but not in a good way. Francesca glared at the guy from the hotel, who looked just as untrustworthy as he had when he'd hit on her there. There wasn't anything specific about him to make her suspicious: he was a little plump with sandy hair, probably around the same age as she was. He could have been any one of a hundred similar male students she'd met while pursuing her degrees. Maybe a thousand of them. Bookish. Socially awkward.

Horny.

Sneaky.

Dangerous. She shivered a little at the unexpected thought, sensing the truth in it, and knew she hadn't imagined the way the guy's smile widened. Could he know what she was thinking? Francesca stifled the urge to shiver and glared at him.

Orion turned slightly, as if he wanted to see her in the periphery of his vision. She had the definite sense that he was aware of her reaction. "Do you know him?" he asked softly, his tone hinting that he'd tear the guy apart if she asked.

Francesca was tempted, but she had no real reason to dislike this guy so much. He just gave her a bad feeling. That wasn't a crime.

"Not really. He was staying at my hotel in Rome and hit on me at breakfast."

Orion's eyes lit with fire and he straightened a little. "He *struck* you?"

"It's a saying," she said reassuringly, brushing his shoulder with her fingertips. "It might not work in Greek. Um, he propositioned me."

That didn't seem to improve Orion's opinion of the other guy. He inhaled sharply, turning his glare upon the guy—who retreated another step.

"Nothing ventured, nothing gained," that guy said in Greek, then smiled. It was a toothy smile, one that seemed more hungry than friendly.

"Sigmund," Orion whispered in a low hiss.

"That's me. And you're Orion." Something changed in the other guy's eyes, giving him a resolute look, and he shoved his hands into his pockets before sauntering into the room. He seemed both provocative and tense, though he was trying to appear indifferent.

If anything, Orion became more taut, Francesca guessed he was poised to respond. That blue light was brighter.

"And I'm thinking, Orion, that you've got a secret." Sigmund raised his brows. "Shall I guess what it is?"

Was there really a blue shimmer around him, too? Francesca might be due for an eye exam.

"I suspect you already know," Orion said taking a step toward Sigmund.

Both shimmers brightened.

"Wait a minute," Sigmund said, looking between Francesca and the glass vase. "This isn't a firestorm."

How did he know the word? He used it the same way as Orion did.

"Either way, it is not your concern," Orion said. "I suggest you leave."

"Mmm," Sigmund said, sauntering closer to the vase. "Problem is I'm not really good at taking suggestions." He stopped in front of the vase with his hands in his pockets, bending to peer at the golden light swirling inside it.

Then he laughed. It wasn't a nice laugh.

"You, poor sucker," he murmured, glee in his tone. "You're having a firestorm with a *jar*." And then he cackled with laughter. He pivoted to face them both, eyes shining. "I guess that leaves Francesca for me."

"I think not," Orion said.

"What are you going to do about it?" Sigmund taunted as he took a defensive stance.

The tension in the room multiplied tenfold and Francesca feared the worst. The light in the vase became frantic, like fireworks snared inside it, which didn't help. The air sizzled, as if lightning would crack and set the whole place on fire.

"No fighting," she said but Orion shook his head.

"Too late," he said flatly, his tone leaving no room for argument. "He has threatened you and will not live to tell of it."

"Orion!"

"Lock the door when we leave," he advised in a terse undertone.

"You can't leave..."

"We won't fight here. There is insufficient space."

That made zero sense to Francesca, but Orion continued before she could ask.

"If there is another exit, take it. You should not witness this confrontation."

"If you're going to fight, I'm going to stay," she said, knowing he'd need an advocate if the security guards came to investigate. None of them spoke Greek as far as she knew. She didn't want him to be in trouble and for things to escalate since he couldn't explain.

Sigmund smiled, and it was clear neither of them had issues with things escalating.

Men!

Orion took a step closer to his opponent, that shimmer becoming blindingly bright. "Now," he said to her, exhaling the word, then he leapt toward Sigmund. He seized the other man and hauled him out of the back room into the adjacent exhibit hall.

Sigmund snarled and jumped toward Orion just as Francesca called for them to stop. The blue shimmers flashed—then Orion became a dragon, right before her eyes, breathing a stream of brilliant orange fire at Sigmund. The dragon's wings beat hard and lifted Sigmund into the air.

Francesca had already lost count of impossible things when Sigmund became a dragon of malachite green and snapped at the black dragon with fury. A heartbeat later, the pair took flight in the gallery, grappling for supremacy as they fought hard.

In the meantime, Francesca's jaw nearly hit the floor. For the first time in her life, seeing wasn't quite the same as believing.

———

"A FIRESTORM WITH A JAR," Sigmund taunted in old-speak as Orion breathed fire at his face. The *Slayer* laughed, seeming unaware that his green scales were being singed black.

"My firestorm is not your concern," Orion replied in kind, hurling the *Slayer* across the exhibit hall.

Sigmund spun in mid-air, laughing at Orion with bared teeth. *"Good thing no one else is here to see your humiliation,"* he said, his tone mocking.

The pair circled, their wings outspread, then locked talons in the traditional fighting pose. They wrestled then, each trying to dominate the other. Orion held back and let Sigmund believe he had a chance of winning this battle.

"Too bad no one is here to see you pay for interrupting us." He said, snapping at Sigmund's chest, letting the *Slayer* feel the brush of his teeth and the fan of his breath.

"But don't you owe me? I gave you a ride, after all." Sigmund sneered. *"Didn't you know?"*

"Of course, I knew you were Slayer," Orion said, letting his tone turn taunting. *"But I don't fear a feeble creature like you."* He laughed as Sigmund bristled. *"Look at you! As soft as a worm. As plump as a pigeon."* He laughed again and lifted a claw, inviting his opponent's inspection. He had to weigh a third more than Sigmund and was all hard muscle. *"Look at me. A seasoned warrior with blood on his talons."* Orion scoffed. *"This will be short,* Slayer, *but not sweet for you."*

"Don't count on it," Sigmund snarled and Orion knew then that his opponent would cheat.

He had been warned.

"Show me your worst." Orion let his old-speak drop low. *"Then I will show you mine."*

There was a faint tang of fear before Sigmund mustered his bravado again, but Orion noticed. *"I will have her once you're dead."*

Orion shook his head, circling his opponent with steady steps. *"She would never accept you."*

"I will take her anyway. I will force her."

The very suggestion enflamed Orion's fury, though he guessed that Francesca was a woman who could defend herself. *"I invite you to try,"* he replied, following his words with a torrent of dragonfire, and the fight was on.

CHAPTER FIVE

O rion had become an enormous black dragon with scales that could have been carved of anthracite or obsidian. They gleamed as he fought ferociously. Francesca blinked, but there was no doubting her new lenses. Sigmund was malachite green and silver, and a much more slender dragon. She had the sense that he was younger as well as slimmer, and he certainly wasn't as muscular.

Orion flung Sigmund across the exhibit hall, then they locked talons and Francesca heard a low rumble like thunder.

Or an earthquake.

Or one of the local volcanoes erupting. She should have followed the safety protocol and checked out the window, but she couldn't tear her gaze away from the dragons.

She doubted she would ever see a dragon battle in real life again.

It was pretty amazing that she was seeing one now.

She couldn't let herself consider how Orion had become a dragon before her eyes. It was too much to believe, though even as she tried to ignore the possibility, she found herself making a list of his dragon-like qualities.

Protective.

Fierce.

Powerful.

His low voice, his intensity, his sharp gaze, how he was completely ripped—they were all traits she could associate with a dragon.

He'd said the firestorm was the mating sign of his kind, and now she realized he didn't mean Greeks. Her mind resisted, insisting that a man could not become a dragon—but she had watched the man-to-dragon transformation happen.

Twice.

The wall was cracked where Sigmund had hit it and the temperature was skyrocketing from the fire Orion breathed. This wasn't a hallucination.

She had to reconsider what she knew to be true, and fast.

There were dragons living amongst humanity, dragons who could take the shape of men at will. What else could they do?

Breathe fire, obviously. Sigmund exhaled a plume of flame at Orion's chest scales, and Orion hurled him across the exhibition hall hard in retaliation. Sigmund slammed into a wall near the ceiling and slid down it to the floor.

There was another rumble, like thunder or a subway passing beneath the building, but there were no subways in Baiae. Sigmund's eyes flashed with fury and he leapt at Orion, who neatly stepped aside. The statue of Ulysses rocked unsteadily but Orion plucked the life-size marble statue off the floor, moving it out of harm's way like a stray action figure.

There was definitely something reminiscent of Orion in his deliberate movement, and in his choice to save the statue.

Then the rumble came again, a longer and deeper one this time.

With a start, Francesca realized it had to be the sound of them *talking* to each other. It wasn't thunder—and she doubted it was a friendly discussion. She watched, fascinated that they had a language of their own, then guessed that they were exchanging taunts. That was what knights did before battle in all the old ballads. It was what Beowulf had done with the monsters he confronted.

There had been inexplicable thunder when Mr. Montmorency followed her and Orion to that alley.

And both Mr. Montmorency and Orion had shimmered blue, just the way Orion and Sigmund had moments before.

Was Mr. Montmorency a dragon shifter, too? The possibility boggled the mind. Just ten minutes before, Francesca could have sworn there was no such thing as a real dragon, much less a man who could turn into one; now she was suspecting that she knew of three of them.

Just how many of these dragons lived amongst human society? Francesca had the sudden sense that the world was not as she had always believed. It made her feel a bit dizzy.

Sigmund must have said something that Orion didn't like, because he was slammed hard into the wall again for his comment—as if Orion was losing his temper. He breathed fire in retaliation, lighting the exhibit hall with orange flames. Francesca smelled burning flesh, then the black dragon looked over his shoulder.

Directly at her.

His eyes were a pale silvery blue and his gaze intense, so much like Orion's look that Francesca gasped. She had no lingering doubt that he was a dragon.

Or that she was in trouble for not following his command.

"Go," he ordered in a voice that made the floor vibrate—as well as Francesca's sternum. "*Now.*"

Francesca retreated, remembering his instructions. Her heart was racing as she shut the door to the workroom and locked the door. She thought about pushing a desk against it, just for insurance, but doubted it would stop a determined dragon. She surveyed the room as the sounds of a fight carried from the exhibition hall. Glass shattered abruptly and she guessed that a display case had been knocked over. If she was going to run, she didn't have time to secure Mr. Montmorency's vase in their storage room and she didn't want to risk it being broken. She seized her backpack and rolled the vase quickly in the protective packing she'd used, then jammed it into the bag and fastened the top.

She glanced between the back exit and the door to the exhibition hall and knew she couldn't resist one last look.

A man shouted in Italian for the fight to stop and she guessed it was a security guard. Francesca wished him luck with that. She bent and looked through the keyhole to find the fight fully in progress. There was smoke in the air and scorch marks on the wall and floor from the dragon fire.

The pair of dragons pummeled each other, rolling across the floor as they struggled for ascendancy, punching and clawing and snapping at each other. Those massive tails swung, sending another display case sliding across the floor as if it was a toy. Both dragons had fearsome arrays of sharp teeth and talons that could shred anyone to ribbons.

Sigmund took flight, flapping massive leathery wings, but even the high ceiling of the exhibit hall didn't give him enough room to escape his opponent. Orion snatched him out of the air by seizing his tail with one claw, tore open his chest with the other, then flung him across the exhibit hall. Black blood flowed from the wound, then sizzled when it landed on the stone floor. Smoke rose from the hot blood and Francesca wondered whether the dragon blood was burning holes in the floor like corrosive acid.

Meanwhile, Sigmund landed hard against a display case, shattering the glass. Though he was breathing heavily—more heavily than Orion—he was only down for a moment before he bounded toward Orion again, breathing a stream of fire that finally set off the fire alarm. The dragons ignored the security guards trying to intervene, the shrieking fire alarm and the flashes of the cameras from the small group of tourists who had gathered to watch. The sprinklers came on and the exhibition hall began to get misty. Orion swung his tail, wrapping it around Sigmund's leg and tripping him, then holding him captive as he exhaled.

Francesca narrowed her eyes. She could almost see something silvery emanating from Orion's mouth, like a sparkling mist. Sigmund struggled as if trying to evade it, but Orion was relentless. His breath glittered as it wound through the air, as sinuous as a snake, and she peered intently through the lock to watch. The sparkling line circled in the air as Sigmund struggled to escape, then dove into the open wound in his chest. He screamed with an anguish that made the hair stand up on Francesca's neck and almost made her feel sorry for him. There was another rumble of thunder. There were also a lot of flashes from cameras. The guards called for the fight to stop but the dragons battled on. Sigmund twisted in sudden desperation and bit at Orion, tearing open the flesh of his shoulder.

Orion's blood flowed crimson red over his scales. Why was it a different color?

Orion tipped his head back and raged fire at the ceiling of the hall, scorching it black. He then seized Sigmund and dragged him toward the wall on the south side. Beyond it was the harbor and the beach, but the only window was very small. He used the green dragon like a battering ram, slamming him into the wall repeatedly. The entire castle shook as a crack widened between the stone blocks of the wall, then he swung his powerful tail once more.

The stone wall broke, a large hole opening around the window. Guards and tourists shouted in dismay as a patch of blue sky became visible and the stone floor began to crumble near the hole. The museum was built on the top of a peak overlooking the harbor, and in this moment, it looked like a long way down.

Orion tossed Sigmund through the hole and let him fall. There was a bellow from beyond the stone walls but Orion reached back to the line of astonished tourists and snatched at their cameras. Some dropped them as they tried to run, but others kept snapping pictures.

He breathed fire over their heads and they fled, uninjured. Most dropped their cameras on the way and he stepped on them deliberately, crushing them to oblivion.

He didn't want to be witnessed, or have his presence recorded.

He then bounded across the exhibit hall toward the hole after his opponent, looking regal as he paused on the lip of the gaping hole.

He turned slowly, sparing one last glance toward the workroom door.

Francesca straightened in alarm and backed away from the keyhole with her heart pounding.

Orion *knew* she was still there and that she hadn't followed his instructions. Feeling caught, she seized the backpack and ran to the emergency exit, racing down the stairs to the staff door of the museum. Once again, she hugged the vase against her chest as she ran. She reached the door, but no one was paying attention. The security guard who should have been monitoring the exit was standing out in the courtyard, shading his eyes from the sun as he watched something overhead.

Francesca darted out of the museum, completely unobserved. Her Vespa was still parked there from when she'd met Dr. Thomas and Larry at the museum to go to Rome. It took her a minute to get it started because her hands were shaking. Her palms were damp and her heart was pounding, but she forced herself to breathe steadily as she rode out of the courtyard. She headed back toward town and her small apartment with relief. She let the Vespa blend into the traffic, meandering as if she didn't have a care in the world.

It was only then that she looked skyward, not really surprised to see the silhouetted figures of two fighting dragons against the late afternoon sky. The larger dragon was clearly winning, his blows effective and relentless, while the other smaller dragon struggled limply against his opponent.

Orion was a dragon shifter.

Francesca parked, then stared and marveled. More importantly, he was flying away. Would she ever see him again? Would he explain everything to her? His dragon nature certainly explained why he seemed so different to her from other guys.

Had he thrown the spark at her?

Who knew what else he could do?

And what did his ability have to do with the glow in the vase?

She definitely needed to know more about this firestorm he seemed to think was so important. She headed toward her apartment, needing to sit down and quietly think.

She recalled his few slips with language. Just how old was he?

Was he immortal?

Did he *remember* ancient Rome or even ancient Greece? Francesca turned and stared back at fighting dragons in astonishment. They were much smaller now.

Was that why his Greek sounded so different?

She drove on, thinking furiously. What if he did remember? What if he could tell her everything she wanted to know? She'd always been a bit envious of other researchers who could do interviews to fill out the details in their area of study, instead of having to sift through a lot of records, seeking hidden truths. If Orion was a survivor of those ancient eras, instead of speculation about the past, he could *tell* her how it had been. The prospect was exciting.

How could she find him again?

How could she convince him to confide in her?

Then her speculation stopped cold. What if Sigmund killed him?

No! That possibility was terrifying. She looked around and noticed a rooftop restaurant. She parked the Vespa then made her way up the stairs to the terrace, pushing through the crowd of people watching the dragons fight overhead.

She gripped the bag as the dragons moved further away, flying toward the south. They were just silhouettes in the distance, but unmistakably dragons, given the way they breathed fire at each other. They dipped low over Bacoli, then Orion dropped Sigmund.

The smaller dragon fell toward the sea, while Orion dove after him like an arrow seeking a bullseye. Sigmund vanished beneath the surface of the Mediterranean with a splash, followed closely by Orion.

There was a furious eruption of bubbles where they had plunged into the water, the sea boiling at that point, then the water stilled and everything seemed normal again. Francesca gripped the bag but neither of them reappeared.

What had happened to Orion? Could dragons drown? Men certainly could and that worried her. How could she find out the truth?

ORION WAS AN EXCELLENT SWIMMER, but he saw no reason to exert himself. He shifted back to human form once he dove beneath the surface, then watched as Sigmund sank to the depths. The Slayer was rotating between forms, shifting rapidly from man to dragon, which indicated that his injuries were severe.

If the salt water hadn't revived him, Orion didn't think anything else would. He held his breath and tread water as he watched Sigmund vanish out of view, finding himself amazed that the water wasn't more clean.

He remembered the Mediterranean being as clear as a crystal, but now it was muddy, despite the bright blue surface. He could see garbage on the bottom of the sea and floating in the water, and turned away in disgust. Perhaps it was a fitting place for Sigmund to rest forever.

He swam to the shore with easy strokes and hauled himself out of the water, wincing at the pain in his shoulder. He took off his shirt and wrung it out, then bound the wound as well as he could. He straightened and looked toward the distant city of Baiae, the fortress that was now a museum distinct.

He had no means of ensuring his own shelter in this time and place, and the sole person he knew was Francesca.

Orion began to walk, hoping she might be persuaded to assist him. She knew his truth now and he could not be at all certain of his reception. He lifted a hand and saw the faint glow of the firestorm's light, a beacon that would lead him to Montmorency's vase.

He could only hope that Francesca was in its vicinity.

———

SIGMUND WAS SINKING, the salt water stinging in his many wounds, ready to surrender the battle to survive. His lungs were screaming for air and he'd reverted to his human form against his own will. The water around him was inky with his own blood and even it stung his burns. He couldn't summon the energy to shift shape, even if that meant he might be able to soar out of the sea. No doubt Orion was waiting for him and would pounce as soon as he appeared.

He'd never been much of a fighter and couldn't see a reason to change now.

Then a whisper of old-speak jolted Sigmund back to consciousness.

"I could save you."

It was Magnus, taunting him with a possibility that would prob-ably be snatched away. Sigmund knew better than to trust the old *Slayer*, but he was tempted to respond all the same.

"No point," he replied, ensuring that he sounded morose.

"You said you'd learned something that might be of interest to me."

So, the wily *Slayer* had been toying with him by turning him down flat. Despite himself, Sigmund felt a flicker of interest.

"Whatever," he replied, letting himself continue to sink toward the bottom. He winced because his old-speak had sounded a little

more vigorous that time. He had to rein that in if he was going to fool Magnus.

"You were ambitious to interfere in a firestorm." Magnus scolded, his tone knowing. *"To challenge a much larger Pyr over his mate showed an audacity I didn't realize you possessed."*

The *Slayer* was coming closer. His old-speak was a little more resonant in Sigmund's thoughts and there was a shadow overhead.

Should Sigmund tell him the truth about the firestorm? He felt a quickening as he considered the possibilities.

"It's not a firestorm," he whispered, then willed himself to sink.

"How can it not be a firestorm?" Magnus bellowed in Sigmund's mind, his old-speak loud enough to give Sigmund a headache.

"I just wanted to know the secret," Sigmund murmured, letting his voice fade so that the last word was almost inaudible.

"Secret?" Magnus echoed and Sigmund smiled at his evident interest. *"What secret?"*

Sigmund didn't reply.

He felt Magnus' shock, timed the duration of the *Slayer's* hesitation, then felt a surge of satisfaction at the sound of the splash. With an effort, he remained motionless, even though he was desperate for a breath of air. He felt the current as the water moved, then a dragon claw snatched him from behind and he was in the clutches of a jade green and gold dragon.

Sigmund remained limp and let his eyes close slowly. Magnus swore, then there was a sudden rush of air. It was impossible but everything spun around Sigmund and he felt nauseous, then he was cast down hard. He landed with a wet splat on a tiled floor and took a big gulp of air, knowing he'd be bruised. He choked up some salt water and coughed as his heart leapt, then opened his eyes.

He was alive!

Magnus, in his human form, was watching Sigmund from the far side of the room, his eyes narrowed and his mood clearly grim. He wore a suit that was perfectly tailored and every hair was in place, his dress shoes polished to a gleam. He could have been a fashionable older Italian gentleman, except for the hungry gleam in his eyes.

That was all dragon.

Sigmund was impressed that the old *Slayer* had spontaneously manifested elsewhere, moving through space in the blink of an eye and bringing Sigmund with him. Even more amazing, Magnus was *dry*.

How had he done that? Spontaneous manifestation was a feat exclusive to the Wyvern, the only female *Pyr* who had mysterious powers of her own, or so Sigmund had always believed. It wasn't as if anyone saw the Wyvern with any regularity or she was inclined to answer questions when she did appear. Sophie was all about the enigma.

He knew she wouldn't confide in Magnus. No, that *Slayer* had figured this out on his own. Sigmund was willing to bet it had something to do with the bloodstone he wanted to see so badly.

"Tell me," Magnus commanded audibly as Sigmund surveyed his surroundings. He knew this room, with its high ceiling, its fresco and its treasures, even though he'd seen it only once—and that had been a quick glimpse. One of the artefacts was missing from Magnus' displayed collection. The vase that he'd just seen in the museum in Baiae had been in that fourth alcove, and he was sure it had been the one filled with golden light.

Had Magnus faked the firestorm somehow?

The bloodstone Sigmund sought was in the other vase, the one inscribed with some chick's name. He itched to hold it, just for a moment. He'd only read about the bloodstone in an old manuscript, a chance mention that made him consider new possibilities—possibilities that seemed particularly likely given that Magnus had the stone.

He let his gaze move back to Magnus, doing his best to hide his thoughts. "This is your apartment in Rome."

"Tell me," Magnus insisted, refusing to be distracted.

Sigmund got to his feet, sensing that his position had become much stronger since his last visit. He was encouraged, even though he knew he looked like a wreck. There was a puddle around his feet and he pushed a hand through his wet hair. Then he shook his head, knowing he had to play it right. "Not unless you make it worth my while," he said and Magnus nearly growled.

"I'll throw you back there and let you drown."

Sigmund shrugged. "Then you'll never know, will you?" He tilted his head to regard the *Slayer* and smiled just a little. "Is it the faked firestorm you want to know about or the secret about the blood-stone? I'm having a hard time keeping track of your demands."

Magnus snarled. "You'll tell me everything."

"Not a chance," Sigmund replied. "I intend to survive, so I have to make sure you need me. I'll tell you one thing for saving me. You choose which it is." He watched the *Slayer* look between the vessel with the bloodstone and the empty display stand, as if undecided, and realized Magnus knew less than expected.

This negotiation could be very interesting.

———

FRANCESCA SAT DOWN HARD at the closest table on the patio and forced herself to loosen her grip on the backpack. It was stone-cold, proof that Orion wasn't in the vicinity. She was surprised by how easily she accepted that to be the case. She wasn't surprised by how much his disappearance bothered her.

She liked him.

No, it was more than that. She hadn't met such an interesting and attractive guy in a long time. He was mysterious in a way, a man with secrets and hidden layers. She liked that. Francesca liked the sense that it could take years to learn his secrets, if she ever did.

It should have worried her that he could change into a ferocious creature made for battle. Instead, she wanted to learn what it was like, how he'd come by this ability, and what else it meant beyond the firestorm he'd mentioned. She wanted to know why the green dragon had black blood and Orion had red blood.

She wanted to know why no one ever talked about dragon shifters living in human society.

Then she recalled that people *had* written about them. In Ovid's *Metamorphosis*, people changed shape all the time. Gods changed into creatures and people. Gods and humans even changed into objects, like women becoming trees when they were pursued by lusty gods. The sources she studied day and night were chockful of shapeshifter stories.

Francesca had assumed they were just stories, but what if there was truth in them?

She couldn't sit in the restaurant then, not with that possibility in her thoughts. She became belatedly aware that the mood in the restaurant was chaotic. People were comparing what they'd seen and talking about the dragons. The staff were pouring drinks as quickly as they could but Francesca held her backpack tightly and left.

As was so often the case, she needed her books.

She made it to her apartment in record time, securing the Vespa, then unlocking the door and flinging the keys on the table. She set down the backpack with care, trapping it between a chair and the counter so there was no chance of it tipping over, then put on her glasses as she confronted her research books. She had only a sampling here, the ones that were most useful to her studies. She grabbed the Ovid, then looked for older references. Ovid had been a first century Roman, though the stories he recorded could have been older.

Francesca was looking for Greek sources. Even as her fingers trailed over the spines of her books, she remembered details that she'd dismissed before. Circe had turned Odysseus' men into pigs in *The Odyssey*; Proteus had been a sea-god known for his shape-shifting abilities. How could she have forgotten Metis, the first wife of Zeus, who had been able to turn herself into any creature at all?

Zeus had challenged her to become a fly, purportedly to test her abilities, but truly because he feared she would bear a child more powerful than himself. He'd swallowed her, but she'd already been pregnant resulting in the mighty Athena springing from Zeus' brow in battle armor when Hephaestus clove open his head.

Shapeshifters seemed to be everywhere once Francesca started to think about them. She chose a book on Greek mythology and turned to the section on therianthropy. The Greek gods had a tendency to change the forms of humans who annoyed them. Zeus changed King Lychaon and his children into wolves for killing Zeus' own children; Athena turned Arachne into a spider for challenging the weaving skills of the goddess; Artemis changed Actaeon into a stag for spying on her in her bath; Hera turned Tiresias into a woman for seven years, then back to a man. Zeus changed form himself in pursuit of sexual conquest, becoming a shower of gold, a bull, a swan, an eagle, a cloud, and a serpent among numerous other choices.

A serpent. Where were the dragons?

It took Francesca a while, but she finally found two in the story of Jason. To claim the golden fleece, Jason had been obliged to fulfill three tasks for King Aeetes who owned it. Jason was so discouraged by this that Hera made the sorceress Medea, also Aeetes' daughter, fall in love with Jason. She then helped him to overcome her father's challenges. First, Jason had to plough a field with fire-breathing oxen that he yoked himself: Medea gave him a potion to protect him from the flames. Second, he had to sow the teeth of a dragon, which would sprout into warriors. Medea told him how to defeat these foes before they could slaughter him. Finally, he had to overcome the dragon who guarded the Golden Fleece and steal the prize: Medea gave him a sleeping potion for the dragon, he stole the Golden Fleece and the triumphant pair set sail. Aeetes gave chase but they killed Medea's brother, casting the pieces into the sea, and Aeetes was distracted from his pursuit to gather the pieces of his dead son.

Sometimes the heroes in these stories didn't seem very noble to Francesca.

There were more dragons in the story of Cadmus, a prince of Phoenicia and founder of Thebes, who Herodotus believed had lived 1500 years before his own time. That put Cadmus circa 2000 BC. Cadmus had killed a sacred dragon guarding a well, and sown the teeth in the soil. Warriors had sprung from the soil, poised to attack, but stones had been thrown among them to make them turn upon each other. (Evidently, they hadn't been particularly bright warriors.) Five survived and helped Cadmus found Thebes. Despite his successes, Cadmus believed himself to be cursed because he had killed the sacred dragon. In frustration, he had said the gods could make him a dragon if that was the kind they favored most, and his transformation had immediately begun. His wife, Harmonia, had begged the gods to share her husband's fate and they had ended their lives as dragons. In another version of the tale, they had been changed to dragons after their deaths.

That was closer to shape-shifting from man to dragon, but didn't provide enough information for Francesca.

Weird how there were two stories about teeth.

Francesca frowned at the shelves of books. There should be more dragons. She had a vague recollection of dragons and maybe dragon shifters in Norse mythology but it wasn't her area of specialty. She was trying to remember a survey course in her undergrad years, when she realized that the vase had begun to glow again.

To her surprise, the sky had grown dark outside the windows. She'd absently turned on a desk lamp as she read and researched, but now saw that the apartment was in shadows.

Except for the golden light emanating from the backpack. She crouched down before the bag and removed Mr. Montmorency's vase. Even as she carefully removed the packing, she could feel its growing warmth. She blinked when she set it on the kitchen counter, the frenzy of golden light almost blinding in its intensity.

And then she smiled, because she knew what—or who—had awakened it.

Orion was coming back.

There was the sound of a man's footfall on the steps outside her apartment and Francesca almost flew to the door. She hauled it open to find the man in question climbing the last of the stairs.

He looked as resolute as ever, if weary. His hair was pushed back, as if he'd run his fingers through it when it was wet and it had dried that way. His T-shirt was stained and bound over his shoulder.

When she opened the door, he glanced up and his slow smile made her feel as if the sun had come out from behind the clouds. He looked younger then and less careworn, the heat in his eyes making her tingle all over again.

Francesca smiled, unable to hide her relief. "Orion!" she whispered with delight. "You're here."

"I followed the spark of the firestorm," he confessed in a low rumble. "You have the vase with you."

"I do. It's here." She hesitated, feeling suddenly shy with him on the threshold of her place. "How did you get here?"

"I walked," he admitted. "I came out of the sea some distance to the south, then I walked." He sobered then, his gaze searching hers with intensity. "You saw," he whispered.

Francesca smiled. "I saw," she agreed easily. "And I have so many questions for you." His eyes lit and the corner of his mouth began to lift in a smile but Francesca wanted to do something other than talk. She impulsively caught Orion's face in her hands and kissed him.

She felt his surprise. He hesitated for a heartbeat and she had time to fear that she'd been too bold, that he didn't want her anymore, that she'd made a mistake. Then his arms locked around her and he lifted her off the ground, deepening their kiss with such tenderness and power that Francesca was lost in sensation.

This man could kiss.

Would she ever get enough of him?

She was only vaguely aware of the crackle of fire within the Roman vase behind her. What was more important was that Orion had come back to her. He was a dragon shifter, a man whose abilities she had only glimpsed, but maybe that was why his kiss filled her with an urgent desire that couldn't be denied.

Maybe it was because his very existence gave her more to investigate and learn.

Then Francesca became aware of the cloth beneath her fingers. It was stiff, as if it had been wet and dried on his walk. She pulled back, noticing the blood stain. She remembered the green dragon tearing open his shoulder and realized that the injury had followed him between forms. "You're hurt!"

"Not so badly as that," he said, as if having his shoulder sliced open was no cause for concern.

Francesca thought otherwise. She seized Orion's hand and tugged him into her apartment, locking the door behind them and reaching for the knot in the T-shirt with determination. She really hoped he didn't need stitches because there would be explanations necessary at the hospital then.

She knew that wasn't the only reason she was taking him home, though.

CHAPTER SIX

Francesca had smiled at him.

She had welcomed him.

Relief flooded through Orion with such power that he felt unsteady on his feet.

The entire way back to her, he had fretted about her welfare. The future *Pyr* believed that observing the shift could drive a mortal insane, though that had never been his own experience. There had been those who came to watch the *Pyr* shift shape in his own time, those who sought a connection with his kind, those who knew more of the *Pyr* than the *Pyr* knew of themselves. He had thought the concern irrational until he realized that Francesca had witnessed his change—and she was a modern person, like those the *Pyr* thought might be driven mad. He had not been able to return with sufficient speed and had worried about her condition the entire way.

Her smile was more welcome than the radiant burn of the firestorm. Its heat had guided his steps, leading him directly to her. He was so glad she had taken the vase from the museum and had kept it with her. Otherwise, he would never have located her so quickly.

His feet were sore and there was salt crusted in his hair. His shoulder ached and he didn't know when he had last eaten. But when Francesca flung herself at him, Orion could only catch her close in gratitude.

He loved that she had initiated their kiss—and she had done as much, even knowing his truth. It was no small thing to be revealed as a dragon warrior to a woman of such good sense, but in the time it had taken him to walk back to town, Francesca had accepted what she had learned of him. She was a marvel.

Her kiss was glorious, a caress that filled him with heat and purpose, with a desire that he knew would be difficult to check once unleashed. It had been hard to let her break their kiss, though her concern for his welfare was heartening. He could not complain when she pulled him into a private space that was obviously her residence.

He leaned down and put his forehead against hers, inhaling deeply of her sweet fragrance. He felt as if he had come home, which made no sense given that he was in an alien time and place. But the connection he felt to Francesca was undeniable.

Orion didn't want to deny it, firestorm or not. He had to move away from her to think clearly and make the right choice, but he could not force himself to step back. Instead, he held her and looked around her home with curiosity. Even tearing his gaze from hers took more effort than it should have.

She was bewitching him, simply with her presence, and worse, he did not care.

Francesca's abode was small and neat, consisting of one large room with a wooden floor and white walls. It reminded him of her with its simple elegance and practicality. Every item had been chosen with purpose but there was a beauty in each detail. There was an area to his left for food preparation, a bed against the wall to his right, and a desk before a large window with a bookcase alongside. She had an enviable view of the harbor from that work space, and the top of the desk was littered with books. A small desk lamp was lit, but its light could not rival that emanating from the glass vessel. Beyond the window was a walled patio that he guessed would bask in the sunlight of midday, and there were potted plants against the far rail.

On the sill of the window was a large quartz crystal, one that startled him with its similarity to the darkfire crystal that was responsible for his current dilemma.

"I'm not a crystal freak," she said, following his gaze and laughing a little. "My brother Gabe is a geologist. He brought it to me when he visited." She rolled her eyes. "At least he didn't talk about aligning chakras like his wife Kathy does. She told him to bring it to me. She's always trying to convince me of the power of the unseen." She shook her head.

This speech made no sense to Orion, but he had no notion what to question first.

Instead, he considered the glass vessel, which was filled with frantic golden light and crackled with captive sparks. It was in the area for preparing food. It glowed brilliant yellow thanks to his proximity, radiating a glorious light and warmth. Orion wasn't technically feeling the firestorm with Francesca, but just being close to that fire turned his thoughts in a predictable direction.

As did the enticing Francesca herself. Orion was keenly aware that they would not be interrupted in this place, that she had allowed him into her sanctuary. Her trust aroused him as much as her kiss.

He wanted her more than he had ever desired a woman before. She was a treasure and a prize, a woman who was both strong and gentle.

A woman to whom he would gladly surrender his heart.

But she was not his mate. Orion had to remember that. The lick of his firestorm stirred his desire, but it was possible that Francesca's doubt meant the gods played a jest upon them both. Could he convince her to compromise? She was so pragmatic. How he wished he could show her the gods, just as he had revealed his own nature, however inadvertently. With one glimpse, she was convinced that he was a dragon shifter, but he knew there was no other argument he could have made to convince her.

She had to see to believe.

She was still talking about her brother, a little smile of affection curving her lips. "Gabe has no ability to plan for his packing. He took home so many rocks and souvenirs that he had to leave a bunch of his stuff behind. I was supposed to take it to a charity or a thrift store, but I haven't gotten around to it." Her gaze flicked to his, her eyes all hazel with specks of green. "Lucky for you."

"Lucky for me," he echoed, unable to tear his gaze away from hers.

She flushed and her lashes dropped. He watched her frown as she pulled the cloth away from his wound, then she paled. Surely her concern for his welfare was a good sign. She moved away to retrieve her glasses from the table on the other side of the small space, and he felt bereft by the lack of contact. As soon as she returned, he put his hands back on her waist and urged her closer. She fit against him and yearning rolled through him with such vigor that he closed his eyes for a heartbeat. She didn't seem to notice that he tightened his grip and urged her an increment closer.

Perfection. Both slender and strong. Quick-witted and fearless. A warrior queen. He could tuck her under his chin, protect her from any foe, shelter her from any storm—or he could watch her slay her own opponents with ease.

"I hope you don't have to go to the hospital," she said, her practical tone making him smile. She winced as she tugged the last of the cloth free of the dried blood on the wound. "Does that hurt?" It stung a bit, but that was nothing compared to infliction of the wound itself. Orion shrugged and she smiled a little. "Men," she murmured inexplicably.

"Hospital?"

"To be treated. To have it sewn up."

"It does not need to be sewn," he said with conviction.

Her eyes narrowed as she glared at him. "Don't get all macho on me. I've seen enough of that with my brothers. It isn't going to get infected on my watch."

"You have more than one brother?"

Francesca nodded. "Two. You're just like them. They always want to tough everything out, like it's a measure of their masculinity to endure pain." She shook her head. "It's just stupid to not take care of yourself."

"I take care of myself," he murmured, surprised by how much he liked her fussing over him. He had always been in the company of men, mostly warriors, and was unfamiliar with the ministrations of women. He always felt rough in their presence, never knowing what to say—as Damien did so readily—if he managed to say anything coherent at all. Francesca was different and he was not certain why.

Was it because she was not his mate?

Or because she could be, if he changed her mind?

She cast his stained shirt into the kitchen sink with a grimace, then took a cloth and wetted it. She looked up suddenly. "What do you do with your clothes?" Orion didn't know what she meant. "When you become a dragon, where do they go? This T-shirt is all salty from the sea, but you went into the water as a dragon."

"You were watching," he said with pleasure.

"Everyone was watching," she said with a laugh. She lifted a brow as she wrung out the cloth. "Where were your clothes?"

"They must be folded away and hidden from view. No one can know where they are."

She looked toward the stack of books. "I remember that from stories. If someone stole the werewolf's clothes, he couldn't turn back into a man." She eyes Orion again. "Is that true?"

"I have no desire to find out."

Her gaze warmed. "No, neither would I." She returned to him with brisk steps, then paused a step away from him to survey his bare chest. He saw the flush in her cheeks and the way she caught her breath, then she swallowed and kept her gaze fixed on his wound. "You must work out a lot," she said and her voice sounded strained.

Orion smiled a little, liking that she was so affected by the sight of him. He was glad to collect each hint of her interest. "My occupation demands it."

"Dragon or warrior?"

"Both."

She met his gaze and he smiled slowly, watching her cheeks pinken. He closed his hands around her waist again, letting his thumbs move in small circles against her. He felt her sway a little then she turned her attention to his injury. Her hands were less steady, though she still worked diligently at cleaning it.

"It's a mess," she said, as if he had contrived for it to be so. Her voice was breathless, though, another encouraging sign. She worked steadily, removing the dried blood, avoiding his gaze so studiously that he knew she was keenly aware of him. He gripped her a little more firmly, then bent to kiss her ear. She smelled sweet and feminine, and he wanted her with a primal vigor.

"You need to stand still," she chided. She flicked a look at him, her eyes sparkling a little.

"Do I?" He held her gaze and let his thumbs slide beneath the waist of her skirt, inhaling sharply when he felt the smoothness of her skin against his own. Her gaze lifted to his as he made those circles again and he watched her lips part.

"You're distracting me," she whispered.

"Should I stop?" he asked.

She shook her head then smiled. "It feels good," she whispered.

"It does," Orion agreed, liking that she was not shy. He slowly slid his hands under her blouse, then when she did not move away, he opened each button in succession, starting with the one at her waist. Her hands stilled on his shoulder, and she held his gaze, transfixed. When her blouse was unfastened, he opened it then surveyed her with satisfaction. Her breasts were firm and high, snared in the lacey white garment he had glimpsed earlier, the one that failed to hide the rosy perfection of her nipples.

She stepped back then and he had a moment of disappointment, then she removed the blouse and returned to his embrace, her chin high. Orion flattened one hand against the back of her waist and pulled her closer, sliding his hand slowly up her back, from waist to nape, then back down again. She shivered, then rolled her hips against him, almost purring with pleasure.

"Who seduces who?" he murmured and she laughed a little.

"Maybe we're seducing each other." She laid one hand on his uninjured shoulder and flattened it against his skin, sliding her palm across him. Her lashes swept down as she watched her own caress, a gentle touch that set fire beneath Orion's skin. She felt his shoulder and his upper arm, then her hand swept back to his chest. She pushed her fingers through the tangle of dark hair there, then tipped her head back to meet his gaze as her fingers slowly slid down toward his navel.

"You explore," he said, his voice a deep rumble.

"Uncharted territory," she said lightly, her tongue running across her lips as her fingertips circled his navel. Her hand brushed down, over the front of his pants, over the heat of his erection, and Orion caught his breath sharply. He caught her hand in his, kissing her palm before placing it on his shoulder again.

"Too fast?" she asked.

"I fear you will think so, once you touch me there," he warned and she smiled, untroubled by his threat.

"This should be stitched up," she said, wincing at his shoulder.

"Is it clean?" Orion asked and she nodded. "Take the vase and sear it."

Her mouth opened, then closed again, her expression one of alarm. Then she nodded and followed his instruction. "I guess you know better than me," she said. She lifted the vase in both hands, the light within it brightening to white fury as she brought it closer. Orion closed his eyes against its brilliant radiance, then he tipped his head back and bared his teeth as she followed his instruction. The heat seared to his very soul and he smelled the burn of his own flesh.

But when she lifted the vase away, he exhaled, feeling that it was better. He turned to look at the wound, running his fingertips over it, then guided her to another place. The skin was swollen and the closed wound an angry red, but he knew it would heal. Francesca followed his instruction, then set the vase back on the counter.

"Wow," she said. "Just like new."

"Not quite," he murmured and she smiled.

"Could you have done that yourself?"

"I cannot light the firestorm myself, but I can endure a temporary pain to achieve an end."

"I bet you can," she said, her gaze sliding over him again.

"My turn to explore," he whispered. He pulled her closer once more, keeping one hand on the small of her back, then cupped one breast with his free hand. He ran his thumb over the nipple until it tightened, then bent to capture the tight peak in his mouth as he had before. The taste of her was exquisite, the feel of her superb. He had fought and he had won, and in triumph, there was little better than a celebration of the senses with a tempting woman. Francesca gasped and quivered, then arched against him, demanding more.

Orion fairly lifted her from the floor, enflamed by her response. He loved that she responded to his touch with a passion of her own, and could not wait for her to make demands of her own. He grazed her nipple with his teeth through the sheer lace and she whispered his name, locking one hand in his hair. She squirmed and reached behind herself, unfastening the garment and dropping it to the floor, smiling when she returned to his embrace. She kissed him then, claiming his mouth with a hunger that Orion yearned to satisfy. The feel of her bare skin against his own, the crush of her breasts against his chest, was almost enough to make him surrender to temptation...

Almost.

There was a crackle of light then, one that made him open his eyes to look. Behind Francesca, he could see the glass vessel, its interior ablaze as the golden lights moved within it with newfound frenzy. It might have been filled with fire, though that made no sense. Fire could not burn without air to sustain it. The light brightened as he watched, becoming first yellow then turning to pure white lightning.

"Lightning in a jar," Francesca whispered, following his gaze and looking over her shoulder. Her hands were on his shoulders but Orion put a little distance between them, needing to think.

She was not his to claim.

In a way, it would be a travesty to take her in the presence of his mate.

Orion winced and pushed a hand through his hair.

Once, desire had been sufficient, but since he had felt the flare of Damien's firestorm, he had wanted more. His encounters with the modern *Pyr* left him convinced that there could be more. Indeed, he had only to recall his father's tales of his mother to know that he might expect more. Orion wanted the burn of his firestorm, but he also wanted the partnership of his destined mate. He wanted a family, a companion, someone at his back come rain or shine—and he was surprised by how much he longed for all of that.

The radiant vessel reminded him that Francesca was not his mate.

If and when his mate truly escaped that vase, he would be obliged to put Francesca aside for the sake of the future of his kind, regardless of his attachment to her, regardless of what a marvel she was.

"What's the matter?" she asked quietly and he felt her studying him.

"I would not mislead you," he admitted, pressing a kiss to her bare shoulder and retreating a step. "I would not have you believe that there is more between us than there can be."

She smiled a little. "Because I'm not your mate? Seriously, Orion, you can't wait your whole life for that one person to suddenly appear. You have to enjoy the moment, live a little..."

"But she is near," he said, gesturing to the vase. "And when the firestorm sparks, I must follow its command."

Her eyes narrowed slightly as she glanced from the vase to him. "It's a vase," she said. "A weird vase, I'll give you that, but a piece of glass can't be your mate. This can't be your firestorm."

"I am not so certain," Orion said.

"What do you mean?"

"It could be a jest of the gods," he admitted. "It could be because you don't show them reverence, or because I insulted them in the past."

"So, you're going to be chaste until I believe in destiny? That could be a long wait."

"I must be with my destined mate, whenever and wherever she appears. It is my duty to my kind to satisfy the firestorm and conceive a son."

Francesca's view of that expectation was clear. She looked exasperated. She reached for her blouse, turning her back upon him. "Honestly, Orion, that's so old-fashioned. It's 1972, for goodness' sake. People can just have sex without worrying about getting married and having babies and all that commitment. Never mind *destiny*." She fastened the lace garment, then turned to face him as she buttoned the front of the blouse. "Live a little. Follow your impulse. Have *fun*." Her hair was loose over her shoulders and her lips were a little swollen, her eyes snapping with frustration.

At him.

But Orion was snared by one thing she had said.

"1972," he repeated. "This is the year?"

She was surprised by the question. "Of course. Didn't you know?"

Orion didn't reply. He moved instead toward the sparkling vase, his thoughts churning as quickly as the light snared within the artefact.

1972.

Assuming that the date was calculated in the same way as in the realm of his brethren in America—the number of years since the birth of a religious leader of whom he had no knowledge—another thirty-six years had to pass before the spell was broken over Drake's company of warriors, including himself.

Orion and his fellows in this year of 1972 were still trapped in the form of teeth, buried beneath modern London in an ancient lost cave.

A cave favored by the opponent of Rafferty, Magnus Mont-morency.

Orion suddenly felt unsteady on his feet. How could he be in two places at once? Or had the tooth that held him captive vanished from that hoard when he appeared in this place and time?

He had the curious sense that he should not be in Francesca's presence at all, but the darkfire crystal had brought him to it, and it looked as if his firestorm burned. Though it did not. As Rafferty had said—or would say in the future—the darkfire turned all upside down, challenging assumptions and testing beliefs. Orion had seen his firestorm spark evidently between himself and an ancient vase. And now he was alive in Italy even as the tooth he had become was forgotten in a hoard in London. How could all of this be true?

What if he had attacked Magnus Montmorency and killed him earlier this day? Would that have changed the future he remembered? For better or for worse? He *had* killed the *Slayer,* Sigmund. What would be the repercussions of that? Orion could inadvertently influence the outcome of the war that his future brethren fought against the *Slayers* for command of the earth.

He might have already done as much.

Panic rose within him.

He might even affect the breaking of the curse over himself and his fellow Dragon's Tooth Warriors. What then? Would he vanish from this era without a trace?

Would he be forgotten as if he had never existed?

Would they be trapped as teeth forever, because of his error? Would the *Pyr* lose their battle against the *Slayers* because of his unwitting deed?

The prospects were horrifying. Orion didn't know what to do. He thought he shouldn't do anything. How could he undo whatever he had already done? Terror rose within him, until he felt Francesca's hand on his shoulder.

"You don't look so good," she said softly. "Why don't you take my brother's stuff and have a shower? Clean up, then we'll get something to eat." He looked down at her, astonished that she could think of food at a moment like this. Against every expectation, she smiled. "I know how my brothers get when they're hungry and I'm starving, too." She gave him a little nudge. "Come on. I'll lock the vase away and you can answer my questions about dragons. I know the perfect place."

Orion was not certain he could eat or make casual conversation. He wasn't sure he wanted to tell Francesca more about the *Pyr*, but going out would remove him from the vicinity of the vase. The firestorm was affected by proximity, and even though this wasn't his firestorm, it shared similarities. The heat of this one could attract *Slayers*, like Sigmund earlier in the day. If he couldn't risk killing another *Slayer*, how would he be able to defend Francesca? The possibility of her being injured or worse was more than enough to prompt Orion to nod agreement.

She might not be his mate, but she was a treasure of the earth and one he would defend to his last breath.

———

WHY HAD Orion stopped kissing her? Francesca had been more than ready for an intimate encounter. She'd been looking forward to seeing him completely naked—and feeling him against her. She wasn't used to being rejected when things got that far along. He really was worried about this mate thing, and she wondered how she could get him to let it go.

But why had he been spooked by the year? She didn't believe for a moment that he could have forgotten. It was almost as if he hadn't even known the year, which made no sense at all.

She could add that to her list.

She studied the vase as the water ran in the shower, fighting the temptation to steal a peek at him. She could just imagine how tanned and muscled he was, how tight his butt would be and—well, there were other parts of him that she wanted to see as well.

Francesca smiled at her own thoughts, then realized that the light in the vase had dimmed. It was a deep orange again, like fireworks against a night sky, and the lights were moving more slowly.

It couldn't be because Orion was in the bathroom, could it?

She considered the distance. That did put him about fifteen feet further away. It had sparked when he had arrived at the doorway of the workroom at the museum, probably close to the same distance. Francesca picked up the vase and took it out to her terrace. It glowed a little in her hands, but the light definitely dimmed as she carried it away from Orion.

She set it down on the tiles and perched on the edge of a chair, watching the light die down to embers. Another ten feet and it would probably be completely dark inside the vessel, as if there was nothing unusual about it at all.

That was definitely a situation she couldn't explain.

She took the vase back inside and tucked it into the back of her closet, hiding it from view. She made sure it was well-padded and couldn't come to any harm there. She'd take it back to the museum in the morning. She changed into a pair of jeans and a white blouse, put on a bit of lipstick and a pair of sandals. She left her hair loose and put her glasses in a small purse, then waited for Orion. She wanted to tempt him to pick up where they'd left off, but she had a feeling that wouldn't be easily achieved.

In a way, it was kind of sweet that he wanted to protect her from disappointment. She had to admire his determination to act upon the firestorm whenever it happened, and she imagined for a minute what it would be like to know that a guy was completely committed.

The problem was that you couldn't be sure of anyone, not until you were involved and in love, and that meant letting yourself become vulnerable in the hope that it all worked out. Francesca had learned that lesson the hard way. She wasn't going to be one of those pathetic women who thought their lives only had merit if they were married. She also didn't like long odds and happy marriages seemed to be a lot less easy to anticipate than a successful career. She could work hard and succeed in academia: working hard offered no guarantees in romance. She wasn't going to give up everything just to keep a man happy either, no matter how much she loved him.

She refused to miss Derek.

She knew he didn't miss her. She knew he'd married.

Good for him—he'd found staff.

What she missed was having someone in her life—as much as Derek had ever been around. It was the idea of him she missed more than Derek himself. The problem was that her experience with Derek had left her uncertain of the point of having anyone else in her life.

In Francesca's view, love went both ways. Of course, two people could make a life together that didn't involve one becoming the slave of the other, but she knew they both had to want it that way. Her brothers made it work, but she'd learned to appreciate how rare they were.

The problem with being practical was that Francesca had to see a thing to believe it, and she'd seen her brothers create enviable partnerships with their wives. That kind of balance was possible—and having seen one meant she couldn't resist the idea that one day, some day, there might be a partnership like that out there for her.

The trick was finding the right guy.

It wasn't Orion, by his own insistence on his firestorm. Francesca refused to be disappointed—he was being honest with her and that was a good thing. So, why couldn't they have a little fun together and enjoy each other's company for a night? She had to think it would be worth the price of admission.

By the time Orion stepped out of the bathroom, a haze of steam following him, Francesca had decided. She wasn't his destined mate, which meant that forever was out of the question as far as he was concerned, but one night together certainly wasn't—and she was good with that.

She was going to seduce Orion.

She stood up and smiled, noting that he had to wear Gabe's chamois shirt open, given the broadness of his chest. Beneath it, Orion wore a red Levi's T-shirt that hugged him like a lover. He'd brushed down his khakis and polished his boots. He'd shaved and his hair was wet, curling against his collar in damp curls of ebony. His gaze swept over Francesca with approval and he smiled that slow smile, which only fed her confidence that he could be seduced.

She couldn't wait.

———

AH, Francesca. If ever there had been a woman to tempt Orion, she was the one. If he could have chosen a mate of all the women he had ever encountered, she would have been his first and only selection.

But she was not his mate, and that detail was troubling.

They walked together to a small taverna that she recommended and got a table at the back. It was a bit noisy but not too crowded, and the food smelled so wonderful that his stomach growled. She had been right that it was time to eat. He already felt better after having cleaned himself and changed his clothes.

The taverna was welcoming and smelled of good food. The tables were simple wood, the chairs straight with woven straw seats. The server lit a candle on their table and gave them large sheets covered with writing.

Francesca must have noticed Orion's expression because she paused in the act of putting on her glasses. She asked the waiter something and Orion listened, catching the gist of the conversation but not really understanding the words. Then she spoke to him in Greek. "They specialize in fish here, fresh from the sea. He says the swordfish is fresh today and the calamari, or they make pizzas..."

"Francesca, you choose."

She considered him. "How hungry are you?"

"Very." Orion didn't realize how much until he answered her. "I have no means to pay," he began. "Save this." He pulled the only two coins from his pocket and showed them to her. She was visibly started. "But one is not mine to surrender and the other, I will not surrender."

"Keep them," she said quickly. "It'll be my treat." She turned to the server again. Orion watched them discuss the food, then warm bread was immediately brought to the table along with two bowls of olives – green and black – and olive oil. Red wine was poured for both of them, the decanter left on the table, and he knew his confidence in Francesca's choices had not been misplaced.

"Can I see those again?" Francesca asked in a whisper and he knew she meant the coins.

He surrendered them to her, trusting her to return them, and watched her examine them.

"You didn't get this from the museum," she said of his challenge coin. "The octopus coin there has a nick on one side. This one is in much better shape." She glanced up and he nodded agreement.

"It is my challenge coin."

"Should I know what that means?"

He pointed. "The other is the challenge coin of a *Slayer*. That I caught and kept it means that we are agreed to battle to the death at some future point."

She blinked. "It's a Roman coin. A *follis*."

He shrugged, not wanting to tell her whose coin it was.

"A fight to the death. Really?"

"Truly, Francesca. There are some battles that must be fought."

She sighed and shook her head. "We can argue about that later," she said, handing him back the coins as the waiter returned.

To Orion's delight, that server brought a large plate of something golden and hot. It was calamari, coated with something that was crispy and delicious, making the dish both familiar and new. The bread and olives were simple but fresh, and Orion had never enjoyed food so much.

"Francesca, you have chosen well indeed."

"It's just the beginning," she said and he knew he would eat it all. "You have to tell me about dragons," she warned with a laugh. "That's my price."

"And I will pay it willingly."

She propped her chin on her hand, watching him as she sipped her wine. She ate the occasional bite, but seemed more interested in studying him. "When did it start?"

Orion looked up.

"Being able to do what you do." She glanced toward the other tables, but no one was listening. Orion found himself doing the same, though he thought it unlikely that many spoke Greek, let alone as he did.

He felt no hesitation in confiding in her. There was something utterly trustworthy about Francesca. "It began in my youth, when my voice deepened. The change was anticipated, for my father had also been *Pyr*, then I was sent to train."

"*Pyr*?"

He smiled at her. "That is what I am. The modern *Pyr* tell a story of our beginnings. Let me see if I remember it." He considered then spoke. "In the beginning, there was the fire..."

"That's not how it usually goes."

"It does for us." Orion watched her smile, then continued. "In the beginning, there was the fire, and the fire burned hot because it was cradled by the earth. The fire burned bright because it was nurtured by the air. The fire burned lower only when it was quenched by the water. And these were the four elements of divine design, of which all would be built and with which all would be destroyed. And the elements were placed at the cornerstones of the material world and it was good."

He paused to eat some more calamari and drink some wine. "But the elements were alone and undefended, incapable of communicating with each other, snared within the matter that was theirs to control."

Francesca was apparently transfixed. "I'll guess this is where you come in."

Orion nodded. "And so, out of the endless void was created a race of guardians whose appointed task was to protect and defend the integrity of the four sacred elements. They were given powers, the better to fulfill their responsibilities; they were given strength and cunning and longevity to safeguard the treasures surrendered to their stewardship. To them alone would the elements respond. These guardians were—and are—the *Pyr*."

"I like it," she said when he fell silent. "So, you came into your powers and were sent to train." Her smile was mischievous. "Learning to breathe fire?"

Orion nodded. "To breathe and weave smoke, to shift quickly, to strike hardest in a fight. There are skills to be mastered in all details of our nature."

"Smoke," she said. "Is that what you breathed into Sigmund's wound?"

"It is a tactic of the modern *Pyr*." Had he just taught the *Slayers* to do as much, and years before they should have known it to be possible?

She eyed him, probably due to his choice of words. "And that rumbling. You were talking to each other."

Orion knew he should not be surprised that Francesca had realized what old-speak was. "Taunting," he agreed. "It is customary before battle."

"This is old stuff," she said, reaching for the calamari.

Orion opened his mouth and closed it again, reconsidering his words before he spoke. "You have no idea."

She looked up, her eyes bright. "Then tell me."

Tell her.

Confiding the details of his own story would reveal his age to her. Would she be horrified? Would she be skeptical? Orion had a feeling she might believe him, and if she did, he would feel as if he had at least one comrade in this place.

He knew how to tell her, as well, so it would not be a shock but her own conclusion.

He finished his wine and put the glass aside, leaning over the table to hold her gaze. "I remember my thirtieth summer. We were summoned by Peisistratus to oust the invader Kleomenes from Athens. He was defeated in the Acropolis and compelled to retreat to Sparta."

Francesca blinked. Orion watched her wrestle with the implication, because she recognized the names just as he had anticipated. He took the opportunity to eat more calamari, content to give her all the time she needed.

It wasn't very much time at all.

She put down her glass and leaned over the table. "The tyrant Peisistratus? Ruler of Athens along with his son?"

Orion nodded.

She frowned. "And King Kleomenes? The Spartan king who retaliated by bringing the Peloponnesian League against Athens?"

Orion shrugged. "I did not witness that retaliation. We were sent to engage the legendary Cadmus, who was mighty despite his advanced age." He waited a moment then continued, seeing her skepticism. "My kind were the warriors upon whom rulers relied."

"I can believe a king would like to have an army of dragons to call," she said quietly.

"We were still revered, but our leaders by my time wished to see us step out of tales and into battle again. Sadly, Cadmus deceived us."

"You were in a company of dragon shifters who were defeated?"

It was gratifying that she had such confidence in his powers. "We were enchanted," he admitted and watched her eyes light with understanding.

"As *teeth*," she guessed to his surprise. Her gaze flitted over the room and he watched her remembering the details. "But the story is that the teeth were sown, that they became warriors and that the five survivors became the Spartans."

Orion laughed. "No. My kind were known long before the Spartans, who fought their way to fame with their valor." He nodded. "There were those of my kind who fought with the Spartans, even those said to be of their lineage, but I was with Chalcis and of another line."

Francesca's eyes were dark as she dropped her voice to a whisper. "You know this was thousands of years ago, right?"

Orion nodded. "In some moments, it is easy to believe. But my comrades and I were trapped in the form of teeth for many centuries." He fell silent as the server brought their meals.

The fish was fresh and looked to be perfectly grilled, surrounded by vegetables. Francesca had a round piece of bread with smaller pieces of meat and vegetables arranged atop it, and something melted over it. Orion was momentarily distracted from his story by the enticing aroma of the food. He speared a piece of an unfamiliar vegetable with his fork. It was grilled yet still firm, a little spicy but very good. He closed his eyes for a moment in appreciation, only to open them to find Francesca smiling at him.

"I have erred?" he asked.

She leaned closer and whispered. "You can't be from Ancient Greece. You're eating with a fork like you've done it all your life. Tell me the truth, Orion."

"Ah." Orion paused, hesitant to confess more but knowing he had to, in order to gain her trust. "I have told you the truth."

She flicked a glance at the fork.

"But the next detail will defy belief."

"You did that at dragon shifter," she noted, then smiled. She moved a piece of her bread—'pizza', she had called it—to the edge of his plate, evidently sharing. He offered the fish and she took a piece with her own utensil, evidently as pleased with it as he was. The pizza was spicy and savory, a choice he would try again.

"The curse upon us was broken by another of my kind, who sowed us into the earth of his garden. We rose from the soil and took flight, following his instruction to eliminate a foul place where *Pyr* were being turned to monsters. We succeeded, though many of our number were lost."

"When was this?" She took an olive and ate it, her expression hinting that she wasn't convinced.

That wasn't likely to improve soon, but Orion continued all the same. "In the year 2008."

Francesca sat back hard and stared at him. "That won't be for more than thirty years."

"And then, two years later, in 2010, something odd happened."

"Oh good." She took a gulp of her wine. "Your story was getting predictable."

Orion shook his head. "I should not be telling you all of this," he said, reconsidering his course. "I know it is an uncommon story, but you asked me for the truth."

To his surprise, she reached out and covered his hand with hers. "Tell me, Orion. I want to know."

He considered her, weighing that. "It concerns how we met this morning."

"Then I really want to know." She smiled. "Please."

A beautiful woman entreated him. *This* beautiful woman asked it of him, and that meant Orion had no choice but to comply.

Let the results be what they might be.

CHAPTER SEVEN

Was Orion delusional?

Or did he have a list of impossible things to believe before breakfast, too? Francesca supposed that being a dragon shifter might alter someone's perception of the world—and she had no doubt of his powers. She'd seen him change shape, she'd seen him kick another dragon's butt and she'd seen him fly.

But having been present at battles twenty-five hundred years ago? Funny how that was the bit that she had trouble swallowing—but then, she couldn't see any evidence beyond Orion's word.

Oh, and that coin in perfect condition, the one that was similar to the coin in the museum from ancient Erétria. The octopus on one side was very distinctive.

She listened, hoping whatever he said would prove that he was right.

He studied her for a long moment, obviously cautious of continuing thanks to her own reaction, then something decided him. "In the year 2010, our commander believed it was our fate to possess one of the three darkfire crystals."

Francesca chose just one item for clarification. "Darkfire?"

"An ancient force strongly associated with my kind. Some would call it magic, but I suspect it merely is beyond our comprehension."

"What does it do?"

"It allows improbable events to occur."

"Chaos," Francesca said. "It invites chaos."

He shrugged. "The darkfire crystal came into the possession of our commander as if destined to be his."

"What does a crystal have to do with it?"

"The darkfire was snared in three crystals, lighting them from within. Drake claimed one of them, then it took us through time."

"There's time travel too?" She took another gulp of wine, already wondering what had happened to the other two darkfire crystals.

"And worse, comrades vanished from the company on that journey. Each time the darkfire in the stone flashed, we were gathered up by a great wind and flung to a new location."

Francesca was thinking of Dorothy and Toto, but didn't expect Orion to understand the reference so kept quiet.

"When the wind faded away, there was always at least one of our number missing. We never knew when the stone would light with darkfire. We never knew who would be left behind." He took a shuddering breath. "There was no reason, no pattern to it."

He looked really agitated, and she knew the experience had shaken him. "That sounds terrifying."

"It was." He fell silent, finishing his meal. "Yet all the same, I left them by choice when I saw you this morning."

She froze in the middle of taking a bite, when she realized the import of what he was saying. He'd been with the guys in the square with the bakery, the ones who had suddenly...vanished.

"Those guys? You were with *those* guys."

"They were my comrades."

And just before they'd disappeared, there had been a blue-green light flashing across the ground.

"What color is darkfire?" she asked.

"It shines blue-green, like strange lightning."

Darkfire. Francesca shivered.

There was evidence she'd seen, after all.

She pushed away her glass of wine, her thoughts spinning. What if his story was true? "They were *all* dragon shifters?" she asked, knowing the answer already.

Orion nodded.

They were the company of dragon shifters who had been enchanted and trapped as teeth, then released from the spell by one of their own kind. "But we can go back to Rome and you can rejoin them?" she asked, fearing she knew that answer, too.

Orion shook his head. "They are gone and lost to me now. The crystal lit again and I have no notion of their location."

"In time *or* space."

He nodded.

She studied him. "So, you're alone now. Because you left them?"

"I followed the spark of the firestorm, or so I believed at the time. Any of them would have done the same. It is our destiny to fulfill the promise of the firestorm, regardless of the cost."

"Destiny," she said, feeling irritated by the reference. "You're always talking about destiny."

"It is a force that cannot be denied."

"I don't believe in destiny. I believe in self-determination." Even as she said the words, Francesca wondered how long her view might survive in Orion's company. He had good reasons for believing in destiny, while she'd never seen many justifications in her own life. "If everything is pre-determined, then we have no choices."

Orion wasn't shaken by this argument. "We have choices, of course, but destiny will overwhelm our errors. I thank you for the suggestion of this taverna and the meal. You chose well."

Francesca wasn't entirely convinced, but she wasn't ready to end their discussion either.

She had questions, so many questions. Even if they disagreed about the role of destiny in their lives, there was still more he could tell her.

A lot more.

"So, you're isolated now."

"No. There are more here of my kind, as you saw this very day."

"Did you know that?"

He shook his head. "Not before our encounter this morning."

"Why did you fight with Sigmund?"

"Because he threatened you, and this is evidence of the firestorm, as well, because its heat draws those of my kind, good and bad." He frowned, moving his empty plate aside. "And yet it is not a firestorm, because the light sparks with a vessel and not a woman. It is a conundrum."

"But according to what you've told me, the mate *is* a kind of a vessel," she said. "Isn't she supposed to conceive your child in the firestorm?"

Orion grimaced in concession to that, but it clearly wasn't a point he found to be of concern.

Maybe that was because no one had ever considered him to be a potential vessel. The idea of this firestorm lighting, and some incredibly hot guy assuming that the woman targeted by the firestorm would be glad to have his son and bring another dragon shifter into the world, the notion that this woman wasn't supposed to have any conflicting views, was more than enough to make Francesca glad that they weren't having a firestorm.

She wasn't sure she would be able to resist Orion if he tried to charm her, but she definitely didn't have time or the desire to have a son.

Nor would she just bear one—like a *vessel*—hand the infant over to his father and forget about him.

Francesca moved the last piece of pizza around her plate, trying to choose the best question to ask next. "What if Mr. Montmorency's story is true?" she asked, then met Orion's gaze. "What if the Sibyl is trapped in the vase? What if *she's* your mate?"

He shook his head. "If all that remains is her voice, then she cannot bear my son either."

It was a little troubling that the Sibyl's inability to be a mate made her less interesting to Orion, but then this conversation was filled with hypothetical situations.

Francesca reached for the wine and Orion filled their glasses again. "Did I imagine that Mr. Montmorency shimmered blue this morning?"

"You did not."

"And the Sigmund guy did the same thing later. So did you."

"It is a sign of agitation, a precursor to shifting shape."

"A warning light."

He shrugged. "If you wish to call it as much."

Francesca had a suspicion, but she needed to hear Orion say it aloud. She leaned over the table. "Why did Mr. Montmorency shimmer?"

"You have already guessed, Francesca. He is a *Slayer*, too, like Sigmund was."

"And the difference between *Slayers* and *Pyr*?"

"The *Pyr* defend the treasures of the earth. The *Slayers* do not. We did not have this distinction in my time, but there were those of us who were inclined to good and those inclined to evil, to be sure."

"Sigmund would have killed me?"

Orion nodded.

"And Mr. Montmorency might, too?"

"I fear he might."

She nodded, unsurprised. All of this detail, and it came back to one key item in her view: Orion recalled the past because he had lived it.

"So, here's the thing," she said, leaning across the table, her eyes bright. "If you're right about destiny, and this isn't your firestorm, or your firestorm can't be with a vessel, then why are you here? Why did this darkfire even bring you to this time and place?"

Francesca thought her question was reasonable, even rational, but it clearly shook Orion. He stared at her in silence, apparently because he did not know.

In contrast, she thought the answer was obvious. She smiled at him. "I have a theory," she said, then finished the last of her pizza in a triumphant bite. He waited, his gaze fixed upon her with expectation. "Maybe it was so you could meet me."

———

WAS it Orion's destiny to meet Francesca?

The notion was entirely plausible, though he could not understand why it should be so.

"Because you had two *Slayers* circling you and were in need of defense," he mused.

Francesca laughed. "No. I don't need a defender."

He gave her a look. "Because you can defeat dragons yourself?"

"That Sigmund guy only attacked because you were with me," she pointed out. "And Mr. Montmorency hasn't done anything to me."

"Yet," Orion felt compelled to note.

"I have a better idea," she said, her eyes sparkling as they hadn't since he'd started his confession. "You're here to help me in a much more practical way."

Orion could not see what was impractical about saving a woman from a *Slayer*, but he chose not to argue the point. Francesca, he could see, was prepared to share her idea and he had only to wait.

"You can tell me," she said with delight. "You *remember* Ancient Greece. You can tell me about the Sibyl and about the agency of women in your time and about the expectation of gender roles."

"Of what merit is that?"

"It's what I study! It's the focus of my doctoral thesis. You could help."

"And people will believe what I say, simply because I have said it?"

She sat back and drummed her fingers. "You're right. It wouldn't be a very credible citation to quote a guy who says he's over two thousand years old and a time-travelling dragon shifter." She smiled.

Orion smiled despite himself. "In these times, there is some skepticism regarding our nature and existence."

Francesca leaned forward. "But what about *things*? Do you know where there are lost items that would support whatever you tell me, artefacts that would provide proof or documents that record stories?"

"My father remembered the stories of our kind. That was his role, and he shared them with me that they would survive his passing from this earth."

"I like stories," she said. "You could tell me another one."

Orion indicated the emptying restaurant. "Not on this night, Francesca."

Her expression immediately became concerned. "How's your shoulder?"

He shrugged, then winced when it pulled. He had to consider where he would sleep this night. He had need of rest, but would have preferred to have been with one of his fellows. It was possible that the other *Slayer* might seek him out in his moment of weakness. All the same, he knew he would not be able to remain awake and vigilant for long.

Would he have time to breathe a dragonsmoke barrier around Francesca's home?

He would ensure it.

She had paid for the meal while he considered this, and put her hand in his as they left the restaurant together. "I hope you're planning to come home with me," she said, bumping her arm against his.

He looked down at her in surprise. "I thought so," she said with a nod. "You wouldn't presume, etc."

"I would see you defended."

"I don't think I need protection," Francesca showed a confidence that Orion thought undeserved, but he would not argue with her. "Does that mean you don't want to come to my place?"

"No, I am grateful for your invitation. A place to sleep would be most welcome." She was climbing the stairs ahead of him to her apartment and Orion could not keep himself from admiring the view.

Ah, Francesca...

She turned suddenly and he felt caught, but she surveyed him in her turn, then smiled. "I'm not inviting you home just to sleep," she said in a wicked whisper that heated his blood, then slipped her arms around his neck. Their faces were level when she stood on the higher stair and all Orion could see was Francesca. There were stars in her eyes and an enticing curve to her lips as she leaned closer. His arms went around her waist seemingly of their own accord and when she laughed with delight, he pulled her closer with satisfaction.

"But you are not my mate, Francesca," he protested in a murmur, even as she lifted her lips for his kiss.

"Exactly," she said with a resolve he didn't understand, then she laughed at his confusion. "I'm not up for love, Orion, or even romance, but I'm definitely interested in sex." Her lashes dropped to hide her gaze and his heart squeezed. He wanted to argue with her, but then she cast him an impish glance. "Especially with you, tonight. Maybe it's your destiny to remind me just how good sex can be. Maybe *that's* why you're here right now."

She kissed Orion before he could answer, her fingers winding into his hair, her breasts pressing against his chest, and Orion groaned as he surrendered, body and soul, to temptation.

Francesca.

———

ORION.

Francesca didn't even care that he was a time-traveling dragon shifter—or maybe that was what made him different from every other guy she'd ever known. Maybe his dual nature made him more earthy, more attuned to physical pleasure. Maybe his great age was what let him appreciate each moment in time and to linger when another might have rushed. Maybe his nature was what made him so vital and male and completely irresistible.

He was built like a sculpture, tanned and toned, confident and powerful. She'd never seen a man's body that was so perfectly muscled, and certainly not up close and personal as they'd been while tending his wound. When he'd sat across the table from her in the restaurant, oblivious to the appreciative glances of other women, she hadn't wanted to tear her gaze away from him. He ate with grace and appreciation, considering each bite he took, and she liked how attentive he was.

It was a good portent for the night ahead.

The sweep of his thumbs, sliding under the waistband of her skirt easily, moving steadily in that endless caress, had driven every sensible thought from her head—and what *hadn't* happened next had been driving her crazy all through dinner. Sex had always been hurried with Derek, more about his satisfaction and need than her own, and Francesca often felt that there could have been more.

She knew that by the time Orion was done, it would be hours later and they'd both be sated.

She couldn't wait.

Maybe this night of pleasure was what she'd been waiting for—or maybe Orion was who she'd been hoping would walk into her life. As much as he talked about destiny and mates, there was only a minute hesitation before he responded to her touch. His kiss was honest, forthright, intense, exactly how she wanted to be desired. There were no games with Orion, no comparisons with other lovers, no past or future—just now, and the thrill of their responses to each other. He was in the moment, *this* moment, unequivocally with *her*—not thinking of someone or something else—and seemed intent on making the interval last as long as possible.

Francesca was in complete agreement.

She was all-in for this night of passion and carnal satisfaction. She was due. In the morning, Orion might leave before she awakened. He'd probably head out to find his mate, whoever and wherever she might be, and Francesca made her peace with that—because right here and right now, Orion was making love with her.

She backed up the steps, as they kept kissing, urging him toward her apartment. When she broke their kiss to unlock the door, he held her captive, his arms around her waist and her back against his chest. He nuzzled her neck and kissed her ear, whispering to her of what they would do. Francesca loved to talk in bed, and Orion's promises almost made her drop her keys.

He closed his hand over hers, cupping her breast in his hand as he guided the key to the lock with the other, and Francesca leaned back against him. He growled against her throat as he pinched her nipple and she knew she'd never gotten so hot so fast before.

Then they were over the threshold and he was locking the door behind them, his eyes aglow as he watched her. Francesca retreated a little, turning on a few soft lights, then kicking off her shoes. She wriggled out of her jeans, too impatient to have his hands on her skin to do a strip-tease for him, and heard him catch his breath. Her shirt and bra were cast on the floor with record speed and she shook out her hair as she met his gaze. She smiled as she pushed her panties over her hips, thinking the heat in his eyes might even be enough to tip her over the edge. Then she touched herself and his eyes blazed silver fire, even as he whispered her name.

Like she was a goddess.

Orion's shirt was cast aside as Francesca watched, marveling at his physique. It wasn't hard to believe that he was a dragon shifter, not when she looked at the muscled power of his body. He was also aroused, his erection straining against the front of his jeans. He smiled when she eyed it, then their gazes met again in anticipation. He took off his shoes but left the jeans on. He moved toward her slowly, giving her time to change her mind. She didn't, but held her ground, smiling. He caught her hand in his, lifting it and putting her wet finger in his mouth as he held her gaze. He suckled it, his eyes glowing, and Francesca felt her knees weaken at the graze of his teeth.

Then he dropped to one knee himself, his hands locking around her waist. He lifted her to her toes and Francesca parted her thighs, gasping when his mouth closed over her in an intimate kiss. His tongue teased her artfully, flicking against her so that she gripped his shoulders in pleasure.

"I will not let you fall, Francesca," he murmured, his breath driving her insane. "Trust me."

She did. Francesca tipped her head back and abandoned herself to his touch, parting her thighs even more as he kissed her more deeply. He teased her clitoris slowly, flicking his tongue across it to drive her wild, his grip resolute upon her waist, heat emanating from him as he coaxed her desire to a frenzy. She wouldn't have expected she could come when she was held aloft, but Orion was relentless and she felt her inhibitions dissolve.

He took his time, ensuring that she came close to climax repeatedly, then retreating and building the heat again. There was a fire beneath Francesca's flesh, a need growing within her that she knew only he could satisfy—and she loved that he would push her over the edge only when he decided it was time. She was out of control, which meant she had no choices to make. All she had to do was enjoy. She lost track of time as he teased and tormented her, then she felt the brush of his tooth and couldn't hold back. The orgasm tore through her like an explosion, making her cry out, then lock her thighs around him convulsively as she came and came and came.

As she caught her breath, Francesca heard his chuckle of satisfaction. It was a perfect dragon sound and she smiled. He stood up, lifting her easily in his arms, his eyes bright with anticipation of his own. Francesca kicked her feet, feeling like a million bucks.

"You are flushed," he almost growled, then bent to kiss her thoroughly before she could reply. She tasted her own arousal, and it was wicked and thrilling. He carried her to the bed without breaking his kiss and laid down beside her, their legs tangling together on the narrow bed. His eyes gleamed with a very masculine satisfaction, a confidence that he knew exactly what he had done to her—coupled with a conviction that he'd soon be doing it again. She dug her nails into his shoulders, urging him closer and loved that he crushed her into the mattress, trapping her against the wall, just as she'd wanted. She felt powerful that a tiny sign of encouragement could see her every desire fulfilled. He was an attentive lover and a thorough one.

"I came too fast," she whispered and he smiled.

"I wanted you wild," he confessed, eyes glowing. "I wanted you to relinquish control."

"I should have held out longer."

"Perhaps this time," he said, his hand sliding to touch her again. She liked the weight of his hand upon her, that he was both tender and powerful. He moved deliberately, paying attention to what she liked, and he already knew how to slide his fingertip across her and make her gasp aloud.

He did it again and she was pretty sure she wouldn't be able to hold out this time either.

She didn't even care.

"So beautiful," he whispered. "So responsive. Francesca, you were made for loving."

She could have argued that, because she'd never been so abandoned before, but his mouth closed over hers again in a demanding kiss. His thumb and finger teasing her so that she squirmed. He crushed her against the mattress and there was nowhere else she wanted to be. She loved the heat of his skin against hers, the feel of his solid power against her body, and the sorcery of his fingers stirring the tempest within her again. Her body was filling once again with fire but this time, she wanted more.

She reached out and ran her hand down the front of his jeans, wishing she could unfasten the fly from this angle. "I want you inside me," she whispered, her voice husky. "I want to feel you Orion."

He smiled down at her. "And I want to feel you lock around me, pulling me deeper, demanding more and more." He shook his head slowly, lifting his head to look toward the closet. There was an unmistakable golden glow illuminating the edges of the door. "But that cannot be."

What?

———

IF FRANCESCA HAD KNOWN how alluring she looked, she would have been shocked. She braced herself on her elbows when Orion moved away from her, her hair tangled over her shoulders, her breasts bare and her nipples pert. She smelled like sweetness and seduction, she looked like a siren, and it nearly killed Orion to put distance between them.

But his mate was in close proximity. And he knew that regardless of what Francesca said about expectations, she might change her mind by morning. Women, in Orion's experience, showed an assurance in assuming that matters would endure, particularly after sexual union. He would not deceive her, even at the price of his own torment.

He wanted her as he had not desired a woman in a long time.

But he also would honor her.

He moved away from her, though it took every increment of his control, and turned his back upon her to tug on the T-shirt again. He would have to relieve himself once she slumbered, for he would not sleep in such a state himself.

Nor could he breathe smoke to see her defended.

He heard her sweep from the bed. She marched past him to the small chamber for washing and closed the door resolutely behind herself. He told himself to be glad but ached that she was insulted.

The firestorm glimmered, the vase clearly secured in the closet. He approached it and the light brightened to yellow, flickering with greater agitation. As much as he would have liked to have studied the vase, Orion knew the light might attract *Slayers*.

He backed away, moving to the furthest point of the apartment, and considered his options.

They were few.

He could leave, without the vase, but that would be an abandonment of the firestorm.

He could leave, taking the vase, but that would be theft.

He could break the seal on the vase, releasing whatever was inside it, but that would vex Francesca. Orion had but one ally in this time and place, and it seemed prudent to maintain her support. He was keenly aware that his refusal to continue might have already condemned that plan.

He pushed a hand through his hair, and Francesca emerged from her sanctuary. She was dressed in a top and pants that covered her from chin to ankle. It was dark green and gleamed with the shimmer of silk, and the top was cut loosely. If she thought this was an unflattering garment, she had much to learn of her own allure. Her hair was pulled back tightly and the tint had been removed from her lips.

She eyed him warily. "I thought you might have left already."

"Should I have?"

She shrugged, waiting.

"You are insulted," he ventured to suggest and she shook her head.

"Why wouldn't I be?"

He raised a hand. "Because it is my intent to treat you with honor, to not encourage expectations that cannot be fulfilled. I would not disappoint you, Francesca."

"You just did."

He had no further argument on his own behalf.

She seemed to realize as much because her voice softened. "It's just that what happened before that was so awesome," she said quietly. "No one ever touched me like that."

"Every man you invite to your feast should touch you thus," he said with conviction and she smiled.

"I'm glad I invited you to my feast," she said, her gaze heating. "Despite your early departure from the table."

"I..."

"I understand, Orion. I just hope that you're not disappointed." They looked as one at the glow from the closet. "What are you going to do?" she asked, suddenly practical again. "Where are you going to go?"

"I do not know but I sense you have a suggestion."

"I do. You can stay here, but the vase goes back to the museum tomorrow."

Orion nodded agreement, but Francesca was not done.

"I assume you want to stick close to it, though, until you know what's going on with this firestorm." She waited for him to nod again. "I think I can get you a job at the museum, just menial stuff, but it pays cash and they won't ask you a lot of questions." She lifted a hand. "But I get to ask questions."

"Your terms are generous."

"I'm in a good mood," she said, then her smile flashed. Orion grinned in his relief and she gestured to the small eating area. He sat and she stood as she prepared some hot beverage. "What happened to the other one, Sigmund?"

Orion hadn't anticipated that question. "He will trouble you no more."

She tilted her head to study him and he knew his reply was inadequate.

"I watched him sink to the bottom of the sea with the other refuse. I knew he would die soon, if he was not dead already."

"How could you tell?"

"Our kind, when fatally injured, rotate between forms. It is a sign of distress, of pending death. He was doing that, so I knew his remaining moments were few."

"Will they find a dragon corpse in the sea?"

"We die always in human form, just as we are born in human form. No doubt, his remains will wash ashore somewhere." Orion didn't really care about Sigmund's fate.

"I saw you dive into the sea far to the south. How did you get here?"

"I swam ashore and walked, guided by the beacon of the firestorm." Again, they turned in unison to look at the glow.

"Good thing I brought it home from the museum."

"An excellent thing. It would have been harder to find you otherwise."

"Harder but not impossible?"

"Our senses are more keen than human senses. I might have been able to smell you."

"I don't smell that much."

"Every being has a distinctive scent. Yours is beguiling, to be sure."

She flushed and looked down as she poured out a cup of that brewed beverage. "Tea?" she asked, offering it to him. He accepted, though he didn't really want it, and she poured another for herself. "Chamomile," she said. "It won't keep you awake."

Orion nodded and sniffed it, noting its herbal scent.

"Why was his blood black and yours is red?"

"Because he was a *Slayer* and I am not."

"It changes the color of their blood? Why?"

"Some say it is because they have chosen selfishness over our quest to defend the elements and the treasures of the earth. Some say they have chosen darkness and the sign of that is in their blood."

"Why did he attack? Because you're *Pyr*?"

"All of my kind are drawn to the sign of the firestorm. *Slayers* do not have firestorms, so it is their tendency to interfere." He hesitated, then saw no reason to hide the truth. "Often by attacking the mate."

"A good reason not to be a mate," Francesca said lightly and Orion strove to hide his shock at her words. "How do you know you will have a firestorm?"

"Because it is destined. We each have a destined mate, and will have a firestorm when we encounter each other."

"And the only measure of romantic success is the conception of a child."

"A son. The *Pyr* have only sons."

She finished her beverage with a flourish and set down the cup on the counter, her gaze filled with challenge. "If I ever had kids, I'd want a daughter."

"Why?"

"Because I'd like to make a difference. I'd like to teach a daughter that she could do anything and help her to achieve her goals, whatever they might be. There are more than enough obstacles to women, and I want to be a force for change." She went to the closet and removed some blankets, the light radiating from the interior space when she opened the door. Her lips were tight when she turned with her burden and Orion didn't want to ask her about opening the vessel. She put the pile of blankets on the floor beside her bookcase, then bent to straighten the covers on the bed.

"You need not bear a daughter to do that," Orion noted and she looked at him in surprise. "My commander, Drake, is a mentor and a guide. He is like a father to each man in our company, though there is no family bond between us. There need not be a blood tie as the foundation of such a relationship, Francesca."

She paused in the act of plumping her pillow. "You're right."

"I am certain there are many younger women who would be glad of your guidance."

"Maybe there are." She turned to him, one hand on her hip. "Are there young dragon shifters who would be glad of yours?" If she was teasing him, Orion did not see the jest.

"If there are, I would gladly mentor them."

"I like that," she said simply, then gestured to the pile of blankets. "You get the floor." Then she got into her bed quickly, reaching to turn out the light, then lying with her back toward him.

Orion went into the small chamber to wash, and returned in only the jeans and briefs. Francesca's breathing was slow, but he didn't believe she was asleep.

No, she was sensible. She would be vigilant until *he* slept.

But Orion would be more vigilant. He would breathe a smoke barrier to ensure her protection when he did sleep. He took one of the blankets onto the terrace and sat down upon it, welcoming the touch of the night air against his skin. The city was quieter and he could smell the sea so close by. He closed his eyes, breathing steadily to calm himself, listening to the rhythm of the earth.

When his pulse had slowed and his breathing deepened, Orion exhaled a long plume of dragonsmoke and began to weave a protective barrier around Francesca, the glowing vase and the apartment. Only when the dragonsmoke barrier was completed to his satisfaction, when the barrier would sound a clear crystalline ring to any of his kind, would Orion sleep.

He suspected that Francesca watched him, but he did not care.

He did not notice the flicker of blue-green light dance in the quartz crystal on her window sill, then vanish again.

CHAPTER EIGHT

When Francesca finally slept, she dreamed.

She was in a garden at night, one with high brick walls surrounding it. She could hear distant traffic and even heard a siren at one point. She felt the rumble of what might have been a subway train and knew she was in a modern city. A house overlooked the garden, although there were no lights in the windows.

A man was digging a furrow in the ground. She had no ability to move closer and could only watch as he worked. His hair was dark and long, and he was muscled—not unlike Orion. He was dressed casually and didn't seem to notice that it was raining just a little. He was ruggedly handsome, with dark eyes and brows. There was something reassuring about him, as if he exuded an aura of tranquility.

He glanced up as another man came out of the house. This man was blond and reminded Francesca of a wrestler. He seemed younger than the first man, though he was just as muscled. They nodded to each other, obviously well-acquainted, then the blond man began to etch another furrow alongside the first one. The ground was obviously hard, given the amount of effort it took them to even make a shallow indent.

They hadn't gotten far when a third man came out of the house, letting the door bang behind himself. The fair one looked up with disapproval, but the dark one kept working. The new arrival seemed indifferent. He was enormous and buff, a veritable Viking with long blond hair and tattoos. He yawned and stretched with enthusiasm, grimacing when the fair one sternly ordered him to help.

Time seemed to accelerate then, the stars turning overhead as the men made progress. Francesca had the sense of a film being sped up, but they never looked silly even at a quicker speed. They were deliberate and serious, which left her wondering why they were making these furrows. When they finally straightened, the entire yard had narrow ditches dug into the soil, each about two feet from the ones on either side. Francesca remembered planting the garden with her grandmother years before and wondered what they were going to sow. With such high walls, she had to believe the garden was pretty dark.

The dark-haired man went into the house, returning with a handful of large items. They might have been stones, but were a curious shape. Pointed. Almost like dog teeth but much, much bigger.

Francesca had a funny feeling then.

Even more strange than the items themselves, the dark-haired man began to hum as he pushed the first one into the soil. It was more than whistling while he worked. It seemed to be an incantation. The furrow was deep enough that the stone disappeared into the soil, then the two other men piled the earth over it and patted the surface smooth. The first man continued to work, planting his stones—or whatever they were—about three feet apart down the length of the furrow. He planted the next furrow and the next, ten furrows in all, each with ten seed-stones, humming more powerfully all the time.

Except the last row. He was one seed-stone short, but that didn't seem to trouble him.

Her dream was definitely on board with Francesca's list of improbable or impossible things, because the dark-haired man then laid down on the ground on his back. He spread his arms wide, flattening his palms against the soil, reminding her of kids making angels in the snow, but then he hummed with greater vigor. It was a resonant sound, one that made the patio stones and the walls of the garden vibrate a little.

The other men joined his song gradually, as if they had to learn it, then the volume of the trio gradually became louder. It was a song that resonated in the soil and in Francesca's bones, a song that made her very marrow resonate. She couldn't understand the words, and wasn't sure it even had any, but the chant stirred her, making her want to rise up and follow the dark-haired man.

No matter where he might lead.

FRANCESCA WOKE UP ABRUPTLY, surprised to find herself in her apartment in Italy and not in that garden. The dream had been so vivid. It was night but the air was warm and there was no rain falling. She definitely wasn't in her dream.

Had those been dragon teeth?

She rolled over and looked across the apartment, fully expecting to see Orion sleeping on the floor.

He was gone.

She had a moment of alarm that he'd left without saying farewell, then saw him sitting on her small terrace and relief flooded through her. He'd only put on her brother's jeans and there was something so gloriously male about him that Francesca just wanted to stare.

No, she wanted to touch.

She told herself to be glad of a good long look. His eyes were closed and he was breathing steadily, so that she wondered whether he was asleep or not. She saw a glimmer of silvery light and was reminded of that battle against Sigmund. Was that how dragons exhaled? Or was it something else? This guy had enough mysteries to keep even a curious person like her intrigued for the long haul.

What would it be like to have Orion as a partner for the duration? In the middle of the night, she could entertain the whimsical idea. She had a hard time thinking it would be a bad situation.

But maybe she was romanticizing it—or him.

One great orgasm was skewing her thoughts about love, romance, Orion and everything. She really was a cheap date. She smiled to herself, admitting that Orion was easy to have around. It was seductive how intently he listened to her and considered her point of view, how honest he was about his own story. She had a hard time believing it would be his way or the highway.

Maybe he would become exactly like Derek in time. Maybe the bloom wasn't yet off the rose. In one night, they'd hardly reach the point of either taking the other for granted. She was being ridiculous, extrapolating from a moment to a lifetime.

This wasn't a relationship. It wasn't a taste of a shared future. It was a moment, maybe even a stolen one. The mistake would be to hope for more of what might otherwise have been the start of a really, really good thing.

He had called it fairly. He would follow his mate, without hesitation, leaving her or anyone else behind, without a backward glance. In a way, Francesca could respect both the intention and the way he had admitted to it, right away.

She would have welcomed him the night before. She wouldn't have seen a one-nighter as him taking advantage of her, but she respected that he had a moral code and that he lived by it.

There was a dull glow coming from the closet, illuminating the crack between the door and the cabinet itself. She didn't want to think about the firestorm, so she recalled the dragon battle at the museum the day before.

She winced, wondering what she'd say about what she'd seen, just as something flashed in the far corner. She straightened a little to look, having just caught a glimpse of green and gold. She was sure that something had appeared in the corner then darted along the edge of the room, where the shadows were deepest and the wall met the floor.

It had been running toward the kitchen, but she couldn't see any sign of it now. Francesca shivered, the hair pricking on the back of her neck, and hoped there were no mice in her apartment.

Orion's eyes opened then, as if he had heard her sit up. He smiled and beckoned to her.

Francesca forgot her dream and the mouse. She grabbed her robe and stepped onto the terrace to join him. The shadows seemed particularly magical when she halted beside Orion.

She admitted to herself that she could fall hard for this guy, even though they weren't destined to be together.

Better he didn't know, then.

He indicated the stars overhead. "Some things do not change so much over time."

She tipped her head back to look at the night sky. The stars were always brighter here than she remembered them being at home. The light pollution had to be less.

Orion pointed. "And see? We are yet here."

He seemed to be pointing toward the North Star, but not quite there. "I don't understand."

"The constellation Draco. He battled the gods for ten years before Athena killed him and cast him into the sky. On the way, he twisted about himself, but in the cold air of the north, he could not become untangled." He traced the line of a serpent with his fingertip and Francesca smiled, remembering old drawings of the constellations. It was a loop with a pointed end, which could have been a dragon's head with a pointed nose, then a long tail trailed behind it. "And so he remains forever, twisted in the north, the tip of his head a pole star for sailors, and his state a reminder of the perils of battling women warriors." Francesca smiled at that. "In Athens, the festival of Panathenaea celebrated the victory of Athena over the dragon, and was held when his head was visible from the Acropolis."

"It's not the pole star now," Francesca felt obliged to note. "We use Polaris now." She pointed to it, at the end of the Big Dipper. "The stars have a precession over time."

He nodded and she realized he had made his peace with his journey through time, accepting it as fact. She was surprised to realize that she had accepted it, as well, though she had no physical evidence to support his claim beyond the coin he carried. Theoretically, he could have bought it, found it, been given it—but Francesca believed it was his and he had carried it from the past.

Her conviction was a bit nuts. She certainly hadn't witnessed his journey across the centuries, much less his release from being enchanted as a tooth. She just trusted him. He didn't seem to know how to lie or be disloyal.

Her dream...could those have been teeth the dark-haired man was planting? And that song. Was that a kind of spellcasting? She shivered and dismissed it, not wanting to ask and sound silly.

Maybe she believed his story because there was something about Orion that couldn't be easily reconciled with the world Francesca knew.

He was different and that couldn't be ignored.

"It is said that the Pyramids in Egypt were built so the entrance passage on the north face would give a view of Thuban, the pole star of Draco," he continued, and she liked that she could both hear his voice and feel its rumble in his chest beneath her fingertips. It wasn't hard to believe he was a dragon, not at all. "But that is less important than the triumph of Athena over the dragon himself." Orion pulled back to look down at her. "Only the goddess of war could defeat the dragon that could have been the forebear of the *Pyr*. Are these the kinds of tales of women you would hear from me?"

Francesca smiled, realizing that he was trying to give her what she sought. "Do you know any others?"

"Many," he said with quiet conviction. "So very many that it would take a lifetime to recount them all."

"Your lifetime or mine?" she asked lightly, then realized what she had said. "Are you immortal?"

Orion shook his head, looking sadder. "No. We age slowly until the firestorm sparks, waiting for that destined moment." He reached out and touched her cheek with a fingertip, his gaze dark. "I am saddened that you are not my mate," he said, his voice gruff.

"I'm glad," she said and his expression was stricken. "Really. I am."

———

FRANCESCA DID NOT UNDERSTAND that they were cheated by the gods. She did not recognize that favor had been withheld. Orion's heart was aching that she was not meant for him, and he could make no sense of the light of the firestorm in the vessel.

"Destiny is no jest, Francesca."

"It's not true, either, Orion. People aren't destined to be together or even not to be together. People have to choose to be together and they both have to work at their relationship to find success."

"You are skeptical of partnership," he noted and she shrugged.

"Live and learn."

"Who has injured you?"

"It doesn't matter."

"If we were mates, I would defend you," he began but Francesca shook her head.

"It's not you," she said gently. "This is about me."

He was puzzled.

"Think about it." She frowned a little. "If I was your mate, you'd expect me to drop everything to have your son."

"You would conceive when the firestorm was satisfied," Orion felt obliged to note.

"The first time?"

He nodded.

"That makes no sense."

"Yet it is true, I assure you."

She bit her lip, as if to keep herself from saying again that she was glad they were not destined mates. "But what if I didn't want to conceive a child the moment we met? What if I had things to do?"

He was mystified by this and it probably showed.

"Orion, I'm not that interested in the traditional path of wife and mother. I never have been. I want my career. I want to make a difference to the world."

"A child makes a difference."

"But a child takes time. Having a child means not doing other things. It means a choice and it's not a choice I want to make right now. I might not make it ever." She held his gaze steadily. "I love my research. I want to be able to pursue it wherever it goes, without having to hold back out of consideration for someone else's needs. I want to follow *my* dream."

"I do not see that it must be one or the other."

She smiled a little. "But I think it is, and if I'm going to be expected or asked to bear a child, to spend nine months pregnant and eighteen years raising that child to adulthood, then I think my opinion matters." Her gaze brightened in challenge. "Don't you?"

"Of course." Orion could not disguise that he was troubled by her comments. At this rate, they would never gain the favor of the gods. "Then you never wish to have children?"

"I'm not sure. I'm not ready to decide." She tapped a fingertip on his chest. "But your firestorm would take away my choice, and I can't love that."

"There is always a choice..."

"Is there? I didn't think that was how destiny was supposed to work."

Orion nodded slowly because he had to concede that.

"Don't tell me that you're disappointed that I don't want to be a mom, at least not right now," she said with quiet heat and he heard her disappointment in his response. "You can't think women only exist to be mothers. I expected more from you, Orion."

"I am disappointed that there might never be another with your cleverness and charm," he said, pushing his fingers through her hair and smiling at her. "But then, perhaps one marvel that is Francesca is sufficient."

Her smile dawned slowly, then lit her eyes, the sight encouraging him as little else could have done. "You are dangerous, Orion," she whispered and their gazes clung for a potent moment before she turned away quickly. "I'm going to sleep a bit more before getting ready for work," she said and hurried into the apartment, as if she was running from something.

Given her view and her determination to cling to it, it probably was better that Francesca was not his mate. Destiny, Orion knew, would not be denied.

———

IN THE DARKNESS of the closet, the golden salamander crept toward the vessel that was his own possession. Neither he nor Sigmund could figure out where Orion had come from or why he had suddenly appeared. The light emanating from Miss Marino's backpack had hinted that something had changed in the vessel she carried. Magnus had come to see for himself.

It felt almost like a firestorm, but not quite. Certainly the heat in his veins recalled many firestorms of his experience, as did his yearning to draw close to it—and to thwart it. He slipped through the protective wrappings until his feet were against the glass itself.

Then he stared into the vase, dazzled by the frantic golden lights trapped within it. It could have been electric fireflies, or miniature fireworks, and the energy radiating from the brilliant light was enough to take his breath away.

A *Pyr* couldn't have a firestorm with a vase or even with the air trapped inside a vase.

What about the Sibyl's voice?

Magnus was sufficiently curious to influence events. He had disguised his scent, but the skill was new to him and he might falter when surprised. If so, Orion would immediately sense his presence and Magnus wasn't interested in having their duel to the death.

Not yet.

He wanted answers first.

He crawled to the top of the vase and began to chew the seal. It was harder than he'd hoped and he had to tear it with his teeth to make any progress at all. He bent and ripped, growled with frustration, then felt his scent flare to unexpected vigor.

He'd only compromised it, but he had to flee immediately and hope the seal would break on its own.

———

ORION ABRUPTLY SMELLED *SLAYER*.

He was instantly awake, well aware of the blue shimmer that surrounded his body. He was on the cusp of change, startled into wakefulness by the scent of *Slayer*. The sun was rising, turning the sky pink, and he had been sleeping hard, even on the floor. Francesca was also sleeping, her hair cast across her face.

He scanned the apartment, remaining utterly still as he sought the intruder.

Nothing.

Save for the golden glow emanating from the closet.

He heard a rustle, a faint sound that would have been undetectable if he had not been *Pyr*. It had come from the direction of the terrace. He crept toward the sound.

Nothing.

He went onto the terrace, halfway expecting to find an opponent on the roof, or even on the building below.

Nothing. The town was still in the dawn. He could see a few boats on the sea, but it was too early for more. He turned in place, scanning the sky for some hint of a dragon, but there was none. He looked down into the streets he could see from his vantage point, but they were empty. He returned to the apartment, securing the door behind himself, and looked out the entry to the stairs. There was no one.

He stood with his back to the door, willing himself to retreat from the cusp of change, and inhaled slowly. It was there, unmistakable, but subtle. He recalled Magnus Montmorency's ability to spontaneously manifest elsewhere and also to take the form of a salamander, and his agitation redoubled. That ability would allow the *Slayer* to pierce a dragonsmoke barrier, by manifesting inside the protected area.

What else could Magnus do? Had he forgotten any of the *Slayer's* abilities gained from the Dragon's Blood Elixir?

Had the *Slayer* visited them and left?

Or was he yet in the apartment?

Orion didn't want to awaken Francesca, but fortunately, her abode was small. He looked around the perimeter of the single room, under the furniture and in the cabinets. He even looked in the cupboard where the vessel was secured, narrowing his eyes at its flare of light with his proximity. He looked in the small washing chamber, but had no success.

The scent faded, even as he searched.

The *Slayer* was gone, but Orion could not be happy that he had visited at all. The glow between himself and the vessel was the beacon, to be sure.

Did he dare to break the seal himself? Francesca did not wish to tamper with the artefact, which was fair, given that it did not belong to her. But Orion knew that the true owner, Magnus Montmorency, was well aware of the source of the firestorm's heat. It could be argued that it was Orion's responsibility to release his mate, if she was captive in the vessel. Of all individuals, Magnus Montmorency would understand that urge—even if he did not endorse it.

But Francesca would be angry if he acted without her approval.

How could he win her approval?

Orion frowned and went into the washing chamber to prepare for the day. When he was clean and had changed his clothes, the sun had risen higher and the apartment was brighter. He could hear more activity in the street below, but Francesca was still asleep. Quietly, he explored her provisions and prepared a meal to break their fast.

When she rose from bed and smiled at him, his heart clenched. If only...

"You probably don't know how to make coffee," she said, coming to his side.

"I do not know what it is."

"There's an argument against time travel." She filled a vessel and set it on a burner to heat, then ground beans in a small implement, pouring the powder into another vessel. The water boiled, a result of the same power Orion had seen used by his future brethren, the one delivered through the walls to the small receptacles, and the air was filled with a scent that had become familiar to him in modern times.

"Coffee," he said with understanding.

"It has to steep," Francesca said then noticed his preparations. "Thank you."

"We must eat and you were sleeping."

"Do you do windows?" Her tone was teasing, but he still didn't understand.

"In a company of warriors, there are tasks that must be done each day, and each takes his turn in fulfilling them."

She ate a piece of fruit, eying him. "And in private life, in your times, did women prepare all the meals?"

Orion shrugged. "I do not know about the homes of others. My mother did not, to be certain."

"What did she do?"

"She was a warrior. Her skill with a bow was unrivaled."

"She went to war while your father raised you?" She seemed to find this amusing.

"They both fought wars. I lived with my father most of the time and visited my mother in summer, when the horses grazed in the plains."

Francesca considered him for a moment, as if she did not know whether to believe that or not. "Interesting." She excused herself and retreated to the washing chamber, returning soon afterward. He could see that she was dressed for the day, and her manner was more purposeful than it had been.

"Do you want coffee?"

He nodded agreement, uncertain whether he wished it or not, and watched her prepare the hot beverage. One sip was not sufficient to convert him but he saw that she favored it greatly.

If they shared another morning in each other's company, he would contrive to make this beverage for her.

"You look concerned," she said, watching him over the rim of her cup.

"I must win your favor," Orion said.

"You did pretty well last night."

Orion knew he could not endure such temptation twice, not with the heat of the firestorm turning his thoughts in an earthy direction. "I wish for you to open the vessel and release my mate," he said, raising his gaze to hers.

"No."

She said it simply, as if her refusal was not of great import to him and his future.

"But my mate..."

"Cannot be a woman's voice, even if the Sibyl's voice is still in there. Something seems to be in there, I'll give you that, but it's not up to me to choose to open the seal. The vase is on loan, Orion. It has to be returned in the same state as it was borrowed."

"The donor knows of this."

"Dr. Thomas doesn't. I can't afford to lose his support."

"Will he agree to open it?"

"I have no idea." She sighed. "I'll ask, all right?"

"Francesca!" He resisted the urge to sweep her into his arms and kiss her triumphantly, but only just barely. "You would know of the past. I can tell you what I remember." He was not certain it would be sufficient for her, for he already understood that she liked evidence and he had none. Stories were not proof.

"I guess it's too much to hope that you might lead me to a lost city, like Troy, so I'd establish my reputation in a flash." She took another piece of fruit, unaware of the import of her words.

Orion frowned at her. How could that great city be lost? "A *lost* city?" he echoed.

Francesca looked up. "Yes, Troy. It was remembered only in stories until Schliemann went looking for it in the late nineteenth century. I'm sure a lot of people thought he was nuts, but he found it."

"It is no feat to discover something where it has always been." On second taste, the appeal of the coffee improved.

"It was *lost*."

"Yet, he undoubtedly *found* it right where it had always been," he said wryly.

Francesca looked at him, then she led him toward her desk. She put on her glasses and returned with a piece of folded paper and spread it on the counter. It showed the familiar shapes of the Greek islands and the lands to the east. Orion recognized the land, though he had never seen a map so detailed. There were many, many names written upon it in small type, most of which he could not decipher.

"Where?" she asked and he realized this might provide her proof.

If it was a test, it was an easy one. Orion dropped his finger to the location of Troy without hesitation.

She looked. The map evidently only marked modern cities as there was no dot at the location of Troy. "How do you know?"

"I was there. My father took me, for he had seen it burn."

She folded her arms across her chest and eyed him with skepticism. "But Troy burned around 1200 BCE. You said Cadmus enchanted you and your friends around 500 BCE."

He considered this interval and nodded agreement. "It was six or seven centuries, to be sure."

"No one lives that long, Orion. Your father couldn't have been at the battle and then taken you to see the ruins."

He smiled at her. "The *Pyr* live so long. I told you. Until we experience our firestorms, we age very slowly."

"And then?"

"My modern brethren say that their aging matches that of their mates. I cannot say. In my time, my fellows seldom remained with their mates."

It was the truth, but she did not like it, he could see.

"Then your mother didn't live with you?"

He shook his head. "My father had great affection for her, though. I visited her each year from the time I was a boy. My father also told me of her people after her passing."

"And of Troy."

"That was where they met."

Francesca returned to her wall of volumes, considered them, then retrieved a small box from a drawer. "This is a tape recorder," she explained as she put the device on the counter between them. Orion

KISS OF ENCHANTMENT 153

was intrigued. She then opened a volume filled with small rectangles. "And these are cassettes. On these cassettes is a reading of *The Iliad*, the epic poem composed by Homer about the Trojan War."

"Truly?"

"It's an important primary source, and this reading is in the original Ancient Greek. I got it to practice my pronunciation." She gave him something she called a headset, and showed him how to work the device, then put in the first cassette and pushed the button with the arrow. Immediately, Orion heard the authoritative voice of a man reading in Ancient Greek.

"'*Sing, O goddess, the anger of Achilles son of Peleus, that brought countless ills upon the Achaeans. Many a brave soul did it send hurrying down to Hades, and many a hero did it yield a prey to dogs and vultures, for so were the counsels of Jove fulfilled from the day on which the son of Atreus, king of men, and great Achilles, first fell out with one another.*'"

He sank into a chair, smiling, because the cadence of the words and the form of the poem reminded him so much of his father. He was overwhelmed by his memories and awed by the power of this small mechanism.

Francesca tapped him on the shoulder and he removed the headphones with reluctance. She showed him how to stop and start the device, and how to change the cassette, as well as the order in which they should be heard.

"I have to go to work," she said. "Will you be all right here for the day? I'll see what I can do about getting you a job and I'll ask Dr. Thomas about the vase. Don't get your hopes up on that part."

Orion nodded, for he trusted her to do her best. He started the device again. He was transfixed by the tale and transported to the life he had left behind. He sat, hands over the headphones, and closed his eyes, savoring every word of the poem. It was beautiful. His father would have admired it greatly.

Francesca meanwhile packed the glowing vase into her back-pack, then signaled to him that she'd be back after work.

Orion had a moment, in which he considered calling her back and insisting that the vase remain with him. The fact was that it would remain dark when it was out of his proximity, and that was safer for Francesca. *Slayers* would only be attracted by the light of the firestorm.

And if he sensed a threat, he could find her more easily if she had the vase with her, just as he had done the day before.

Reassured, Orion settled back to simply listen. As the poet's version of events unfurled in his mind, awakening his own memories, he could only smile with pleasure.

Francesca, once again, had given him exactly what he desired.

Was her refusal to believe in destiny the reason why the firestorm wasn't real? He found it hard to believe that any god could be displeased with Francesca for long.

Perhaps her reluctance to bear children was at root.

The darkfire had brought him to her for a reason. It had marked her with the spark for a reason. There was a riddle to be solved and he suspected he would only find the solution with her assistance.

Could there be another justification for his presence in this time and place? Had the darkfire brought him here so that he could help Francesca in her research? The only way to find out was to assess what she knew of his time and his kind, then identify any gaps in her understanding.

He simply had to trust the darkfire, though Orion didn't like that one bit.

———

IT WASN'T OFTEN that Francesca was forgotten in favor of a primary source in Ancient Greek. She found herself smiling as she rode the Vespa to work. She couldn't be offended, not when Orion had looked first surprised and then enraptured. The way his gaze had intensified as he listened had been a gratifying sign that they were both intrigued by Homer. Orion had a full day of listening ahead of him.

In a way, she envied him the discovery of that poem. The first time she had read it, she had been similarly captivated. It had almost been as if she could see the battle happening before her eyes.

How would it compare to his father's stories of that event? Francesca couldn't wait to find out.

The bustle of activity around the museum was impossible to miss, as was the hole in the exterior wall. That was sobering. Francesca stood in the crowd looking up at it and listened to snatches of the conversation around her. Some talked of dragons. Some were skeptical of that story. Some speculated upon the cost of repair. Still others had conspiracy theories to share, and grim predictions for the days ahead.

Francesca wondered what she was going to tell Dr. Thomas. She was supposed to have been in their workroom, so might have been a witness to the destruction. Could she really tell them she'd watched dragons fight it out in the exhibition hall? What would that do to her reputation as a scholar?

In the end, she didn't need a story at all.

A number of people were in the exhibition hall, some of whom she recognized as museum staff and others who looked like contractors assessing the damage. Larry was helping to gather artefacts from shattered display cases, and Dr. Thomas seemed to have taken charge of the restoration, at least for the moment.

"Francesca!" Dr. Thomas greeted her with obvious relief. "I was afraid you might have been injured in this horrific incident. You really need to get a phone in your apartment."

Francesca didn't have to pretend to be surprised by the damage. The exhibition hall was a bigger mess than she'd noticed at the time, and the hole in the wall was spectacular. It looked as if someone had put a tarp over the hole the night before, but it was coming loose and flicking in the wind from the bay. She glimpsed an impressive view, despite the efforts of the workmen trying to secure the tarp.

"Do you have the vessel?" Dr. Thomas demanded after she'd reassured him. "Is it still intact? Even if he is deluded, I wouldn't want Mr. Montmorency's possession to be damaged. I was worried when I arrived this morning and saw that it wasn't here."

"It's fine. It was really warm in here yesterday and I was tired after the drive. I took it home to make my notes."

It was a ridiculous excuse, but Dr. Thomas swallowed it. "I'm so glad you did. Look at this place! I don't even want to think about what could have happened to you if you'd been here." Francesca had a moment to feel gratified by his concern, then he continued. "And the artefact could have been stolen."

"What exactly happened?" Francesca wanted to hear the official story.

Dr. Thomas ran his hand through his hair, which made him look rumpled, agitated, and even more handsome than before. "There are stories, ridiculous stories of two dragons fighting here then crashing through the wall. It's impossible, of course, but it will take time to unveil the truth." He sighed. "People find this dramatic tale very appealing, when likely it was just thieves."

"Has anything been stolen?"

"We don't know yet. It's hard to be immediately certain with all of the debris, but I want to be careful with our own artefacts."

"Of course."

"I've had calls this morning from three of our donors, seeking reassurance that the items they have loaned to us are intact and safe. I gather this incident has been on the news. They haven't been easily reassured." He frowned. "I wonder, Francesca, if you might begin to move our workspace to Cumae? It's possible that the visitor's center there has a place where we can work while repairs are attempted here." He pushed his hand through his hair again. "We might even have to move the exhibit there, depending how long the reconstruction takes, although that will vastly diminish its visibility." This clearly troubled him, making Francesca realize that her supervisor was ambitious as well as interested in the research itself.

"It *is* Italy, sir," she felt obliged to note. "Construction projects tend to proceed slowly." They'd been fixing the curbs on the street where she lived since before her arrival several months before, and she would have expected that job to take only a few days.

"I know! And the opening is only three weeks away." He swore under his breath, which surprised her a little. "The publicity people are supposed to photograph the four vases today, but it will be impossible, given the state of the exhibition hall."

"Why don't they photograph them at Cumae?" Francesca suggested. "We could have them in the cave. With the right lighting, it would be dramatic."

Dr. Thomas' eyes lit. "That's a wonderful idea, Francesca, but I'm tied up here for the day."

"I'll take the vases and meet them there," she suggested. She knew it would mean a lot of carrying of the packed vases, but maybe Orion would help. Mostly, she wanted to get out of the museum. Someone might realize she had been a witness and insist upon asking her questions.

"I'll need to borrow the car," she added.

"Yes, of course. It's parked in the courtyard." He handed her the keys, then frowned at the noise in the exhibition hall beyond. "So much time wasted!"

Francesca didn't point out that more than time had been lost. The museum might not even have the funds to finance the repairs.

"Should I call the Cumae site and let them know about the change in plans?"

"Yes, please. We still have pictures to develop from yesterday of that newly discovered mosaic, and I'd hoped to get back down there today. That's what I wanted to concentrate on, not *this*."

"You know, I met a guy yesterday who is looking for casual work. I told him I didn't know of any, but..."

"But with this damage, we'll need some more hands. He could take his papers to the office."

"I don't think he has papers, sir. I think he's Greek."

"Do you think he would work hard?"

"I do, sir. He really wanted a chance to make some money. He was outside a restaurant. Big guy."

"Sounds like exactly what we need and cash would be what he needs. Please arrange it, Francesca."

"Of course, sir."

A phone rang in the workroom they usually used but nobody moved to answer it.

Francesca knew that was because they were all men. She excused herself and answered the phone, only to be greeted with a barrage of furious Italian. She asked the gentleman to wait, and called to Dr. Thomas. "The curator of Roman antiquities at the Vatican Museum for you, Dr. Thomas," she called, watching him wince. "He seems a little upset by the news this morning."

That was an explanation she was glad to surrender to someone else.

CHAPTER NINE

It was just after noon when Orion felt the heat of the firestorm increasing. He realized that Francesca had to be returning to her apartment. That meant she was bringing the vessel, as well, which maybe meant she had permission to open it. He smiled in anticipation of her arrival.

Perhaps she was right that it was good they were not having a firestorm. He found her argument compelling. He was not at all certain that he should endeavor to change her thinking: should it not be a woman's choice whether or not she bore a child?

Perhaps that was why the darkfire modified their firestorm, to give Francesca that choice. If she decided to bear his son, would the mating sign spark in truth? Or had he been right that the gods withheld their favor because she did not acknowledge the truth of destiny? If that was the case, he doubted she would ever change her view.

And as much as he desired a firestorm, Orion did not wish for Francesca to change at his urging. He liked and admired her, just as she was.

The matter was far more complicated than Orion had ever believed it to be. In his time, most *Pyr* had followed the spark, satisfied the firestorm, conceived a son, and returned to the mate years later to collect the boy for his training. Simplicity itself.

Although when he considered the matter, it might not have been so simple for the mate to be left alone to bear and raise a child who would develop powers beyond her own.

His father had been unusual, in that he had taken custody of Orion from birth, and perhaps provided an example for his own future.

The odd situation made him more aware that he was alone. Orion missed the companionship of his fellows and the opportunity to speak with them. Drake might have wise counsel in this circumstance.

Meanwhile, in the poem, the Amazon queen, Penthesilea, came to the aid of the beleaguered Trojans. Orion's attention sharpened, for this had been his mother's sovereign.

And in that instant, he knew. The tales he had been taught by his mother and of her kind, his experience in his annual visits, might provide the lost history that Francesca sought. She was, after all, interested in women of the past.

He met Francesca at the door to her abode and she looked up in surprise, caught in the act of lifting the key to the lock. "What do you know of the Amazons?" he demanded.

———

FRANCESCA WAS STARTLED. Orion, in contrast, looked jubilant. She considered his unexpected question. "You mean the society of female warriors who shunned men?" He nodded. "That at best, their details are exaggerated and that they were simply female warriors among the Scythians."

Orion shook his head with unexpected resolve.

Francesca entered the apartment and closed the door behind herself. "Or at worst, they never existed."

His eyes sparkled with humor. "They existed, to be sure, and were fierce beyond all others. Who has told you that these women didn't exist?" He nodded toward her small library. "What do your books say of them?"

"Why? Do you know stories of them?"

"Yes." He spoke simply, a hint that he knew more than he was admitting. His expression was that of someone with a secret, one that threatened to burst free, so Francesca humored him.

She crossed the apartment and reached first for a favorite volume. "Herodotus wrote in the 5th century BCE. He said the Amazon's homeland was in Pontus—" she checked the index, then flipped through the book to find the reference "—near the south shores of the Black Sea, that their capital was Themiscrya on the Thermodon River, which is near modern Terme. He tells a tale of how they became known to the Scythians..."

"They were originally *of* the Scythians," Orion said flatly, dismissing this claim with authority. "Where is this Terme?"

Francesca spread the map across the counter again. She pointed out the modern city, which was in the vicinity Orion had expected. Orion's fingers ran over the map to Greece, where he named the islands in Ancient Greek, one after another.

"It is said that Hypsicrates claimed that the Amazons abandoned their city and moved into the Caucasian Mountains, beyond the lands of the Gargareans. They were a society of men who met in secret each spring with the Amazons to conceive children, the girls being kept by the Amazons and the boys by the Gargareans." At Orion's raised brows, she pointed out the mountains on the map, which stretched from the Black Sea to the Caspian Sea.

She reached for another volume as he studied the map, his brow furrowed.

"How great are the distances on this illustration?"

Francesca showed him the scale before she realized it wouldn't mean much to him, both miles and kilometers having been fairly recent inventions. "How far does an army walk in a day?" she asked.

"From Marathon to Athens on a good day. Progress depends upon the weather and the terrain."

Francesca checked the map and discovered that was thirty kilometers. She measured out that increment on the scale, and marked it on the edge of a piece of paper. "That's one day's march, then," she said and he smiled, bending over the map with his new guide. He was measuring from Troy and to the east, his fingertips running over the lines of mountains and the dots that marked their peaks.

"The Talmud says that Alexander the Great confronted the Amazons. In some stories, their queen bore his child. In another, the two armies confronted each other and the Amazon queen taunted him. She said that if he conquered them, people would say that Alexander killed women, and that if they conquered his army, people would say Alexander had been defeated by women. He chose not to engage in war with them as a result of that conversation." She looked up.

Orion laughed. "This is the wit I recall of them. Their humor was quick and sharp, like a well-honed knife."

"You met them?"

"My father met one, at Troy." He tapped that location again and smiled crookedly at her. It was incredible to believe that he had actually seen it so many centuries before. "And I visited them each summer thereafter."

Francesca sat down hard as she understood his implication. "Your father's firestorm was with an Amazon," she guessed, not really daring to believe it. His mother had been an Amazon!

Orion's smile turned mischievous. "Perhaps this is why I have such admiration of strong women." And when he looked at her, his eyes shone so that her mouth went dry. "Iphito was her name. She was the most valiant of warriors and the best of mothers."

"Iphito," Francesca whispered in amazement.

"You know this name?"

"Mostly we have lists of the Amazons who died in battle at Troy, but there's a vase in the collection here, one that was found at Cumae. It depicts an Amazon and lists her name as Iphito." She looked at Orion. She believed him, and yet, it was incredible that he remembered these details. "What can you tell me about her?"

He lifted a brow. "That she was magnificent. And to my recollection, Francesca, she surrendered nothing at all in choosing to bear a son."

"We're not having a firestorm," Francesca protested.

"No," Orion agreed. "But if we did, perhaps it might be considered an opportunity instead of an obligation." He looked down at her, his fingertips on her cheek, and she felt her knees weaken. "What of the vase, Francesca?" he whispered.

"We can't open it." Disappointment lit his eyes. "Because we have to drive to Cumae, so it can be photographed. Maybe after that." She didn't want to give him false hope. "Maybe not, though. The car is parked downstairs with the vases from the museum."

"Is it secured?"

"Yes."

"And it is the time when everyone rests after the midday meal, is it not?"

Francesca nodded.

"I would rest with you, Francesca, perhaps show you my admiration of strong women." There was a wicked glint in his eyes, one that made her heart skip.

"I'm not in a rush to leave," she said, her voice husky.

Orion held her gaze as he eased closer. She could feel his heat and smell his skin, her entire body responding to his proximity. His fingertips slid from her shoulder to the front of her blouse and he met her gaze, his own fiercely silver.

He was asking permission.

She smiled a little and nodded, not moving away at all.

Orion inhaled with satisfaction as he opened her blouse and looked down at her bra. "I like this garment," he confided in a low murmur. His fingers eased across her breast, and he cupped its weight in his hand. "It both disguises and displays."

"Lace and elastic," she said, watching as he bent to take her nipple in his mouth. He kissed it, teasing it, launching molten lava through her veins. She knew she should step away, but his touch felt so good.

"Will you linger here with me?" he murmured against her breast.

"Yes," she said, tipping her head back with pleasure. His hands locked around her waist, then swept downward, taking her skirt and panties over her hips. His kisses followed the downward path until his mouth closed over her persuasively.

Francesca moaned at the tide of sensation. It was early afternoon. Everyone was taking a break. No one expected them at Cumae soon.

"Then let me pleasure you first, Francesca. Let me give you this." Orion flicked his tongue against her, his hands holding her captive to his caress, and Francesca couldn't think of a single reason to object.

Cumae and the publicity team could wait.

———

IT WAS difficult to find much fault with the world, in Orion's view, as they drove north out of Baiae. The sun was shining and the air was warm. They had opened the windows in the little car so the wind blew through, bringing the scent of the sea. Francesca said the distance was not great. The road they took bent to the north, winding out of the city and into the hills. He liked that they drove at a slower speed on this smaller road, for he had time to appreciate his surroundings.

This was familiar. Olive trees and low buildings, an azure sky and the sea in the distance. The small businesses were becoming more familiar to him, as well as the signs advertising their wares. He could not read the words, but it was clear that the establishment on the right served confections and beverages, perhaps like Francesca's coffee.

He could live happily in this place and time, with the right company.

Much of his good mood was due to his conviction that he made progress in persuading Francesca of his merit, perhaps even of convincing her of the virtue of the firestorm. After all, the most obvious reason for his presence in this time was the prospect of his firestorm. The car was filled with the golden glow from the vase and its radiance filled him with both desire and hope.

Just because the darkfire had made it different from expectation, didn't mean his firestorm was cursed, much less doomed. On this day, with this woman, Orion had hope.

Francesca drove, which gave him the opportunity to study her from the passenger seat. When they had turned onto a smaller road, he saw her smile.

"You're watching me."

"I can do nothing else, Francesca. You are a marvel."

"There are lots of other things you could do, though."

"Ever practical," he teased and her smile broadened. "I assume you have a suggestion."

"You could tell me more about Amazons."

"What would you know of them?"

"Everything. Anything. Where they lived. How they lived." She paused. "How I could find proof of their existence and their ways."

Orion considered this. "So much of what we know and love becomes dust with time," he mused. "And it has been hundreds of years."

"Thousands," she corrected. "But you survived it."

On the cusp of agreement, he snapped his fingers in realization of the truth in her words. "Because we were buried in a hoard."

"Excuse me?"

He straightened to look at her, excited by his realization. "Bone erodes if left atop the soil. If buried, though, if *stored*, it endures. The teeth survived in that hoard because it was buried in the earth. We need to find a grave of the Amazons for your evidence."

"Good luck with that," Francesca said with considerably less enthusiasm.

"How so?"

"Well, if there is one, it's probably in the Soviet Union. They're not really big on hosting American researchers or archeologists." She frowned. "Where were the dragon's teeth found?"

"The hoard was in England and dated from Roman times, we were told. It was discovered during the excavations for an underground train station."

"A subway line," Francesca said. "Or the Tube if it was in London."

Orion nodded, recalling what Rafferty had told the Dragon's Tooth Warriors. "Greenwich and Deptford were to be the new stations on the Jubilee line." The words meant little to him, but Francesca nodded understanding.

"I don't know those stops, but you said it would be 2008." She turned to watch Orion nod. "So, they might not even be planned yet. Whose hoard was it?"

Orion was startled. He hadn't considered that detail before Francesca asked, but it couldn't be irrelevant. No coincidence was. "The *Pyr* said it belonged to Magnus Montmorency."

She halted before a gate and turned to look at him, her eyes wide. "Not the same Magnus Montmorency, the collector who loaned us the vase?"

"The same."

"But a Roman hoard would have been buried almost two thousand years ago—" She caught her breath. "He shimmered blue in that cul-de-sac because he's *Pyr*, too."

"*Slayer*," Orion corrected. "He is *Slayer*."

"You didn't tell me."

"There is a limit to how many times per day I can shake your assumptions, Francesca."

To his surprise, she laughed. "I like how you shake my assumptions, Orion." She smiled at him, a dazzling sight that made his heart thump and his blood run hot, then drove through the gate as if she hadn't stirred him in turn. "How many of you guys are there?"

"Not enough," he said grimly, hearing an echo of Erik Sorensson in his voice. How could he locate the *Pyr* who would become the leader of his kind? Would contacting Erik imperil future events? Orion wished he knew for sure.

She parked in a small paved zone beside a modern building, then got out of the car. There was a larger vehicle in the parking lot with script on the sides of it. "Good, they're here." She gestured for him to wait and Orion stood beside the car, so accustomed now to the golden heat emanating from her backpack that he barely paid any attention to it.

He reconsidered that as two people came out of the building with Francesca and decided that he could carry one of the other vessels, to ensure the light did not attract attention. He picked one up and retreated a step, which made the light dim. Francesca introduced the photographer—a redhead named Gina—and her assistant—a young man named Paolo—then spoke to them quickly in Italian, pointing down a wide walkway that headed south. They went to the van and packed up their equipment on a cart.

"We're going to go to the Sibyl's grotto for the photographs," Francesca told him. "Although it's unlikely to actually be where the Sibyl delivered her message to Aeneas, the lighting is dramatic.

There's speculation that it was actually added later as a defensive structure." The photographer's assistant added two of the packed vases to the cart and secured them to Francesca's satisfaction, then they began to walk together. Francesca carried her backpack with the vase that continued to glow faintly, and told Orion about the site.

"This structure that contains the grotto was originally a fortress defending the southwest face of the cliff," Francesca told him. "It dates from the end of the fourth century BCE or the beginning of the 3rd century BCE. From its vantage point, you could look over the city of Cumae below. The fortress was originally smaller but was extended by the Romans to include cisterns to gather water." She gestured to them. "In the early Christian era, the cisterns were used as burial sites and the chamber we're about to visit was used for worship." As she spoke, they entered the darkness of the structure to follow the downward path to the so-called grotto.

It was a relief to step into the cool shadows, though it took a moment for Orion's vision to adjust. As the photographer talked to her assistant, presumably about the task ahead, Orion followed Francesca into deeper darkness. Even without her comments, he would have known that the place was very old. There was something in the scent of it that told him it was ancient.

"The grotto was discovered during excavations in the early 20th century, made in search of the locations mentioned by Virgil in his poem, the Aeneid. That poem is about a Trojan who fled to Italy and became the forebear of the Romans."

"There is an Aeneas in this poem you shared with me."

"There is. Same guy, supposedly, but he's the hero of the Aeneid. One of the things he does is consult with the Cumaean Sybil. Ultimately, he asks her how to visit the realm of the dead."

"Why would he wish to do this?"

"He wants to ask his dead father for a sign. A portent. The Sibyl tells him how to enter that realm, and more importantly, how to return from it."

"And this excavation was for the entry to the realm of the dead?"

Francesca laughed. "It was assumed that Virgil meant a specific place. This was a popular area for Romans. So, when an archeologist found this gallery, with its lateral openings, he believed he had found the cave with the thousand mouths from which the Sibyl delivered her predictions."

Orion stopped at the end of the corridor to stare. The carved passageway had a strange shape, wider in the middle and narrower at the top and bottom, like a pinched hexagon. The openings at intervals on the one side created alternating bands of light and shadow down its length. He felt as if he approached a site of great importance, and looked about himself when the corridor widened into a chamber.

"And there are three small rooms," Francesca gestured. "Which prompted people to conclude that those were oracle rooms."

Orion shook his head. "It is not the same as Delphi where the Pythia was oracle."

"No," she agreed. "What do you think is the biggest difference?"

"There are no fumes. At Delphi, the air is thick with smoke and scent, and the oracles leaned over the openings to breathe deeply of the fumes that rise from below. The fumes fed their visions and gave them insight beyond that of most men." He surveyed the chamber. "The Sibyl cannot have given her forecasts here."

"I don't think so either," Francesca agreed.

Gina arrived and spoke with obvious approval, gesturing to the light and indicating a spot to Paolo for them to set up.

It was dramatic. The afternoon sun slanted through those openings, creating bands of light. Orion had to believe that there was a lost passageway leading to another chamber, one filled with the fumes from the earth. Though the oracle and the Sibyl were different, they both served Apollo and pronounced predictions of future events. He knew there was a Sibyl at Delphi but had only ever visited the oracle.

In the oracle's sanctuary at Delphi, there was water for seekers to wash before approaching the oracle, images painted on the walls, attendants sworn to Apollo's service and crowds of seekers. This place seemed barren and empty, devoid of the reverent atmosphere he would have expected.

But then, were there still believers after so much time? This might not even be the right location.

As his thoughts spun, he followed instructions. He put down the packed vase in place and unwrapped it. The photographer's assistant worked quickly, setting up lights and other equipment, arranging the vessels against the carved stone walls.

It was a shame there were no paintings. The paintings at Delphi had always been powerful to him. In the light of the lanterns and with the fumes rising, they often seemed to move on their own.

Gina was photographing one vase, the flash from her camera illuminating the space at intervals, even as her lights heated the space. Orion saw Francesca frown and went to her side. She was unwrapping the vessel that responded so vehemently to his presence, and the light within it brightened as he came closer. They looked as one at Gina and Paolo, who were too absorbed in their task to notice.

"The seal is breaking," Francesca whispered to him, her concern clear. "I don't understand. I've been so careful with it."

Orion bent closer. "It has been chewed by some vermin," he said, surprised by that.

"Ew," she said, recoiling. "But where and when? I don't have mice or rats in my closet."

"But why would such a creature eat this?"

"It's wax and linen," Francesca said. "It's not even dyed. It can't have any flavor at all." She caught her breath then. "You know, I thought I saw something last night. It was very quick, but might have been a small lizard."

Orion stared at her as his alarm rose. "A salamander?"

"Maybe. Why? Is that important?"

He had no opportunity to reply for the golden light suddenly grew brighter. The vase was brilliant, radiating light of palest yellow and a heat that might have made it glow.

"You're too close to it," Francesca whispered, flicking a glance toward Gina.

"No, it is more than that. Something has changed." Orion bent closer but did not touch the vessel, awed by the frenzy of yellow and orange light within it. Even before he reached a hand toward the surface of the vase, the radiance brightened to a blinding white. The contents swirled frantically, seething inside the vessel as if seeking an escape.

The heat emanating from the vase grew and he almost felt his face burn, then he heard a sizzle. The wax around the seal was melting before his very eyes. The binding unfurled from where it had been damaged and the stopper in the mouth of the vase quivered. It began to move, the light bubbling beneath it to push it out. Orion reached to clap his hand over it, but he was too late. The contents suddenly churned, all white light and shooting sparks, then boiled.

The vase shook and the stopper popped audibly as it broke free.

It hit the interior of the cavern with force, then ricocheted down to bounce across the floor. Meanwhile, the vessel's contents spilled forth like pale yellow lava. The stream didn't flow over Orion's hands, though, but floated through the air, like a banner of silk, and headed for Francesca. She gasped as the light swirled around her in a thousand shades of yellow and white, lifting her hair and obscuring her from view behind radiant white light.

Then Orion heard the faint sound of a woman's voice, like a whisper on the wind.

The Sibyl!

It was a rhyme, but not in a language Orion knew. He heard the faint words, but he didn't understand them. Francesca dove for her purse, seized a pen and paper from its depths and began to write, the pad of paper braced against her knee. Her lips were moving as she tried to remember the words and record them all, but Orion could barely see her for the flurry of sparks that surrounded her. Francesca was enveloped by the sparks, almost as if she had stepped into the vase herself.

Gina barked a question, but Orion simply raised his hands. He could guess what the photographer was asking, but he had no reply.

He had to see what the sparks would do.

The banner of light shimmered, countless flecks of white and yellow illuminating the shadows of the grotto, as it embraced Francesca. She pushed up her glasses, looked at what she had written, and scribbled a bit more, apparently oblivious—or more concerned with recording the verse. Her lips moved and she frowned, the golden light of the sparks making her look like the statue of a goddess he'd once seen. Athena, majestic and gilded, formidable and beautiful.

Did he dare to hope his firestorm would light with Francesca?

He had a moment to think of the possibility, then the sparks abruptly winked out. The vase went cold in his grasp, the interior so dark and still that Orion knew it was empty. He stood blinking in the shadows, feeling chilled.

The Sibyl was gone.

The firestorm was gone. Extinguished forever and never to be satisfied.

Disappointment flooded Orion's heart, followed by a wave of regret so potent that it left him dizzy. He had failed his kind. He had sacrificed the promise of the firestorm.

And he could not help but dread the result of that.

It was not his fault that he had not been in the right time or place to meet his destined mate, but the darkfire had thwarted his destiny all the same. Its spark had dimmed, probably centuries after it had first lit, and it could not be kindled again.

His mate was no longer of this world.

Later, he might be bitter, but in this moment Orion was only shaken.

What would happen to him now?

Would the darkfire snatch him away again?

What did it mean for the future of the *Pyr* that he had not fathered a son?

Francesca looked up, her eyes alight with her discovery, then she obviously noticed his dismay. She frowned and looked around herself, realizing belatedly that the shimmering light was gone. "But..." she began.

Orion smelled *Slayer* in that instant. His woes were immediately forgotten, his duty to this particular treasure of the earth at the fore.

"You're doing that shimmer thing again," Francesca whispered, worry in her tone. When she saw the *Slayer*, closing fast, she would be even more worried.

The approaching dragon was jade green and gold, his teeth gleaming and his eyes glowing with menace.

Magnus Montmorency.

Orion hovered on the cusp of change, more than ready to fight to the last.

Gina took Orion's picture, given the flash of light. Actually, she took a lot of them from the sound of her camera. Paolo was running back up to the top of the fortress, apparently terrified.

Orion flicked the *Slayer's* challenge coin back at him and watched Magnus snatch it triumphantly out of the air. The *Slayer* breathed a stream of dragonfire as he laughed, then Orion shifted shape in his turn. The darkfire flashed but neither of them changed their course.

Orion had just been cheated of his destiny.

Let Magnus Montmorency do his worst.

———

IN A HIDDEN CAVERN behind a house on Bardsey Island, Donovan Shea and Rafferty Powell stared down at the man sleeping on the stone floor. The dark-haired man might have been thirty-five years old, except that he'd looked the same for as long as Donovan could remember and that was a long time. Donovan had brought a light, which sputtered in the darkness, casting shadows on the curved walls.

"So, he's okay?" he asked. "I mean, he always looks the same, and has ever since I took over this place for you."

Rafferty shrugged. The older *Pyr* had been Donovan's mentor and knew many secrets, but Donovan guessed that he wasn't going to share any on this day. Rafferty opened his mouth but didn't say a word before a spark of blue-green light slid around the perimeter of the room before extinguishing itself. The flame swayed in the lantern but otherwise there was no sign that the other light had been there.

"What was that?" Donovan asked in a whisper.

Rafferty frowned. "It might have been darkfire." He indicated the sleeping man, who had rolled to his side while their attention was diverted.

Donovan shivered. "I didn't even see him move."

"He has some connection to the darkfire," Rafferty murmured, bending closer to look. "Was he smiling before?"

"No," Donovan said, taking a step back. "Definitely not."

"How curious," Rafferty mused, his gaze following the same path that the blue-green light had taken. "I wonder..."

Donovan would rather get back to the house than stand around here and wonder. This place gave him the creeps. "I got some steaks," he said. "Since he's okay, why don't we get out of here and have something to eat?"

"Why don't we?" Rafferty agreed with a smile.

Donovan headed straight for the passageway, only glancing back when he realized Rafferty wasn't right behind him. The older *Pyr* was studying the sleeping man again, whose breathing remained slow and regular, so soft that only a *Pyr* would hear it.

Then that blue-green light blinked again and Rafferty turned away. As they walked together along the passageway to the house, Donovan unexpectedly remembered another cavern, a magnificent pearl—and a deceptive woman named Olivia.

He shivered again. He hadn't thought of Olivia in years, and there was absolutely no reason to do so now.

By the time they reached the house, he had a persistent sense that he'd forgotten something, that there had been something unusual in the cavern that he'd already forgotten.

But the mysterious guy that he guarded for Rafferty had just been sleeping the way he always did. Nothing had happened at all.

Even though Donovan —and Rafferty—forgot the darkfire completely, the Sleeper saw it in his dreams.

That was why he smiled.

IT WAS A DISASTER.

Francesca couldn't imagine how the situation could be worse. The seal was broken on Mr. Montmorency's Roman vase, the stopper had rolled away into the shadows, Orion had shifted to a dragon to fight another dragon that had abruptly appeared—and Gina was taking pictures of all of it. Paolo had fled, which might have been the only sensible thing to have happened in the previous ten minutes.

Even as she worried, Francesca couldn't help but admire the view. Orion was magnificent in his dragon form, his black scales gleaming like anthracite, his nails and teeth tearing at his opponent— a jade and gold dragon that was almost the same size as him. The floor was rumbling with the sound of distant thunder and she knew the dragons were exchanging taunts and threats. Gina was taking pictures as quickly as she could, even though her lights had been trashed by the battling dragons.

Francesca wondered about the golden lights that had swirled around her before extinguishing themselves, then about the words she'd written down in Latin. If those lights were from the Sibyl, she'd been released and her voice let out of the jar. The lights had gone out, but did that mean the voice wasn't having a firestorm with Orion or that the Sibyl had vanished into the ether? Francesca didn't know and that bothered her. She'd shoved that piece of paper into the pocket of her jeans and could feel the crumpled shape of it against her hip. It had to contain a clue. If there was a mystery about Orion's firestorm, she wanted to figure it out for him.

If the lights weren't from the Sibyl and her voice, then what were they? Why had they responded so vehemently to Orion's presence?

The strange thing was that a firestorm between a dragon shifter and his fated mate, reduced to a voice in a jar, made the most sense.

There were too many things happening at once. Francesca needed it all to stop so she could think things through.

That wasn't likely to happen anytime soon, though.

She held Mr. Montmorency's vase with one arm and reached for the stopper, which had come to a halt against the stone wall. It was silly, but putting the stopper back in the vase seemed to be the most sensible small action she could take at this time.

"Let me help you with that," said a man whose voice was not quite familiar. Francesca spun to find the guy from the *pensione*, the other student who creeped her out, right behind her. He really did have an oily smile.

Things had officially gotten worse. He was Sigmund, the other dragon Orion had fought in the museum, and a *Slayer*.

His smile broadened, probably because Orion was too busy to defend her. He shimmered blue a little and his eyes glinted, making Francesca wonder that she hadn't guessed sooner that he was a dragon deep down inside—and an evil one at that.

"I thought you were dead," she said and he laughed.

"Not quite yet." His eyes glinted, making him look very dragon-y. "Unfortunately for you, Signora Marino."

He snatched for her and Francesca hurled the stopper at him. It was of goodly size and solid glass, heavy enough to leave a bruise. It hit him in the face, which made him swear and shimmer more brilliantly blue around his perimeter.

She knew what that meant: he was going to become a dragon in a hot minute and that would seriously shift the odds in his favor.

Francesca surveyed the cave and realized the closest adjacent room was too small to accommodate a dragon. She lunged toward it, ducking inside just as she felt the swipe of a dragon claw through the air behind her. Sigmund's talons must have slipped through her hair. She retreated to the back corner of the small round chamber, hoping there was enough distance from the opening that he couldn't reach her. Her heart was racing and her palms were damp.

She realized she was still holding the vessel and put it down. It was dark and empty now, not interesting in the least.

The very prospect of the Sibyl being lost forever saddened Francesca, even though—at best—she'd only been a voice just minutes before.

A malachite and silver dragon claw appeared in the opening to the cave and snatched toward her. Francesca flattened herself against the wall. She could hear the sounds of the other two dragons fighting and didn't want to distract Orion, but she couldn't defeat a dragon on her own.

Or could she?

Francesca didn't need to be rescued, not even from a fire-breathing dragon.

On impulse, she hurled the empty vase toward the ground, feeling only a twinge of remorse when it shattered. She picked up the biggest shard of glass and retreated around the perimeter of the room so that she was alongside the opening. She held her breath as she waited, hoping he couldn't hear the pounding of her heart.

Suddenly, Sigmund's claw swept into the cavern again. He muttered something under his breath that could have been a curse, then he withdrew his claw. She heard his breath become louder and guessed that he would put his eye to the opening. She had to move quickly, and she'd probably only get one chance.

Francesca said a prayer, stepped into the opening and stabbed the glass shard into Sigmund's eye. She buried it as deep as she could before he roared with fury and retreated. His tail slammed against the walls of the outer chamber as he howled with pain. There was black blood flowing across the stone floor, black blood that smoked as it burned a crevasse into the rock. He was thrashing in agony, striking the walls and floor repeatedly with his claws and tail, even as Francesca remained safely in the smaller room.

When he stilled against the far wall, moaning, he changed shape. He turned back to a grad student and then to a dragon, shifting between forms with dizzying speed. He was holding his injured eye either way, the black blood flowing between his fingers or his talons.

If he was dying, it couldn't happen too soon to her thinking.

Francesca had bigger problems than Sigmund, though. The rock of the fortress had cracked with the force of his blows. Even as she stood there, the rock groaned and the cracks widened. She watched in horror as a fissure opened in the floor and gaped open, the shattering of the rock seeming to happen in slow motion right before her eyes. The rift yawned wide, and a fathomless darkness below was revealed. The scent of sulphur rose through the opening along with a whiff of steam. The ground beneath her feet began to crumble, like she was in an earthquake.

This was not a good thing.

Francesca lunged for the openings in the outer wall that looked over the ancient city, racing toward the closest band of sunlight. She wasn't quick enough. The rock walls around her cracked and shattered with increasing speed, everything falling into the ever-growing hole. The floor tilted before she'd taken three steps and she slid toward the gap, unable to grab anything to stop her fall. She screamed as she lost her footing and tumbled into the newly-revealed abyss, just as Sigmund vanished through one of those gaps into the afternoon sunlight.

Francesca was alone, falling into a pit in the earth, and no one even knew where she was.

CHAPTER TEN

"We meet again," Magnus said in old-speak, a chuckle beneath his words.

Orion didn't reply. He was assessing the *Slayer*, who was of a size with him and might have once been as strong. It appeared that Magnus had not fought a great deal of late, for his middle was soft. His eyes shone with malice though, and Orion knew he would cheat if he saw the chance. Magnus was still formidable, a splendid dragon of jade green and gold, and one that moved with deliberation.

Gina was snapping pictures as quickly as she could, but Orion would concern himself with such evidence later. For the moment, there was only Magnus and the gleam in that dragon's eye. The flashes from the camera lit the cavern, illuminating the scales and talons of both dragons so that they looked like splendid treasures. Their scales might have been jeweled, their talons carved of precious metals, but they circled each other with athletic grace.

If Orion failed, if he was defeated by the *Slayer*, Francesca would pay the price, and that was a result he could not tolerate.

"How is it that we did not meet before yesterday?" Magnus asked.

"*I was certain I was acquainted with all my brethren,* Pyr *and* Slayer." A thin stream of dragonsmoke unfurled from his nostril but Orion saw it and guessed his intention.

"*Perhaps an oversight on your part,*" Orion said.

"*Perhaps a deception on yours.*"

"*I am not the deceptive one in this battle.*"

Magnus laughed, the dragonsmoke surged forth, but Orion moved with lightning speed. He breathed a plume of dragonfire, trapping Magnus against the wall as he raged flames at his opponent. Magnus did not reply, but the dragonsmoke darted toward Orion, targeting his eyes with deadly accuracy. He felt the sting but lunged away from Magnus, dropping to his belly and sliding across the stone floor to rise up suddenly and snap at his opponent. His teeth closed on Magnus' leg and he tore into the flesh with gusto, then spit out the vile taste of black *Slayer* blood. Magnus fell upon him and tore at his wings, but Orion dealt him a trio of quick blows, the first in his soft belly, the second and third in his face. He heard a tooth crack before Magnus roared with fury. Orion seized him and slammed him into the roof of the cavern, battering at the stone with the captive *Slayer* until he heard a bone crack.

Then suddenly he held nothing at all. A salamander slipped through his talons and fell to the floor. Orion roared and fried the reptile so that its flight was halted and it was scorched against the stone. He snatched its tail and surveyed the chamber, his gaze falling upon the vessel that had been unwrapped and staged for photographs. He pulled the stopper from its neck and shoved the salamander into the vessel, then jammed the stopper back into it. He then held the vase in his talons, watching the salamander frantically run around the interior. He smiled as he breathed dragonfire on the glass, heating it so that he thought he heard the salamander squeak.

Orion did not care. The salamander was Magnus, a *Slayer* who would finish him without a moment's hesitation. He heated the glass even more. He felt the glass scorch his nails. He felt it soften. He heard the outrage of the salamander and then suddenly, the creature was gone and the vessel was empty.

Magnus was not defeated but he was gone, at least for the moment.

Orion cast the vase aside just as Francesca screamed.

He realized with horror that the walls were crumbling on all sides. He caught a glimpse of someone leaping through one of the openings into the sunlight and realized it was Sigmund. The scent of *Slayer* had been so strong that he had not realized both of them were present. Gina took one last picture of him, the flash of her camera blinding him for a moment, then she fled up the ramp to the surface.

The rock crumbled, a crack opened beneath his feet and Orion could smell sulphur. He shifted shape and raced into the chamber where Francesca had retreated. He could only see her hand, waving for help from the crevasse. He lunged toward her and snatched her hand, pulling her back to steady footing.

Her excitement was evident, though he could not explain it. The cracking slowed, then stopped, dust rising on all sides as the rock settled in its new position.

"No, the other way," she protested.

"But there is danger..."

"There's a room down here, Orion," she said quickly. "A cave with paintings and an opening for the fumes from the earth to rise. It's a hidden sanctuary." He lowered her so that she was on her feet on a level below him, and felt her shake with excitement. Her eyes alight. "Orion, *this* is the Sibyl's cave! We've found it!" Then she tugged him closer. "Come on!"

Her mood could not have been at greater variance to his own. His mate was gone, his firestorm extinguished, his destiny thwarted, and he had no notion of his own future prospects, but Orion followed her all the same.

———

MAGNUS WAS GONE.

Worse, he'd left Sigmund behind.

The miserable *Slayer* had abandoned Sigmund to his own fate. If Magnus made a recovery, though, and Sigmund witnessed the change, he would know for sure that the *Slayer* had figured out the ancient formula to create the Dragon's Blood Elixir. It had to do with that bloodstone, Sigmund was certain of it. He was pretty sure he was smarter than Magnus—if not as vindictive—but even Magnus might have figured out the secret in a couple of hundred years.

If so, Sigmund wanted to know. He had experiments he wanted to perform with the Elixir, tests he wanted to make to know the fullness (and limits) of its capabilities.

The only good news was that Sigmund's wounds weren't as bad as they could have been. He might be blinded in one eye, thanks to that bitch Francesca, but otherwise he was pretty much intact. He just needed to get this shard of glass out of his eye and even a human doctor could do that.

He flew to the highest level of the fortress, hoping he wouldn't be spotted, then ran after the fleeing photographer in his human form. "Can you help me?" he shouted in polite Italian. He'd beguile her so that she forgot his blood was black.

The photographer halted in her flight to look back, her dismay evident when she saw his eye. She swore and her expression turned to concern. "But what is wrong? Your blood is so dark."

"It looks black in the sunlight," Sigmund said, dropping his voice to the melodic tone necessary for beguiling. It was tough to summon the required serenity, given the pain in his eye but he did his best. He met her gaze, letting the flames light in his pupils. She leaned closer for a better look and he knew that she was snared. "The sunlight can be deceptive."

"The sunlight can be deceptive," she said, echoing his words in a mechanical tone as she held his gaze. "It only looks black in the sunlight."

"I need to see a doctor."

"You need to see a doctor."

"You can drive me to a doctor."

"I can drive you to a doctor." They started to walk up the hill toward the parking lot and she averted her gaze, frowning at the ground as they walked up the hill. "I didn't know there was anyone else here."

"I came to help with the display," Sigmund lied. He lowered his voice again and she looked toward him, snared once again by the flames in his eyes. "I am friends with Francesca."

"You are friends with Francesca," she repeated. "You came to help with the display."

"You can drive me to a doctor," he said again.

"I can drive you to a doctor."

"I need to see a doctor."

"You need to see a doctor."

"You can drive me to a doctor."

"I can drive you to a doctor."

"I'll get you to the hospital. Don't worry." She patted his arm reassuringly as her assistant appeared beside a van from the museum. "He's a friend of Francesca's who came to help with the display," she told the younger man. "He needs to see a doctor."

Her assistant's eyes widened, but Sigmund would beguile him in the van. He knew the emergency team would take the glass shard out of his eye and that he could dismiss it as an accident. In the end, he'd beguile everyone he encountered into forgetting he had ever been there.

And he'd 'accidentally' pull the film from her camera, too.

He couldn't wait to see if Magnus made a miraculous recovery, proving that he had the Elixir. He might have to visit the old *Slayer* and remind him of the price of betrayal.

EVEN BEFORE THE DUST SETTLED, Francesca could discern the ancient paintings that adorned the walls in the revealed space and she was awed. There were illustrations of snakes and clouds, flowing water and blazing flames. There were women dancing in a line, the lines of their garments and their features still wonderfully clear. She felt as if she was stepping into the past and was thrilled to be the first to see this cave's wonders in centuries.

Orion followed her, taking care to ensure his footing was solid, then eased past her. "Let me check the ground first," he insisted.

Even in her excitement, she could understand the value of that—and appreciate his protectiveness. Who knew how far the fall might be—and she couldn't shift into a creature with wings. She stood where he had left her, itching to go further but knowing she had to be sensible.

Orion vanished into the cavern below and she saw a blue shimmer when he was out of view, then his dragon wings unfolded against the darkness. He worked quickly, pulling stones free and arranging a kind of path for her, one that led down to the cavern that had been hidden below.

When she followed, it was even more amazing than she'd hoped. Francesca could only stare about herself and marvel. "They must have sealed it away in early Christian times," she said. "Hiding the pagan past." Even in the poor light, she could see that the chamber was larger than the one above and elaborately decorated.

Orion was noticeably quiet, even after he shifted back to human form. His eyes glinted and she knew he was alert, watching for any hint that the crumbling would begin again.

She smiled at him. "Is it the way you remember Delphi?"

He nodded, decisive and matter-of-fact. "The roof is high, higher than six men, an ancient design. When our kind attended the oracles, that gave us room to shift shape." He indicated the central well. "From here, the fumes rise to inspire the oracle." He pointed to a shadow in the wall. "The approach might have been there, and the seekers might have gathered here, on the lip of the abyss."

"And the Sibyl?"

He pointed across the dark well to an outcropping on the other side. "Her throne might have been there, overhanging the abyss. And there, you see the thousand mouths from which she might offer her prophecies."

Francesca eased her way around the well, wanting a better look. There was a corridor leading away from the opening, one with a wall perforated with hundreds of round holes. As she stood there, a wind passed down the corridor, stirring the dust as once it must have stirred the leaves of prophecy. It whistled and whispered, even though there were piles of tumbled rock that kept her from following it. She couldn't see anything in the shadows in either direction. "I wonder where this goes—or where it comes from."

"There is always a ritual path," Orion said. "A route for pilgrims." He pointed to the end that rose higher. "That must emerge on the hillside."

Francesca nodded. In the other direction, the path was blocked by the avalanche of rock. She wondered whether it terminated there, or continued onward. Would there be more hidden chambers? She understood how it must have felt finding Tut's tomb, or the remains of Troy.

"These images are incredible. Look at the detail!" She considered the dragon on the wall beside her, a beast of fable and myth, with a long tail, fierce claws and numerous teeth. It breathed fire into the air, like a spouting whale. It was painted in dark hues, the lick of flame in red, which made her think of Orion's dragon form.

"A guardian," she whispered, her heart glowing that Orion and his kind had served good for many years.

She glanced back to see that Orion was looking down into the central well. It was a round opening with no discernible bottom. He took a stone and dropped it into the abyss as she watched. It was a long time before Francesca heard a faint splash. In the meantime, the fumes rose to surround them, making her feel a bit light-headed.

Orion straightened and shook his head. "We should not linger in this place," he said then offered his hand to her. His manner was brusque and she could not understand why he wasn't more excited about the newly-revealed chamber.

He had to be disappointed that the light of the firestorm had gone out, even though he could never have satisfied it with a voice. "Do you think she was in the vase?" she asked when she stood beside him. He would have climbed over the rubble, but she gave his hand a tug, urging him to stay.

He gave her a simmering look. "If so, it is my fault she is lost. I should never have touched the vase. My proximity compromised the seal."

"No. You said it was damaged by something first."

He shook his head grimly. "Even if that was so, I will not dismiss my part in this, Francesca. She is lost and the fault is mine." He frowned. "I have failed my kind."

Francesca couldn't let him blame himself. "You didn't chose to be enchanted. It's not your fault that you didn't meet her when you should have," she argued, but he would not be consoled.

"The darkfire cheated us both," he said, his gaze dancing over her. "Perhaps all three of us."

"I haven't been cheated of anything," she said quickly and she meant it. "Without the darkfire, I would never have met you."

He paused then, considering her and her words, then smiled sadly and kissed her palm. "You are kind, Francesca. I am glad also that we met."

He turned to test the fallen rock, placing one foot on the debris to find a solid place. From there, he stepped upward again, seeking another foothold. Francesca held his hand and followed him, gasping when the brilliant blue-green of darkfire flashed like lightning in the cavern behind them.

It sparked around them both, crackling and jumping, illuminating the space like a fireball. It then surged upward and into the chamber above. Francesca heard a tinkle, then the light vanished so suddenly that it might not have been. Francesca blinked as Orion pulled her over the wreckage and into the chamber above.

Magnus Montmorency's vessel was standing against the wall, the iridescent shimmer of Roman glass as evident in its smooth surface as when she had picked it up from his apartment.

"How can that be?" she demanded and hurried to it. The stopper was in the neck of the vessel, the seal was intact, and the inscription was identical. It was as if she had imagined shattering the vase, or using the shard of glass to hurt Sigmund.

Orion came to her side and lifted a hand toward the vessel. Nothing changed. The interior of the glass remained dark and still.

"She *is* gone," Francesca whispered.

"But the darkfire repaired the damage," he added huskily before he turned away. "It is as if she had never been."

Francesca watched him, admiring his silhouette against the sunlight even as she had no idea what she could say to console him. What if you spent your whole life anticipating a destined meeting, then couldn't capitalize on it when it happened?

She could imagine that anyone would believe they had lost an opportunity, but the firestorm's satisfaction was so important to the *Pyr* that it could only be more. It was only natural that Orion felt he'd failed his kind, though Francesca didn't see that he'd had a lot of choice in the matter. She couldn't think of a way to make him feel better.

Then she remembered the verse she had written down. She pulled the piece of paper from her pocket and went to her glasses, where they had fallen on the ground. They weren't broken, thank goodness, and she put them on to read the message.

"What does it say?" Orion asked, coming to stand beside her.

"I'm not sure. My Latin is okay, but my Greek is better. I'd like to ask Dr. Thomas..."

"No." He was emphatic. "No one can learn of this, not before we know what it says."

"Okay. I have to tell him about the cavern, though. It's a huge discovery."

"Perhaps not as magnificent as that of Troy."

Francesca laughed. "Well, it won't hurt my reputation, that's for sure. I wonder how I'll explain the dragons." She bit her lip.

"You need not. Look at the hole. This soil must be unstable. Perhaps the hot lights of the photographer provoked a reaction."

Francesca winced. "She took pictures of you."

His expression turned grim. "Perhaps they will vanish. Perhaps she will not believe them."

"There were photographs taken in the museum and when you fought Sigmund in the sky."

Orion bowed his head. "Another betrayal of my kind. Perhaps it is best that the darkfire ensured I did not father a son."

Maybe this last message from the Sibyl—if that was what it was— would give him hope.

"This is going to take me a while to translate." She adjusted her glasses and peered at the paper. "I wish I had my dictionary. This is the nominative..." she murmured.

A flash of blue-green light slid across the floor of the cavern again, the light making Francesca jump. She was learning to distrust the darkfire, that was for sure. Orion turned in place, following its course, his posture defensive and his expression wary. She wasn't surprised that he was shimmering blue, and poised to defend her. The light illuminated the perimeter of the space then the paper she held began to shine blue-green.

The writing on the paper blinked, like letters of flame, then the darkfire did its thing and abruptly faded. The chamber felt dark and still, and the hair on the back of Francesca's neck prickled.

"Wait! It changed!" she whispered, holding out the piece of paper. "It's in English now!" She eyed Orion in astonishment, but he looked just as surprised as she felt. "And it's still in my handwriting. How did that happen?"

"Darkfire," Orion said grimly.

Apparently, he was right because the verse was also about darkfire.

Francesca read it aloud.

> "*Darkfire follows its own quest*
> *The force of the* Pyr *knows their fate best;*
> *Throughout the ages and the years*
> *Darkfire feeds their hopes and fears.*
> *When the firestorm sparks in Cumae*
> *The Sibyl will have a new part to play.*
> *When truth and myth find common ground*
> *Both choice and fate find their footing sound.*"

She looked up expectantly but Orion frowned. "There is no firestorm in Cumae," he said. "Not any more."

"Maybe not yet," Francesca said with false cheer. She nudged him. "You can't have a firestorm with a vase or a voice. Maybe that was just a precursor to the real thing. Maybe you'll meet your mate here tomorrow or the next day." He looked up, considering this. "You said yourself that there had to be a reason why you were here. You should wait and see what happens next." She waved the verse at him. "It says there will be a firestorm in Cumae, after all."

He nodded, clearly finding appeal in her argument. "I will stay," he said. "You have found me labor."

"Stay with me," she said quickly, smiling at his hot glance. "After all, I still want to take advantage of opportunity."

His smile was slow and warmed her to her toes. "How so, Francesca?"

"You can tell me about the past. You can give him hints for my research." She smiled and leaned closer to whisper in his ear. "You can help me regain my faith in men."

He turned slightly to look at her, his eyes that intense silvery-blue that made her shiver. "And how would I do this, Francesca?"

"With sex," she said. "Lots of great sex. Your mate isn't around, so we can just enjoy each other. No strings attached. I'll get some condoms..."

"Condoms?"

She sought an older word. "Prophylactics."

He shrugged. "If this is your choice, Francesca, I will pleasure you."

"You make it sound like a duty," she teased, but his slow smile was more than seductive.

"It will assuredly be pleasure, but there will be no child. The *Pyr* father children only during the firestorm."

"And only sons."

He nodded once.

"Then stay with me, for as long as you're in Cumae." When he hesitated, she plunged on. "I don't believe in destiny, but I believe in making the best choices I can. There's here and there's now, and we're together. I like you and I think you like me. Let's make the most of the moment, and not worry about tomorrow before it comes. That's opportunity and we should take it."

Her knees weakened when he smiled finally, then Orion caught her in his embrace. "I find your suggestion irresistible, Francesca," he murmured, bending to touch his lips to hers. He searched her gaze for a long moment. "You are certain?"

Francesca had never been more sure of anything in her life. "Yes," she said.

Orion grinned then captured her mouth beneath his own, kissing her so thoroughly that she was almost tempted to forget the newly discovered cave.

But not quite.

———

THEY RETURNED to Francesca's apartment where she showered and changed, then continued to the museum to share the news with Dr. Thomas. Orion also washed, glad yet again that her brother had left so much behind. He shaved, taking satisfaction in the smoothness of his face without the bristle of whiskers. This razor was similar to those he had learned to use in the future world, and he admired the tool greatly. Then he paced, considering what had occurred and disliking its implications.

Destiny had been thwarted by the darkfire.

This could not be good.

Orion considered that perhaps he had always been destined to suffer this fate. He could not regret having met Francesca, and he would never betray her. She spoke good sense that there was no reason to avoid intimacy in the absence of his firestorm. Just because she was not his mate did not mean there could be no merit in their partnership.

Perhaps this was the reason for his presence in her time. His memories might help with her research.

In that moment, he recalled the poem about Troy. He had almost listened to it all. He could perhaps finish while he awaited Francesca's return.

Orion was sure he imagined the similarity between the crystal on Francesca's sill to the one Drake had carried. At least the stone held no spark. He picked it up and examined it more than once, but it was cold and dark.

The loss of his mate was making him fanciful. Surely the darkfire had caused enough chaos on this day? Surely it should be exhausted and vanish for an interval to leave him in peace? He set the crystal aside, still distrusting it, and started the tape recorder.

The sun was sinking by the time Orion finished listening to Homer's poem. Francesca still had not returned, though he was not surprised. The find had been exciting for him and he knew it was more so for her. She had planned to take Dr. Thomas to Cumae, and doubtless they had lost track of time in their mutual enthusiasm.

In time, she would return.

He had need of a quest.

He liked the poem on tape, of the rousing details it had contained and the vivid depiction of the battles. He favored his father's versions, of course, but there was much to be said in favor of this one. What troubled him were the omissions. There was no mention of the *Pyr* and their valiant role in the dispute. Even the Amazons had been included, but not the *Pyr*.

He composed a list in his thoughts, arranging the omissions so he could present them coherently to Francesca. He reviewed it, committing it to memory, and was content with it.

Perhaps he could solve the riddle of his presence in this place. He paced the apartment, restless, then stood on the terrace looking over the city and the bay. Why had he been brought to this time and place? It was not to meet his mate, evidently. He recalled the verse and recited it to himself.

> *Darkfire follows its own quest*
> *The force of the* Pyr *knows their fate best;*
> *Throughout the ages and the years*
> *Darkfire feeds their hopes and fears.*
> *When the firestorm sparks in Cumae*
> *The Sibyl will have a new part to play.*
> *When truth and myth find common ground*
> *Both choice and fate find their footing sound.*

How could the Sibyl play a part in his firestorm, when she no longer existed? Was Francesca right that his true firestorm might still spark here in Cumae? Orion was skeptical. What was this of truth and myth? He had told no lies, and the *Pyr* were not myths. It was a conundrum he could not solve alone.

Once he would have asked Drake for counsel, or even Damian, but they were both lost to him. Once he might have consulted with Erik Sorensson or even Rafferty Powell, but he dared not reach out to either lest he influence the future of his kind. In this time, he knew only of two *Slayers*, and he had no notion where to find either of them. He could have sought their scents and followed them, but he much preferred waiting for Francesca.

It seemed there was nothing he could do but wait.

Orion was enough of a warrior to find that situation vexing.

Then he had an idea. He was in this time, at least until the darkfire sparked again. He should learn of it, and navigate it better than he had done thus far. He could not be so reliant upon Francesca and he might discover the reason for his presence. He and his fellow warriors had learned their way around the future world by observation. He could do the same here. And it made good sense to understand one's situation as well as possible. He might even locate one of the *Slayers*.

He was also hungry and activity would make that easier to ignore.

Orion left the apartment, taking the spare key from the hook and locking the door as he had seen Francesca do. The Vespa was parked in the corner below, and he knew she would be walking back from the museum when she did return. Without the vase filled with light, he had no notion of her location or proximity.

He didn't like that much, or the reminder that she wasn't his mate. He also wasn't one to rail against the fates and bemoan his situation. It was, and he would make the best of it.

He considered the Vespa and decided it was better to walk.

There were small fishing boats in the harbor with men working upon them, much the way he remembered from home. He headed in that direction, delighted when he heard them speaking Greek.

———

FRANCESCA RETURNED HOME LATE, but in a jubilant mood. To her relief, Orion had not left. He was sitting on her terrace, seemingly lost in thought. He looked up at her arrival and smiled, which made her feel a thousand times better that he was there, and much worse that he'd been waiting without knowing what to expect.

"I'm sorry I'm so late," she said. "But there was no way to let you know what was happening." She had brought pizza and a bottle of wine, assuming he'd be hungry. She was.

Orion inhaled appreciatively. "I can only assume that Dr. Thomas wished to visit Cumae with you, and that later, perhaps you celebrated your discovery."

"And I couldn't tell you. Even if I had a phone, you probably wouldn't know to answer it."

"A phone?" He was taking plates and glasses off the shelf, arranging for their meal on the counter.

"A device to contact people in other locations. It rings when someone calls and when you answer, you can hear their voice."

"No matter where they are?"

She nodded.

His skepticism was clear, which made her realize she wasn't the only one confronting details that seemed impossible.

That was funny, in a way.

"Did you explore more of the cave?"

"Yes and it's wonderful!" she said, unable to hide her enthusiasm. "That grotto is fantastic, an epic find, and you'll never guess what else."

"Then tell me," he invited with a smile.

Francesca knew that she was chattering but unable to help

herself. "Dr. Thomas has assigned me to supervise the documenting of the site. Every element will have to be itemized and photographed, and then there will have to be interpretations made of the paintings, the artefacts and the site." She got the corkscrew to open the wine as she talked, and Orion set out plates on the counter.

He sniffed appreciatively when she opened the box. "This is similar to the bread you ate last night."

"Yes, pizza. This one has sausage on it and olives. This could be my big chance, Orion. People spend their whole careers hoping for a discovery like this one, and here it is, right when I'm finishing grad school..." When she fumbled with the corkscrew, too excited to make it work, Orion lifted it from her hands. He examined the corkscrew, then nodded.

"Ah, an augur," he said under his breath. After a false start, he opened the wine, nodding appreciatively as he poured it out.

"I have considered that this discovery might be the reason for my presence," he said.

Francesca laughed. "Only dragons could have broken open that wall," she said and lifted her glass. "Let's drink to the future."

"Let's drink to your future," Orion countered, his smile heating her blood.

He ate and she talked, remembering only occasionally that she should eat, too. She told him about the paintings, about Dr. Thomas' excitement, even about Larry's envy. She told him about the curator of the site coming to see it and the preparations being made for further excavation. She was chattering and she knew it, but her excitement couldn't be held back. She'd ensured that he'd be able to work there the next day, as planned, and he was appreciative of that.

Orion listened and nodded, he smiled in the right places, but she sensed that he was distracted. He didn't eat as much as she expected either.

Finally, she fell silent, all out of words, and just smiled at him. She noticed the tape recorder. "Did you finish the poem?"

Orion nodded. "It is, as you said, a fine work. My father would have enjoyed it greatly."

"But...?" she invited, sensing that there was more.

"They omitted us from the tale," he said, without looking at her.

She understood immediately. "The *Pyr* were at the Trojan War?"

Orion gave her a glittering glance. "We were the *reason* for the Trojan War," he said with heat. "How could we be removed from the tale?"

"You don't remember this, right?"

He shook his head with impatience. "It was before my time, but I remember my father's recounting of the tale."

The Trojan War, Francesca knew had been a real battle as well as one romanticized in Homer's *Iliad*. The ancient city of Ilium or Troy, located by Schliemann in the northwest of modern Turkey, had been razed around 1200 BCE. How much of Homer's tale was truth and how much was fiction? No one knew.

But Orion might.

None of the versions or interpretations Francesca had read included dragon shifters. She would have remembered that.

"Tell me," she invited and he turned away from the window, scanning the room as if he had never seen it before. She guessed that he was recalling his father's words and waited for him to begin.

"Our tale began with the fire," Orion said and Francesca looked up, not having expected those words. Orion smiled slightly when their gazes met. "We are *Pyr*. We are lit by the spark from Hephaestus' forge, his first gift to our kind."

Francesca was intrigued. She began to take notes in her personal shorthand. She just hoped she could keep up with him.

"It began with the fiasco of Pandora," Orion continued. "Hephaestus felt an obligation to men to improve their situation, even though he could not undo what had been done. And so he retreated to his forge and he labored day and night, designing men who could become dragons at will. He hammered our dragon scales into perfect shapes and crafted us for both beauty and strength. He shaped our talons and our teeth, he made our wings larger and stronger than those of any known bird, he made us the marvels that we are. He decreed that we should defend the treasures of the earth, including mortal men and women, and that we should be the custodians of the elements. He filled our hearts with valor, sharpened our senses beyond expectation, and endeavored in every way to ensure our superiority as guardians of mankind. And when he was content with his design, he breathed flame into the first three of us, igniting their souls with his fire, then dispatching them into the world."

Francesca was scribbling furiously.

Orion came to sit across from her, his elbows braced on his knees as he watched her. "My father could not write like a scribe," he said and she looked up. He tapped one temple. "He said he remembered every tale he was ever told and I always believed it."

"And you?"

He shook his head. "I remember only my own tales, by and large. I was taught to remember poems and stories, to memorize whatever I might need to know later."

"That's true in most cultures where people don't keep a written record."

"My father's memory was beyond impressive. I do not believe he ever forgot a detail." He frowned and looked down at the floor. "Our last words were exchanged in anger," he confessed quietly. "And that can never be undone."

"What did you fight about?"

"Stories. He wished to tell me one of Cadmus when we were leaving to hunt that viper. I had no time to listen to a mere story. I told him that stories were for old men in their dotage, and that young men had battles to fight and stories to live." He grimaced. "He told me that I would have a tale to tell one day, but I was dismissive." He sighed. "I remember how he flinched at the anger in my words."

"But you didn't return from that battle with Cadmus," Francesca said softly.

He looked up, his gaze clear. "And now that I finally have a tale to tell, one that he would not know and which he would admire, I cannot share it with him. Worse, I know that he died uncertain of the fate of his only son." He frowned again, then continued with his tale. "But I was telling you a tale. Hephaestus was married to Aphrodite, against that goddess' desire. She had no wish to be wed to a lame god, but the wedding had been held all the same. She had less interest in being wed to a man who could ignore her for long intervals, as Hephaestus did when he retreated to his forge to craft the *Pyr*. In need of attention, she was unfaithful, embarking on an affair with Ares."

"And she was caught," Francesca recalled.

"Hephaestus learned of their trysts and sought them out, discovering them in the midst of their lovemaking. He cast an enchanted net over the entwined lovers and carried them to Olympus, where they were displayed to the other gods. Aphrodite was humiliated and vowed to seek vengeance against her spouse.

"She had to wait long for the opportunity, but the divine have patience and time to spare. And so it came one day that the mortal Peleus was to wed the immortal Thetis, a match arranged by the gods."

"To thwart the prediction that a son conceived by Thetis by a god would rule Olympus," Francesca said. "At least they *try* to avoid destiny."

"But seldom succeed, and there is the lesson," Orion reminded her before continuing. "But in dispatching the wedding invitations, an omission was inadvertently made and Eris was not invited to the celebration. She sought vengeance upon all, and contrived a means to make trouble. She had a golden apple made, inscribed with the words *For the Most Beautiful*, and she cast it at the feet of the goddesses Hera, Aphrodite and Athena. Each strove to claim it and a great argument ensued, all three finally agreeing to accept the choice of an impartial judge. Paris of Troy, judged the most handsome of mortal men, was granted that task."

"Aphrodite, however, was not inclined to leave matters to chance. She resolved both to see herself triumphantly named as the most beautiful and to avenge herself upon her husband. She knew that Hephaestus had arranged for one of his beloved *Pyr* to have a remarkable wife and mother to his children. By his design, the beautiful Helen, daughter of Zeus and Leda, would be the wife and partner of King Menelaus. Menelaus was King of Sparta and one of the most powerful and noble of our kind. From infancy, Helen's beauty was renowned in all the world. Aphrodite promised Paris that when he chose her as the most beautiful of the three goddesses, Helen would be his reward. She would thus thwart the scheme of Hephaestus and gain the golden apple."

"It would have been nice if Helen had been given a choice," Francesca muttered.

"She was a child, Francesca, and her future was her guardian's responsibility to arrange." She looked up at this detail, but Orion continued with the tale. "And so, Aphrodite claimed the apple and shortly thereafter, Helen's guardian, Tyndareus, sought to arrange Helen's marriage. Menelaus sent his brother Agamemnon to argue his suit, suspecting that his conviction that Helen should be his by grant of the gods might be perceived as undiplomatic."

Francesca smiled as she wrote. She hadn't thought of the dragons as being very concerned with diplomacy.

But then she was learning a lot of new things about the dragons who called themselves the *Pyr*.

CHAPTER ELEVEN

Orion continued his story and Francesca managed to keep up with him as she took notes.

"Suitors came from all of Greece to seek Helen's hand and Tyndareus feared that there was no good choice to be made," he said. "He knew of Hephaestus' plan and he himself believed that Menelaus was the best choice for his foster daughter. He feared he had no good options. If he made a choice, the unsuccessful suitors might attack the winner, but also if he sent the suitors away without awarding Helen's hand, there might still be violence. Paris was there and creating strife in the court, insisting that Helen should be his betrothed. There were tales of him visiting her secretly and charming her to his view, as well." He paused. "She was yet a young girl."

A child, he had said. That was different from many of the versions Francesca knew.

"Odysseus arrived as a potential suitor though he soon was convinced that he had little chance of success. He offered his assistance to Tyndareus in finding a peaceful solution in exchange for that king's assistance in Odysseus' courtship of Penelope. Once they agreed, Odysseus insisted that all the suitors pledge to defend the man who won Helen as his bride, whoever that man might be. Once they did so, Tyndareus awarded Helen to Menelaus and Agamemnon escorted her to Sparta. There she would be the guest of her betrothed until their nuptials. Paris followed, however, met with Helen and seized her, taking her to his father's kingdom of Troy."

"But there was the alliance. Surely Paris expected repercussions."

"Perhaps he did not care."

"The others could have left them alone."

"No, it was a matter of honor." Orion was emphatic. "They had sworn to defend the successful suitor by the determination of Tyndareus and that man was Menelaus. They had given their word, and that could not be set aside. Menelaus summoned all the suitors who had pledged their alliance to him, and a fleet of black ships sailed across the Aegean to avenge him. The siege lasted ten years: many men and *Pyr* of merit died on those battle fields."

Francesca lifted her pen. "Is the part about the Trojan horse true?"

He nodded once. "The Greeks chose deception to end the battle. My father said there was dissent in the ranks. There were those who insisted they had kept their word in defending Menelaus. Many believed it was unnecessary for more men to die over a woman, regardless of her beauty. There was no easy truce, though, not so long as Paris defended his intended bride."

"They were not married yet?"

"It is said that she was still a maiden, though a woman fully grown, at the end of the hostilities." He cleared his throat. "The Greeks sailed west, giving every appearance of abandoning the fight, but left a large wooden horse on the beach, as if it were a gift. The Trojans accepted this as a peace offering, and brought it within the walls of the city to marvel at its artful construction."

"Wait," Francesca said. "Laocoön, the priest of Poseidon in Troy, warned them against doing so and was attacked by serpents."

Orion smiled. "Not serpents."

"*Pyr*," she breathed.

"Apollo had no fondness for Laocoön and heard of his warning. He summoned the *Pyr* to defend those loyal to him, and two of our kind rose from the sea to silence the priest and his sons forever." Orion's expression was grim. "The war had endured for ten years, Francesca. It had to end."

"So, Hephaestus and Apollo both favored the *Pyr*."

Orion inclined his head. "Among others of the divine. Athena smiled upon us in her time." He cleared his throat. "After the horse was brought into the city, the Trojans realized it was filled with warriors, who streamed into the streets to fight. The ships had also returned to bring more forces. The Greeks defeated the Trojans in a fierce battle, until Menelaus himself pursued his errant bride. His heart was filled with only fury and the thirst for vengeance, and he blamed her for the loss of many valiant warriors. But when he raised his sword, Hephaestus granted another gift to our kind.

"Hephaestus loosed the fire again, sparking the first firestorm. He knew it was the sole way to dismiss the fury within Menelaus, to push anger aside with desire. That blaze filled both Menelaus and Helen with a surety of their destiny together, enflaming their hearts and fusing their very souls as one. Each brought out the best in the other and their partnership was greater than the sum of the parts. Their match was heralded as a perfect balance, for he was governed by earth and fire, while she had affinities to water and air. He was fierce in his protectiveness and his love, while she spoke to him of mercy and newfound ideas, of dreams and tenderness. They ruled Sparta in happy harmony for many years, and she bore him three sons, all handsome and valiant warriors who filled their parents' hearts with pride."

"And they lived happily ever after," Francesca said with a smile.

———

ORION LOOKED UP SLOWLY, struck by Francesca's dismissive tone. "You find no merit in that?"

"It's just hard to believe, that's all." She did not like to be challenged, he could see, but she also did not find happy partnerships to be plausible. He wondered again who had betrayed her trust. Hers was, he thought, a learned response. She continued quickly, as if endeavoring to convince herself. "Maybe she was making the best of the situation she couldn't change. Maybe she hated Menelaus her whole life."

He wagged a finger at her. "Maybe she discovered that a man of less charm might have a more steadfast heart."

"Maybe she was trapped." Her eyes flashed at that, a telling choice of word.

"There have always been ways for people to influence their situation. They can flee. They can choose another ally. They can end their own life or that of another. A beauty like Helen might have found a man to steal her away from all she despised. There are choices, Francesca, and if her life was so lamentable, I believe she would have selected one of them."

"You're just convinced of the power of the firestorm. You want to believe in happy endings."

He would have wagered that she did, as well, but no longer dared to do so. She was sitting on the stool at the counter and he moved closer, watching her swallow in awareness of his proximity. Oh, there was something else she desired of him, and Orion would gladly satisfy her desire, now that there was no immediate prospect of his destined mate appearing.

"Is that such folly?" he asked gently, leaning against the counter near her. Her gaze flicked over him, her lashes sweeping down to hide her thoughts. She caught her breath, though, and pink stained her cheeks, such a sure sign of her interest that Orion had no doubt of her thoughts. The conviction multiplied his own desire a hundred-fold. "I find the notion appealing that a man and a woman can become partners as well as lovers, and to build a life together that suits them both."

Her gaze flicked to his. "I think it's wishful thinking."

Orion smiled slowly and it seemed that Francesca could not look away. He could have drowned willingly in her eyes and he eased closer, watching her lips part. "Why? Do you not know happy couples?"

"Sure, but they didn't have a firestorm. It wasn't an instant attraction that worked forever. They met and talked and fell in love as they discovered they had things in common. It was a *process*."

"And because there is no destiny, there can be no gods who locate your ideal mate and ensure that you cross paths with that individual. You must wander through your life alone and hope for happy coincidence instead." He shook his head. "I think your view is bleak, Francesca. I would rather have interfering deities."

"Of course, you would," she chided and he chuckled. "But how do they *know*?"

"Because they can see into our hearts, of course. Because we are revealed to them in all our truth."

"Okay." She lifted her chin in challenge. "What would ensure you and I were destined to be a happy couple for all time?"

"Nothing. We are not destined mates."

"But if we were? What else would be in our favor than destiny, if it was? There has to be more at work than meddling deities!"

"You say that as if there is opposition to such a notion."

"I think we're about as different as two people could be."

"But there can be strength in that." He chose his words with care. "There could be a balance of our affinities to the elements. Our strengths would then complement each other so that we would be greater together than individually."

"Teamwork is better than working alone."

He nodded, watching her consider that.

"It's definitely better to have you around when *Slayers* attack, but I haven't needed to be rescued until I met you. Both good and bad turned up together." She held his gaze. "And the whole argument that they're attracted to the firestorm, so it should be consummated as soon as possible for everyone's safety, is kind of self-serving. It also omits the detail of the mate having the obligation of bearing a child. That shouldn't be a flash decision."

Orion smiled. "And so you prove your affinity to the element of air."

"How so?"

"You are rational, logical, decisive and clever. These are the gifts of air." His brows rose. "As are intuition, foresight and dreams."

"I don't dream," Francesca protested.

"Everyone dreams. You might not recall your dreams, but you have them."

"There you go again, convinced of something with no evidence of it." She eyed him. "It's weird that I'm not afraid of you, though. I never was."

"Because you know to trust your intellect."

"Some people would dismiss that as a woman's instinct."

"There is nothing to dismiss about instinct," Orion said. "An intuitive conviction is not a whim. It is usually based upon many thousands of observations, distilled into a sense so reliable that it can save your life." She turned to look at him in surprise. "I never dismiss instinct, whether that of man or woman. It is a powerful and protective force, though in any given instance, it may not be possible to list the observations that have contributed to the conclusion."

"Maybe that's why I like you," she said. "You don't treat me like an idiot for knowing what I know."

"On the contrary, I have only admiration for those with knowledge."

"Aha!" she said, eyes flashing with triumph. "You must have an affinity for fire."

Orion laughed. "Because of my nature? I do, but that is not the proof."

"What is?"

"Fire is allied with passion and compassion, with emotion and sentiment and resolve. Those who are imbued with fire follow their hearts and trust in their feelings."

"Believing in the firestorm because you like the sound of it."

He reached out and touched her shoulder with a fingertip, letting it slide down her arm. Her eyes widened but she didn't move away. "I think you like the sound of it, too, Francesca. You argue most vehemently against it."

"The lady doth protest too much?" She shrugged, then met his gaze. "Or the lady has been fooled before."

"I make no jest with you."

"No, you really believe in it. I'm just not a romantic like you."

At least not any more. Orion heard the words she did not utter.

"That's only two elements," she prompted.

Orion surveyed her. "Earth must be yours. Earth is pragmatic and practical." He smiled. "Earth demands proof that can be touched and held."

Francesca laughed, her eyes dancing. "That's me. I need evidence to believe anything."

"While water is more intuitive, more sensitive to greater forces and more trusting of them, more accepting of the wisdom of dreams and visions."

"That sounds like you."

He held her gaze. "And so, what could we accomplish together, Francesca, though we are not destined mates? There are other reasons for alliance than the conception of children."

"Exactly."

"You might study your books and sources, while I might

remember tales I have heard or places I have seen centuries ago. The combination might aid in your research and studies of the past. This might be the reason for my presence here."

"You could find me a Troy," she said. "But really, you've already stepped up with that. The Sibyl's grotto is amazing."

"Perhaps it is only the first discovery to result from our alliance."

"When do you think your firestorm will spark?"

"It could be years. Decades." He let his fingertips slide up her arm again as he held her gaze. "Centuries." He could feel the heat emanating from her. Even without a firestorm, he was filled with yearning for this woman all over again. "It might be extinguished already, if you recall," he whispered and her eyes widened with awareness of him. It was spellbinding to know that she felt as aroused as he was.

"I think you should seize the day," she said, her words breathless.

Orion leaned closer, moving slowly so she could evade him if she so chose. He was aware that she might have changed her mind about her earlier invitation, and to him, the choice was hers to make.

She just watched him draw near, seemingly holding her breath as she waited.

He brushed his lips across hers and felt her shiver. When he spoke, his lips were close to her ear, his hands closing over her shoulders. "I think, Francesca, that we should seize the moment together," he murmured and she caught her breath.

"It must be that affinity to water that makes you able to read my thoughts."

He laughed as he pulled her into his arms, his fingers spearing into her hair and cupping her nape. Francesca wound her arms around his neck and arched against him, parting her lips in invitation. "Or perhaps your affinity to air gives you the power to guess mine," he suggested, before he silenced her laughter with a slow and very satisfying kiss.

———

NO ONE HAD EVER TOUCHED Francesca with the reverence Orion showed. He was protective but she knew he would release her if she made one gesture of protest. He was a powerful dragon shifter, but she felt as if she was the one in command.

That was as seductive as his touch.

She halfway thought she'd imagined how amazing it had been with him the night before or that she'd at least embellished the recollection. Maybe it had seemed better because it had been the first time between them and a long time since she'd been intimate with anyone. But she watched his eyes begin to glow as she opened her blouse, revealing her bra to him, and knew it had been remarkable.

And this night would be even better.

She'd chosen a pink satin bra when she changed, hoping she'd have the chance to show it to him. He flicked a hot glance at her, his approval clear, then lifted a hand to cup her breast. "This one disguises more than the other," he said, stroking his thumb across the satin that covered her nipple. His throat worked as he watched his own hand and Francesca's pulse fluttered like a butterfly. "Though I like it as well. Such softness," he added, then eased his finger beneath the elastic to caress her nipple and tease it to a peak.

It was hard to believe that it had been only a few hours since he had touched her like this. Francesca felt as if it had been a year.

"The clasp is at the front on this one," she managed to say and almost laughed at his delight when he opened it. He surveyed her breasts with satisfaction, then bent to kiss her nipple, suckling it so that she moaned with pleasure. He gripped the back of her waist with one hand, his other easing beneath the waistband of her jeans. She knew his plan and heartily approved. She unfastened the front of her jeans and he pushed them over her hips, chuckling when he saw that her panties were the same pink satin.

"Did you dress to tempt me, Francesca?" he growled.

"Yes."

"You need not do as much. You are a siren in your own right."

"But we didn't *finish* before."

"Because my mate was close. It would have been unkind, both to her and to you."

"But now she's gone," Francesca reminded him in a whisper.

There was a flash in his eyes, and she feared she'd said the wrong thing. Then he smiled at her as his fingertips moved against her and she gasped with pleasure.

"You do that so well."

"I begin well, by your response, but I would do it perfectly for you, Francesca." He kissed her, his embrace a little rougher and more demanding than it had been, even as his fingers moved persuasively against her. "I would make this ideal for you, just as you want it to be. You must tell me exactly what you like best."

"That," she said as his thumb slid across her clitoris. "A little harder and faster."

He did exactly as she instructed, making her gasp, then he slowed. "There must be a tease, to ensure ultimate satisfaction," he murmured, then bent to kiss her nipple again.

Francesca peeled off her shirt and kicked off her jeans, wriggling out of her bra and her panties. Orion lifted her in his arms and carried her to the bed, stretching out beside her. She was a little bit crushed beneath him, trapped between his hard body, the mattress and the wall, and she loved it.

"What else?" he demanded, his breath against her ear as he kissed her there. She could feel his erection straining against his jeans, pressing against her hip.

She ran her hand over him, feeling him grow larger beneath her caress.

"I want you inside me," she confessed. "I want to feel the heat of you filling me up."

His fingers eased inside her and his thumb pressed on her, the move making her gasp and arch her back. "You will find your pleasure first," he threatened. "Twice."

Francesca might have argued but he claimed her mouth with a crushing kiss, his caress becoming more insistent. She grabbed the back of his shirt and pulled it up to his shoulders.

"I want you naked," she said when she had the chance to speak. "I want to feel you against me and inside me."

"Francesca," he whispered then stood up abruptly. He looked down on her as he peeled off the T-shirt and flung it aside, the gleam in his eyes making her feel beautiful. She reached for the front of his jeans, but he stepped back, unfastening them with haste and discarding them along with his briefs. He moved back toward her, more confident and glorious than she'd even imagined a man could be, and she reached for the drawer in the nightstand.

She offered him a condom, which he accepted and considered.

"We only father sons during the firestorm," he said with complete confidence.

"You can't know that."

"I do." He looked utterly convinced of it, though it didn't seem rational to Francesca.

She would be the one to have to deal with the result if he was wrong, after all.

"Humor me?"

He chuckled and handed it back to her. "Of course. Show me, Francesca."

She opened the package as he watched with interest, then reached for him, liking how he caught his breath at her touch. She caressed him first, liking that she could so arouse him. She eased the condom over him, hoping as she did so that it was big enough, then laughed as he admired the fit. He smoothed it himself, then granted her a playful glance.

"Do *not* talk about sheep guts," she said. "It would spoil the moment."

"Nothing can spoil this moment, Francesca," he said after he laughed, then beckoned. "Come here," he invited in an irresistible low growl.

Francesca she stood up, then approached him slowly.

"Now you choose," he said as he caught her close. He kissed her roughly, his hand in her hair, his other arm locking around her waist and lifting her to her toes.

"I chose you already."

He murmured in her ear, his breath making her shiver. "The bed. The wall. The floor."

"The counter," she said, and pointed. Orion's hands were beneath her butt and he lifted her easily from the floor. Francesca wrapped her legs around his waist as he kissed her and he held her there, his heat against her. She moved, rubbing herself against him and he inhaled sharply, then lifted her higher. His eyes gleamed as she reached between them and guided him into her slick heat. She saw the fire in his gaze as he eased inside her and felt his entire body taut with need. His gaze was so intense that his eyes were almost silver. She gasped at the size of him, moving so that he was drawn deeper, watching his jaw tighten with restraint as he buried himself fully. He shook as he exhaled, then he met her gaze again, his own simmering.

"Perhaps we have no need of the counter," he murmured.

Francesca smiled and pumped against him, watching him grit his teeth. "Perhaps not," she said and rolled her hips, loving the feel of him inside her.

He whispered her name, then drove deeper, his eyes glittering as he moved. He lifted her high then ensured he rubbed against her, his every thrust feeding the desire within her and stirring it to a fever pitch. She gripped his shoulders and kept her legs locked around him, loving how they rocked together, loving his power and tenderness. His gaze burned into hers, his tempo increased, the fire in her veins became a tempest.

She whispered his name, certain they'd combust but he continued with persuasive power, pushing her higher than she'd ever been, waiting until the tumult overcame her. She cried out and clutched him closer, feeling him bury himself deep within her then roar with satisfaction at his release.

She was clinging to him limply and he leaned against the counter, pressing a kiss to her shoulder. He said her name on a sigh that made her smile and she straightened to look into his glorious eyes. She pushed her hand through his hair and kissed him sweetly. "But you said twice for me first," she teased him.

He sighed, as if with remorse. "Then we must begin again, to get it right."

Francesca laughed and watched him smile.

"And it will be better the next time," Orion vowed. "For each time, I learn better how to feed your desires." He kissed her again, his embrace possessive and demanding, and Francesca wondered how long she would survive a more intense bout of lovemaking.

Then she couldn't wait to find out.

———

FRANCESCA DREAMED.

She was in that garden again, the one where the dark-haired man had planted the big seeds. The scene was just as it had been in her previous dream, as if she had never left. He and his two companions were still singing that low infectious song and she wondered how long it had been going on. The light was different, as if at least one night had passed as they chanted. It might have been close to the dawn.

The earth rumbled suddenly, causing their song to falter as they turned to look. The dark-haired one urged the others to continue and they sang with greater vehemence, as if they'd gotten their second wind.

The ground shook, much as it had done earlier that day in Cumae, but the earth in this garden split open. Francesca gasped when a man emerged from the soil. He was naked and muscular, like Orion, his expression inscrutable, his hair trimmed short. He stepped out of the crevasse as if there was nothing usual about that at all. He reached back toward the earth, and his outstretched hand was seized by another. He pulled a second man to stand alongside him.

The original three sang a little louder. These two warriors cleared their throats, then raised their voices in song, as well. A third and a fourth man emerged from the soil, crowding the garden as the soil cracked open even more.

As a fifth man rose up from the ground, the first one pointed to the second and third of the arrivals. Something passed between them, not a word but a glance, and the pair leapt into the air as one. They moved in perfect synchronization, as if they had been trained to work in unison. Francesca was amazed when they both shimmered blue and became dragons when they were six feet above the ground, but she realized she shouldn't have been.

These were the teeth, the cursed *Pyr* who were released from the spell by one of their fellows.

In 2008.

She watched in awe as the dragon's mighty dark wings flapped and they soared into the dark sky together, then turned their course to fly out of view. When she looked back, the garden was packed with impassive dark-eyed men.

Was one of them Orion? She couldn't identify him easily. There were too many shadows.

The next pair took flight after the first, then another pair and another. Dozens more men sprang from the earth as the original trio sang, more of them leapt into the sky and became dragons. Francesca lost track of their number. She noticed how similar the dragons were to each other, all of them graced with scales as dark as anthracite and talons like dark steel. They looked more ancient than the *Slayers* she had seen fight with Orion.

They looked just like Orion.

There had to be one with silvery-blue eyes, but she couldn't tell. It was night and the shadows were long. All of these men looked similar to her, as impassive and powerful as a warrior should be. It was clear they were dispatched on some mission. When only the first of them remained, he spoke to the three who had summoned them, but she couldn't hear their words in her dream.

Then those four took flight as well, flying in pairs after their fellows.

Francesca found herself alone in the walled garden, staring into the night sky as the last of the dragons vanished from view. She wondered at their destination, then guessed. Orion had told her that they had defeated a foe together, after their enchantment had been broken by the *Pyr*.

Was she dreaming his memories?

Or was she seeing the future?

FRANCESCA OPENED her eyes to find Orion's heat behind her. He was spooned against her, trapping her beneath his body and the wall. She felt both warm and treasured, and liked the fan of his breath against her shoulder. It was dark outside, the hour late, and the city was quiet.

She felt safe.

She was happy. That was a surprise and she had to think about it for a minute or two.

Who would have guessed that a powerful dragon shifter would make love so tenderly? Who would have imagined that any man could begin to undermine Francesca's convictions so quickly as Orion had? She liked how he touched her. She liked how he listened.

She liked that he didn't try to force her to agree with him, about anything. He was principled and steadfast.

And persuasive.

Orion was giving her precisely what she said she wanted but Francesca already felt that it might not be enough. In a teeny tiny corner of her heart, she dreaded the prospect of his firestorm sparking, because that would be the moment he left her forever.

If his firestorm sparked, she couldn't blame him for following it, though. He'd been honest with her from the beginning about his obligation to the firestorm. But Francesca was already starting to realize that Orion would be impossible to forget.

She admitted to herself that he was eroding all of her barriers, and doing it with ease.

She heard his breathing change and knew he wasn't sleeping. "How can you be here *and* there?" she asked in a whisper.

"I am here," he murmured, pulling her closer as he kissed the back of her neck.

She twisted around, trying to discern his features in the shadows. "And you're in Montmorency's Roman hoard near London, enchanted in the form of a dragon's tooth. It's not 2008 yet. You must be *there*." She frowned. "But you're *here*. Does that mean you're not *there* right now? Or does it mean that you're not really *here*?"

"I do not know." Orion nuzzled her again. "I believe that I am here."

"What are you going to do?" she asked after a moment.

"I will wait in Cumae for my firestorm." He spoke slowly, but she could hear that he'd decided upon his path.

"What if it *is* over and you missed your chance?"

"Then I have failed. But I must wait to seek out my fellow *Pyr*."

"You don't want to mess up their chances in that war."

"Indeed. I must not encounter them again before my departure in 2011."

"That's a long time. Almost forty years."

She felt him shrug. He gave her a caress, his fingers warm against her skin. "Perhaps I will not be lonely, Francesca," he murmured in a soft rumble that made her smile. He kissed her then, a sweet searing kiss, but not one that eased her concerns.

She wasn't going to be in Cumae forever. This summer, her second, should be her last. What would Orion do when she went back to the States?

How could she ask him that when she was the one who said she didn't want a commitment?

She turned over and he pulled her closer again, his breath becoming deeper as he dozed off again.

It seemed as if there was no hope of them being a couple for long, which should have pleased Francesca more than it did. Maybe that was why the darkfire had brought Orion here. Maybe he would help Francesca heal so that she could fall in love when the right guy came along for her.

Funny. She hadn't believed in the right guy before or in waiting for The One. That sounded too much like a destined mate. She thought relationships were made not found, but this dragon shifter was shaking up her assumptions—and she liked it. She didn't even want to think about the end of their partnership, however it happened. She snuggled closer to Orion. She was going to follow her own advice and enjoy the moment.

She'd worry about the future when it happened and not a moment before.

———

ON SATURDAY, Francesca chose to work. It would be a good day to get some clear photographs of the newly discovered sanctuary with the workers off for the day. Orion was mysterious about his plans and she teased him that she hoped they included dinner.

Before taking the Vespa to Cumae, though, she went to the post office.

She called one of her big brothers every Saturday to check in.

Today, it was Rafe's turn.

Francesca only had to wait about twenty minutes for the operator to get a trunk line, then she was sent to a numbered booth for her call. The phone there rang and she picked up.

"Frannie!" Rafe said, his usual cheerful self. There was a bit of a delay on the line, as usual. "I'm glad you called early. We've got one crazy Saturday lined up and I was afraid I'd miss you."

"What's happening at Chez Marino today?"

"Maddy's taking Mike for a mom-and-baby swim at the Y..."

Francesca smiled. "Blowing bubbles together."

"Pretty much. She went last month, too, and they both seemed to like it."

"And you're being the house husband?"

"Ha. I've got a racquetball tournament, then I'll make dinner. How about you? You don't have anything to do with this fabulous new discovery in Cumae, do you? Or did the competition beat you to something cool?"

"It's in the news?"

"Not on the front page, but as soon as I saw it, I thought of you. The pictures aren't very good."

"Because I'm still taking them. We haven't let the media into the site yet."

"Then you are part of it."

"I found it, Rafe. It's amazing..."

"Wait a minute. Wait a minute. The article says that some guy found it. Hang on." There was a distant rustle. "Dr. Thomas. You know him?"

"He's my advisor for my thesis, so kind of my boss."

Rafe gave a mirthless laugh. "Well, this makes it sound like he's working alone, in all his considerable brilliance."

Francesca gripped the phone. "It has to at least *mention* me."

"Not a word, sister dear. Like I said, it sounds as if he's all alone in the hidden cave."

Francesca's ire rose. "I found it," she said. "I'm running the team that's documenting it."

"Meanwhile he's writing all the articles and not sharing credit. Very nice. Look, Frannie, I know you're not supposed to rock the boat and all that, but if that's the situation, you need to stand up for yourself. You need to ask questions and worst case, get some witnesses and documentation of your part in this. He should at least be giving you credit, even if he takes all the credit because of seniority."

"I know." She took a breath. "Okay, I'll talk to him today."

"Is he old?"

"Not very."

"Then maybe it's just an oversight. The press don't always listen to the details, and sometimes they get them wrong."

"Sometimes. I'll look up the article and talk to Dr. Thomas. Maybe it *is* just an oversight."

"That's it. Nobody ever had to tell you to stand up for yourself." There was pride in his tone and Francesca smiled at the sound of it. "What else is going on?"

She took a breath, then decided to confide in him. "Well, I met this guy."

"Excellent. You need someone to appreciate you." Rafe cleared his throat. "Assuming that he does?"

"He does. He's kind of great." Francesca found herself smiling.

"Tell me."

"His name's Orion. He's Greek and he knows all the stories." She left out the dragon shifter bit.

"Aha! Another history buff."

"He tells the myths as if he was there, like he knew the gods personally. He's a great storyteller. He says his dad was a storyteller, too."

"Sounds perfect."

"But it's not a thing, you know. It's just casual."

"You never can tell. I never thought Maddy and I would have a thing. She ticked me off so much, but then I ended up finding the day kind of flat if she didn't set me straight on something. I guess it was inevitable after that."

Francesca smiled. Her brother and his wife had their stormy moments, but she knew they both enjoyed the drama and the passion. "The course of love never runs true?" she teased and he laughed.

"But it doesn't have to be the same for everyone, Frannie. Follow your heart. Do what feels right."

"I am, but I think he might leave."

"Visa problems, huh? Enjoy the moment. You don't have to always be planning for your retirement together. And maybe you can follow him home when and if he does." Rafe chuckled. "Maybe he'll come back for you in the end. I can believe that you'd be hard to forget, little sister."

"Thanks, Rafe. I'm just taking it a day at a time."

"Excellent plan. I'm glad you're happy." Someone shouted in the background and he covered the receiver to reply, then spoke again. "I'm late, Frannie. Gotta go."

"It's good talking to you. I hope you win that match."

"Me, too. Chuck is always too sure of himself. It's fun to take him down a notch. And hey, be sure you speak up about getting credit. We all know you're a star, but sometimes other people have to be reminded."

"Okay. Will do."

"Go for it, Frannie. I'm ready to have some fame in the family. You could be like that guy who found King Tut."

"Howard Carter," Francesca said. "As long as I don't have to be Lord Carnarvon."

"Why?"

"He's the one who died of an infected mosquito bite, and started the rumor of the curse."

"Right. Don't go that way, Frannie. Take care and I'll tell Gabe you called."

"Bye, Rafe." Francesca ended the call then went to pay for it, thinking about her brother's advice. He was right. She'd talk to Dr. Thomas today.

IT WAS clear to Orion that Francesca did not cook. The kitchen in her apartment was woefully equipped—and he was from centuries in the past. His expectations of implements and pots were low, but her kitchen was beneath even his threshold. He understood the stove to an extent from his time with the future *Pyr*. The refrigerator, he knew, should have contained more than cream for her coffee and left-over pizza.

Perhaps she had never learned. Perhaps she did not care.

Orion not only knew how to cook—within limits—but he enjoyed it. He also liked to eat and while pizza was not a bad meal, it had already lost its appeal with repetition.

When he was paid his wages on Friday, he knew he had the power to create a change.

Armed with his cash and a shopping bag he found in the cupboard, Orion sought a market. Some things did not change through the eras and he found one in a plaza, filled with tables that were loaded with local produce. Although he did not speak Italian, he learned some phrases that morning and there was much that could be accomplished with the point of a finger. He offered coins to each vendor to pay for his choices, watching what they chose and learned something of the currency, as well. He recalled the meal at the taverna, the garlic and tomatoes, the olives and the other vegetables, and sought to reproduce it.

He bought bread and cheese, rice and lentils, lemons and a fresh chicken to roast the next day. One farmer who sold him a lot of vegetables gave him a bouquet of wildflowers as well. He bought table wine, relying upon the recommendation of the shopkeeper and carried home his purchases.

They would now eat like kings.

He had seen a shop with women taking in laundry, a service which also had not changed. He gathered his clothing from the apartment and took it to them in another bag. Their conversation involved a lot of hand signals, but he understood that he could collect it later in the afternoon. The one woman frowned at the blood in his T-shirt, but he showed her the healing wound. She clearly thought there couldn't have been so much blood from that injury, then her companion made a wrenching motion with her hands and laughed.

Perhaps he had been killing chickens. Orion laughed along with them and let them believe what they wished to.

He met his new friends, the Greek fishermen, when they docked that afternoon and chose from their catch, as arranged. He knew the small sea bass, each large enough for a single serving. *"Lavraki,"* he called them and the fishermen agreed, then told him they were "branzino" in Italian. He bought four, then returned to the apartment, venturing out again for a larger pan for the oven. He happily made a sauce that afternoon, letting it simmer, pinching herbs from the pots on the terrace.

While the sauce simmered, he retrieved his clean clothing from the women in the shop. He didn't have to feign his delight. It was soft and clean, folded and smelled like sunshine. He was fulsome in his appreciation and even with the language barrier, the women were beaming with pride when he left.

Back at the apartment, he chopped vegetables to make a bed for the fish, then cleaned the fish when he thought Francesca might soon return. He had to watch the oven closely, but that was much like watching a fire in his view, ensuring that it was neither too hot nor too cold. He set two places on the counter, put the flowers in the only vase Francesca possessed, and his stomach growled at the smell of the roasting fish.

Now he could fret, as his father once had worried, that the meal would be ready before anyone arrived to eat.

To his relief, Orion heard the key in the lock. He looked up as Francesca entered and noticed that her eyes were flashing with fury before her expression changed to astonishment. She stepped into the apartment, surveying his preparations with a kind of awe, and then slowly, she smiled. He did not imagine that she blinked away a few tears, but any confession of whatever had troubled her could wait. She set down a large envelope on her desk and he wondered what it contained.

Whatever concerned her, a good meal always went a long way to improve one's view of the world. Orion knew this meal would be delicious.

CHAPTER TWELVE

W hen she headed home Saturday night, Francesca was hot and tired. Worse, she was angry after her conversation with Dr. Thomas. She felt defeated and resentful that she couldn't change a thing. She supposed she'd have to figure out a solution for dinner, but didn't really feel like it.

She was done with men again.

How could Dr. Thomas think his choice was justified?

How could he criticize the first draft of her thesis so harshly?

She was afraid she'd be revising it and having him find it unacceptable for the rest of her life. She'd thought that having him as an advisor would be a great fit, but his comments were scathing.

And it hurt.

Her apartment door was locked, which she hadn't expected. Was Orion gone? Maybe he'd left for good while she was at work, but then, she doubted she'd be good company on this particular night. All the same, it was hard to believe that he wouldn't say goodbye.

That had to be why she felt disappointed by the prospect of his absence.

She frowned and unlocked the door, even as she acknowledged

that someone nearby was going to have a fantastic dinner. She could smell fish and vegetables roasting, but she didn't have the funds to eat out every night. She felt a stab of jealousy for that lucky individual.

Then the door swung open and she saw Orion in her kitchen.

Her apartment looked different. It seemed warmer and more welcoming, but maybe that was because of the vase of wildflowers on the counter. Several candles had been lit and the window to the terrace was open, the sky darkening beyond. Two places were set at the counter and that wonderful smell was coming from her apartment. She couldn't quite believe it, but she blinked and he was still standing there, watching her as if he was concerned. "You cooked," she said, even though that was obvious.

He bowed slightly. "As much as I appreciate the pizza and you providing it, Francesca, I would vary the fare."

She smiled. "I get tired of pizza, too."

"I am relieved not to be alone in this."

She sighed. "But I don't cook so it's often pizza."

"This is clear, Francesca, but I gladly assume this task." He gestured to the counter and she smiled as she approached. There was a dish of olives, some fresh bread and an array of cheeses. There was a bottle of wine and that heavenly smell of even more.

"You cooked," she said again as if she could not comprehend it.

"Do men not cook in these times?"

"Only my brothers as far as I've seen. That smells fabulous."

"And why would I cook a meal that did not smell appetizing?" he asked and she laughed.

She put down her purse, kicking off her shoes, feeling better already. She washed her hands and offered to help but he indicated her seat. Francesca opened the wine and poured two glasses, stealing an olive from the small dish and a piece of fresh bread. "I'm starving."

"I am hungry as well," he said. "I guessed when you would arrive, but feared I might be mistaken."

"Perfect timing?"

He cast her a smile that warmed her to her toes. "Perfect, Francesca."

She inhaled with appreciation when he removed the roasted fish from the oven, already feeling more cheerful. She then shook her head at the quantity of food. "Who else is coming?"

"No one."

"There are *four* fish, Orion."

"But they are small. Two each, surely."

Francesca didn't think they were that small. "Just one for me."

"Then I will eat the other. Fear not. It will not be wasted." He indicated a whole fish, then glanced at her. "Are you in the custom of removing the skin and bones, or should I do it?"

"You're probably better at it than me."

He nodded and slid the fish to a cutting board. He made quick work of removing the head and tail, the skin and bones, working with a pair of knives. He then placed the filets on a bed of rice. He surrounded the fish with vegetables and set the plate before her, then prepared another plate for himself. It was lovely to be served, and once again in his presence, she felt spoiled. When he sat down and she'd thanked him, they toasted each other with the wine then dug in.

"Ah, the timing was excellent," he said with satisfaction after he'd tried the fish. "You need this," he instructed, offering her a wedge of lemon. She dutifully squeezed its juice over the fish, echoing his gesture.

It was delicious. "It's really fresh. Where did you get it?"

"When you returned to the grotto the other day, I went for a walk. I met some Greek fishermen at the wharf. They offered to sell me fish fresh from their catch if I arrived in a timely manner today." His brows rose. "I was timely."

"I'm glad."

Orion told her about the vegetable market, which she vaguely remembered was held each Saturday morning in a nearby square, and enthused about his purchases. He had found the bakery and the wine store, as well as the funny little place that sold everything at a discount and was so crowded with merchandise that there was hardly any room for customers.

"And what of your day?" he asked. "Did you finish the photographs?"

"Not quite." Francesca put down her fork and eyed him as she had an idea. "Will you answer a question for me?"

"If I can."

"You've been to the future."

Orion nodded.

"Is it different?"

"It is different in many ways, of course. All matters change with time."

"But is it different for women? Or do men still expect them to be barefoot and pregnant, cooking and cleaning and being subservient all the time?"

He looked up, his expression puzzled. "The women wore shoes then as now, and I do not think all of them were with child."

Francesca smiled despite herself. "I mean traditional gender roles. Do women still do all the housework, run the errands, act like everyone's mother? Or can they make choices of their own?"

"You dislike that I cooked?"

"No, I think it's great. I love that you don't expect me to cook. And you didn't make a huge mess for me to clean up."

"I clean my own tools," he said firmly and if she could have fallen in love with a man, Francesca would have fallen for Orion right in that moment.

"I mean about work. Are women equal in the future? Do they get equal pay for equal work and have equal opportunities? Can they pursue their career, if they want one, the way that men pursue their careers? Or do they always have to be the one to make sacrifices?"

Orion considered this as he finished his meal. "I do not know. We were warriors and spoke to few women in that time." He shrugged. "Save, of course, for the mates of the *Pyr* of future days."

"And what are they like?"

"They all had work of their own before the firestorms sparked," he said. "In fact, the *Pyr* of the future are partners with their mates. The women are not merely vessels, as you have previously suggested."

"But they did conceive when the firestorm sparked, regardless of what they were doing at the time?"

He nodded. "The firestorm does not compromise in its essence."

But maybe being with a dragon dude was worth it. Francesca could definitely see the appeal. "Tell me about them," she said, still thinking.

Orion moved aside his plate. "The spell was broken the first time during the firestorm of Donovan Shea, the Warrior of the *Pyr*. Only one of our kind was freed then, Nikolas."

Francesca thought of the guy planting the weird seeds and how he had been one short.

"Donovan's mate is a scientist and inventor. She had created a vehicle fueled by water instead of..." He snapped his fingers, searching for the word, appealing to her.

"Instead of gasoline?"

He nodded. "That was the word. The 'Wizard', they called her, though she insisted there was no sorcery among her skills. Alex Madison in the city of Minneapolis." He smiled. "Named for a warrior and wed to one. It is apt. She was not to be deterred."

Francesca got her pen and notepad and began to make notes. "Who else?"

"There was one *Pyr* already mated when the spell was broken, Quinn Tyrrell, the Smith of our kind."

"Smith?"

"He has the skill to repair our scales. It passes from father to son.

His mate is Sara Keegan, the Seer. She receives prophecies about our kind, though I believe she was skeptical at first."

"Didn't she always have that ability?"

"I believe she gained it during the firestorm."

How interesting that the firestorm could provoke more changes than the conception of a child. "Does she have a career?"

"She owns a bookstore."

Francesca nodded approval of that. A woman running her own business, whatever it might be, was all good in her view. The future *Pyr* were two for two.

Orion continued. "The spell upon the dragon's teeth was broken during the firestorm of Erik Sorensson, the leader of the *Pyr*. His mate is a scholar, like you, though her work favors myths and stories." Francesca looked up with interest. "I remember her saying that the best tales have their toes in the truth."

"I like her already." Francesca couldn't help thinking of Schliemann and Troy.

"Their firestorm was in London."

Francesca thought about the teeth being sown in her dream. That could have been London.

"Her name is—or will be—Eileen Grosvenor." He paused, frowning. "I wonder if she has even been born in this time."

"I don't think we should start thinking about that," Francesca said. "It's too confusing."

"Indeed."

"Who else?"

"The next firestorm was that of Delaney Shea, Donovan's brother. His mate, Ginger, had a farm for milk."

"A dairy farm."

"Yes. It was organic and the cows were of certain breeds."

"Heritage cows?" Francesca asked, thinking she would like these mates a lot.

"This is it. We did not know them so well as the *Pyr* who had his firestorm next. Niall Talbot. He lived in New York and we aided in his quest to eliminate the shadow dragons, of which his twin brother was one. His mate, Roxanne, created the art on people's skin."

Francesca left the question of shadow dragons for the moment. "Tattoos?" she suggested.

"Yes! She had a shop and considerable skill, especially in the depiction of dragons." He frowned. "Imagination Ink," he said and Francesca wrote it down, assuming it was the name of Roxanne's tattoo shop. "Rafferty Powell was next, of the line of the Cantor. His mate, Melissa Smith, spoke on the bright screens of the news."

"Television. She was a newscaster? A reporter?"

He shrugged. "Something of this nature. She persuaded Erik Sorensson to allow her to create a show about the *Pyr*. There was much debate about this, but the war against the *Slayers* was going badly and the darkfire was allied with Melissa in this."

"When was this?"

"2011."

"And there was darkfire then?"

"There has always been darkfire, Francesca. It is associated with our kind, but it vanishes for long intervals. Rafferty's line have a connection with it, and his forebear was the Cantor, but I do not know the details." He shook his head. "Much was said that I did not understand."

"Does he have long dark hair?"

At Orion's nod, she continued. "I think I heard him sing."

Orion's surprise was evident.

"In my dream."

"Ah, the one you did not have," he teased and she laughed.

"He planted things in his garden and sang to them. His song made the ground tremble and leap."

Orion's eyes gleamed with pale fire. "And what happened?"

"The ground split open and men stepped out of the soil. Warriors." It sounded crazy, proof that it was a dream, but Francesca had a feeling it was another impossible thing for her list. "It was night and they were hard to see, but they kept stepping out of the furrows. And they took flight in pairs, shifting into dragons when they leapt into the air."

"Francesca! You say you do not dream, but you have dreamed of our release! What else?"

"Nothing. Just that. In one dream, he planted seeds and in the second, the warriors came from the soil. I've only ever had two dreams." Their gazes met and held, then she continued softly. "I couldn't tell if one of them was you."

"One of them *was* me," Orion said with heat.

She was afraid that he might become grim again about lost opportunity, so urged him to continue. "Tell me more about mates."

He inhaled and frowned, looking into the distance. "If there was another firestorm and mate, we did not witness it. That was when the darkfire carried us into the past. Drake, our leader, collected the stone from Lorenzo. He was a magician for the theater with a show in Las Vegas."

Francesca made a note. "So, it was different for the mates," she said, looking over her list. Here she'd thought that being a destined mate would mean that the women were chattel, but they sounded like they were on more equal footing with their partners than most women she knew. "All of these women had careers." She glanced up. "And the firestorm means that they all had sons, too."

Orion nodded. "Save Erik, whose mate bore a daughter."

"I thought the *Pyr* only had sons."

"There is a single exception. At any time, there is one female *Pyr*, who has the powers of prophecy among other gifts."

"Like the Sibyl."

"Yes, that is so. But during Erik's firestorm, the Wyvern died. She chose to sacrifice herself, for the good of the *Pyr*, but also because she had made a transgression."

"What was that?"

His lips tightened to a grim line. "She loved the first of my fellows to break free of the spell."

Francesca flipped back through her notes. "Nikolas?"

"And he loved her, but it is forbidden for there to be congress among our kind. They violated our customs."

Forbidden love. Francesca made a note.

"And so, when she perceived that someone would die in the quest to destroy the Academy, Sophie willingly took that role." He looked down. "And Nikolas could not be halted from following her into peril."

"Was this Academy destroyed?"

Orion nodded. "But they were both lost. They died together."

"Maybe that was what they wanted."

"Perhaps so, but in the absence of a Wyvern, when Erik's firestorm was satisfied, his mate bore a daughter."

"A new Wyvern!"

"So it is suspected, but she had as yet no powers when we departed. Our sons come into their *Pyr* skills at puberty and it may also be thus for her. I cannot say. The Wyvern and her ways are shrouded in mystery."

Francesca looked at her notes. "When does this Dragon's Tail War start?"

"It was said to be linked to an astrological event, a time of reconciliation and restoration. I do not know the date it began, but it was to end in November 2015. After that date, there would be only *Pyr* or *Slayers*, no longer both."

Having met two *Slayers*, Francesca could understand his concern about the outcome of that battle. "You could kill Mr. Montmorency and Sigmund now, then they wouldn't be a threat in the future."

Orion winced. "Though it is tempting, I am not sure of the merit of this notion. Sigmund, as I recall, was the lost son of Erik Sorensson. There was a reconciliation between father and son during Erik's second firestorm. When I thought I had killed Sigmund, not realizing his identity, I feared that my actions would cheat Erik of that appeasement."

Francesca could understand that. "What about Mr. Montmorency?"

"He has a large part in the war ahead," Orion said. "It is impossible to anticipate all the repercussions of an early demise on his part. Plus, I remember now, he and Rafferty were ancient adversaries. Again, much was resolved in their final confrontation."

"Can you tell me who won?"

He smiled. "Rafferty triumphed, but speak of this to no other before such events occur."

"Wait a minute. You said Erik had a second firestorm."

"His mate was reincarnated. It was, or will be, most unusual."

"She's the one who collects stories," Francesca remembered. "Eileen Grosvenor."

"Yes. She was from Chicago, though they met in London."

Francesca made a note.

"And now I have surrendered many tales," Orion said, leaning across the counter. "I ask only one of you in return, Francesca."

She met his gaze, dreading what he would ask.

"Tell me what angered you this day," he invited.

And she smiled in relief, more than glad to do that.

———

ORION POURED MORE wine while Francesca frowned at her plate. "I called my brother today, like I always do, and he'd read about the discovery in Cumae."

The speed that tidings traveled in the modern world still amazed Orion, but he knew better than to comment upon it. He simply nodded.

"But the thing is, he asked if I knew about it. And he did that because the article gave all the credit to Dr. Thomas for the discovery." Francesca took a large sip of wine, her eyes starting to flash again.

"He was not even there."

"No! He wasn't. I stopped at the newsstand and found several articles on it. Every single one was the same. They all said it was Dr. Thomas' discovery and several had comments from his assistant, Larry."

She was fuming and Orion guessed why. "But there was no mention of you?"

"Not a word! So, I asked him today at the museum, and he had a lot of excuses. Finally, he said that he let Larry give a quote because Larry needs to establish his career. He'll have a family to support so it's important for him to get a solid footing."

Her eyes were ablaze.

"And you presumably will not experience this concern?"

"Not according to Dr. Thomas. He made some comment under his breath that I'd probably be pregnant in a couple of years, maybe teaching adult education classes in history at a community college after my kids grew up, and they had a good chuckle together. I wanted to punch them both."

"I assume you did not," Orion said mildly and she smiled.

"No. There wasn't a lot of time to respond, anyway, because he'd finished reading my thesis."

Orion guessed that his lack of comprehension showed.

"It's a composition about my research, which hopefully will result in my getting my doctoral degree." She gestured to the fat envelope. "He doesn't agree with my thesis, which is fine, but I thought his criticism was harsh."

"It is not fair and I believe you are justified in your anger. But I think I am right in saying that you are reliant upon this Dr. Thomas?"

"He's my advisor for my graduate degree. He could make my life miserable if he wanted to, and he could keep me from advancing at the speed I want."

"And so you are beholden to a leader whose tactics you do not admire. The situation frustrates you, doubly so because you believe you cannot change it."

"Pretty much."

Orion nodded and chose his words with care. "Though my labor is different from yours, still I have experienced something similar. I have had commanders whose judgement I did not trust, and whose orders I did not find suitable. Still, when you are a warrior, it is your obligation to obey. A wise man told me that I should learn from such foibles and errors, so that if and when I was in a position of authority, I could lead my men better."

She eyed him, sipping her wine. "That's actually good advice."

"It is. When you are in this position of authority, you can choose differently. You can mentor those beneath you. You can encourage them. You can ensure that they receive credit for their efforts." He smiled at her. "And they will love you for it, Francesca. Such a course breeds loyalty like no other."

"Do you think so?"

"If this Larry were to be offered an opportunity he perceived to be better, would he remain with Dr. Thomas?"

"Probably not. I doubt I would."

"Exactly. But those leaders who treat their soldiers with respect will find those soldiers following them, independent of other offers. Their loyalty will not permit them to do otherwise."

He watched Francesca nod. When she smiled at him this time, her gaze was warm again. "The best part of that advice is that it gives you a plan. Something to do rather than just fume about injustice."

"It does." He dared to continue. "And it is true that one who is skeptical of a scheme or a notion can be your ally in the end."

"How so?"

"Because you cannot be casual with your references and arguments. You must build a stronger case to convince the skeptic, and buttress your argument. It is a good practice to seek every possible objection before presenting any plan, to be prepared for the greatest possible obstruction."

She was thinking about this. "So, you end up making a better argument, because you need to convince someone who doesn't agree with you?"

"Exactly."

"That's really clever." She spun on the stool a little bit. "You see, my thesis is about women with special powers, like the Sibyl, having more agency. Agency means they can make choices that affect their lives and situations." She snapped her fingers. "Helen had no agency. Men made choices for her. But the Sibyl declined the favors of Apollo. She must have believed she had the right to do that."

"Perhaps because she had prophetic gifts that she was not obligated to share," Orion said. "While Helen was a beautiful child that all could look upon, regardless of her opinion."

Francesca nodded. "And the Amazon queen could challenge Alexander, because they had fighting skills. So, these women's abilities influenced their amount of agency." She turned to look at the wall of books. "I have to look for more examples. I have to broaden my perspective to make a better argument. I can check out all the other mortal women who declined the advances of gods and look for patterns..."

Orion could feel her excitement and was pleased he had been able to assist. He began to clean up the kitchen, stealing glances at Francesca. Her eyes were alight, her enthusiasm a tangible force. She moved quickly, making a stack of books on her desk, murmuring to herself. Her expression and posture were completely transformed.

"This is great," she said finally, coming back to the counter. "Who gave you that advice?"

"My father, of course. He was wise beyond all others." He turned his attention to the pan he was washing, ignoring the tightness in his chest.

"You miss him," she said finally.

Orion wasn't in the habit of speaking from the heart, not in the company of his fellow warriors, but he trusted the impulse to confess this weakness to Francesca. "I dislike that we parted in anger. It haunts me. If I could have one wish, it would be the opportunity to reconcile with him."

"Even more than your firestorm?"

"Even more."

"That's surprising."

It should have been, but it didn't surprise Orion. He turned to her then chose to speak his mind. Once before, he had not said all that he could have said, and he regretted that. He would not regret it again. "My firestorm will not be with you, Francesca, yet I know that no other woman will capture my heart with such speed and power as you have done. Thus I cannot yearn for my firestorm as once I did."

"Orion!" She left her chair and came around the counter, backing him into the wall as she kissed him with a fervor. Her passionate reaction to his confession filled him with joy. He caught her close and lifted her from her feet, kissing her deeply.

His father also said that a man's deeds were a more reliable measure than his words. He would show Francesca of his admiration for her, even if it meant neither of them slept on this night.

Indeed, he could not resist the temptation to please her, again and again.

————

IT WAS Thursday of the following week that Francesca had unexpected company. She was working alone in their private space at the museum, creating the display panels for her segment on the Cumaean Sibyl. Dr. Thomas was in Cumae and Larry was at the underwater city, documenting that mural. After her discussion with Dr. Thomas, she'd left the subject alone, agreeing to disagree—and taking Orion's advice to plan for the future. The students she advised and mentored were going to adore her.

She was working whenever she could on the revisions to her dissertation and just as Orion had forecast, she could feel her argument becoming stronger with every addition. Dr. Thomas had done her a favor with his critical comments.

She and Orion were living each day to the fullest. He worked at Cumae in the daytime, then cooked dinner at night. They talked and walked and made love, and Francesca didn't think she'd ever been happier. On this particular morning, she'd awakened to the smell of fresh coffee and thought she'd died and gone to heaven. She just wanted this magic to go on and on.

"Signora Marino?" a man said from the doorway, his voice more than familiar.

Francesca jumped to her feet. "Mr. Montmorency. How nice to see you here."

It was a lie. There was nothing nice about welcoming Mr. Montmorency on her own. He exuded an aura of menace that had Francesca ensuring she didn't turn her back on him.

He was wearing a navy suit that had to be too warm for the sunny spring day they were enjoying. His shirt was crisp and white, his cuffs French, his shoes polished to a gleam. His tie had to be silk and was perfectly knotted, but the gaze was as cold as that of a lizard.

"I was in the area and thought to visit my prize," he said silkily. He approached Francesca as a predator might advance upon lunch. Even in human form, his smile seemed very dragon-like. "I do miss it in my little collection and can't help fearing that something will befall it when it's out of my sight."

He'd come to make trouble. He knew it had been broken in Cumae, and he wanted to make sure that Francesca was blamed.

She smiled. "Of course. It's such a lovely piece. Come and see the display. It's not completed yet, but it is coming together. Your vase will be here, in the first alcove, in the place of honor."

He stood in front of the display, his gaze flicking over the array of photographs, even as he exuded impatience.

Francesca had gathered images of the Cumaean Sibyl, including paintings and sculptures, even some illustrations from marginalia of medieval manuscripts, and created a collage background of them all. In each of the four sections, a saying about the Sibyl or attributed to her was on a banner above that section, then there was a block of copy on each panel, discussing some detail of her story. Recessed into the middle of each panel, about chest-high, was a glass-fronted mirrored and lit box where one of the vases would be displayed.

"'The last age, sung of by the Cumaean Sibyl, is coming; the great cycle of ages is beginning again from the beginning...'" Mr. Montmorency read from the top of the panel above the space for his vase. "Vergil."

"From the Eclogue, yes." Francesca gestured to the display. "You see, each vase will be visible but also secured, so that there can be no threat to it. Dr. Thomas is very serious about security."

Mr. Montmorency harrumphed but she ignored him.

She indicated the type beside that first display box, which thanked Mr. Magnus Montmorency for the generous loan of the piece for the duration of the exhibit. "I was going to ask you if you would like the attribution to be like this, or if you would rather it was anonymous. The other lenders are museums, but in the case of a private supporter, we can withhold your name."

"I don't care about my name on the display," he said, spinning to face her. "I want to see my vase."

"Of course. I'll just get it from the secured storage room." Francesca smiled, well aware that he was puzzled by her attitude. She knew as well as he did that it had been shattered. She had been the one to break it, after all.

He stood, tapping his toe, as she retrieved the vase. She enjoyed that it had been wrapped up again for its return from Cumae and that she could stretch out the delay until he saw it again. The temperature seemed to rise in the room as she patiently unwrapped the padding. She finally removed the last piece and the vase was revealed, stopper in place, seal intact.

He made a choking sound.

Francesca sighed. "It is lovely. The patina on this piece of Roman glass is truly admirable. I predict that it will be a favorite among attendees."

He seized the vase while she was speaking, lifting it to his eye as he examined it. He took it to a brighter light and peered at the seal, then at the stopper, then seemed to struggle to compose himself. When he returned to place it on the table again, his smile was taut. "Not so much as a speck of dust upon it."

"We take care of our prizes, Mr. Montmorency, even if they're only borrowed."

Their gazes locked them, his own filled with animosity, and Francesca willed herself to remain serene. She held his gaze as if she were completely innocent, fully aware that he knew otherwise.

He was the one to clear his throat and avert his gaze first. "You had a workman here," he said tightly.

"We have many workmen here, Mr. Montmorency. Even more since the need for repair here at the museum."

"A Greek. Dark with silvery-blue eyes." He eyed her, a challenge in his glance.

"I think I know the man you mean," Francesca said. "He isn't here anymore." It wasn't a lie. Orion wasn't at the museum. He was working at Cumae.

"Where did he go?"

"I have no idea," she lied, holding his gaze steadily. "Perhaps he returned to wherever he was from."

She saw the flash of annoyance in Mr. Montmorency's eyes and the way his nostrils pinched at his sharp intake of breath. Then he spun on his heel and marched away, crossing the hall at a crisp pace. He slowed in the exhibit hall beyond, probably to consider the damage—or maybe the corrosion from *Slayer* blood etched in the floor.

"Have a nice day, Mr. Montmorency," Francesca said, unable to resist taunting him a little.

He pivoted to glare at her. "Thank you, Signora Marino," he said, biting off the words. "Perhaps we will meet again soon."

Perhaps he was unable to disguise the quiver of rage in his tone. With one final hard look at her, he pivoted and left the museum.

"Perhaps not," Francesca said under her breath as she lifted the vase to return it to the storage room.

———

MAGNUS MONTMORENCY WAS FURIOUS.

How could the vase be repaired? He had gone to the museum to ensure that Signora Marino was humiliated in the hope of drawing out her *Pyr* protector. But his vase was intact. Even the seal that he had damaged himself was as perfect as the day he had surrendered it in Rome.

How could this be?

And she knew, she knew there was some trickery. He could see as much in her eyes, in her manner of superiority. She believed he could not find her protector.

Magnus was tempted to hunt down that *Pyr* and see him dead. But he was a formidable opponent.

Two would be better in that battle, and he could smell Sigmund in close proximity.

———

SIGMUND WAS FEELING sorry for himself. He was sitting in his hotel room in Baiae, wishing he'd never left Rome. Unlike Magnus Montmorency, he couldn't spontaneously manifest elsewhere, and unlike Magnus, he didn't have endless supplies of cash. He was running a bit low on resources, too low to race back to Rome in the hope that Magnus was at home.

And his eye still hurt like hell. It had been almost a week and the eye was still bloodshot. Worse, the pupil was dark. He was afraid he was going to lose the vision in that eye and that it would permanently look different from the other.

Someone knocked on the door to his room and he didn't even have the energy to be cautious. He opened the door, astounded to find Magnus Montmorency there.

The *Slayer* smiled. He was neatly attired but there was a fire in his eyes that didn't bode well for somebody. Sigmund had to hope that wasn't him.

Magnus was also in perfect health, which meant he had figured out how to make the Dragon's Blood Elixir—and he had access to it.

Then Magnus put his hand into the pocket of his suit jacket, removing a small bottle, like one that might be used for eye drops. There was no label on it.

"I believe you need this," he said, offering it to Sigmund.

Sigmund looked at the bottle in awe. "That isn't..."

"It is. There's only one drop. I wouldn't want you to develop *needs*."

The Dragon's Blood Elixir. Sigmund took the bottle with a shaking hand. The Elixir was said to have remarkable healing powers, to be able to bring a wounded *Pyr* or *Slayer* back from the cusp of death and make him whole again. There were mysterious allusions in the old sources to additional powers that came with prolonged use, which was what he wanted to know more about. "Why are you giving this to me?"

"I thought it was what you wanted." Magnus moved to take the bottle back, but Sigmund held it out of the *Slayer's* reach. Magnus chuckled. He nodded and Sigmund opened the bottle. He took a breath, fearing the worst, then quickly put the single drop into his eye.

He could feel the eye healing. If he had a mirror, he was sure he could have watched it. As it was, he could only watch the dawning satisfaction in Magnus' expression.

"It's miraculous," he whispered.

"No. It's an ancient formula of remarkable power. There are no miracles here."

"I still don't understand why you gave it to me."

"Because I want you to be in my debt, of course." Magnus' smile faded. "Do you know who he is?"

There was no doubt who the *Slayer* meant.

"No. I thought you did."

Magnus shook his head. "Was it a firestorm?"

"No, but there were similarities."

"I don't like surprises," the *Slayer* said with impatience and Sigmund nodded agreement. "Do you know where he came from?"

This time, Sigmund shook his head. "It's as if he came out of thin air."

"Then I think he should return there." Magnus lifted a brow, inviting Sigmund's opinion. "Shall we offer encouragement to that effect?"

Sigmund, his eye completely healed, was ready to agree.

———

ORION SAT ON THE TERRACE, staring at the sky, after Francesca went to bed. The moon was full, its light shining on the sea, and the sight, for some unexpected reason, made him yearn for all he had lost.

Was that why he could not sleep?

No, he felt that something was amiss. He felt a sense of pending doom, perhaps a portent. He had smelled *Slayer* several times on this day, and he did not like it. He had roasted a chicken on this night and Francesca had eaten well, telling him about the progress of her research. Orion had found it difficult to concentrate. While she worked in the evening, he had fortified his dragonsmoke barrier around Francesca's apartment, then they had loved slowly.

He listened to her breathing and could not dismiss his sense that all came to an end.

But why?

And why in this moment?

What observations were feeding his intuitive sense that this night was a crossroads of a kind?

There was a flicker of light behind him and Orion glanced back at the darkened apartment. This time, he was quick enough to see a blue-green spark in the quartz crystal. He moved slowly to the stone and picked it up, only to find it dark again. He knew so little of darkfire, but still he distrusted it.

He disliked the darkfire almost as much as he disliked his lack of anyone to ask for advice. He had to chart a course alone, with little information, darkfire and no counsel.

Orion put down the stone with impatience and turned away. His gaze lingered on the tape recorder where he'd left it after finishing the Aeneid, and he realized the solution was right before him.

In the poem, Aeneas had asked the Cumaean Sibyl to take him to the underworld, so he could confer with his father. They had departed on that journey from the grotto that he and Francesca had discovered, not an hour's walk from this very place.

Orion could ask his father for advice. Consulting with the dead could not change the future or influence the fates of his fellow *Pyr*. He looked toward Francesca, who was sleeping deeply. Her eyes moved beneath her lids and he knew she dreamed, despite her insistence that she never did as much. His heart squeezed tightly as he watched her. Her expression was so serene that he did not wish to disturb her.

Indeed, he could not ask anyone to visit the realm of the dead with him.

His smoke barrier was buttressed.

The *Slayers* were unlikely to attack again in the absence of a firestorm.

The Sibyl had departed from her glass vessel in Cumae, when the new grotto had been revealed. If Orion was to find her or her voice anywhere, it would be there. Impulsively, he picked up the quartz crystal from the sill and put it in his pocket, kissed Francesca's temple, then left before he could change his mind.

CHAPTER THIRTEEN

F rancesca dreamed.

She saw a company of men, much like the group in the square where she had first glimpsed Orion. There were perhaps twenty of them, dressed in that unusual garb that Orion had been wearing when she met him. They stood in a courtyard of vaguely Italian design, but the sunlight was very bright. It reminded her more of the American Southwest than Italy, despite the design of the house.

Was this Lorenzo's home, the place Orion had mentioned?

She thought she could identify Orion in the ranks of the men by his stance. He stood near the back of the company, his manner wary and watchful. The leader opened his hand, revealing that he held a large quartz crystal with a blue-green light trapped within it.

It looked like the one Gabe had given her, but then quartz crystals probably looked much the same.

The light within the stone brightened to blinding intensity then flashed once. The company of men vanished. Francesca blinked, but they were gone. The sun shone down on the empty courtyard as a dark-haired man stepped out of the house. He frowned as he surveyed the courtyard, clearly as disconcerted as Francesca by their disappearance.

Maybe that was Lorenzo.

Her dream shifted then, the courtyard dissolving into a mist.

A moment later, she found herself in an apartment with modern furnishings and brick walls. It could have been in a converted ware-house and the ceilings were high. The same leader was there, though his features were careworn and he appeared to be tired. No, more than tired. He looked defeated. On the table before him was a cup of coffee that he might have only tasted. There was also a crystal, presumably the one he had carried before, but it contained no spark of any kind.

There was no sign of the other men who had been with him, and she couldn't see Orion.

A little girl climbed onto a chair beside him and offered a drawing of a plaza, not unlike the one where Francesca had met Orion. The man smiled wearily at her. There was another man sitting opposite him, a man with an intense expression and dark hair, with silver at his temples. His expression melted when he looked at the little girl, and Francesca guessed this was his child.

Was this Erik Sorensson, the leader of the *Pyr*, and his daughter, who might be the new Wyvern?

There was a knock at the door and the men looked up. A woman with a cloud of dark red hair appeared and stretched out a hand to the little girl, who went to her side.

Eileen Grosvenor.

The man with the silver at his temples answered the door. The other man's face lit with wonder as a company of young men surged through the door. Each and every one of them had a tattoo of a dragon. As Francesca watched them flow into the apartment and pledge themselves to the command of the dark-haired man, she thought they shimmered blue around their perimeter.

Dragon shifters. *Pyr*!

Francesca thought of the battle between *Pyr* and *Slayers* that was yet to come, and Orion's uncertainty of who would triumph. If their leader had returned to the future alone with the exhausted stone, his company of men must have been scattered through the ages, like Orion.

Who were this unexpected and welcome influx of warriors?

Francesca guessed when she saw one with silvery-blue eyes and dark hair, one with a smile so familiar that her heart clenched.

Orion's son.

FRANCESCA'S EYES FLEW OPEN. Her dream was a vision of the future and Orion's *Pyr* son was in that future. He hadn't missed his firestorm, after all. He couldn't have, if this vision was a true glimpse of the future. There was no doubt that the other two men had been glad of the arrival of the young *Pyr*.

What if those *Pyr* made the difference in the war against the *Slayers*?

Only a week after learning of their existence, Francesca didn't want to imagine a world without the *Pyr*.

She thought about the dates of the Dragon's Tail War and realized this vision had to be of sometime between 2011 when Orion had left the future with his fellows and November 2015, the end of the Dragon's Tail. Orion's son was an adult in her vision. He looked to be in his thirties, and though she knew that the *Pyr* aged differently than humans, that had to mean that Orion's firestorm would spark soon. It was thirty-nine years to 2011, and she hated having anything like an end date to their time together.

His firestorm hadn't happened yet, and it would spark soon. He'd have to leave her. She wanted him to fulfill his obligation to his kind, but she already knew it would finish her to see him walk away.

She turned to tell him about her dream and realized that he

wasn't on the terrace anymore. He wasn't anywhere in the apartment at all. She felt a moment of alarm that he had left her, but then she knew that couldn't be the case. He would have said farewell.

If he'd had a choice. What if he'd vanished as unexpectedly as he'd appeared?

No, there was no darkfire. He'd gone on an errand.

The tape recorder was on her desk, because he'd been listening to the Aeneid. He'd said he had no one to consult and that he would have loved to talk to his father again. The Sibyl had guided Aeneas to Hades from her grotto at Cumae—and they'd released the contents of Mr. Montmorency's vase in Cumae.

Francesca had a good idea where she'd find Orion. The firestorm would help her to locate him more precisely than that. She dressed quickly, then pursued him on the Vespa, not caring about the lateness of the hour.

If Orion was going to find the Sibyl, if he was going to the underworld, Francesca wasn't going to be left behind.

———

ORION WAS WALKING along the road to Cumae, which he already knew well. He wasn't entirely certain how he would get to the underworld, much less what he would find when he got there, but only his father's wisdom might help him in this situation.

He regretted leaving Francesca, but he couldn't ask anyone to venture into the realm of the dead with him, not at any price. He wished he had learned to write, because then he could have left her a message. As it was, he was glad to have committed her features to memory even though he doubted he would ever forget her. He feared he would never see her again, but perhaps it was better to part sooner than later. He was glad, at least, that he had not disappointed her.

Perhaps she would find happiness with another, a man who

could give her the daughters she craved, a man who would cherish her as Orion had.

Orion's mood was grim as he trudged to Cumae in the darkness. The quartz crystal felt heavy in his pocket and he wished he had not impulsively taken it. He felt now like a thief in taking this possession from Francesca's home. Was that how she would remember him?

Would she remember him at all?

Would he survive this journey? Aeneas had only managed it with the guidance of the Sibyl, and Orion was alone.

No, not quite alone.

Orion heard the machine Francesca called a Vespa behind him. It could have been someone else as the vehicles were popular, but at this hour, he hoped otherwise. Francesca couldn't have come after him—it wouldn't have been a logical choice and Francesca was sensible.

But it *was* Francesca, he soon saw with his keen *Pyr* vision. She drove toward him, accelerating as she came closer, and he smiled at her typical resolve. Her presence felt so right. He knew he had only been able to leave her earlier because she had been asleep.

Orion stood and waited, smiling like a besotted fool. When she halted beside him, he realized that her expression was fierce.

"You left without saying goodbye." Her tone was accusing. "I hate when men do that."

"Surely there cannot have been many who have abandoned you."

"One, and it was enough." Her tone was hard and her lips tight. "But that's old news. I thought you had left too, and I was upset." She took a breath. "Where are you going? You don't have much money and you don't speak Italian. It's crazy for you to walk away in the middle of the night, but you're not crazy."

"I thank you for this." Orion could not take offense. He was filled with satisfaction to simply be in her company and could not hide his pleasure.

"I'm not kidding. You must have a plan."

"I will need neither coin nor fluency in Italian in Hades' realm."

Francesca caught her breath, her expression becoming concerned. "You're not going to kill yourself." There was only a hint of a question in her tone.

Orion shook his head with impatience. "This Aeneas visited his father's shade in Hades with the aid of the Sibyl. I would do the same."

She nodded. "What an interesting and unexpected idea."

Her composure was so at odds with Orion's frustration and uncertainty that he could not restrain his response.

"I have need of counsel, Francesca! I am both here *and* there and I fear the ramifications of every choice I make. Why am I here if my firestorm was a failure?"

"It wasn't," she said with complete confidence. "I dreamed of your son, so it can't have happened yet."

Orion was shaken. He whispered her name.

"But it must happen soon, because it looked like he was an adult when he rejoined the *Pyr*." She recounted a dream to him so filled with marvels that Orion could scarcely believe it. But she had seen Drake and the child, Zoë, and Erik. She described Erik's lair so well that he had no doubt.

"An entire company of warriors," he said in wonder. "That would change all."

"The darkfire must have taken you all into the past so you could have your firestorms and have sons. Then depending how far back in time it was, those sons would have sons, etc., and they'd all turn up to help with the war."

"This is a marvel of a tale. But how do I join them?"

"I didn't dream that part." She smiled. "Maybe we should try to ask your dad." She softly quoted a passage from one of her sources.

"The descent of Avernus is easy.
All night long, all day, the doors of Hades stand open.

But to retrace the path, to come up to the sweet air of heaven,
That is labour indeed."

"Indeed," Orion said. "But you cannot join me."

"You're not going without me."

"I could not put you at risk, Francesca. That was why I left you this night, for your safety. I did not think of it as abandonment."

She studied him, then she smiled just a little. "What if I volunteer to come with you?"

"You should not."

"I might insist." Francesca smiled and waited, her manner expectant.

He surrendered the battle, knowing it was one he would not win. "Then I would be glad of your companionship."

Orion glimpsed her smile of pleasure before she gestured to the seat behind herself. "Get on. The sooner we start, the sooner we'll be back."

Orion was not certain that was true, but he did not argue the point. He got on the vehicle behind her, aware that his weight would slow its speed, and sighed as he slid his arms around Francesca's waist. Her hair was bound up, but her ponytail swept across his face as they rode, the soft heat of her so near that his thoughts turned in a predictable direction. It was remarkable how he never had sufficient of this woman, that mere moments after making love to her, he desired to do as much again. She was a madness in his blood and one he hoped was never dispelled. His grip tightened upon her waist as he caught his breath and his thumbs slid beneath the waistband of her jeans seemingly of their own volition. He felt her laugh a little but she didn't pull away.

How would he leave her for another when his firestorm sparked? How would he bear the loss of her?

Her tone was practical when she spoke. "So, let's review the Aeneid. The first thing the Sibyl told Aeneas when he came to her was that he should sacrifice seven bulls in exchange for her prophecy."

"I have surrendered my fellows, my time, my place and all I know of life. I believe I should not be required to surrender more," Orion said tightly.

"There is that," Francesca ceded. "Then the Sibyl had a vision and she predicted war and ultimate triumph, etc., then she advised him to be stalwart in the face of adversity."

"He need not have paid for such counsel."

"He said pretty much the same thing."

"I thought him wise in this."

Francesca chuckled. "And he insisted the Sibyl accompany him to the underworld that he might confer with his father who had died in Sicily. He told her how he had saved his father, Anchises, at Troy, and insisted that his father had told him to appeal to the Sibyl."

"Because of the truth of her counsel," Orion remembered.

"Yes. The Sibyl was said to be unable to tell a lie."

"You have this in common with her, Francesca, for you are forthright beyond all others I have known."

She drove through the open gates of the archaeological site without speaking. She took the turn toward the grotto, the headlight of the Vespa shining into the darkness ahead of them. They didn't really need it, not with the light of the full moon. The route was uneven, more of a path than a road, so she slowed down.

"And what did the Sibyl say to Aeneas after his appeal?" she prompted, like the teacher she was destined to be.

"She agreed to take him to the underworld, but first he had to bury one of his dead comrades."

"Then he had to get the golden bough, which was sacred to Persephone. Taking a gift to the goddess of the underworld was supposed to encourage her to let you leave. The golden bough is hidden and evidently only those destined to enter the underworld can even find it, as well as break off the branch easily. As soon as it is broken, another branch grows in its place, which seems to indicate that the road to hell was pretty popular." She shrugged. "Maybe it was even paved."

Orion did not understand this, but he refrained from commenting upon it. "And this tribute to Persephone was the sole way to ensure one's retreat?" he asked. "For I have no golden bough and do not know where to seek it."

"Perhaps it's not your destiny to visit."

"Perhaps I will make it my destiny," he said with heat and she glanced back.

"Now, there's a perspective that makes sense to me. Forget destiny. Make your life be what you want it to be, even if it means walking through hellfire." She eased the Vespa to a halt by the entry to the old grotto and turned off the engine.

"There are supposed to be three ways to leave the underworld," she told him, her tone reassuring. She counted them on her fingers. "Those who succeed do so either because of the love of Zeus, because of their own goodness, or because they are born from gods. Orpheus, Heracles and Theseus visited the underworld and were sons of gods."

"I still count a deficit," Orion said, his tone grumpy. "Zeus loves none in truth. I am both good and bad, like all men. And I am not divinely spawned. My parents were both mortal warriors."

She eyed him. "But where did the *Pyr* come from in the first place? You said that Hephaestus favored your kind. Maybe some divinity had a part in your creation."

"The tale was always that we were created a race of guardians for the elements and the treasures of the earth. There was no more measure of divinity in our making than in that of mankind."

"Aeneas was the son of the goddess, and his mother helped him find the golden bough."

"Again, I sense this quest may be ill-fated. Do you still insist upon accompanying me?"

"I do. I might remember something that helps you come back."

He considered her with a smile. "And you want to see."

Francesca laughed as they stepped into the darkness of the cavern. The air was cool, even though they still had to descend the ramp to the grotto that had been known for years. Francesca had something in her hand and she touched a switch so that it cast a beam of light on the path ahead. "Flashlight," she said. "Seemed like a good idea at night."

"It is unfortunate that it is not a golden bough."

"And so the Sibyl led Aeneas to the opening to the underworld, which was supposed to be near Lake Avernus, which is just to the east of us. Aeneas made sacrifices at the portal to Nyx, Gaia and Persephone and created altars to Hecate. They waited all the night long."

"Then Hecate opened the ground before them to admit them to the underworld."

"It reads like an earthquake, so obviously the path was blocked until Hecate, or somebody, cleared the way."

They continued into the newly exposed grotto. A lot of debris had already been cleared and Francesca played her light over the paintings on the walls. "It's incredible to think that these images are over two thousand years old," she whispered in awe.

"As am I, Francesca," Orion rumbled and she laughed, surprised into it.

"Just graffiti to you then?"

"No, they are beautiful, but I have other concerns on this night." He was both glad of her presence and felt tense that she accompanied him. He feared for her welfare on this quest, but knew she would not be left behind in safety.

"Of course." They walked together along the path that descended into the earth. Her hand was cold and it shook a little in his grasp, despite her bold words. That hint of her fear fed Orion's urge to protect her and he moved slightly ahead of her, leading the way.

The path went down, twisting its way seemingly into the heart of the earth. The temperature rose slightly and the darkness seemed more impenetrable. He helped Francesca climb over several rocks in their path and they moved around others. There was more loose gravel beneath their feet and the ceiling of the tunnel became lower. Orion's sense of doom seemed to grow with every step.

"Bad time to recall that this is a volcanic region," Francesca said, her voice a little breathless. He saw her glance back at the shadows behind them and realized he couldn't see any hint of light from above. "Being deep in the earth in the *Campi Flegrei* might prove to be a bad idea if our timing is unlucky."

"When did the volcano last erupt?"

"I forget," she said. "But they say it's due." She nodded. "Let's hurry."

They moved more quickly then, her urgency infectious, but after another twist, the passageway ended suddenly in a wall of rock.

"It can't be a dead end," Francesca said, then laughed under her breath at her own words.

"The way is obstructed," Orion said, taking her flashlight and shining it on the ground. The path was hewn and fairly smooth, until it reached the rock blocking their way forward. He ran the beam of the flashlight up the wall, seeking the edges of the large stone, and thought he could discern them.

"It is a rock rolled into the path," he said. "Perhaps we do not need to await Hecate after all." He gave Francesca the flashlight and she held it so he could see. There wasn't enough room to shift shape, so he leaned against the offending stone, bracing all his weight against it until it shifted slightly. He fit smaller stones beneath the edge, kicking them further beneath the rock and leveraging its weight. Gradually, he made progress until finally he was able to shove the stone hard and feel it move.

Francesca braced the flashlight against the ground and moved to help him. They pushed and shoved and grunted, then suddenly, the stone moved aside with a rumble, revealing a gaping abyss of darkness. The air was hot and smelled of sulphur.

"Fire and brimstone," Francesca said, picking up her flashlight. "Looks like this is the place."

Orion seized her hand. "You need not accompany me. I will not think less of you."

"But I want to know what happens next," she admitted with a quick smile. "I want to see what's there, if anything." She eyed the darkness. "The River Styx, the shades on the bank, Charon, Cerberus, Persephone. What if it's all real? What if it's different than we've been told?" She wrinkled her nose. "What if this is just a tunnel that leads to nowhere?"

"What if the price of entry is no ability to return?" Orion couldn't stop thinking about their lack of a golden bough. Annoying a goddess seemed like a bad strategy to him.

"I still want to know," she said, gesturing to the opening as she quoted another passage. "'*Now you need all your courage, now your stout heart.*'"

Orion smiled, never having doubted that.

He would have moved onward but Francesca stepped into his path. "Just one last thing," she said, her voice breathless, her eyes bright. She kissed him suddenly on the mouth, her impulsive move taking him by surprise. His response was immediate and visceral.

If this was to be his last taste of Francesca or his last kiss in this lifetime, Orion would make it one to remember. He caught her close and deepened their embrace, not surprised in the least when she opened her mouth to him and pushed her fingers into his hair. Their kiss turned hungry with predictable speed, and he admired again how honest she was in her passion. He could feel her sweet curves against him, and his yearning shook him to his very marrow.

When she broke their kiss and stepped back, he released her with an effort. They stood staring at each other, her eyes filled with unfathomable shadows, the light of the flashlight making the darkness seem deeper. He reached out and touched her cheek with a gentle fingertip and she closed her eyes, cradling her cheek against his hand. "No regrets," she said softly and smiled at him.

"Who was he?" Orion asked. "The fool who abandoned you?"

She frowned and looked away and he thought she would not reply. Then her gaze collided suddenly with his. "This might be my last chance to tell you," she said softly. "His name was Derek. We competed for top honors all through high school, then kissed for the first time at prom. We went to the same college and lived in the same dorm. We were going to graduate and get married, have a family, buy a house, teach history." She swallowed. "I loved him so much. I thought I would die when he was invited to do a semester in England. At Oxford. It was the chance of a lifetime, and I insisted he take it." She shook her head slowly. "Four months apart then a lifetime together. It seemed so simple, even if it was awful to watch him leave."

She fell silent, her throat working and Orion saw her blink back tears.

"But it was not simple," he guessed.

"Oh, it was simple. He never came back." Her tone was bitter and Orion heard that she still hurt over this loss. "He fell in love and he got married and he never even had the balls to say goodbye. He just vanished. I heard about his wedding from a friend of a friend." She faced the darkness. "I loved him and I trusted him, but I was wrong about him. That was when I decided that I would throw myself into my work and my research, and that my career would never ever let me down."

"But you will be alone."

"Maybe that's better," she said, but there was less fire in her words.

Then she vanished into the shadows of the grotto, leaving Orion with a much better understanding of her reasons for not wanting a firestorm. He waited a moment, composing his thoughts. Surely, one's intentions had to be clear in descending to Hades. He knew his goal, and hoped to speak with his father, but he also knew he would do whatever was necessary to defend Francesca.

If one of them was destined to remain behind, it would be him.

Orion followed Francesca, hoping for the best and fearing the worst.

He had not taken three steps when the light of her flashlight was suddenly extinguished.

———

FRANCESCA FELT raw after telling Orion the truth about Derek, but in another way, she felt lighter for having said it aloud. The simple fact of it was that she didn't think Orion was like Derek at all. He listened to her, for example, and didn't talk about himself all the time. He wasn't always comparing and measuring, assessing her against himself. Everything had been a competition with Derek, even lovemaking. Orion seemed to be more about partnership and mutual satisfaction.

That was part of why he was nearly irresistible.

He was better company and an easier person to live with, one who compromised and played his part. He didn't expect her to be the one to do the menial tasks or to surrender her goals for his. It was true that she didn't particularly want to have kids, but Orion, she knew, would be a good father and partner. He was intent upon doing his duty and acting with honor, but he would see fatherhood through that lens. She'd only known him a few days and she trusted him more than she'd trusted anyone in a long time. Francesca was pretty sure she hadn't been deceived either.

Orion was just one of the keepers.

The prospect of his son—their son—being part of the team that ensured the *Pyr* triumph over the *Slayers* made her want him to have that firestorm soon, even though it had to mean him leaving her.

She felt Orion come to a halt behind her as the flashlight went out. She shook it and tried the switch, thinking the batteries couldn't have chosen a worse moment to give it up. Orion's hand landed on the back of her waist.

"The path was reasonably straight," she said. "We could find our way back to the surface."

"Or we could continue," he said softly. She opened her mouth to protest, but he touched her lips with a fingertip. "I can see them." There was wonder in his tone, but when Francesca looked around, all she could see was darkness.

"I can't see anything."

"The senses of my kind are more acute," he said softly. "You will see them in a minute." He chuckled under his breath, a reassuring sound. "I should have expected them."

Francesca didn't understand, but finally, she saw the pricks of golden light in the distance. The way they moved—like fireflies—swirling around each other, almost dancing, was very familiar. The color of them, all gold and orange like sparks from a bonfire rising into the night, was also familiar, and she smiled.

"The sparks from the jar!"

"Indeed."

"She's here," she said, as if it was perfectly logical that the Sibyl should exist only as a voice, that the voice should appear as lights in the presence of her destined mate, and that those lights should be sufficiently sentient to anticipate their arrival in this place—and their destination. Evidently believing impossible things could become a habit. "She wasn't dispersed!" she said with excitement. "She was released. And she's *here*!"

"I hoped that she would remain in a familiar location, even that she would join us on this journey if she could," Orion said easily, keeping his hand on the back of her waist to guide her.

Those lights dove into darkness ahead, vanishing from sight, then darting back toward them, urging them ever onward. They seemed to be dancing, swirling with an enthusiasm that made Francesca smile.

The path sloped abruptly downward after the next turn and into deep shadows. Fumes rose from it, looking silvery in the light. If there was a pathway to Hades, that would be a likely candidate. She wondered whether anyone else had discovered and explored it, but had never heard any stories about it.

Except the Aeneid.

A blue-green light flickered suddenly in the distance, as if from the terminus of the path far ahead. It illuminated more of the jagged path that descended into the earth. Francesca glimpsed pits on either side of the path and openings, perhaps to caves, and smelled hot sulphur. There were stalactites and stalagmites, the combination obscuring sections of the pathway from view.

She grabbed Orion's arm, not sharing his confidence. "This can't be safe."

"That was darkfire," he said, indicating where the light had flashed. "As well as being a beacon of chaos, it is associated with the dead, the ability to converse with them, and the territory of dreams. Perhaps if we venture along this path, we will dream of Hades, defended by the darkfire." He smiled at her, his gaze intense and his expression inscrutable. He was dragon to his marrow in this moment and Francesca was reassured to be with him. "Again, I say you need not accompany me."

If he was going, so was she. "Let's go." She slid her hand down his arm so that her hand was in his again, and Orion clasped her fingers. His grip was warm and comforting, and the faint shimmer of blue around the perimeter of his silhouette didn't hurt either. She knew he'd shift in a heartbeat to defend her and that was just fine. The orange lights darted ahead.

"And what did the Sibyl tell Aeneas when they entered the underworld?" he asked in a low rumble. Francesca appreciated his question and the distraction of replying to it. He'd just listened to the poem. He had to know this, but it settled her nerves to talk about it.

"That he would see shades, that they would seem real and he might wish to attack them, but that they were forms without substance."

"Ghosts," Orion said.

"Visions," Francesca agreed. "They saw Hynos, Thanatos and Geras, as well as diseases and hunger and grief. The Sibyl noted they were all visions that men did not have to visit the underworld to experience."

Orion nodded. "And then?"

"And then they reached the river Acheron and the ferryman, Charon."

"The river Styx," Orion said, using the Greek name for it. "We should know it when we see it."

"At the very least, we won't be able to cross it alone," Francesca agreed.

───────

THERE COULD BE no time in this tunnel, upon this seemingly endless path that wound ever deeper into the earth. Orion had no notion of how long they had walked. His feet were sore and the weight of Francesca's hand within his own was most welcome. The lights raced ahead, seemingly gleeful as they led the two of them silently onward. The heat rose and the fumes grew stronger. He heard rumblings in the earth and a bubbling that might have come from lava. He was well aware that this was an area of high volcanic activity, but he hoped Francesca could not hear the sounds evident to his keen *Pyr* hearing.

Without warning, they stepped into a large round cavern, one that might have been carved of white stone. There were arches on every side, dozens of pathways opening into darkness, as if a thousand paths converged on this one place. Orion could not say whether the openings were natural or had been carved by men—they were rounded but irregular, some larger than others, and only arranged roughly in rows. He had seen swallows make similar patterns of holes in cliffs. Once they stepped into the cavern, it was impossible to guess which path to take.

The sparks were swirling in a column in the middle of the space, one that extended from the highest height to what might have been a well in the middle of the space. They walked toward the dark hole, which was three times as wide as Orion was tall and perfectly circular. Cold air rose from it, against every expectation, and the soft moans of a hundred beings, if not more. Orion realized that water streamed from some of the openings around the circumference, flowing toward the great hole and running down its walls to some lower point. He could hear the distant drip of water from the bottom and shivered despite himself.

"A well of souls," Francesca said, dropping to her hands and knees to peer into its darkness. "There's a staircase winding around the edge," she said, pointing to it in the shadows.

Orion knew better than to descend it, at least not before he had explored other options. "And its depth is unfathomable," he noted. "I would not take the risk of a slip on those steps."

Francesca nodded and drew back a little, her gaze roving over the cavern and the column of dancing fireflies. "We have to have reached this place for a reason."

Orion almost smiled at her conviction but knew better than to tease her about destiny. He took the coin from his pocket, the one his father had given him so many centuries before, and rubbed it between his finger and thumb. Francesca glanced toward him, noting his gesture. "For the blessing of the gods," he said, then flicked the coin into the abyss before them. He said a prayer to Apollo as the coin glinted in the light of the fireflies, tumbled end over end, then fell into the darkness and vanished.

For a long time, too long a time, there was no sound at all.

Orion heard a distant splash, a sign that the coin had landed far beneath them. He had no notion whether Francesca had heard it or not, for the sound had been faint, but the lights swirled with sudden speed. As he watched, they took the shape of a tree bough before them.

"The golden bough," Francesca whispered before the lights scattered and tumbled into the abyss, seemingly in pursuit of the coin.

They were abruptly extinguished, leaving Orion and Francesca in fathomless darkness.

Then a woman spoke, her voice as insubstantial as the wind.

> *"Command the spark*
> *To kindle the flame*
> *Darkfire's loss*
> *Is destiny's gain."*

Her voice faded over the course of the verse, so that the last word was barely discernible.

Orion knew it was the Sibyl and that she was gone.

"That makes no sense," Francesca whispered. The cavern was completely still and dark, the air turning cold. The hair pricked on the back of Orion's neck and he could hear the thunder of his pulse in his ears. He stood motionless, knowing he awaited something but uncertain what it might be. He thought of the verse but could make no sense of it.

The darkfire sparked suddenly, illuminating the cavern with a bolt of blue-green light, just as a bellow rose from the dark well before them. Orion seized Francesca and pulled her back from the lip, feeling the shift muster within himself. He saw the blue shimmer that heralded his own change just as a dark cloud rose with a vengeance from the well. It churned before them like a storm cloud, its depths lit by cracks of darkfire, and he shifted shape with a roar even as he feared the worst.

Then Orion's own challenge coin shone as it was flung toward him. He caught it by instinct, snatching it out of the air, before the rumble of his father's old-speak echoed in his thoughts.

"You dare much in this journey, son of mine, but your valor was never in doubt."

CHAPTER FOURTEEN

"Father!" the dragon that was Orion spoke with reverence and Francesca should not have been surprised that he spoke aloud in Ancient Greek.

Orion's father had risen from the dead to confer with his son. Maybe she would soon believe anything, because it did seem that anything was possible.

She stayed a little behind Orion, wanting to see what was happening but also wanting to be able to run if necessary. She wasn't sure she could run fast enough to escape a dragon ghost, but she'd try, if it came to that.

Because it was undoubtedly a dragon ghost that had risen from the dark well. The figure was insubstantial, but definitely dragon-shaped and of a size with Orion in his dragon form. The ghost dragon's scales were dark, like Orion's, but his chest was golden and his eyes were clear green. She could see the other side of the cavern through his form, but he'd cast that very real coin at Orion. He was both there and not there. She watched the crackle of darkfire sparking around the cavern like lightning and didn't trust it one bit.

There was a rumble before Orion spoke and another one after it.

She hated that she couldn't understand what they were saying. That old-speak sounded like thunder or an earthquake wasn't the most reassuring coincidence in this particular place.

She wasn't going to speculate on how deep they were beneath the surface in this volatile and volcanic region, not until she was home again.

She also wasn't going to wonder whether she would *ever* be home again.

Orion, to her surprise, shifted back to his human form. He reached for her hand. "Francesca has to hear your counsel, Father," he said and her heart warmed at his concern. "Why does the Sibyl say to command the spark?"

"Because it is your legacy to command the darkfire," the dragon ghost boomed, his voice so loud that the ground shook.

"I do not know of this legacy," Orion protested.

"Because I was to pass it to you on my deathbed, but you had vanished."

Francesca watched Orion bow his head. "We were enchanted, Father..."

"A ploy of the darkfire to see itself free."

"It was Cadmus..."

"All can fall prey to the seductive power of darkfire, Orion," his father chided. "Listen to me! Hephaestus favored our kind with a weapon against the darkfire cast by Zeus to cause disharmony and strife. Hephaestus feared darkfire's unpredictable force would be the ruin of men, and so, as we were chosen guardians of the elements and the treasures of the earth, he chose three from our number as his allies."

"How can I not know of this detail?"

"It was a sworn secret, only the defenders themselves knowing of their role until the duty was passed to their successor." The ghost dragon held up a claw, counting three items. "The first, and his descendants, would have the ability to gather the darkfire. This is the line of the Cantor, whose skills lie in the charms and chants, and the ability to conjure. In my time, Cyrus, a *Pyr* warrior with a rare skill for shifting, wielded this talent and could sing to please the gods themselves. It was said he pursued the spark of the firestorm to the distant north."

"Rafferty's line," Orion murmured softly and Francesca recalled that *Pyr* singing in his garden. Was his legacy the reason he'd been able to break the spell over the teeth?

Orion's father continued. "The second appointed *Pyr*, and his descendants, would have the ability to disperse the darkfire and send it forth into the world. One of the four sons of Magnor, Marcellus showed the greatest skill with this power in my time. He lived near these parts, though I did not know him well."

"This must be the line of the Sleeper," Orion said beneath his breath, which made no sense to Francesca.

"The third *Pyr,* and his line, have the power to both gather and disperse the darkfire, to be its commander in all times. This was a safeguard, in case one of the other lines should die out or the ability not shine brightly in one of its sons. In your absence, I could pass the tale to none, but you, Orion, son of Erebus, who am myself son of Orpheus, have this duty to fulfill to our kind. Command the darkfire and ensure that the treasures of the earth are defended!"

Saying thus, the dragon ghost faded abruptly and vanished, and even the booming echo of his voice faded.

"But how?" Orion asked, and there was no reply.

Francesca thought she knew the answer. She gripped his hand.

> *"Command the spark*
> *To kindle the flame*
> *Darkfire's loss*
> *Is destiny's gain."*

Orion shook his head, uncertain.

The darkfire illuminated the cave in a sudden flash. "Sing to it," Francesca said. "Command the spark." She hummed a bit of a tune that she remembered from her dream and Orion eyed her as the darkfire flashed brilliantly again, bouncing around the perimeter of the cave. "Now would be a good time to start," she added with a smile.

SING TO THE DARKFIRE.
  Summon the darkfire.
  Snare the darkfire.

Orion remembered that song, though he had no notion how Francesca knew it. He remembered Rafferty's chant to them in the garden of his London home, the chant that had broken the curse over the Dragon's Tooth Warriors. Had Rafferty summoned the darkfire to do his will?

It did not matter. Orion hummed the chant along with Francesca, remembering even the notes she did not know, then sang it again with greater vigor. The darkfire sparked and crackled and he remembered the crystal. He held it out in one hand, holding Francesca's hand with his free hand, and he sang with all his might. The stone floor vibrated. Vapor rose from the well of souls. The darkfire snapped and flashed.

Then a deep voice sang with him, bringing tears to his eyes as it emanated from the abyss before them. His father joined the song and the darkfire responded with vigor. The chamber was lit completely, the darkfire bouncing from the walls and ceiling of the cave, its light growing in the crystal Orion held. He shifted shape and the song had more resonance in his dragon form, and the darkfire grew even brighter.

No sooner had Orion marveled at this than he heard another voice rise from the abyss to join their chorus. His grandfather! Orion,

Erebus and Orpheus sang together, his grandfather's song the most elaborate and skillful of the three. Orion strove to learn every nuance and variation to the tune, even as the darkfire gathered closer. His grandfather added a different chorus, one that made Orion's very blood leap, and he sang it with all his might.

The darkfire seemed compelled to obey him with this addition, even against its considerable will. It snapped as if to battle the summons, flashing irregularly and cracking like lightning. When Orion sang the new chorus again, the darkfire struggled against him for ascendancy, flaring so brilliantly that the sun might have ventured into the cavern with them.

Then it snapped, crackled, and the crystal flared with blue-green light. The darkfire was agitated, flashing in the stone, but it was trapped there. Orion closed his hand more tightly around the stone feeling triumphant as the voices of his father and grandfather faded.

A drip of water echoed in the darkness. The temperature in the cavern cooled, and the darkfire in the stone was merely a furious spark.

The cavern was dark and still, more peaceful than it had been. Orion shifted shape again, amazed by what he had done, feeling his exhaustion.

"I knew you could do it," Francesca said, giving him a nudge. "There's nothing like that dragon magic."

"It is not sorcery, Francesca," he protested, then was silenced by a sudden flood of orange light rising from the well before them. It bubbled and seethed, boiling toward the lip of the abyss and he flung Francesca toward the path. "Run!" he cried, but she didn't.

"No," she said softly. "Not this time."

She slipped her hand from his grasp and stepped back toward the abyss. She opened her arms wide, her posture triumphant, and he watched in awe as a tide of orange fireflies rose from the abyss and surrounded her, obscuring her from his view for a heart-stopping moment. The banner of flaming light surrounded her, just as it had when the vessel had broken, and Orion discerned her silhouette within the glow of light.

She tipped her head back and opened her mouth, her eyes alight when she turned to face him. The sparks swirled in a frenzy, then cascaded into her open mouth as Orion feared the worst.

Francesca!

———

FRANCESCA HEARD the rumble and she saw the light. The Sibyl's voice was clear in her thoughts and she knew exactly what she had to do.

The Sibyl had told them, after all.

Orion had commanded the spark of the darkfire.

Now the flame of the firestorm would kindle, and this time, she would welcome it. She would step up and volunteer. If anyone was going to give Orion a son, it was going to be Francesca. She knew they'd make it work, that their partnership would be more than the sum of the parts.

And his son would help to win the war against the *Slayers*. She wanted to be a part of that.

She had the opportunity to give the man she loved his most heartfelt desire. There was no other option than to choose.

Francesca chose.

She lifted her arms as the lights surged from the abyss with sudden speed, catapulting over each other in their haste, their hue darkened to reddish-gold. They hurled themselves toward her, then swirled around her in a deep gold curtain that blinded her to everything else. She laughed at the touch of them against her skin, then the Sibyl whispered in her thoughts. She opened her mouth, welcoming whatever change they brought and felt them slide down her throat. She knew that the Sibyl had chosen her as a vessel and she embraced the chance to be more than she had been thus far.

When the lights had poured into her, swirling inside her so that her very veins felt alight, the cavern was again in darkness.

"'*To such a degree will I be changed that I will be visible to no one; but I will be recognized by my voice,*'" Francesca found herself saying, her voice a perfect echo of the one they had just heard. "'*My voice the Fates will leave me.*'"

The Sibyl was within her, somehow.

It wasn't logical, but Francesca knew it was true.

And she welcomed it.

Because she felt the shimmer of the firestorm mustering deep within her. She had the chance to change the future, to assure the survival of the *Pyr*, to give Orion the destiny he craved.

She turned to him in triumph, her voice returning to its normal tones. "Propertius wrote that." She smiled at his astonishment and reached out a hand, her gesture casting a spark in his direction.

She laughed as an arc of flame sailed through the air and struck him on the chest, sending a surge of heat, dizzying power and desire through her. She was aflame and aroused, her thoughts filled with the prospect of Orion's kiss and his touch, her need for him enough to dismiss all coherent thought from her mind.

She'd just add that to her ever-growing list of impossible things.

The firestorm heated to a radiant glow between them, illuminating the cavern with its light. It flickered and brightened as Orion strode toward her, his gaze filled with wonder, the sparks turning from orange to yellow and finally to white. Francesca burned for his touch as she had never wanted anything or anyone before.

She was his destined mate, by choice.

She laughed as Orion caught her close and kissed her, knowing that the promise of the firestorm was just the beginning of their adventure together.

———

ERIK SORENSSON FELT the spark of a distant firestorm. He was in Chicago, moving his few belongings into a previously abandoned warehouse. He planned to renovate it and gradually turn it into apartments, keeping the upper floor for his own. It was in a lousy neighborhood and access to the roof would provide a measure of privacy for his own dragon activities. The zoning would allow him to use the main floor for his pyrotechnics business. Given his *Pyr* nature, he wasn't worried about being victimized by vandals. He was sorting boxes in a former office in the northeast corner of the top floor late that night when he felt the spark.

Who was having a firestorm?

Erik immediately turned and looked out the windows, though he knew the firestorm was too far away to see from his vantage point. The heat was faint, perhaps in Europe, and he immediately reviewed his mental list of *Pyr* who might be there. He had been on edge since the total lunar eclipse at the end of January, a blood moon so spectacular that he'd immediately thought it might be a portent.

He was excited by the possibility of one of his fellow dragon shifters having the opportunity to breed, no matter who or how distant the firestorm was. Their numbers were too few in these times.

He quickly located the Dragon's Egg in his possessions and unpacked it, exposing its smooth obsidian surface to the moon's light. It was said to reveal the location of each firestorm as it sparked, but thus far, it had been only a big piece of stone to move around. Despite that, even holding it in his hands filled Erik with a sense of wonder. It was so large, bigger than a basketball, so heavy and so black, polished to perfection. The globe of black stone gleamed as he turned it beneath the moon's light, offering him no vision or insight. He frowned at it, tired of being constantly confronted with the loss of knowledge of his own kind. He wondered whether he was doomed to watch the *Pyr* fade from the earth completely, unable to gather his fellows or lead them in any way. He had a heartbeat to feel defeat, then a blue-green light flicked across the stone.

Had he imagined it?

Erik leaned closer, peering at the stone, and the light flashed brighter. Its light flooded his vision and his thoughts, filling his heart with hope and possibilities—then it winked out, vanishing as surely as it might not have ever been.

And Erik immediately forgot about it.

He stood in the darkness, feeling foolish. He had no idea why he'd unwrapped the Dragon's Egg. It was the middle of the night and he was moving. Had he wanted to check that it was undamaged? That was ridiculous. He'd packed it very well. Impatient with himself, he replaced the precious stone in its velvet bag and packed it away again.

Why had he wanted to look at it?

It wasn't as if a firestorm had sparked anywhere. No. There was just the light of a full moon, the distant glimmer of Chicago's downtown, and a pile of his possessions in the corner of this old warehouse. He braced his hands on his hips and looked over the vacant top floor of the building. There was work to be done, for sure, and that didn't include staring into stones that never revealed anything of importance.

———

NIALL TALBOT WAS IN STOCKHOLM, trying to figure out how he could get into the upcoming United Nations conference on the environment. Being passionate about the subject evidently wasn't enough and the security was crazy. He wanted to be a part of it though, to help save the planet. He just had to figure out a way to get inside, and not as an usher. He wanted to make a difference.

He'd been in Sweden for a week and already had a morning routine, which including a stop at a little café for breakfast and the chance to read the papers. The smell of chocolate, coffee and butter had drawn him in the first day, and he'd returned every day since. On this morning, he'd been gestured toward the table he'd taken the day before and felt like he was becoming a regular. The waitress brought him a French press of hot coffee and a basket of pastries, but Niall was frowning at the headlines on the first newspaper he'd grabbed.

A pair of dragons were fighting in the sky. Who were they? He didn't recognize either of them and didn't know of any *Pyr* being in— he scanned the caption—Baiae, Italy. He wasn't entirely sure where that was. He peered at the picture as the waitress laughed.

"How stupid do they think we are?" she asked with a shake of her head.

"You think it's fake?"

"Of course! There aren't really any dragons." Her eyes twinkled and she turned away, confident in her belief.

Niall wasn't quite so sure. He read the article, which said just about nothing, and made a mental note to buy a copy of the paper later, just in case.

When he left the café though, there was a shimmer of blue-green light. Niall blinked, but it was gone, then he spotted one of the organizers of the conference just ahead. He hurried to make his case for admission, not even realizing that he'd forgotten completely about the dragons in the news.

———

IN A ROUGH BAR in the meatpacking district of Manhattan, Thorolf was arm-wrestling with a biker. The other guy wore studded black leathers and most of his visible skin was adorned with tattoos. His hair was long and dark—while Thorolf's was long and blond, braided into dreadlocks—and he was almost as big as Thorolf. He was missing a tooth, and his tattoos featured skulls and roses. Thorolf thought he could use a Norse god or two among the collection. They'd disagreed about that, about the brand of beer each favored, and the superiority of motorbikes over bicycles. As a bike courier,

Thorolf had strong opinions about his ride of choice. When they'd nearly come to blows, the bartender had insisted they arm-wrestle instead.

The two glared at each other over the small table, the biker's buddies gathered around. Not all of them cheered on their friend: some bet on Thorolf instead, much to the biker's outrage. The bar was smoky and loud, the floor was sticky, and it smelled of a combination of fried food and body odor. It was Thorolf's favorite place.

He was just easing the biker's hand back, just at the point of seeing his opponent falter, just letting his triumphant smile begin when he felt a shock. Whatever it was sent a shudder through him, like he'd been hit by a jolt of lightning. He felt warm to his toes with no good reason, and the biker took advantage of Thorolf's distraction to slam Thorolf's wrist to the table.

The biker shouted in triumph and jumped up to accept the back thumps from his fellows while Thorolf shook his head in disgust.

"What shook you?" the bartender demanded. "I thought you had that one."

"Someone walked over my grave maybe."

The bartender shook his head sadly.

"Gimme another beer," Thorolf said, only to find the biker right beside him.

"Make that two," he crowed, giving Thorolf's shoulder a bump. "Because you owe me, loser."

"Only if there's a rematch," Thorolf replied, and the biker guffawed.

He didn't have a chance of winning twice, though.

———

SLOANE FORBES WAS PACKING up in what had been his cottage in Ireland. His father had been born and raised on this property and Sloane had been born on the kitchen table. He'd kept it over the centuries since his father's death, tending the garden and annotating his father's many journals and books. He went away at intervals to feign his own death, returning as his own heir to live in peace and tranquility for another thirty or forty years.

Sloane was the Apothecary of the *Pyr* and had been born in 1655, the only son of Tynan Forbes, the previous Apothecary, who had died in 1735. He still missed his dad and wished he'd had more time to work alongside him. It seemed as if many secrets had been buried with his father and Sloane was endlessly trying to recover lost knowledge about healing the *Pyr*. He was glad of his longevity, as he'd learned many languages in order to decipher the works in his father's extensive collection.

And now the city approached with increasing speed, the suburbs seeming to spread closer by the minute. He'd sold the land to a developer, even though he didn't want to leave. Sloane couldn't be who he was and live as he did with so many people—and watchful eyes—so close. He would miss this cottage and all its quirks, but he would miss the garden most. Some of the herbs had been planted by his father and the beds had been laid out before Sloane's time. He was looking forward to starting over in America, in California, but he knew he would miss the pervasive sense of history in this place.

It was home.

He was organizing little envelopes of seeds, taking as much of the past with him as possible and lingering over the task, when he felt a sudden flush of heat. It was more than the sun coming out from behind a cloud, and he hoped it wasn't a bomb.

He went to the window and looked out. The garden still looked beautiful, even with more traffic on the far side of it and the haze of buildings beyond. He stepped outside, but nothing was amiss, nothing but the nagging sense that he'd missed something. He stood in the garden, closed his eyes and listened.

There was a tingle in his fingertips that was almost familiar. Could it be a firestorm? He wondered whose it might be. He was pretty sure there were no *Pyr* close by. That was part of the reason he wanted to go to America. He was going to stop in Chicago and talk to Erik Sorensson, the *Pyr* who wanted to be their leader. Maybe it was time for them to keep better track of each other than they had in recent centuries.

Maybe they would become relevant again. His father had warned of that. Sloane smiled at the memory and went back into the house. He almost saw a glimmer of blue-green light slide along the empty bookshelves. He moved closer to investigate, running his hand over a dark wood cabinet that dated from his father's time. It was part of the wall, an immovable barrier, as well as a piece of carved furniture. It was built right into the house and featured in some of his oldest memories. Sloane would regret leaving it behind, though there was no way to take it.

Only in this moment did he see a slender gap he hadn't noticed before. He ran his finger along the vertical space, realized it was the edge of a door and thought he could see the glimmer of a latch of some kind.

Within half an hour, he had it open and lifted out another of his father's journals. This one was leatherbound and dusty, the pages crowded with Tynan's familiar spidery writing. Sloane was awed and relieved that he'd discovered the treasure in time. He set it aside then went over the cabinet again, making sure he hadn't missed anything else.

He was so absorbed in his task that he forgot the surge of the distant firestorm.

———

AT HIS FORGE IN MICHIGAN, Quinn Tyrrell felt the heat of a firestorm flare in his veins. He knew exactly what it was, but he also knew that the *Pyr* and their firestorms had nothing to do with him.

He continued to work, albeit a little more grimly, and ignored the indication that there were more of his kind still in the world.

He had no use for any of them, just as they had no real call upon him as Smith. Let their scales become damaged beyond repair. Let them learn the price of betraying his father.

Quinn had his own fires to tend.

———

ORION AND FRANCESCA were retracing their steps, bathed in the glow of the firestorm. Orion could not believe his good fortune. He stole glances at Francesca, but her confidence in choice was complete. He had no doubt that she had followed her own desire—and in so doing, had granted his own.

The firestorm crackled between himself and Francesca, burning with a golden vigor that seared his very soul. His mate! His firestorm!

And she had chosen it.

Orion was humbled and honored, even as he burned with need. He wanted to savor every second of the firestorm, just as he wanted to surrender to its temptation. It brightened steadily, becoming a luminescent cloud that enveloped them both. Even as they returned to the grotto, the firestorm's intensity grew with every passing moment. The flames flicked and danced, brightening to a white radiance, the intensity of his need for Francesca obliterating all other concerns from his mind. He closed his eyes, savoring the tide of raw desire that filled him, as they crossed the newly discovered grotto.

Then Francesca gripped his hand more tightly. She did not have to utter her warning, for Orion smelled *Slayer*. She was his mate and his treasure, and he would ensure she never regretted her choice.

Once Sigmund was defeated.

"Flee," he instructed her so softly that there was only the motion of his lips.

Francesca nodded, resolve dawning in her gaze.

Orion bounded onward, shifting shape in a brilliant shimmer of blue as soon as he entered the upper grotto. The firestorm filled him with power and a sense of invincibility, and he roared at the sight of Sigmund in his human form.

The *Slayer* shifted quickly, but not quickly enough. Orion snatched at him, tearing open his arm. The injury followed him to his dragon form and black blood dripped to the cavern floor. Sigmund's eyes flashed with fury even as his tail flicked. *"A firestorm,"* he sneered in old-speak. *"Is it real this time?"*

"As real as this," Orion replied and blew a plume of dragonfire of blinding intensity. He smelled burning scales and exhaled even more, backing Sigmund toward the openings in the side of the cliff. The *Slayer* jumped, half-stumbling and half-flying through one opening, but Orion was right behind him. They locked talons and tumbled down the side of the cliff together, snapping and biting at each other. Orion had no interest in exchanging taunts.

His firestorm awaited.

He saw Francesca emerge at the top of the ramp and watched her hurry toward the parked Vespa. The firestorm had dimmed with distance, but she would only be safe when Sigmund had no ability to injure her. Orion slammed the *Slayer* into the face of the stone cliff, glad to hear a bone crack. He couldn't kill his opponent and risk the future, but he could ensure that Sigmund did not interfere in any matters for a long time.

Sigmund twisted and bit at Orion, tearing his thigh. When Orion recoiled, the *Slayer* twisted from his grip and flew high, like an arrow loosed from a bow. Orion charged after him and seized the end of his tail. He swung the *Slayer* so that his wings lost their rhythm and Sigmund coiled back to grab at Orion, talons outstretched. They wrestled until Orion flung his opponent away, then he tore at Sigmund's wings. Sigmund screamed as his right wing was shredded, and when Orion released him, he dropped toward the ground. He flapped his remaining wing wildly in his panic, but he still fell.

Orion saw the glint of water in the distance, which gave him an idea. Lake Avernus was almost a perfect circle of dark water, its surface utterly still. Orion seized Sigmund, tore his other wing, then dragged him through the sky to the lake. He plunged Sigmund into the dark water and held him beneath the surface. The *Slayer* twisted and fought. He struggled against Orion's grip. He thrashed and clawed at Orion, but he could not escape.

When he stilled, Orion hauled him from the water, still holding him captive. *"You will not steal my firestorm,"* he said in old-speak, then plunged his captive into the water again. He waited and watched, knowing his triumph was close when Sigmund shifted to his human form then back to his dragon form again. He began to cycle between forms, his resistance diminished, his death eminent.

Orion hauled him from the water and flung him on the bank. He studied his opponent, belatedly thinking that the *Slayer* had been defeated too readily.

In his dragon form, Sigmund chuckled, his eyes opening to slits of malice. *"No, I will not be the one to extinguish your firestorm,"* he said, his satisfaction clear even in old-speak.

Orion did not understand, then he heard Francesca scream.

It had been a trick!

———

FRANCESCA KNEW the firestorm had to be real this time, because she felt more aroused than before. It wasn't just in her vicinity this time, it was her firestorm, and she tingled and hummed right to her toes as they walked back to the grotto together. Her imagination was filled with memories of Orion's seduction and the conviction that making love would be even better in the light of the firestorm. Her mind was in the gutter, and if they hadn't been in a cave at night, she might have jumped his bones right then and there.

No doubt about it: the firestorm was a dangerous force.

Then she heard the Sibyl's warning. *"Danger,"* that voice murmured in her thoughts, and she knew immediately what the peril would be. She didn't even have to tell Orion, for he had obviously discerned the threat as well.

She didn't need to be told to run. She couldn't resist the urge to look back once, to see him battling with the malachite and silver dragon that she knew as Sigmund.

Orion was magnificent. The glow of the firestorm gilded him, making him look bigger and more imposing. He breathed fire in a stream of brilliant orange and Sigmund flinched, but Orion was merciless.

He was defending her.

Francesca pivoted and ran up the ramp. The dragons were outside the fortress by the time she reached the surface, and she looked up as they soared into the night sky together. Orion shredded one of Sigmund's wings and she almost cheered, then a man cleared his voice.

She spun to find Magnus Montmorency, impeccably attired, standing between her and the Vespa. "We meet again, Signora Marino," he said, as oily as ever.

She retreated a step, trying to make a plan for her own escape.

She came up with nothing.

And he knew it. He smiled his cold dragon smile, his eyes lighting with anticipation, then shimmered blue.

Francesca turned to run, even knowing she wouldn't get far enough fast enough. She couldn't even see Orion and Sigmund anymore and the firestorm had dimmed to a faint yellow. She felt the hot breath of a dragon behind her and gasped when she was snatched up by a jade and gold claw. The *Slayer* soared effortlessly into the sky with her in his grasp, his dark chuckle filling her with terror. She struggled and kicked. She pounded on his chest, but her efforts made no difference. Being carried away against her will infuriated Francesca, but she could only change her situation in one way.

She screamed for Orion.

———

TOO LATE, Orion realized he'd been tricked. He left Sigmund and flew hard in the direction of the grotto. In the distance, he could see a dragon flying out to sea. The Vespa was abandoned and there was no heat of the firestorm.

Orion cursed and flew after Magnus with all his might. The *Slayer* surged upward after he had flown over the long strip of beach that lined the west coast. His wings flapped hard as he raced to higher altitude.

Francesca was in his grasp, her expression furious. The firestorm blazed more brightly as Orion flew closer and she struggled against the *Slayer's* grasp.

"*And the battle to the death will be fought in the light of the firestorm. I cannot imagine a more fitting scene,*" Magnus said.

"I can," Orion replied simply. "*Release my mate.*"

Magnus laughed, then he tossed Francesca aside. She flailed then fell toward the churning surface of the ocean with alarming speed. Orion dove toward her to catch her, but Magnus blocked his course. They locked talons with such force that they tumbled end over end, Orion keenly aware that Francesca needed his help. *Pyr* and *Slayer* struggled for supremacy, trading blow for blow, striking each other with their tails and snapping with their teeth. The firestorm dimmed and Orion knew there wasn't much time to save Francesca.

He wouldn't be cheated of his firestorm again.

"*Such an attractive mate,*" Magnus said softly. "*Too bad you won't be able to savor her.*"

Orion drove his head against the *Slayer's*, hard enough to make them both dizzy, then he flung Magnus aside. He dove after Francesca, scooping her out of the air and holding her against his chest. The firestorm blazed golden fury, sending heat and power through him along with desire. He was fortified just by her proximity and determined to triumph.

Magnus collided hard with Orion's back, his teeth tearing into Orion's wings. He felt the blood flow and turned a somersault in the air, flinging Magnus from his back. The *Slayer* circled around, eyes blazing, and dove toward Orion again.

"You have to put me down," Francesca said. "You can't fight while you're holding me."

She was right. Orion pivoted as if he meant to flee and raced toward the beach. He set Francesca down on her feet, then soared back into the air, colliding hard with Magnus. Once again, they tumbled through the air, then Magnus snapped at Orion, tearing a hole in his chest. The *Slayer* laughed then bared his teeth again, his old-speak slipping into Orion's thoughts.

"*I will enjoy Signora Marino,*" he vowed. "*At least so long as she lasts. Perhaps Sigmund will savor a taste of her, as well.*"

That Magnus would dare to threaten Orion's mate like this was too much.

Orion roared with such fury that even Magnus' eyes lit with alarm. It was too late for Magnus to evade Orion's wrath, though. He seized the *Slayer* with speed, gripping the *Slayer's* claws and bending them backward with all his might. He wound his tail around Magnus' tail to ensure his rival couldn't escape and continued to crush his claws. Orion heard bones crack and did not care. When Magnus faltered, Orion ripped open the *Slayer's* chest with one vicious bite, then exhaled smoke at the wound, driving it deep. Magnus thrashed in his grip in agony. He begged for mercy. He offered riches for his release.

It was too late for any of that.

It had always been too late for that.

Orion breathed dragonfire on his opponent, savoring the smell of burnt scales, then laughed when Magnus changed shape. He was a dragon. He was a man. He was a salamander, but Orion had been ready for that. He pierced the tail of the salamander between his talons, hearing the creature yelp in pain, and carried him back to the beach. Magnus shifted through his sequence of forms twice on the way, but Orion did not release him. Francesca stood on a rock and when she saw him coming, she picked up another rock.

Orion smiled at the perfection of her idea. "We cannot kill him," he reminded her, and her expression was grim.

"But we can make him wish he was dead."

"*This is for my mate and my firestorm,*" he said in old-speak and Magnus fought him with all his remaining strength, such as it was. Orion dropped the salamander and held him captive as Francesca brought the rock down upon Magnus hard. Then she released the stone and backed away.

Orion looked at what remained of Magnus. The *Slayer* was not dead, but his recovery would take a long time—even if Magnus had access to the Dragon's Blood Elixir in this place and time.

Francesca offered him a rock, but Orion shook his head. "It is sufficient," he said. "Neither of them will interfere with the firestorm, and that is all that is of import on this night." He offered one claw to her, and she smiled, stepping into his embrace as the firestorm flared to brilliance between them.

Magnus moaned softly, but Orion cared only for his mate. He lifted Francesca into his embrace and took flight, carrying her home like the precious burden she was.

Nothing had ever felt so good as the firestorm, but Orion suspected that satisfying it would be even better.

CHAPTER FIFTEEN

Magnus was in his salamander form but so crushed that he was barely moving at all. The gold and green salamander was smeared on the rocks that lined the beach, black blood around him, eyes closed. His bones were broken, clearly, and the open wounds were numerous.

Sigmund wasn't feeling so good himself. It had taken him a long time to reach Magnus, partly because he'd steered a wide course around Orion and the brilliant beacon of the firestorm. His lungs ached from the strain of struggling to breathe, and he knew he'd be bruised all over. Why hadn't Orion just killed them both?

Sigmund poked Magnus with a stick, and he wasn't very gentle about it. He could hear the faint beat of Magnus' heart, a beat that would stop soon without help. "Wake up, Magnus. You're going to owe me a favor."

When Magnus stirred, Sigmund picked him up, grimacing at the mess on his hands.

"Think about it," Sigmund said when the salamander's eyes opened slightly. "I could fry you to a crisp right now and finish you off." He started to change shape, knowing that Magnus had seen the blue shimmer that was a precursor to his shift because the salamander's eyes widened. "Or we could make a deal."

"*What do you want?*" That Magnus used old-speak was indicative of his weakened state.

"Take me to Rome with you."

"I can't," Magnus whispered, but Sigmund didn't trust him. "Put me down. Leave me alone."

"No. Either we both go, or you get cooked." Sigmund watched the *Slayer* closely as he felt the change come over him. The blue shimmer of light lit the deserted beach, but Magnus suddenly moaned in protest.

"Not in dragon form," he whispered. "I can't take us both when you're in that form."

"Then you'd better be quick," Sigmund threatened, hovering on the cusp of change. "As soon as I shift, you'll literally be toast."

Magnus' eyes flashed, then a wind snatched them up. Sigmund barely had time to catch his breath before they were slammed into a hard tiled floor. On the beach? That made no sense. His grip loosened on the salamander and Magnus slipped from his grip and scampered away. The hair on Sigmund's neck prickled as he heard a door slam and lock against him.

He was in Magnus' apartment in Rome. It was night and all the doors in the main room were closed against him. Embers simmered low in the fireplace, but the floor was chilly.

"No one threatens me," Magnus said darkly from behind the secured door.

"You have to give me more of the Elixir!" Sigmund said.

The *Slayer* laughed, his amusement fading to a cough. There was a sound, like a bottle being uncorked, glass against glass. Sigmund crawled toward the sound, desperate for a taste.

"You have to earn it," Magnus said darkly.

A moment later, there was a sigh of satisfaction.

Magnus' laugh was stronger then and Sigmund knew what he had done. He'd taken the Elixir and he'd heal. He had to share!

Sigmund began to beg, but Magnus spoke crisply.

"It's gone," he said with glee, unlocking the door. He stood in his human form, visibly growing more vital by the instant. He wore a black silk dressing gown and as Sigmund watched, his skin healed, his wounds vanished, his hair grew back where it had been burned off. His eyes glittered the whole while. He held an empty glass, one with a reddish residue at the bottom of it, and waved it at Sigmund. "I've had it all and am going back for more." He feigned astonishment. "Oh! You don't know where the sanctuary of the Elixir is, do you?"

"No!" Sigmund cried, throwing himself toward the *Slayer* to beg.

"Oh well." Magnus feigned dismay, waved, then vanished before Sigmund's very eyes.

"No!" Sigmund spun in fury and kicked over the closest pedestal. The stone dragon twined around the pillar cracked when it hit the floor and Sigmund, for some reason unknown to himself, caught the vase that had been sitting on top of the pillar. He eyed the inscription.

Aurelia.

Who *was* that?

It was hard to believe that Magnus had ever cared for anyone other than himself. *Slayers* didn't have firestorms and Magnus had been a *Slayer* for a long, long time. She couldn't have been his mate.

Could she have been a particularly special victim?

Did it matter?

Something rattled in the ceramic jar, and Sigmund lifted the lid. He smiled when he saw the bloodstone resting within the vessel, because he knew exactly what it was.

This would change everything.

He pocketed the stone, confident that Magnus wouldn't return soon. He cleaned up in the luxurious bathroom, then helped himself to a meal in Magnus' well-equipped kitchen and a change of clothes from the *Slayer's* extensive wardrobe. He liberated the cash Magnus had foolishly left in his lair, and left the apartment forever, whistling.

Sigmund's satisfaction would be considerably less when he discovered, months later, that the bloodstone he had stolen was a copy, devoid of the powers of the original.

His bitterness against Magnus Montmorency would only be redoubled.

———

SHE COULD HAVE LOST ORION, and with him, an opportunity.

Francesca felt a new urgency, one that was fed by the insistent heat of the firestorm. She trusted Orion. He wasn't like other men she'd known and he certainly wasn't like Derek. If this relationship led to heartbreak, it wouldn't be because Orion had chosen to hurt her or cast her aside. She knew that he would do whatever he could to defend her and their son.

She smiled at the idea that Orion was her destiny.

She could get used to dragon flights with him. It was wonderful to fly back to Cumae in Orion's protective grasp, to feel the wind on her face and to hear the regular sound of his wings beating against the night. She could feel the pounding of his heart beneath her hands, and she looked down on the city as they approached her apartment, feeling blessed to experience this magic. The firestorm sparked beneath her hands, sizzling between the two of them, flaring from orange to yellow and iridescent white, a glorious sign that they were alive and vital. It filled her with a yearning and a conviction that her choice had been the right one.

Francesca touched her lips to Orion's chest and closed her eyes, feeling his heart skip and his embrace close more tightly around her. She felt the beat of his heart match the pace of her own and felt a potent sense of unity, as if their bodies and hearts were one. It shook her and made her a little dizzy in a very good way. He circled over the site of the apartment, then descended in a graceful spiral. She laughed aloud when he shifted shape in the last moment and landed in human form on her terrace, with her cradled in his arms.

"They will not follow us," he said in that confident rumble she had come to rely upon. He scanned the sky then set her on her feet. "Not now."

"Tonight, Orion," she said, reaching for his face. He looked down at her, never assuming, and when she smiled, his eyes lit with silver fire and hope. "I want you, tonight."

"You cannot evade the promise of the firestorm, Francesca," he warned but she kissed him to silence, loving how the passion flared immediately between them. The light of the firestorm burned white and incendiary, a perfect indication of the heat of her desire for him.

"I know."

"But there will be a child..."

She adored that he was arguing her side, even as his arms wrapped around her, and she felt his body respond to her touch. "A son," she said and he nodded. "I want you," she whispered. "And whatever comes of that will be." She smiled up at him. "I can't think of anything more perfect than giving you what you desire most."

"But..."

"We'll make it work, Orion. I trust you."

"Francesca!" he murmured with awe. She saw his eyes glow, then he captured her lips in a triumphant kiss, one that could not disguise the joy in his heart.

"We could use a condom again," she suggested when she had the chance to speak again. She was breathless and filled with desire. "You've waited so long. We could make it last a day or two." Even as she made the suggestion, she wasn't sure she could hold out.

Orion shook his head. "It will not matter."

"You can't be sure it will happen the first time," she argued. "We could be careful and watch my cycle, use protection..." Her voice faded as he shook his head with resolve.

"The first time, Francesca. It is always thus with my kind." He raised a finger. "And so, you must trust me in this truth, and if we satisfy the firestorm, you must accept the price."

"I do, though. I just want you to enjoy the firestorm."

"Francesca," he chided, entwining his fingers with hers. "How could I not?" Then he swept her into his arms again and carried her into the apartment, kissing her senseless as he carried her to the bed. The firestorm's light danced between them, sparking at intervals, gilding them both and even making her apartment look more like an exotic refuge than she knew it was.

Orion took a steadying breath when he set her down, then unfastened her blouse slowly, his eyes glowing with anticipation. She let him undress her, enjoying the sweep of his hands over her bare flesh, liking the way he smiled at the sight of her lacey white bra. He cupped her breasts in his hands and leaned closer to kiss her nipple, teasing it to a point, then laving his attention upon the other. His hands were a little rough and warm, the heat of the firestorm making every point of contact hum with urgency.

"No," she protested. "We need to tend your injuries first."

Orion was clearly impatient with this notion, but Francesca ignored his protest. She untucked his T-shirt and pulled it over his head, casting it aside with impatience. The firestorm sparked at each point of contact, its demand so distracting that she almost forgot her intention—then she saw the wound from Magnus' teeth.

She retreated to the bathroom and returned with a wet cloth to clean the wound. "It's not as bad as the last one," she said and he shrugged.

"A mere scratch."

"More than that," she chided and he chuckled, his hands rising to bracket her waist. His eyes darkened with obvious intent and she felt her own desire rise. Then she remembered his earlier move with the vessel.

She placed her hand flat against the wound and watched him catch his breath, even as she saw the firestorm flare and flash beneath her touch. She did it twice, ensuring that the wound was closed, then he caught her up and returned her to the bed. He kissed her protest to silence and she surrendered to him willingly.

His hands bracketed her waist again, his kisses moving lower. He swept away her bra, then her jeans and panties. Francesca shook out her hair, hearing the clip hit the floor and not caring where it landed. He trailed kisses of fire across her torso, then turned his attention to her feet. He kissed her instep and traced a line of heat up her calves, growling at the softness of her thighs, inhaling with satisfaction when she parted her thighs in welcome. He feasted upon her then and Francesca abandoned herself to the pleasure of his caress, loving how he teased her with his tongue. Already, he knew what she liked best and he used that knowledge against her, driving her almost to the edge, then retreating, building the tumult within her steadily.

Mercilessly.

Until finally he caught her closer and cast her over the edge, the firestorm flaring to such brilliance between them that she thought it might singe her very soul. She cried out, clinging to him in her release, and heard his proud chuckle. She reached for him before she had even caught her breath.

It was her turn to torment him with pleasure.

————

ORION DID NOT EVEN WANT to blink, lest he miss one detail of the marvel that was Francesca. Her eyes were shining, her hair flowing loose over her shoulders, and her lips a little swollen from his kisses. She was flushed and her nipples were taut, but she was purposeful. She smiled into his eyes as she unfastened his jeans and he kicked off his boots, liking the feel of her hands upon him. Even without the firestorm, he knew her caress would be intoxicating.

She ran her hands over him, flattening them against his skin so that the firestorm was a tsunami of fire beneath her palms. Her hands swept over him from waist to shoulder, healing the small nicks and cuts from the dragonfire, searing him with a desire that he suspected would never be fully sated.

And then she closed her hands around his strength, caressing him so slowly that Orion thought he would die of temptation. She tormented him, moving her hands slowly over him, making him harder and hotter with every stroke. He knew she needed to be in control of the moment, so he clenched his fists by his side, staring down at her, taut to his very marrow.

When she bent to touch her lips to him, Orion could only whisper her name, his voice shaking.

She laughed and urged him to the floor, caressing him ceaselessly as she climbed atop him. He was lost in the marvel of her eyes and the sweet sensation of the firestorm, so beguiling and seductive, almost as irresistible as Francesca herself. When she straddled him, he smiled and let his hands fall to her waist again. He lifted her even as he savored the view, and she took him within her, her eyes shining as she lowered herself and sheathed him completely. They caught their breath as one, gazes locked, then Francesca moved atop him.

In that moment, as the fervor rose and their bodies clamored for release, he felt his heartbeat match the pace of hers again. He was dizzy with the sensation of their breathing finding the same rhythm, with the conviction that they joined as one—a union far greater than the sum of the parts. He gripped her waist as she bent down to kiss him, her breasts against his chest, her hair across his face, her lips upon his and her sweetness wrapped around him. He moved once, twice, three times, the firestorm flared to furious brilliance, and there was only Francesca in his universe.

He rolled her to her back, rubbing himself against her so that she cried out once more with pleasure, then buried himself within her and surrendered to the torrent of fiery pleasure. The firestorm suffused him, tempered him, made him stronger than he had been and more *Pyr* than he had been.

And it sealed their hearts together forevermore.

Orion could ask for no more. The gods had smiled upon them, indeed.

———

"YOU'RE NOT *THE* ORION, are you?" Francesca asked when they were lying on the bed afterward. The apartment was lit only by moonlight and Orion felt complete as he never had before. Their legs were entwined and Francesca was leaning against his chest, her hair tangled around his fingers, her breasts pressed against him. Orion could imagine no better place to be.

"*The* Orion?" he echoed with amusement. "I am no giant, Francesca."

"That could be argued," she said impishly, trailing a hand down the length of him. Orion chuckled. She pulled out of his embrace and leaned over him, her weight on her elbows and her eyes filled with stars. Orion was filled with awe that this brilliant beauty was his mate. He ran a fingertip down her cheek, then let his fingers slide into her hair. Their kiss was long and sweet, its power undiminished by the satisfying of the firestorm.

"*The* Orion," she repeated moments later. "The son of Euryale, daughter of Minos of Crete, and Poseidon. The legendary hunter who could walk across the seas, thanks to his father's gift."

Orion smiled, liking that she knew the stories of his time. "The one who was promised the hand of Merope, the daughter of King Oenopion if he cleared the island of Chios of all wild beasts in a day."

"The one denied by Oenopion after he had done the feat."

Francesca took a breath and her eyes darkened with concern. "The one who raped Merope, taking what he believed was his to possess."

Orion put a fingertip over her lips and shook his head. "Again, you have heard the version of the tale that omits our very nature. That Orion was my forebear. He was deceived and denied, then given drugged wine, falsely accused, then blinded and dumped on the beach like so much offal."

Francesca caught her breath. "He walked across the water to Lemnos, where Hephaestus had his forge."

Orion smiled. "Seeking the aid of one who has always favored us, and Hephaestus did not deny him."

She wagged a finger at him. "He had Celadion, one of Hephaestus' apprentices, stand on his shoulders to guide him to the forge."

"But Celadion followed his master's instruction and guided Orion to the east, where the light of Helius cured his blindness. Orion then returned to Oenopion's court to seek vengeance, but Hephaestus defended him from his own fury, hiding Oenopion from Orion's thirst for vengeance."

"A protective god," she said, settling back down beside him. "I like that. A lot of the time, they seem exploitative."

"We are his children."

"You still believe in gods?" she asked softly, kissing him after her question.

"How could I not? They have brought me to you."

She laughed, her eyes dancing. "Don't imagine you've convinced me to believe in destiny." He knew, though, that she teased him, for their union was so right that it could only have been fated.

"What do you call it, then, that we should find each other against all odds?"

She propped her elbow on his chest, unexpectedly playful. He watched as she kicked her feet and considered the question. "Good sense," she said finally, meeting his gaze with satisfaction. "We're good together. It's only reasonable that we should find each other."

"You forget that I am not of your time."

She sobered then. "Can you bear that?"

He rubbed her cheek with his thumb. "I will endure any challenge for you, Francesca. You are my destined mate, and I am yours."

She smiled then reached to kiss him, her touch igniting a fire within him that would never be quenched.

"The firestorm's not burning anymore," she said when she finally lifted her head. "Does that mean we conceived a child?"

"You know it does. A son, and he will be strong."

She nodded, considering this, and he was glad to see that she had no second thoughts. "What should we name him?" she asked, to his surprise.

Orion smiled. "The choice must be yours, Francesca." He cupped her cheek in his hand, then stared at a glimmer of blue-green darkfire. It flared between his hand and her face, then slid beneath Francesca before vanishing—and leaving Orion chilled.

She yawned, unaware of that he had observed. "We should get some sleep before the sun comes up," she said, reaching for the coverings. Orion pulled it over her, smiling at her obvious contentment. The tips of his fingertips disappeared as he adjusted the covering, then he blinked and they were as they had been.

Had he imagined it?

He said nothing to Francesca, but held her close, lying awake long after she had slipped into dreams, his own thoughts churning.

———

ORION DREAMED of a late autumn day when the plains stretched golden all the way to the mountains and the sky was fiercely blue overhead. He felt the chill of the wind in his hair as his father carried him far to the east, and he knew from the weight in his heart which particular day he was recalling. His father was a dark shadow against the sun, a powerful black dragon with sharp talons and teeth, but on this day, there were tears in his dark eyes.

They flew toward a gathering of women, women armed who stood with their horses. There was a circle of tall poles, each one driven into the soil, the circle of women inside that boundary, the horses tethered outside of it. They stood in silence, watching as Orion's father descended. He shifted shape just before his feet touched the ground, becoming a warrior in simple armor. The priestess, adorned in skins and carrying a mighty staff, gestured to him, indicating a place reserved for him, and he set Orion on his feet.

Orion, all of seven years of age, was invited by the priestess to a place of honor as the drums began. He looked about himself, his eyes filling with tears, taking note of those who had taught and played with him on his annual visits to his mother's people. He had spent summers with the Amazons, learning to ride and to shoot, hearing their stories, being challenged to set fires, to hunt and to track. He studied the surrounding mountain peaks, seeing that they were crested with snow. He knew their names, the names given to them by the Amazons, and he recited them beneath his breath in the verse his mother had taught him to remember them all.

At the priestess's gesture, he stepped forward. She led him to the grave, his father following behind, and looked upon his mother for the last time. She might have been asleep, her eyes closed and her hands upon her bow, but she was too still. Even with his keen *Pyr* senses, he could not hear her breath or her heartbeat. She wore her crown, an elaborate arrangement of flowers and spirals that was as tall as a man's hand, spired and glorious. He saw the wound in her side, the one that had been her last.

His father had told him that she had been killed in battle, defending her kind, and that her passing was of the highest honor. Orion saw that many had fallen with her, even horses, and that they were all to be honored and entombed together. The corpses were all arrayed in their finest weapons and armor, the horses in their fine headdresses and saddles. There was food for the gods, as well as offerings of honey, salt and wine.

The priestess raised her hands and began to sing a lament and a farewell, and Orion felt his father's hand land upon his shoulder. He couldn't look away from the dark scale on his mother's breast, the one that he knew perfectly fit the gap in his father's armor.

Then the other women of the tribe added their voices to the priestess's lament and Orion bowed his head, feeling hot tears scald his cheeks. He would never forget her, the way she laughed as they rode together, the way she challenged him to try harder, the way she hugged him fiercely each time he arrived or departed.

This time, there would be no embrace from her and he wished with all his heart that there might have been just one more.

ORION AWAKENED SUDDENLY in the night, Francesca sleeping against his side. That day was vivid in his mind, as clear as if it had just occurred, the ache in his heart as potent as if the wound had just been made.

But his mother had been Amazon, and her grave would provide the evidence Francesca desired of their existence. He eased from the bed, ignoring the blue-green spark of darkfire that danced around the perimeter of the apartment. It seemed it would never leave him be and he had best get used to it.

It was almost dawn, light enough that he could see his way around without turning on the lights. He found Francesca's map and spread it on the counter, running his fingertip across the mountain peaks. He had to find the right combination, to imagine how they looked from the ground and not from above. It had to be in this area, for it seemed the right distance from his father's home and the plains were broad.

Perhaps here, or here.

He picked up a pencil to mark the likely locations. Francesca might have pictures of the area or they might travel there, so he could provide the clue to her Troy. Excited by the possibilities, he began to draw a circle around the potential area, but the pencil fell to the counter as his fingers vanished again. The pencil rolled to the floor, his mark only barely begun, but Orion had no means of reaching for it. His arm was gone and the side of his chest was vanishing.

He opened his mouth to call for Francesca, but no sound was emitted. The darkfire flashed, its tempest blinded him and he seized the quartz crystal. He shouted into the storm even as he shifted shape to battle the invisible force.

"Francesca!" he roared and his mouth filled with flying sand. "I love you!"

But he was not with Francesca anymore.

———

FRANCESCA AWAKENED SUDDENLY, Orion's voice loud in her dreams. What had he said? Had he said he loved her?

She wasn't sure. She sat up abruptly, unable to miss his absence. The bed beside her was cold. He wasn't on the terrace. There was no glow of the firestorm to guide her to him, not anymore, and she was keenly aware of his absence. She couldn't hear him or see any sign of him. but she knew in her heart that she wasn't going to find him. She searched, all the same, increasingly frantic when there was no hint of him.

No, that wasn't quite true. The big map had been spread on the counter and there was a pencil on the floor. She found a mark on the map, as if someone had started to circle a location but had been interrupted.

Her blood ran cold at the portent of that.

She also found a single dragon scale on the terrace. It was obsidian and hard, obviously a piece of Orion's protective armor in his dragon form. It was bigger than her hand, curved slightly to fit against his skin, with a dark thorn at the bottom of it. She could see a lined pattern in it, like growth lines in a fingernail or the rings within a tree, and she ran her hand over this evidence of his age.

And of his existence.

A wave of golden light filled Francesca's thoughts suddenly, a reminder of the light in Mr. Montmorency's glass vessel and the way it had flowed into her in the grotto the night before. Had they really visited the underworld? She remembered the ghost of Orion's father, the song of the darkfire, the spark of the firestorm, and knew it had all been real.

Then she heard a whisper of Latin in her thoughts.

"For your choice, I grant you the gift withheld from me, Francesca Marino. You will not age until you are reunited with your destined mate."

Francesca felt a touch on her cheek, like a chaste kiss from lips she could not see, then the fireflies swirled and soared, unfurling from her lips and vanishing into the sky high above her.

Even the Sibyl had left her.

She was alone, with only a dragon scale to remember Orion.

No, they had satisfied the firestorm. She let her hand curve over her stomach, guessing that she had one other souvenir of the man who had stolen her heart away.

Francesca would have Orion's son.

She recalled the Sibyl's words and wondered at them. When would she and Orion be united? She had to hope it would be soon, not when they met in the afterlife.

She turned to look at the papers on her desk. Until he returned, she had plenty of work to do.

———

THE DARKFIRE SWIRLED around Orion in a maelstrom, the wind whipping at his hair and clothes as it tore him away from

Francesca. He railed against it, even knowing it was futile, hoping against hope that the tempest would deposit him in her apartment again.

It did not.

When the wind finally stilled, he found himself in the temple at Delphi as a warrior entered the sanctuary. He knew that dark-haired *Pyr* and recognized Alexander immediately. A woman walked with him, their movements revealing even at a distance that they were together. Two boys accompanied them, one of them favoring Alexander and the other so like Drake that Orion knew this was the son Drake had been compelled to leave behind.

He raised his hand and would have shouted, but the darkfire sparked and the wind snatched him up again.

He had no notion of how much time passed or how long he had been subjected to the darkfire's relentless storm. Eventually, the dust stilled and he found himself on a hilltop, with a circle of stones and a woman cradling a child that looked newly born. The man with her was *Pyr*, Orion smelled the truth of his nature, and he thought this dragon shifter to be a stranger, until that man looked up. It was his former comrade Damian, his hair turned to a fair blond, and he smiled as a company of dragons appeared in the distant sky. Orion knew that he and Alexander had found each other, then, as well as their mates, and that the darkfire had served them well.

He had time to be relieved before his ordeal began again. It seemed interminable this time, and that several eternities passed before he was relinquished from its grip again.

And then he knew what he should do. He had been taught the song of the darkfire. He could command the darkfire. He could use his skill to bring tidings to his fellow *Pyr*, and maybe in time, to return to Francesca.

First, he suspected, he had a destiny to fulfill.

His fellows were scattered through time. The darkfire had shown him Alexander's fate. He would visit all the others. He would talk to all of the others, gathering their tales and bringing them tidings. He would encourage them that they bore many sons to aid in the coming war against the *Slayers*.

And in this, he would see the *Pyr* triumph.

Orion held out the crystal and raised his voice in the song his father had taught him, ordering it to surrender to his will.

———

IN LONDON, Rafferty read the newspaper with disapproval. Who was this dragon who had damaged the museum in Baiae? The pictures were grainy, so there was little chance of Rafferty identifying the offender. It made no sense that a single dragon would go berserk in an exhibition hall and destroy so many artefacts and exhibits.

The article said the floor had been corroded by the dragon's black blood, which meant he was a *Slayer*. Rafferty shook his head, even as he admitted the explanation made sense. *Slayers* showed no respect for the treasures of the earth and the marvels of history. There was nothing he could do about the damage, but the article hinted that the museum might not have the funds for a restoration.

Rafferty stood up with purpose, intent upon calling his bank. He'd make a donation, an anonymous one, to help with the repairs. He wasn't responsible for the actions of *Slayers*, but he hated to see such destruction and couldn't just stand aside.

He left his study so quickly that he didn't see the blue-green spark flare in the large quartz crystal entrusted to him by Pwyll so many years before, the crystal that had always remained dark.

By the time Rafferty stepped into his study again, the crystal was dark once again, holding its secrets close.

———

IN THE SANCTUARY of the Dragon's Blood Elixir in Ohio, Magnus blinked. He felt something, then questioned his own observation. He turned to survey the grotto, wondering whether he had imagined the sudden glimmer of blue-green light.

Then he wondered why he was in Ohio. Hadn't he been in Rome?

And how had he been injured? He recalled no battle but felt as if he had survived a dragonfight.

What had just happened?

And why didn't he remember?

CHAPTER SIXTEEN

I n the early days after Orion's disappearance, Francesca couldn't stop looking for him. She couldn't stop hoping for his sudden reappearance. She certainly had moments of doubt.

The weirdest thing was that it was as if Orion had never been in her time. No one remembered him. She sat at the same table at the restaurant where they had eaten together, and the waiter teased her gently about always eating alone. The damage at the museum was blamed upon a single dragon, no one apparently remembering that there had been a second one. The pictures in the newspaper, which had never been very good, had changed and now showed only a single dragon in flight over the sea.

She sought out Gina the photographer, but she looked at Francesca as if she was crazy when Francesca asked about dragons. She complained that her film had all been ruined by her assistant before being developed, while Paolo insisted that he hadn't exposed the undeveloped film to light. Either way, there were no pictures of that day at Cumae. They'd had to photograph the four vessels all over again.

The one thing that remained was the enameled cast iron casserole he'd bought. It was large and rectangular, with a lid, made by a famous manufacturer. But the enamel was the most horrible hue of apple green, shading to vivid yellow on the handles. It might have been the ugliest pot Francesca had ever seen, but it was entirely functional. Its color was probably why it had ended up in the funny little store at a very low price for its quality.

She started to learn to cook, just simple ingredients, roasted in that pot. She knew she'd never relinquish it, even though it was heavy.

There was no sign of Sigmund, which she couldn't regret at all. Dr. Thomas said that Magnus Montmorency had sent his regrets in response to the invitation to the opening of the exhibit. Evidently, he was away from Rome for the summer, with no plans to return in time to see the display. Francesca didn't feel very badly about that either.

She worked hard on the revision of her thesis and even Dr. Thomas confessed to being impressed. She defended it in May, returning to Cumae for the summer to keep working on the grotto excavation. Dr. Thomas brought her the letter with the good news of her degree, smiling at her delight, then gave her an article about the grotto to proof-read for him.

In the article, he'd given her credit for the discovery.

Francesca caught her breath as she read it again, unable to quell a sense that her career was mustering speed.

If only she could have shared the moment with Orion.

———

FRANCESCA HAD two excellent job offers, evidently because word of her thesis had spread rapidly. She also had a publication offer for the thesis and the sense that her star was rising fast. She accepted the post that began in the fall. She liked the department head, a brusque woman of fifty or so with a wicked sense of humor. She liked the position, because she'd be teaching in the history department and be cross-appointed to Classical Studies and their new Women's Studies department. She liked that the college in question was close enough to her brothers' homes that she could call for help if she needed it, but far enough away that she'd have her privacy. She talked to her new boss about her pregnancy and was relieved that it was taken in stride. They immediately planned for her to take on two teaching assistants, who would have the first semester to come up to speed. If she needed to take some time in the winter, everything would be covered.

Her brothers were more surprised by her pregnancy, but she met them for dinner at Rafe's place to explain. She told them that it wasn't the father's fault that he couldn't be with her, and that she loved him with all her heart.

"If he makes you happy, Frannie, that's all good," Rafe said and Gabe nodded.

Maddy squeezed Francesca's hand. "You just call if you need us."

It was another gift and one she appreciated. As her pregnancy progressed and she had questions, Maddy or Kathy were always glad to reassure her.

The green pot was one of the few items she'd moved back from the apartment in Cumae and it was in steady use. Francesca knew she'd never be a great chef, but she ate better than she had in the past. Their son needed the best start he could get.

She also took Orion's scale and kept it close at all times.

She talked to Orion when she was alone in her apartment. She had no idea whether he could hear her or not, she wasn't sure how closely the strands of time entangled, but she talked to him anyway. Doing so made her feel less like she was facing this challenge alone. She also remembered things when she talked to him, as if his memories were sliding into her own thoughts. She thought of that first dinner, of his earnest expression as he confided that he had lived in the past. She recalled the glorious golden shower of the firestorm breaking free. She was awed all over again by the memory of the first time she had heard the Sybil's voice. She debated baby names in those discussions with Orion, knowing that he would support her choice.

Francesca decided upon her grandfather's name, Balthasar.

Christmas that year seemed particularly magical, filled with the wonder of the season and Francesca's own awareness of the miracle of her son. She spent the season at Gabe's house, enjoying the chaos of small children and the comfort of good food.

Francesca went into labor a week later, on Epiphany. She would always remember the Christmas lights in their myriad colors shining in the darkness. She would always remember the snow falling gently and the quiet of that night. Her labor was long but not much worse than she had anticipated—she had, after all, done her research and was prepared for whatever might happen.

What did happen was absolutely textbook.

When she gave the final push at the doctor's order, her mind flooded with blue-green light and she felt Orion's lips against her ear. The warmth of his hand seemed to brush her shoulder and there was awe in the whisper that only she heard.

"He is perfect, Francesca." His chuckle rumbled so close that she didn't want to open her eyes and see that he wasn't there. Her tears rose. "He takes after his mother," he added in a murmur, then she felt his kiss upon her temple. It was a gift beyond all expectation and she opened her eyes, certain that Orion would be back by her side.

Of course, when she opened her eyes, there was no sign of him, and no hint that anyone else was aware of his presence.

And she ached with the loss. The Sibyl had said they would be together again, but when? Francesca was impatient for that reunion and hated that she couldn't influence its timing.

There was always work—and her beautiful son to raise.

———

FRANCESCA.

Orion was haunted by his memories of Francesca and tormented by the way he had been stolen away from her. There had been no chance to say farewell. For the first time in his life, he resented the notion of destiny. Even though he knew he could contribute to the future of the Pyr, he hated that his own partnership seemed to have been sacrificed to the greater good. He felt that he had betrayed her, by satisfying the firestorm in good faith, then leaving her alone to bear and raise their son. The result had been precisely what she had not desired.

He halfway feared to witness her disappointment, but in another way, he could not stay away. He commanded the darkfire to show him Francesca, only to arrive by her side as she was delivering their son. How had so much time passed?

Like a shade or a ghost, Orion was both in attendance and not truly there. He could watch. He could hear, but he could not interact with those in attendance. He watched in wonder as his son was born, as Francesca delivered a beautiful boy with grace and strength. He watched the tears slip from her eyes when the infant was placed in her arms and wished he could truly be with her. He spoke, knowing no one would hear his words, and kissed her temple with awe, knowing she would be unaware of his touch.

But she looked up, as if she sensed his presence, and he had a moment's wild joy before the darkfire crackled again.

He hated to go, and yet, this glimpse sustained him as he continued his labor for his kind.

He commanded the darkfire to show him more. He entreated it to let him see his beloved, and though it was erratic in obeying his demand, the darkfire took him to her at intervals.

Orion saw their son take his first steps, and his heart swelled with pride when the boy's first words were in Greek. He watched Francesca pursue her work with passion and dedication, and when he could, he helped her. He found that he could sometimes nudge a small item or flutter the corner of a map, guiding her attention in the direction of success. She returned often to the mark he had made on the map, seeking the clue he had tried to give her to her Troy.

If only she could find Iphito's grave. Then he would have given Francesca her heart's desire.

———

AFTER BALTHASAR WAS BORN, Francesca's dreams began.

On the anniversary of her first meeting with Orion, she dreamed of their first lovemaking so vividly that she might have been with him again and awakened with tears damp on her cheeks. It was bittersweet to feel that he had been so close but was still lost to her, but in another way, his presence at intervals gave her strength. To know that he would make love to her at intervals, as if it was both the first and the last time, even if it was in her dreams, gave Francesca the strength to continue.

She felt the Sibyl's presence at intervals, though those incidents were less predictable. She would dream of a verse, or a riddle, or envision a site she knew and realize some detail about it. Over the years, Francesca gained a reputation not only for thorough scholarship but for remarkable finds, ones that she might not have made without the Sibyl's hints.

Balthasar was a healthy boy with dark curly hair and silver-blue eyes that reminded Francesca always of Orion, though there was something of her brother's in his mischievous smile. He was active and curious, clever and honest, and even though Francesca knew her opinion was biased, she knew he would become a wonderful man. She taught him Greek from the cradle, wanting him to be able to speak his father's tongue, and he showed a gift with languages that she could only admire.

They traveled to Europe each year, to Greece and Italy, for her studies, and her son had an enviable education thanks to her own connections. When he reached puberty, Francesca watched for any hint of his emerging powers—and routinely scanned their vicinity for *Slayers*—but it seemed that some power watched over them. She often glimpsed a spark of darkfire from the periphery of her vision and she believed Orion was protecting her son.

This was another gift of the firestorm: Francesca had changed from a woman who had to see a thing to believe in it, to one who could take many concepts on faith.

Balthasar finished college with honors, choosing to continue his studies at Cambridge England. His dexterity with language made him uniquely qualified to study ancient literature in all its versions and variations. He often joined Francesca on her research projects. He learned to sail and built his own boat, showing a passion for sailing that made her think of Orion.

And every year that Francesca turned the page of the calendar on December 31, she hoped that the moment of her reunion with Orion was coming closer.

When her co-workers began to tease her that she'd found the fountain of youth and not shared it, Francesca realized she wasn't aging at the same speed as those around her. She hadn't considered the implications of the Sibyl's gift before that, but now she did. She started to have her hair colored, with a touch of grey.

It seemed that in her career, she went from triumph to triumph. Under her direction, the grottos for three other sibyls were found and explored, though only Francesca knew the prize she was always seeking: proof of the Amazon warriors. Orion's half-drawn circle was a clue but an incomplete one. She had to ride the tide of politics and alliances, but she felt she was coming closer to something remarkable.

In the meantime, they were stepping into the history of the *Pyr* that might bring Orion back to her, and Francesca had her notebook as a guide. When she saw the announcement, she ensured that she attended a lecture given by Dr. Eileen Grosvenor in Chicago on comparative mythology. Mindful of Orion's concern about changing the future, Francesca sat in the back and listened to this articulate woman in admiration. The lecturer would soon be the mate of the leader of the *Pyr* and the mother of the new Wyvern, but as yet, she had no notion of the future before her.

Orion would be with her soon and Francesca could not wait.

ORION FOUND himself in the company of a *Pyr* he did not know, one who lived in a cave in some colder clime. He chanted and sang to himself, a *Pyr* well acquainted with spells and songs. When Orion first manifested, he expected to be unseen as usual—but that *Pyr* glanced up, aware of his presence as others had not been.

Indeed, he beckoned to Orion. Though Orion could not understand his words, the *Pyr* showed him two large quartz crystals lined up on the floor of the cavern. He began to sing and the blue-green of darkfire flickered in Orion's peripheral vision. He had the sense that the darkfire was being summoned by this *Pyr*, that it could not resist his song, and he listened avidly as it was mustered.

He was of the line of the Cantor, Orion guessed.

The darkfire responded to his summons, but it did not linger. No matter how they sang together, the darkfire extinguished itself when they fell silent. Orion knew this was because his companion did not know all of the song.

He put the third crystal on the floor of the cave and the other *Pyr* eyed the darkfire within it. His curiosity was clear. Then Orion sang, first the song this *Pyr* had sung, then the one his own father had taught him. The other *Pyr* soon learned the new tune and when Orion sang his grandfather's song, the darkfire cracked in the stone. It illuminated the cave with its brilliant light, then when their voices fell silent, a spark of it remained in the crystal. It crackled and snapped, seemingly fighting its bond, but the darkfire was snared.

The other *Pyr* chuckled and nodded approval.

Then he shifted shape, becoming a dragon first, then a salamander, a stag then an eagle. He became a dragon again, the glint in his eyes revealing that there was far more to this *Pyr* than Orion had expected.

They sang together, the darkfire in the stone growing ever brighter and stronger as more of it was mustered. Orion lost track of time. Beyond the entrance to the cave, the sun rose and set, the night passed and the dawn came again. There was only the song, only the gradual gathering of the darkfire. He thought perhaps it was three days later that the entire cave was alight in blue-green fire. The other *Pyr* shifted shape with dizzying speed as the radiance grew blindingly bright, then they fell silent, hoarse from their efforts.

The darkfire was snared within the three crystals. It sparked and flashed, trapped there so completely that the air in the cave felt still.

The other *Pyr* became a man again and nodded satisfaction at his deed, then the maelstrom snatched Orion away. The other *Pyr* raised a hand in salute, his expression one of resignation.

The storm swirled around Orion, but he was too tired to direct the darkfire. He let it take him where it would, hoping that it would lead him to Francesca now that his destiny had been fulfilled.

———

IN 2005, Francesca changed the focus of her main studies to the role of women in the outflung Roman colonies like Britannia, simply to justify a move to London. She sought out information about the new subway line being built near Greenwich and went to the construction site regularly, hoping the Dragon's Teeth would be found. She was there the day that they were salvaged and watched, her heart in her throat, as they were carried away to be secured with the other relics.

She and Orion were in the same thread of time.

In 2008, Francesca saw the auction notice from the Fonthill Foundation and cut it out of the newspaper, pinning it to her bulletin board where she could see it every day. The address was listed and she knew Orion was *there*, so close and yet so inaccessible. She walked past the building countless times, her yearning so acute that she could taste it. This was the period that it was hardest to follow his instructions and ensure that she didn't meddle in events.

There was an eclipse and on impulse, Francesca went to Fleet Street on the night in question. When she was near the dragon statue that defined the boundary of the city, she saw the spark of a firestorm and caught her breath even as she remained hidden in the shadows. Her entire body responded to the familiar signal and she was filled with both yearning and desire, a longing for Orion so acute that it brought tears to her eyes. She saw a man with dark hair, silvered at his temples, and the woman who had given that lecture several years before. The flame sparked between them, illuminating the woman's surprised expression and the man's grim one.

Erik Sorensson and Eileen Grosvenor. Francesca closed her eyes, leaning back against the brick wall to keep herself from following them.

That night, she dreamed of making love to Orion.

Rafferty Powell was in the phone book, both his antique shop and his residence in Hampton Heath. Francesca took to walking in Hampton Heath, near that *Pyr's* home, watching and waiting. It looked like it had a back garden with a high brick wall around it. She gripped her hands together on the night that she saw a phalanx of dragons taking flight in pairs, barely discernible against the darkness of the night sky, as they flew silently to a battle in defense of their own kind.

She knew that Orion was in their number, but she feared he would not yet recognize her. She clutched his scale, hidden in her pocket, and prayed that he would not be injured in the battle ahead.

There was a gap in his armor and it would be bittersweet to lose him in this moment.

The darkfire sparked around the perimeter of Francesca's life for the next few years, glimmering on the edges of the dawn, limning the shadows, taunting her with the proximity of her beloved. When it vanished so suddenly that there was almost an audible crack, she knew that Orion was or would be soon in that piazza in Rome in 1972.

Her annual dreams of him vanished and the Sibyl's voice fell silent. Francesca told herself that this was the darkness before the dawn and willed herself through it.

Her consolation was the increasing visibility of the *Pyr*. She saw the YouTube videos of dragon shifters, along with the rest of the world, and watched Melissa Smith's feature series about the *Pyr* with more avidity than most. She wanted to reach out to them but she had waited so long already and she didn't want to lose Orion now.

When Balthasar called, his voice filled with enthusiasm, and told her that he would be going to Chicago with a guy named Theo, Francesca knew her son had stepped into the modern history of the *Pyr*. He said that Theo was 'just like him', which reassured Francesca, but she asked the color of Theo's blood. Red. It was all she needed to know to give her blessing.

The threads of time were weaving together, her vision was coming true, and Balthasar would know the community of his fellow dragon shifters. She prayed then as she never had before, prayed that the *Pyr* would triumph over the *Slayers* and that her dragon shifters, father and son, would return to her unscathed.

Where was Orion? He was lost to her in this moment, neither in the Dragon's Teeth, the past of 1972 or the present. He undertook his own journey and Francesca knew his path would lead to her if he had any choice about it.

In the silence of those years, she feared the unpredictability of the darkfire and the possibility that the choice might not be his to make.

After the triumph of the *Pyr* in 2015, Francesca visited Drake with Balthasar and was welcomed into the extended family of the *Pyr*. Orion's commander was just as Francesca had imagined he would be, though he had little to tell her of Orion's fate. He welcomed every detail she could share of the fate of his men. She took solace from Drake's relationship with Ronnie and that it hadn't come together easily.

It was Ronnie who told her to never lose hope.

––––––––

ORION'S VISIONS changed after he ensured that the darkfire was snared. They were more like a sequence of images shown to him by the darkfire. He no longer felt hurled through time and space, but as if he remained in one place, in a kind of limbo, while incidents and images were shown to him. He assumed these were the results of his deeds.

First, he saw one of the crystals on a shelf in a library.

Then he saw a dark-haired man sleeping in a cave, the flicker of darkfire illuminating his features as he smiled in his sleep.

A moment or an eternity later, he saw a crystal in a different cave, one lit with torches that blazed fire. Was it the same crystal or another one? He could not say, but this stone was cracked in half by a red and gold dragon. The darkfire filled the cave with radiance, then vanished and extinguished the torches at the same time, leaving the cave in impenetrable darkness.

Orion understood that the darkfire had been freed.

He saw the crystal in the library again, still intact, which meant it was a different one. The darkfire flared in it, like a pulse, then faded from view. He had the sense that it bided its time.

The dark-haired man touched by darkfire had evidently awakened, for he used a crystal as a weapon, shooting darkfire at dragons that had to be *Slayers*, as a woman watched. She then took the stone, using it to injure a red and gold dragon. Was it the same one who had broken one of the crystals?

Next, Orion saw another crystal and caught his breath in recognition of both the scene and the crystal. He sensed that the crystal in Drake's hand, in that courtyard in Las Vegas, was the one he had filled with darkfire himself. Drake and the Dragon Legion were outside the home of the *Pyr* and master illusionist, Lorenzo. This had to be the third stone. The darkfire flashed and the company of the Dragon Legion vanished from view.

Orion knew where they had gone.

He saw Alexander and Damian again. He caught a tantalizing glimpse of that plaza in Rome, then he watched Drake, alone and weary. The leader of the Dragon Legion surrendered a crystal to Erik Sorensson, its heart so dark that the darkfire had to be expired or at least spent.

Then the dark-haired man was in the cavern of the red and gold dragon, and he broke the second crystal, his manner as triumphant as the red and gold dragon was dismayed. Darkfire danced around the cavern again as dragons battled for supremacy.

Orion counted two stones broken, their darkfire freed.

He saw the same man break the third crystal. The *Pyr* were in a modern city, perhaps in America, and his heart caught when he thought he glimpsed Francesca with the mates of the *Pyr*. His view followed the darkfire, though, and the way it touched the dragons flying high above the city. It reminded him of a blessing or a benediction, then the darkfire flashed and faded.

Gone.

Or dispersed.

Lost? He did not know and he feared the truth.

He found himself then in yet another cavern, one that smelled different from the others, one that emanated the chill of old stone.

There were seven men in the cave, seven warriors who looked to be asleep. He could not stir them. He could not escape. Once again, Orion feared that he was an observer and not a participant.

He could not help but think of his father and all the shades of the afterlife as he waited.

He could not help but fear that he had become one of them, and that his choice to follow his destiny had cost him everything else.

Francesca!

————

FRANCESCA BOUGHT a house on the coast in Greece. It was on the island of Euboea, south of Chalcis, where Orion had been raised. Drake and other members of the Dragon Legion visited her there, and she was glad the house had a guest suite, for it was usually occupied by a dragon shifter. Balthasar came, as well, often with his *Pyr* friends. He kept his own room in the house and rented a slip for his boat in the closest harbor.

Francesca liked being able to walk along the water's edge, regardless of the weather, and she liked the wildness of the storms. It was a place that felt both wild and honest, a place she could imagine a dragon shifter with an affinity to water. She continued to do her research, but she didn't travel as much anymore.

She was waiting.

In the spring of 2019, one of the scholars she had mentored found the grave. Francesca knew the truth as soon as she read the email requesting her assistance and expertise. She immediately went to Russia for the excavation of the burial mound, the one she had been seeking for almost fifty years. The first reports had the tomb was for female Scythian warriors, but Francesca knew they were Amazons.

The barrow was virtually untouched and located near modern Terme, within the area Orion had begun to mark. She stood on the site and surveyed the mountain peaks, knowing Orion had been in the same place centuries before. The scholars she had mentored over the years, the ones who had become her friends and family, had found this prize with their joint efforts. It felt like a personal triumph and the culmination of her career.

Francesca was given the honor of opening the tomb and its contents were more than could have been anticipated. There were more than a dozen female warriors in the tomb, armed, their golden headdresses intact. They were exquisite. The *calathos* headdresses were engraved with spirals and flowers, one still upon the skull of the woman who was clearly the most important of them all.

Upon the leader's breast was a large dark scale of familiar shape, as if it had hung on a thong that had long since disintegrated. Francesca brushed the dust away, blinking back her tears. The scale would cover this woman's heart when she rode into battle, which told Francesca all she needed to know of this warrior queen. She didn't even need the Sibyl to whisper in her ear, although she did.

Iphito.

"In the findings from Cumae, there is a vase showing an Amazon queen," she said to the team. "Her name is recorded there as Iphito, though we know nothing else about her. I wonder whether this could be her." There was discussion of this possibility as more debris was removed from the site, as inscriptions were revealed, and more warriors found. The excitement was palpable and she was impatient to see what else was uncovered.

In her heart, though, Francesca knew she had found Orion's mother, where he had told her there would be a grave. He must have attended the funeral with his father. He would have been young, so his memory less accurate, but he had guided her to the find of a lifetime.

It was her Troy, and Orion had given it to her.

Now if only he would return to her, too.

ORION HAD no notion of the time and date when the seven sleepers stirred. He followed them into a world that was reassuringly modern, and one that made him hope for his reunion with Francesca. He was glad to find them in Rafferty's company and to see other familiar *Pyr* from the future.

He saw the children come out of the house as the Seven Sleepers danced under Uther's direction. He knew they were Donovan's son and Rafferty's adopted daughter, but they had grown considerably since he had last been in their company. He watched the Seven Sleepers banish the red light of Regalian magick. He watched them fly high and circle the constellation of Draco, then vanish. He smiled as he felt the shimmer of darkfire light again, vibrate through the land and begin to regain its power. It sparked across the soil and surged through his feet, lighting him body and soul with a newfound under-standing of its power.

When it filled his mind's eye with a vision of a house that could only be in Greece, Orion knew that the darkfire brought him a gift.

There, he would find Francesca. As the others in the house on Bardsey Island slept, Orion shifted shape and took flight, turning his course to the south.

The promise of the firestorm was past due.

BALTHASAR CAME to the house in Greece for Christmas and told Francesca of his adventures with his fellows, their journey into Fae and the dismissal of the Regalian magick. She loved watching him as he spoke, seeing his passion for his kind, his enthusiasm for justice and his conviction that all would be right. She saw Orion in his every gesture and she had no regrets of her choice.

They were sitting in two of the big chairs on the porch, watching a storm build over the ocean, when lightning cracked in the distance. It was blue-green and Francesca felt a shimmer pass over her skin. She straightened, hoping.

"What is it?" Balthasar asked.

"Darkfire," Francesca whispered with reverence. She would always associate that force with the *Pyr* in general and Orion specifically.

"But there isn't any darkfire anymore," her son protested. "It was extinguished in the last crystal, the one that Marco broke at the end of the Dragon's Tail Wars. No one has seen it since."

"Maybe it was hidden from view," Francesca said. "Maybe it was obscured by the Regalian magick."

"Maybe," he ceded. "The timing would be right."

But Francesca wasn't interested in theories. She stood up, watching the clouds with fascination. They churned, their undersides dark, then rolled closer, almost touching the surface of the sea. The Greek mainland was lost to view as the tempest gathered. The ocean roiled and the waves began to crash on the beach with greater vigor.

The lightning, though, was indisputably blue-green.

Francesca walked toward the water, her heart leaping. She heard Balthasar shout behind her, but she ignored him, her gaze searching the horizon until she saw it.

Him.

A black dragon appeared for a heartbeat then soared into the clouds and was hidden from view.

She felt Balthasar's attention sharpen and knew there was a blue shimmer around his perimeter. She stepped into the cold water and reached out her hands as the distant dragon appeared again. The darkfire struck the water close to him and he was illuminated with its blue-green light, his scales as dark as obsidian. She knew his eyes were as silvery as the sea. He dove into the water with power and grace, cutting a path directly toward her, and she gripped her hands together, hoping with all her heart.

She saw a blue shimmer and knew he'd changed back to human form.

The minutes until she saw the swimmer were painfully long, then she spotted Orion's dark figure as he swam steadily toward the shore. He was all sleek power, and his resolve was so potent that Francesca could almost taste it. She smiled, heart in her throat as he came closer and closer, then surged out of the water like Poseidon himself. His gaze raked over her even as the water streamed from his hair and he whispered her name like a benediction.

"My Francesca," Orion said, striding toward her. "You waited."

"Orion!" She was knee-deep in the cold water when he reached her and caught her close, one hand cupping her jaw as he stared into her eyes with a wonder that made her heart pound. He murmured her name again, as if he couldn't believe they were together, then he kissed her triumphantly, his mouth sealing over hers and stealing her breath away.

Francesca kissed him back, more gloriously happy than she'd been since Cumae.

Orion swept her into his arms and carried her to the shore, never breaking his kiss. Francesca ran her hands over him, needing to reassure herself that he was truly with her, that they were finally reunited. It was only when their son cleared his throat pointedly that Orion broke his kiss and looked up.

His slow smile, so filled with pride, made Francesca's heart race. He kept one arm locked around her waist as he set her on her feet, but offered his hand to his son, then gathered Balthasar close in a tight hug. They were crushed together in his embrace, Francesca's vision blurred with tears, and there was nowhere else she wanted to be.

"You were waiting for him," Balthasar said finally. "All this time."

"I knew he would come," she said, running a fingertip down Orion's cheek. "The Sibyl said it would be so."

"I gave you my word," he reminded her.

"And you gave me my Troy."

His eyes lit. "You found it?"

"I found *her*," Francesca said. She gave him a towel and he wrapped it around himself, then she tugged him toward the house. "They're already talking about a traveling exhibit," she said. "It'll be funded by the Metropolitan Museum in New York and will open there first." She stopped suddenly. "Do you mind? Is it your mother?"

"My mother's spirit is with my father, Francesca. She has no need of her armor any longer and would be glad of it proving the existence and power of her kind."

She hugged him again with relief. "Come and see the pictures," she urged, hearing her own excitement. "She had a dragon scale, hanging over her heart, and a golden crown..."

"There are *thousands* of pictures," Balthasar warned his father with a smile. "Brace yourself."

Orion chuckled. "I remember this enthusiasm and passion well," he said with a nod. "Perhaps we might eat first, my Francesca."

"Of course. *Of course!*" She hugged him tightly, her heart full enough to burst, and her voice dropped to whisper. "I was afraid you would be kept from me," she admitted. "Because I have your scale."

He kissed her then, a rough and possessive kiss, a sweet reassurance in his touch. "Nothing could keep me from you, Francesca. Did we not walk together in the underworld and return?"

"But there is a gap in your armor."

"And my modern brethren have the skill to repair it, with your aid." He sighed contentment as he surveyed her house. "As ever, Francesca, you have chosen well. Have you visited the dragon houses yet?"

"Drake and Ronnie took me there last year and told us of their history."

Orion nodded then spoke to Balthasar. "It was there that my father recounted his tales."

"He certainly was eloquent in my recollection."

His grip was firm upon her hand, as if he would never let her go. "He was a skilled storyteller, a man who held his listeners rapt."

"I hope you remember his stories," Balthasar said. "I'd like to hear them."

"I recall them all," Orion said, matching his pace to his son's. It gave Francesca such pleasure to see them together. "Do you know this *Iliad*?"

Balthasar smiled and quoted from the poem in Greek. "'*Sing, O goddess, the anger of Achilles son of Peleus, that brought countless ills upon the Achaeans. Many a brave soul did it send hurrying down to Hades, and many a hero did it yield a prey to dogs and vultures, for so were the counsels of Jove fulfilled from the day on which the son of Atreus, king of men, and great Achilles, first fell out with one another.*'"

"Ah!" Orion said. "Music to my ears!" He kissed Balthasar on both cheeks, his enthusiasm making the younger man smile. "And I know the song of the darkfire, as well as the fate of the lost members of the Dragon Legion. I must report to both Drake and Erik, and consult with Rafferty."

"And Marco," Balthasar said. "The Sleeper," he added and his father nodded.

"He who broke two crystals. Yes." The first drops of rain broke free as they entered the house. By the time Orion had washed and dressed, Francesca had laid out their meal. Orion laughed when he saw the pot she had used to roast the fish, and Balthasar looked between them in confusion. The rain came down in a torrent as the three of them sat together, gathered as a family for the first but not the last time.

Francesca could not imagine a greater joy.

She could think of one excellent way to celebrate that joy.

When the bedroom door was secured behind them hours later and Orion drew her into his embrace, her heart soared. "I love you," she whispered before he kissed her to silence.

"And I, Francesca, love you." He pulled back to survey her, his eyes sparkling. "We were destined to be. The firestorm knew it well. It just had greater plans for both of us."

"And now that it has seen its objectives achieved, we can savor the promise of the firestorm."

"Indeed, my Francesca. Indeed." She laughed and he kissed her thoroughly, sweeping her into his arms and carrying her to the bed for a loving that was long overdue.

EPILOGUE

T he *Pyr* met at Francesca's home in Greece that Christmas, gathering from all corners of the globe to celebrate the season and the repair of Orion's scale. Drake was first to arrive, with his mate Ronnie and their sons. They would become even more familiar guests, Francesca knew, and she enjoyed watching Drake and Orion walk the beach together in deep consultation each evening. She saw that Drake was relieved to know the fate of his soldiers, and realized that the faith of both men in the beneficial power of the darkfire had been restored.

Erik Sorensson, the leader of the *Pyr*, came from Chicago with his mate, Eileen and their daughter Zoë. He was as decisive as ever, and Francesca thought the glitter of his green eyes revealed his true nature. She hadn't anticipated that Eileen would bring a copy of her compilation of stories about the *Pyr* as a gift, much less that Francesca would be able to add to it.

Quinn, the Smith of the *Pyr*, came from Michigan with his wife, Sara, and their five sons. He had dark hair and blue eyes, and was an artisan blacksmith. Sara was the Seer of the *Pyr* and Francesca found it fascinating to hear of her gift for prophecy, then shared what she knew of the Sibyl. She suggested that they take a trip to Delphi together before the *Pyr* returned to the States and as others heard of the plan, it became a bigger excursion.

Rafferty and his mate Melissa, who Francesca recognized from her television shows about the *Pyr*, were enthused about the expedition, too. Francesca didn't think Rafferty looked any older than when she'd dreamed of him planting the dragon's teeth in his garden.

The younger *Pyr* who were close friends with Balthasar came, as well. Rhys, a chef who owned restaurants in New York, took over the cooking with a natural authority and skill that Francesca could only welcome. Kristofer, a stone mason, worked on extending a wall that encircled the house and provided more privacy. Hadrian, a blacksmith, befriended a local blacksmith, and worked on a gate for Francesca's home. Of course, Theo had arrived at the house, as well, and often could be found conferring with Drake, Rafferty and Orion, as they sifted through his visions of the darkfire at work through the history of the *Pyr*. Rafferty was making copious notes and there were plans to muster the darkfire and secure it in crystals once again.

Francesca found strong women in their mates. Kristofer's mate, Bree, was a former Valkyrie, Hadrian's mate Rania was a swan maiden and Rhys' mate Lilia was a selkie. Eileen knew more stories of shapeshifters than Francesca and they gathered each morning on the beach to swim and talk.

Francesca counted two more gifts of the darkfire in the friendship of this group of remarkable women and the community of the *Pyr*.

She told her brothers about Orion's arrival, and other than Rafe's snort of "about time", her brothers and their families were glad to hear the news. They would come later in January to celebrate Francesca and Orion's wedding, at the house.

But first, the repair of Orion's scale had to be done by the *Pyr*.

On the chosen night, they all gathered on the beach after the moon had risen, its full orb shining silver on the sea. Quinn had spent the first part of his visit assembling the necessary parts for a small forge and he shifted shape first to light a fire within it. He was sapphire and steel in his dragon form, majestic and powerful, and he lit the forge with a quick exhalation of dragonfire. The flames crackled orange and gold, sending sparks into the night sky. His son, Garrett, stood close beside him, watching every detail, and Sara stood with the other boys on Quinn's other side.

Erik shifted next, becoming a dragon of ebony and pewter. He offered one claw to Eileen and the other to Zoë, drawing his mate and daughter close. Zoë's eyes were wide with wonder and Francesca wondered whether she truly would be the next Wyvern of the *Pyr*. If her abilities developed with puberty, they would know the truth soon.

Drake shifted next and Francesca was struck by how much more ancient and formidable he looked in his dragon form, with his obsidian scales. Ronnie's pride was evident in her smile. Her oldest son was from her first marriage, but Jimmy was obviously fond of Drake. Their younger son, mimicked his father's gestures, clearly hoping for his own transformation.

Rafferty shifted next, becoming a massive dragon of opal and gold. His partner, Melissa, ran an admiring hand over his scales, her expression revealing that she and Francesca felt the same awe for their mates.

Kristofer, a veritable Viking who was blond in his human form, became a dragon of peridot and gold. Rhys, who had dark hair and an intense manner in his human form, became a dragon of garnet and silver. Hadrian, who had auburn hair and green eyes, became a dragon of emerald and silver. Theo, who had dark hair and eyes in human form and an impressive dragon tattoo on his back, changed to a dragon of carnelian and gold.

Francesca watched with pride as Balthasar shifted shape, becoming a dragon of citrine and gold with silvery-blue eyes.

The nine dragons stood in a circle around the forge, then turned in unison to look at Orion and Francesca. Orion squeezed Francesca's hand and shimmered brilliant blue before he shifted shape in his turn. He became the dark dragon she recalled so well, his scales gleaming like anthracite, his talons like dark steel, and his eyes as silvery a blue as they were in human form. He turned his gaze upon her, such pride and love in his expression that Francesca felt fortunate beyond all.

He offered his claw to her and she gripped his talon as they approached the forge. Quinn put out his own claw for the scale Francesca had kept all these years. It was strange to relinquish it, yet absolutely right that it would be returned to its destined place.

Quinn held the scale over the fire, murmuring to it. His son Garrett mouthed the words of his father's chant, memorizing it. Francesca realized he was serving an apprenticeship, for Orion had told her that the role of the Smith was hereditary.

He reached out his claw again and Francesca surrendered the token she had chosen to offer for Orion's scale repair. She knew it should be a symbol of what she brought to the firestorm, something unique to their partnership, and she hoped she had chosen right.

She heard Orion's chuckle when he saw what she held and she felt Quinn's approval.

"A quartz crystal or a darkfire crystal?" Quinn asked, looking around the company.

"As yet it holds no darkfire," Rafferty provided. "Francesca suggested it, and both Erik and I agreed it was ideal."

Drake nodded. "There could be no better custodian of that force."

Quinn held the crystal to the flame of his forge. He worked quickly, binding it to the scale by some wizardry that Francesca couldn't explain. Then he heated the combined scale and crystal until the scale glowed red.

"In the darkness, there was the fire," Quinn said, his low voice rumbling. He breathed a plume of dragonfire at the scale and the other *Pyr* did the same, the scale lost to view in a volley of flames. "And the fire burned hot." He lifted the scale and placed it in the gap on Orion's chest. Francesca heard the flesh sear and smelled the hot scale. Orion bared his teeth and tipped his head back at what had to be searing pain. "And it was cooled by the air," Quinn intoned.

Francesca leaned toward Orion's chest and blew on the scale, providing her own element of air to the repair.

"And it was washed by the water," Quinn continued, reaching with one talon to lift a tear from Orion's cheek and drop it onto the scale. It sizzled as it turned to vapor.

"And it was nurtured by the earth," he concluded.

Francesca took a breath, trusted in the *Pyr*, and leaned close to kiss the crystal now fused to the scale. The quartz was cool to her lips, against every expectation, but as she pulled back, blue-green lightning flashed outside the circle of the *Pyr*.

They turned as one to find a dark dragon there, one with black scales that seemed to have an iridescent light to them.

"Marco," Rafferty said softly.

The new arrival held out a claw and a blue-green spark danced upon the tip of his talon, then the spark jumped toward Orion. It reminded Francesca of the spark that had jumped toward her in that plaza in Rome so many years before, but it struck the quartz crystal on Orion's chest. Light flared so brilliantly that she had to close her eyes, then the light faded away.

Marco had vanished with it, as if he had never been there at all.

Francesca met Orion's gaze and saw the glow in his eyes.

"It seems the darkfire will continue to defy expectation," he said.

"In one matter, expectation won't be denied," she said and he laughed, a throaty dragon chortle that made her smile. He then changed shape in a glorious flash of blue and gathered Francesca into his embrace. He kissed her thoroughly as the *Pyr* changed shape and hooted with approval, his fingers sliding into her hair and his kiss searing her very soul.

Their adventure was just beginning, and Francesca felt blessed indeed.

It was as if their happiness was destined to be.

———

AUTHOR'S NOTE

Although this is a work of fiction, the stories about the Cumaean Sibyl are from classical sources. There is a cavern in Cumae, which is believed to be part of a Roman fortress, although when discovered in the 1920's, it was thought to be the Sibyl's grotto. As far as I know, there is no second grotto hidden beneath it, but nearby Lake Avernus was believed by the Romans to be the entry point to the underworld.

There was also a tomb discovered in 2019 near the Russian city of Terme, which contained a number of female warriors. Much of the tomb remained undisturbed, so their crowns and armor were still intact. There was a female leader, though she has not been named Iphito as in Orion and Francesca's story, and it is still considered a Scythian tomb. There is, though, a vase discovered at Cumae in the collection of the museum in Baiae depicting an Amazon warrior named Iphito.

———

ABOUT THE DRAGONFATE NOVELS

The adventures of the *Pyr* continue in the *DragonFate Novels* with the prequel, **Maeve's Book of Beasts**, then **Dragon's Kiss.**

Her kiss could be his doom...

When dragon-shifter Kristofer feels his firestorm ignite, he eagerly follows its spark to his destined mate. To his surprise, the heat leads him to a Valkyrie intent on claiming his soul. Even so, Kristofer has never met a woman as alluring as the fierce warrior before him. Trusting in the firestorm, he must convince her to fight with him instead of against him.

Trading the life of a dragon shifter for that of her sister Valkyrie is an easy choice for Bree... until she meets Kristofer. Experience taught her that dragons are evil, but in him she sees a bold and noble warrior. Finding his confidence as irresistible as his touch, Bree fears she is being tricked into abandoning her sister. But how can she take Kristofer's life when his very presence makes her burn with desire?

When they're compelled to join forces, Kristofer seizes the chance to convince Bree that they're stronger together. Yet as a sinister plan unfolds, an ancient dragon is roused from his slumber.

With danger closing in, can Kristofer convince Bree to surrender her immortality for their forbidden love? Or will Bree's distrust of dragons prove justified?

Dragon's Kiss
The DragonFate Novels #2
Available Now!

———

ABOUT THE AUTHOR

Deborah Cooke sold her first book in 1992, a medieval romance published under her pseudonym Claire Delacroix. Since then, she has published over fifty novels in a wide variety of sub-genres, including historical romance, contemporary romance, paranormal romance, fantasy romance, time-travel romance, women's fiction, paranormal young adult and fantasy with romantic elements. She has published under the names Claire Delacroix, Claire Cross and Deborah Cooke. **The Beauty**, part of her successful Bride Quest series of historical romances, was her first title to land on the *New York Times* List of Bestselling Books. Her books routinely appear on other bestseller lists and have won numerous awards. In 2009, she was the writer-in-residence at the Toronto Public Library, the first time the library has hosted a residency focused on the romance genre. In 2012, she was honored to receive the Romance Writers of America's Mentor of the Year Award.

Currently, she writes paranormal romances and contemporary romances under the name Deborah Cooke. She also writes medieval romances as Claire Delacroix. Deborah lives in Canada with her husband and family, as well as far too many unfinished knitting projects.

Learn more about her books at her websites:
DeborahCooke.com
Delacroix.net

———